THREE SISTERS OF GLENRIDGE

THREE SISTERS OF GLENRIDGE

How WWII Changed Their Lives

HELEN HENDRICKS FRIESS

iUniverse, Inc.
Bloomington

Three Sisters of Glenridge
How WWII Changed Their Lives

iUniverse books may be ordered through booksellers or by contacting:

iUniverse
1663 Liberty Drive
Bloomington, IN 47403
www.iuniverse.com
1-800-Authors (1-800-288-4677)

ISBN: 978-1-4620-2813-9 (sc)
ISBN: 978-1-4620-2814-6 (ebk)

Printed in the United States of America

iUniverse rev. date: 08/01/2011

THREE SISTERS OF GLENRIDGE

THE EARLY YEARS

Emma Wilson was not quite seventeen when the train pulled into the Glenridge, Michigan station. Most young girls did not travel alone in 1914. Emma had traveled many places as a child. She was very independent and didn't realize it was unusual for someone of her age to be alone. She just ignored most of the glances that came her way. Some people did ask her if she had a traveling companion or family. Little did they know that she was not only alone on the train, she was alone in life. She was about to start on an adventure which would become her life. She came to attend Glenridge College. She asked the train porter to help her retrieve her trunk from the baggage car and secure transportation to the college. He looked at her with a look of surprise, but she didn't notice.

Emma was happy. She had waited for this day since she was eight years old. Her life plan was now underway. She would live in the dorm room for four years; she would move into a boarding house (maybe get two rooms if she could afford it); get two cats for companionship and teach English Literature. She would have a wonderful life.

Emma was used to living in boarding houses. She was born in a boarding house and most of her early years were spent living in one. Her dad was a career soldier who volunteered for special assignments and was moved to a new post every nine months or so. He and her mother had decided they would not be separated so her mom would move to the town closest to his post and live in a room or two so that she could be near him.

Her mom and dad, Rose and Archie Wilson, had an unusual but real love affair. Rose had come from Wales with a group of young women who were brought over to America to serve as governesses for the rich families in the early 1880's. Supposedly, she would send money home and other family members would come over. That was the only fact Emma ever knew about her mother's early life. Her mom would not talk about her past to others and she died before Emma was old enough to really ask her about it. By the time Rose got to the States, there were too many girls for the jobs.

Eventually Rose heard about a family in eastern Pennsylvania (the Wilson's) who needed a girl to help them on their farm. Bertha and Charlie Wilson were an older couple with ten children. All the children had married and left home except for the youngest, a young man named Archie. Bertha spent most of her time in a wheelchair and needed help. Rose came to help. She soon fell in love with Archie. Archie was a dreamer who wanted to see the world, not live on a farm. He enlisted in the Army and soon came home to marry Rose. Rose left the Wilson home to be with him. Emma was born the next year.

Emma grew up thinking that all families lived the way they did. Sometimes Rose and Emma might not see Archie for a week or even more; then he would come bouncing up the stairs of the boarding house calling out for his beautiful wife and child. He was a man full of charm who would use that charm to try to get them two rooms instead of one. Usually, it worked quite well. Two rooms meant a bedroom and a room with a sofa, table and chairs and a hot plate. When her dad came home Emma slept on the sofa.

It may sound dreary to some. To a child who had never known another type of life it was magical. They would get up in the morning, tidy up the rooms, have a piece of toast which Rose made by holding the bread on a fork over the hot plate, and then start their adventure. They would walk around the town or into the countryside. Each day they would go to the store to buy their food for that day. Sometimes they took their meals with the other people living in the boarding house. If the town had a library they would spend time there. They would check out books: classics for Rose and kid's books for Emma. Rose must have come from a home with educated people because she started reading the classics to Emma long before Emma could understand them. Emma loved the sound of her mother's voice as she made the characters come to life. Emma would always remember sitting at a table at the library or at home with a big thick tablet with a red cover and lines on the sheets learning how to print her letters. They attended any free activity that might be happening. Her mother was a stranger to no one and soon learned their names. They certainly knew almost everyone in town. About the time they would feel comfortable, Archie would be transferred. This gave them a chance to start over again – see new places and do new things.

Boarding houses were boring to some people, but to Emma they were fascinating places. Some would have people who made it their permanent home. Other boarding houses had transients in for a few days at a time. Emma and her mother got to know them all. No one was a stranger to them. One time a theatre group came to town. Some of the cast stayed at their boarding house and one night entertained the residents. They gave Rose tickets to the theatre and let Emma and Rose go backstage. Emma never forgot one special performer, a man dressed like Abraham Lincoln, who recited the Gettysburg Address. One time a salesman stayed for a few days. He said he was just back from China. Her mother always doubted what he said, but he had with him suitcases full of trinkets he was trying to sell. He gave Rose a beautiful silk fan that opened up to make a scene. He gave Emma a set of three china elephants that he said would always bring her good luck because the trunks of the elephants were turned up. Another time a man and his wife came to town to present a concert. They took turns playing the piano and singing. They sang after dinner for all the guests at the boarding house. Emma always remembered the tears in the eyes of the people who heard their beautiful music. At one boarding house the owner was a woman who gave music lessons on the piano and organ. Because many of her clients were students who came in the evening, the owner made a deal with Rose. If Rose would clean up after the evening meal each night, she would give Emma piano lessons. Both Rose and Emma were thrilled. Emma learned the basics of reading music and always enjoyed playing the piano. One day the circus came to town and some of the performers stayed with them. Emma thought life could get no better.

They were never sure when Archie would be coming home. When he did come home he would regale them with stories of what fascinating missions he had been on or something unusual he had seen. He saw the world as one big interesting place full of enchanting people. He never talked about the bad things or troubles he saw. At least in front of Emma he didn't. It was a time of play. As the years rolled on and Emma entered school she knew that when Daddy came home she skipped school. He was usually able to be with them for Thanksgiving and Christmas. Neither Rose nor Archie talked much about their past. As a child she didn't realize most people do know about their heritage.

When Emma reached school age she started to have real interaction with kids her own age. Up until then, most of her time had been spent with adults. There were no kindergartens in those days. After a week in first grade, the teacher moved her to the second class since she already knew how to read and could do sums. Emma loved school. For the first time in her life she had friends her own age. She had to learn how to play group games. Just about the time she got settled it was time to move to another state and she had to leave her friends behind.

At one boarding house something happened to change her forever. One resident was a young woman named Alice. She was a teacher. She had two rooms and two cats. She was a very happy person who really cared about her students and tried to help them with their lessons. Alice took Emma under her wing because Rose seemed very tired all the time. Emma spent lots of time with Alice, who had come from Michigan to Kansas to teach school. She had been asked to teach classes to the older students. If a student came to see Alice at the boarding house for extra help, Emma was invited in also. She would sit and do homework while Alice worked with students. Emma absorbed what Alice was teaching. She taught world history and made it so interesting to Emma that Emma wanted to see the world. Her dad loved this idea and kept encouraging her to learn more and more. Someday, he told her, they would see the world together. At that time they lived in Kansas.

One day Emma overheard Alice talking with Emma's dad and mom about Emma's future. Her mom had always forbidden her to listen in on other people's conversations. Since it was about her, Emma thought she should hear what Alice said. Emma was very afraid Alice didn't want her hanging around so much. Instead she heard Alice tell them about going to Glenridge College in Michigan. It was a small school. She said it was a wonderful place for an education. There were only four big buildings in her day. The school sat on a hillside that overlooked the Birch River which flowed in the valley below. The town itself was located between the river and the school. Alice talked about the beauty of the river and how blue the sky was. Alice was gifted with words and painted a picture that made it all seem like the most beautiful place on the earth. Emma was very young then and thought it must be a dream place. Kansas had a different kind of beauty. Kansas had no hills where they lived. But you seemed to be able to see for miles across the plains. Alice thought plans should be made and money saved so that Emma could go to school at Glenridge. She thought

Emma had great potential for becoming a teacher. Emma was only about seven or eight at the time and hearing the conversation made her happy. This became her dream. Her folks liked that idea and said they would start a college fund for her. Then they moved again. Emma thought it was the end of her dream.

About that time Rose seemed to need a lot of rest. She seemed listless most of the time. One day Emma was given the news that they would be moving again. Archie was taking them back to Pennsylvania to live with his oldest brother and his wife. Uncle Tom and Aunt Kate had five children. Their children were married and had their own homes. Uncle Tom and Aunt Kate had moved back to the farm where Dad's parents had lived; the place where Archie and Rose had met. Emma's grandparents had passed away by this time. Emma asked her dad if he would still be in the Army. He said he would. He said that Rose and Emma would stay with the family and he would come to visit them. Usually Rose and Archie made moving a big adventure for Emma. This time most of the talk was about aunts and uncles and living on a farm. Emma helped pack up their few belongings. Alice had promised to write and she did for a few months. Eventually the correspondence stopped. But Emma never forgot her and wanted to live the same kind of life. She would go to college in Glenridge, become a teacher, live in a boarding house and have two cats for company. She would be just like Alice.

Emma was surprised when Uncle Tom and Aunt Kate greeted the family with open arms as they got off the train in Pennsylvania. No one had ever met them before. Aunt Kate wasn't much taller than Emma. She had a round soft body and arms that she wrapped around Emma. It felt so good. Aunt Kate had a smell of cooked apples and cinnamon. When she smiled it seemed to light up her face. Her hair was gray and pulled into a bun. Little wisps of hair fell forward on her face. Uncle Tom was tall and stocky, much bigger than Archie. He was like a larger version of Archie. They both had the same thick hair and same shaped chin. He lifted their suitcases as if they were empty and put them on the back of the truck. Dad and Emma climbed onto the back and Rose sat in the front seat with Uncle Tom and Aunt Kate. In less than five minutes they were out of town and on their way to the farm. Emma could tell her dad was happy to be back on the farm. He kept pointing out places he recognized and even called out and waved to the people he knew. This was his first trip home since he and Rose had gotten married.

"There it is. There it is," he called out as they turned off of the main road.

In the near distance Emma saw a big white house sitting in what looked like the middle of some fields. It was two stories high and had a big front porch. She wondered if it was a boarding house. Emma could not see another house. Emma was used to city living with houses close together. *The people who live here must be very lonely*, she thought. Archie was really excited. Emma soon realized that this was his old home. He jumped from the back of the truck and lifted Emma down and told her that this was to be her new home. Emma felt a bit overwhelmed as she remembered that they were not playing the games they usually played when they moved to new places. This looked like a different world.

Uncle Tom and Aunt Kate really fussed over Rose. They helped her out of the truck and into the house very quickly. Uncle Tom came back out to help with the luggage. Archie just stood looking quietly all around without saying much. He reached out for Emma, swung her around and said, "We're home, Emma. We're home."

As the truck had pulled to a stop they had been greeted by three big dogs who barked a joyful welcome until told to be quiet by Uncle Tom. Emma was glad they didn't jump on her. She saw some horses and cows in a field nearby and she saw what looked like a large cage that had many, many chickens that were making a racket. Her dad told her it was the chicken coop.

As they went up the porch steps Emma saw a big front porch with chairs and a tall table with a large fern on it. On the other end was a large swing with cushions and pillows. Sitting on the cushions were two cats who gave her the once-over and then closed their eyes. Once inside they were in an entryway with rooms and a hallway. Emma looked to her left and saw a big parlor with lace curtains on a big picture window. She saw a sofa, some chairs and a pump organ. On the other side of the entry was another room with a big window that also had lace curtains. This room held a big table with chairs all around it. She saw a breakfront with fancy dishes behind the glass. When she saw the big table she was certain that this had to be a boarding house. She looked left and right trying to absorb it all. Through a door in the living room she saw another room. She could see her mom and Aunt Kate so she walked that way. This was another large room with a big bed in the middle with brightly colored quilts. She saw a closet and a bureau with drawers. A fireplace was on one wall and in front of it was a rocking chair and a lamp on a small table that had some books on it. The window was open, the curtains were blowing gently, and a wonderful smell of freshly cut grass filled the air. Emma saw no hot plate or kitchen table. It was a larger room than most places they had lived. Aunt Kate was helping her mother into bed. It wasn't bedtime. Emma didn't know what to think.

"Come give me a hug," her mother said when she saw Emma in the doorway. "I'm feeling tired after the trip and your Aunt Kate thinks I should rest a while."

"You must be hungry," Aunt Kate said. "Emma, would you like to come with me to the kitchen and help me fix some tea and sandwiches for your mom?"

Her mom nodded at her so Emma went with Aunt Kate. The kitchen was another big room. She saw cupboards around the room and a big kitchen table in the center. *This house must be a mansion or a castle,* she thought.

"Maybe you'd rather explore the house than make sandwiches," Aunt Kate said. "Go look upstairs and down and see all the rooms. We thought we'd let you sleep in the pink bedroom. If you'd like a different room we can move you tomorrow. Take a look at them all."

The staircase had a landing half-way up. *My room,* Emma thought as she climbed up the stairs. She had never had a room all by herself. She entered the first bedroom at the top of the stairs. It was decorated in pink. When she entered she saw two windows with a view of the fields that seemed to have something growing in them. Beyond them was a wooded area. She could see a field that seemed to have yellow flowers. Since she had only seen flowers blooming in small groups she decided they must not be flowers. She and her mom would have to explore it together. She looked around inside the room. She saw an actual bed, not a cot pushed against the wall. It was painted white and had a pink and white quilt. Emma would always remember that quilt. It was called Sun Bonnet Sue: little girls wearing pink and white dresses and pink and white sunbonnets. She saw a white chest of drawers and a desk. Above the desk were shelves with books on them. She saw a rocking chair with a baby doll and teddy bear sitting on it. Emma was too stricken to move at first when she saw such beauty. She quickly left the room and ran downstairs to tell her mom about it. Aunt Kate brought a tray for Rose that was nothing like Emma had ever seen at boarding houses. The tray had a plate of tiny sandwiches with the crusts cut off the bread and soup in a beautiful flowered bowl. A teapot and matching cup and saucer were on the tray. Aunt Kate had added a pink rose in a small vase. Rose looked like she might cry. *This wasn't like her mother to lie around.* Emma was torn between excitement over all the new things she was seeing and worried a bit about what was happening.

The next morning Archie came into Emma's, room, pulled up the shades to let the sun shine into the room and woke her. He said they were going on a breakfast hike to explore the farm. Aunt Kate handed Archie a bag with food inside. He put it over his shoulders and hand in hand they started off. Every so often he would stop to look at a scene. He would see something special from his childhood to tell her about. She learned about her dad that day. She saw the pond where he learned to swim, the stream where he learned to fish and a hidden meadow where the most beautiful flowers filled the area. Emma was excited at the beauty of it all.

"Momma needs to see this," Emma told her dad.

"Your momma needs to rest today. We'll take her back a bouquet. You know, Emma, your momma has not been feeling very well these last few weeks. She is not able to be up and about for very long at a time." Archie paused and then went on, "I have to leave to return to Kansas tomorrow morning."

"Do we have to leave so soon?"

"I do. You and your mom will be staying here with your Aunt Kate and Uncle Tom. Your mom is very sick, Emma, and she needs lots of care. Kate and Tom have said they will take care of you both. You will need to help them. You will probably have chores to do each day. That's the way things are on a farm."

"What kinds of things?"

"Aunt Kate will tell you. When I was a boy I had to help milk the cows and feed most of the animals before I left for school."

"Why can't Momma and I go with you? I can take care of her."

"Emma, your momma is very sick and needs a special kind of care. I know your help will make her feel much better. Aunt Kate will know the right things to do."

"Is momma going to die?"

"We hope not."

Emma never forgot that talk. She thought her dad was going to cry so she decided she wouldn't ask any more questions. She watched as he bowed his head and placed his hands over his face. They sat quietly for a few minutes and then walked back to the house.

Life settled into a new routine after Archie left. Some days her momma stayed in bed all day. Sometimes she would sit in the chair in her room. On occasion Uncle Tom would pick Rose up in his arms and carry her to the front porch to sit on the swing. Emma's life was very different now. As Emma got older she realized that Aunt Kate was very, very good to both Emma and her mom. If Aunt Kate was disappointed about suddenly having an invalid and small child around after finally raising her own family, she never let it show. She kept Emma beside her, showing her how to run a home, how to plan and cook meals, clean a big house, and even be a nurse.

After a time Emma had to gather the eggs each day. She got to keep half the money from the sale of them once a week. Uncle Tom put her in charge of feeding the dogs and the house cats. He wouldn't let her feed the barn cats. Uncle Tom said the barn cats had to find mice to eat or the mice would eat the grain that was used to feed the other animals. Every afternoon Aunt Kate and Emma would have a tea party with Rose. Sometimes, Aunt Kate would tell Emma to go read to her mother. Aunt Kate was a very special woman. Without her knowing what was happening, Emma was letting Aunt Kate become a mother to her.

Emma started school in the fall. Because most of her dad's brothers and sisters had settled in the area, it seemed as if the entire school was made up of Wilson children. Sometimes they would fight each other or even fight her. But if one of the Wilson's got picked on by an outsider, the Wilson cousins would gang up like an army against that outsider. Sometimes Emma fought with them, but it really felt good to know those cousins would be around if someone picked on her. Their school consisted of two rooms. Grades one through four were downstairs and grades five through eight were upstairs. Each grade was in a separate row of desks. Classes started each day when the teacher leaned out the upstairs window and rang a bell. This meant get in your seats immediately. The teacher then read some verses from the Bible. They prayed the Lord's Prayer and then recited the Pledge of Allegiance to the Flag. They had lots of fun at recess. Emma probably walked about a mile and a half to get to school. She didn't think it was very far.

Albert didn't make it home for Christmas and Rose spent almost all of her time in bed. They had a big Christmas tree in the parlor and all her dad's brothers and sisters and their families came by.

One day Emma asked Aunt Kate about her momma. "Is she ever going to get better?"

Kate gently pulled Emma onto the sofa and put her arms around her. "I'm afraid your momma is so sick that she cannot get better."

"What will happen to me?" Emma asked.

"You will live right here and sleep in your own room just like you are doing now," she answered.

Emma was never officially told what was wrong with her mother. As she learned more about illnesses, Emma always suspected that Rose must have had cancer. The word *cancer* was never spoken but Emma did hear talk about the big *C*. One day her daddy came home. The family had sent for him. Together, Emma and her dad sat by Rose's bed for a couple of days before she died. She and her dad were each one holding one of Rose's hands as she breathed her last breath. Aunt Kate and the doctor were in the room. Aunt Kate gently took Emma from the room and held her as Emma cried for the loss of her mother. Rose was buried in the church cemetery along side all the other family members who had already gone to Heaven. Archie left to go back to the Army right after the service.

Emma felt like her life changed forever after her momma died. Sometimes she felt like she was one of the hired hands; maybe like her mother had felt when she came to live and work at the farm years earlier. The animals always need to be cared for. From early spring to late fall they were busy with gardens: plowing the ground, planting seeds, the hoeing and weeding that never ended, and picking the produce and canning it to preserve it for the next winter. In between they always had meals to prepare and laundry to wash and hang out on the clotheslines. Many times Emma thought they were being unfair to her and making her work harder because she wasn't their *real* child. She soon learned this was the normal way of life for the child of a farmer. And sometimes it was even fun.

One fun thing about the Wilson's was their love of music. They were all singers, some better than others. No matter what chore you had to do, you sang while you were doing it. Most of the songs they sang were hymns. Some were folk songs that had been handed down through the years. On hot days one of Emma's jobs was to take a glass jar of water out to the fields where Uncle Tom was plowing so he could have a drink of cool, fresh water. Emma always knew where to find him. She would follow the sound of his voice as he sang. He always sang very robustly but . . . . he was always off key. He accepted the good-natured teasing from everyone. Aunt Kate had a sweet, smooth voice. She and Emma would harmonize together when they were doing dishes.

They always sang as they would prepare vegetables for canning. One time there were six bushel baskets on the back porch, three filled with green beans and three filled with corn. They pinched the ends off the green beans, and washed them in lots of clean water. They snapped them (or sometimes cut them) into small pieces so they would fit in the jars. Aunt Kate would cook them quickly and place them in the jars which had heavy metal lids. When the jars were cool they carried them to the dark cool room they called the fruit cellar which was in the basement. The fruit cellar had a dried mud floor and was lined with shelves. It was their *store* for the winter. Corn was a little more work. It was not easy to shuck the outer leaves and remove all the corn silk. The kernels had to be cut off the cobs. Cucumbers had to be made into pickles. Cabbage was made into sauerkraut and stored in big crocks. Tomatoes were Emma's favorite vegetable. She probably ate one for every one she processed. She would scald the tomatoes in boiling water for less than a minute. The skins would peel off in one piece in a smooth motion. Her all-time favorite smell was when Aunt Kate made ketchup. Nothing ever smelled so good. They canned cherries, (after pitting them), peaches and pears. Crops like potatoes, squash, and carrots and apples were put in baskets in the cool, dark fruit cellar. They always had enough food in that cellar to carry them through to the next summer.

While they worked hard they had fun times too. Every Sunday the family gathered at one home or another in small groups. No one worked in the fields that day. Almost always someone from church would come home for dinner. Someone would play the organ and everyone would sing during the afternoon. On holidays, the family gathered as one big group. Emma would always remember one Thanksgiving when almost sixty people came for dinner. Aunt Kate put all the extra boards in the dining room and kitchen tables. Uncle Tom put the long flat boards they used for wall-papering on some sawhorses and created another table. They had at least one huge turkey and mountains of fried chickens and a few roasted chickens which were served with noodles. A couple of the men and older boys had gone hunting and brought back many rabbits. Each family brought a lot of food. They brought chairs so they could all sit down together. Well, almost everyone. Emma noticed that usually about four women didn't get the chance to sit down until everyone else was done. After some sassy remarks about women from one of the young male cousins, Emma realized that not only did the women have to do all the cooking and serving, they also had to do the cleanup. Hmmmmm. Something seemed wrong.

After the day of her great *realization* Emma began to notice other things. While the family had fun and seemed close in many ways, they were often mean to each other. They came up with cruel nicknames for almost everyone. One tall thin girl just a little older than Emma was always called *Beanpole*. Young Jim (not Old Jim, his dad) was always called *Four Eyes* because he wore glasses. Maurice was born with a foot that turned inward. He was called *Clubby*. Francis, who had a generous rear anatomy, was always called *Fat Fanny*. And so on and so on. Even the parents used these nicknames. They called Emma *Miss Know-it-all*. Emma also noticed the family as a group made decisions for everyone else. The family's politics were decided as a group.

The family knew that Emma's college fund had been established. They knew that she added to it with her egg money. That meant she needed to go to High School first. Usually only the boys got to go to High School. The girls rarely went. The feeling was that the girls were married before they were eighteen and had no need for an education. The family finally decided Emma could go with the two older boys into town to high school. She looked upon that event as a major milestone. The headmaster, Mr. Sims, when he learned of her plan to go to Glenridge, wrote to the school to learn their requirements. He helped her plot her studies so she would qualify. When she heard about how much it would cost, she began to worry that her egg money wasn't going to be enough. She decided that if she could get just one year there, somehow or other she would get the rest. She studied hard. Soon she got a new nickname – *Miss Bookworm*. Cousin Will, just two years older than she, told her he wished he could go to college too. That little bit of encouragement made her feel so good.

One Sunday, after dinner, Emma heard her uncles discussing her father. It was painful to hear their opinions of him – none very nice. "He doesn't accept responsibility for his family." "He's a dreamer." "He always hated farming." "He only cares about himself." The most painful one of all was "He doesn't care about his daughter or he'd come visit more often."

From the doorway Emma cried out, "He does so. He loves me." She ran to her room. She slammed the door shut.

The uncles were greatly embarrassed that she had overheard their conversation. With great humility and apologies they tried to make things right. She would have no part of them. She decided she needed to leave the house and family right away. She got an old suitcase and started to pack her clothes. Aunt Kate came and knocked on the door.

"Go away," Emma told her.

"Emma, let me in. We must talk."

"I'll be out of your way tonight."

"Emma, your mother taught you manners. We must talk. Dry your tears. Wash your face. I sent all the family home. Your Uncle Tom is in the barn. We will be alone. Please come downstairs."

Emma couldn't decide what to do. At that moment she felt like a slave, an intruder. She was someone entirely alone in the world. She wanted her mother and father. Her mother was dead. She had no idea where her father was. It was true; he was not good about staying in touch to let anyone know where he was. She couldn't go to him. She reluctantly made her way downstairs.

Aunt Kate said, "Let's take a walk up through the meadow to the top of the hill."

"I'm still going to leave tonight," Emma told her.

"If you feel that's best for you, I will help you. Let's walk first."

It was a beautiful sunny afternoon, not too hot. A soft breeze was blowing in the air. They walked through the meadow of daisies, blue chicory and pink and white clover as they made their way up the gentle slope that led to the top of the hill. Once they got to the top they could see for miles. Aunt Kate had brought an old blanket. She spread it on the ground. She cut a big red apple in half and handed Emma a piece. Not a word had been spoken.

"My dad does love me even if he doesn't come to see me very often," Emma told her. "He's very busy with a very important job to do."

"I know," Kate told Emma gently. "Your uncles were very, very unkind to say what they said. Their punishment for saying those things is that they will have to live with knowing they said it for the rest of their lives. I know they regret it. There may come a time when they will again apologize to you. Whether or not you accept their apologies will be up to you."

They sat quietly for a few minutes.

"Emma, let's play a mind game."

"What's a mind game?"

"It's such a nice day and the view is so beautiful, for two minutes I want you to look at it. I'll close my eyes. Then you tell me everything you can see and I'll do the same while you close your eyes."

Emma decided she needed to play along. She looked around the scene. She began to talk. "I see a beautiful blue sky with puffy white clouds drifting by. I see dark green spruce trees and lighter green locust trees. I see the pasture where some cows are grazing. I see a cornfield."

Aunt Kate opened her eyes. "I see everything you saw. With words you painted a lovely picture. Now it's my turn," she said. "Close your eyes while I look for two minutes."

She began to talk. "I see a farmhouse that's not too big. In the yard a clothesline is hanging full of clothes. I see a woman's dress and a man's work overalls. I see diapers, so a baby must live there. I see some little children's clothes. I see a pile of wood next to the back porch and a few chickens running through the yard."

"I see all that, too," Emma told her.

"Who was right and who was wrong when we told what we saw?"

"Well, we both are right," Emma answered her.

"We didn't see the same things."

"Aunt Kate, we're two different people."

"So . . . ."

"I get your message, Aunt Kate. Each of us sees things differently."

"Bertha and Charles Wilson, your grandparents, were very special people who gave birth to ten children. Each of them was very different in how they looked. They are a lot alike in how they think. They are all hardworking people who are mostly kind and considerate. Nine of the children fell into the accepted pattern and got a limited education, got married early in life and became farmers. The youngest son, your dad, did not fit into that pattern. He let it be known early on that he could never be a farmer. He wanted to see the world. He read adventure stories constantly and was always trying to build a new craft to carry him far away. He was also very, very intelligent. His parents and older siblings decided he would be the one to go to college, become famous. This was set up as a family plan and money was set aside to make it happen. Archie decided college would be boring and instead left to join the Army. The family was crushed because they had made sacrifices to build the college fund. When Archie fell in love and married your mother the family was sure that he would now come back to the farm and re-join the family. It didn't happen. When your mother got so ill and you came back to the farm, his brothers and sisters were sure that at last he would be back to stay. It was not to be. I know that your dad could never be happy living on the farm. Yet in his own way, he knew our ways were good ones and wanted that for you. Your uncles had held on to the dream that they would remain one big family. It is paining them to let go of that dream. I believe they let their frustrations get out of hand today. No one can make dreams for someone else."

It was hard for Emma to imagine her dad making someone sad. He was always so full of charm and laughter when he was around her. She was very lonesome for him. At first he tried to get back to the farm at least once a year. Now it had been two years since she had seen him. She rarely got mail from him and had no idea where he might be.

Emma was still stinging from the hateful words she had heard but slowly, she began to soften in her attitude.

"I still want to go to college. Will the family think I'm running away?"

"Our family expects you to go to college. You will make us all proud that you are the first in our family to get a higher education."

"Will wants to go to college. He told me so."

"I wonder if his father knows that. Tell him to talk to his dad. Maybe we can find a way to make it happen."

Aunt Kate began to gather up things to return home. "Emma, it is our wish that you will stay on with us until you leave for college. We do want you to be happy. If you feel it is too painful here I will try to help you find a place to go."

"Then I couldn't go to college."

"That is probably true. Your mother left home and came across the ocean at a very early age. She got a job and I'm sure you can find someone you can help so you'll have a place to stay."

Emma thought about her own special room. The Sunflower Sue quilt had been replaced by a nine-patch she had made by herself. She thought about the food processed and ready for winter. She thought about the times they sang together. Should she give all this up just because she's angry? She also thought about how hard Aunt Kate and Uncle Tom worked to keep a good home, how much they taught her, and how they took both Emma and her mother in when they had no where else to go. Didn't she owe them something?

"Aunt Kate, I'd really rather be here with you than anywhere else till I go to college. I'll try to work as hard as I can to help you."

They stood on the top of the hillside that beautiful day with their arms wrapped around each other. Slowly, they made their way home and the incident was never mentioned again.

Emma seemed to get a little more respect after that day, yet the hurt never completely went away. She prayed to God to help her find the strength to get through the next year when she could leave for Glenridge. Years and years later as she thought about her dad she realized that she needed to accept him as he was and not expect him to be the kind of person who would be there for her.

The year did pass quickly. Her instructor at school seemed to make most of the arrangements for admission to Glenridge College and Aunt Kate tried to help her get together the things she would need to take with her. When she worried about the money, Aunt Kate told her not to worry about it; just take one day at a time.

The day before she was to leave, the family had a big party for her. Every member of the family came that day, even Cousin Lois who had a new baby the day before. At one point in the afternoon Uncle Tom called all the family to the front lawn and asked Emma to step to the porch. He told Emma she made him and Kate feel young and happy. He told her how much they appreciated all the hard work Emma had done over the years. He presented an envelope to her and asked her to open it. It looked like a legal document. Emma couldn't quite understand it at first . . . . then she did. The money the family had saved for a college education for her dad had not been touched for almost twenty years. They always hoped he would come back and use it. Now the funds were being transferred to a bank in Glenridge for her to use for college. Emma must have cried for half an hour. Each aunt, uncle and cousin came to hug her goodbye and wish her well. The children had drawn many pictures and made many trinkets for her to take with her. Emma realized that even if it was only for a few years, she had a family.

Well, at least for a while she did. The following spring after she left the farm, the Brill Company came to their section of Pennsylvania and bought up many of the farms to build a big manufacturing factory. They built things like railroad cars, trolleys, ambulances and trucks. World War I had started in Europe and these things were needed. Soon another builder came and bought more farms to build row houses so that the people who worked in the factory would have a place to live. The Wilson family sold the farms and scattered away. They stayed in touch by letter at first. Now the big family farm was gone.

Emma felt very independent as she arrived in Glenridge that August morning in 1914. New buildings had been added to the campus since Alice had attended the school. There was now a building where female students had rooms. Alice had given Emma a visual picture of the area that had stayed with her through the years and surprisingly enough it was pretty accurate. Only everything was much bigger than Emma expected.

She was given a room number and a list of instructions when she arrived on campus. She made her way to her room. It was a rather small room with two beds. She would now have a roommate. She unpacked her trunk and got help taking it to the basement for storage. Some of her things she left in a suitcase that she stored under her bed. Life would surely be different. Very different, she soon found out. Her roommate was a very pretty girl named Jewel, whose first question to her was to ask if she had a boyfriend. Jewel didn't want to be at college; her family had insisted. She was just the opposite of Emma. Emma was excited and eager to begin her new life. Jewel was there because her parents insisted she go to college.

The first morning she couldn't stop smiling as she made her way to her first class. She found most of the seats had already been taken. Emma went to the back of the room without speaking to anyone and found a seat. A young handsome man came into the room, stood in the door looking around. He made his way to sit at the desk opposite Emma's.

"I bet you're not from Glenridge," he said.

She saw him turn to a young lady who had beckoned him to sit beside her. Emma heard him say, "I like this seat best." He turned and smiled at Emma, "I'm Albert Martin."

Emma could feel her face getting red but she managed to mumble back, "I'm Emma Wilson."

Despite his smiles to her, she made it through class only to find him by her side when she left the building to go to her next class. She learned that his next class was in the same building as hers. She didn't want to be rude so they walked together.

They only had one class together yet he seemed to appear magically wherever she was for the next few days. On that first Friday he was waiting to walk her back to her room. He told her he lived in Glenridge and was going home for the weekend. He would see her on Monday. Then in plain daylight in front of her building, in front of the world, he reached over and kissed her. She was so shocked. She didn't know whether to slap his face or enjoy the kiss. It was her first grown-up kiss and she had to admit she liked it. With a salute to her he was on his way to the trolley stop for the ride home. He called back to her, "Have a good weekend. I'll see you Monday. Someday we'll get married and I'll see you every day."

Her head was spinning and her cheeks felt like they were on fire. The nerve of this strange young man unsettled her. *I should have slapped his face so he'll never pull that kind of stunt again. He'd better stay away from me*, she thought. *My boy cousins taught me how to take care of myself.*

Emma's roommate, who had been watching from the window, had another opinion.

"You are so lucky to be kissed by that Romeo. Every girl I know would die for that chance," she told Emma.

"I'm not interested in boys," Emma told her.

"I wonder if I can make him notice me," Jewel said as she looked into her mirror. Emma didn't know what to think. She was very naïve about flirting.

On Saturday afternoon Emma went to the library to work on her first term paper. It was for the history class she shared with Albert. She looked up from her work and saw him walking across the room to the table where she was working. He had a package with a big bow in his hand.

"Get away from me," She told him.

"My mother told me I had to come and apologize to you."

"You told your mother what you did?" Emma was aghast.

"I had to tell her. I told her I had met the woman I would marry."

"Why, you arrogant . . . . ." Emma stumbled trying to find the right words to say.

"My mother said you have the right to slap my face. Go ahead." He put his face down in front of her as she sat at the table.

Living on a farm in Pennsylvania surely had not prepared her for this. He was persistent. "I'm very sorry if I hurt your feelings or embarrassed you. I was afraid that if I didn't move fast some other guy would and you wouldn't even see me." He handed her the box.

"Please accept this box of candy with my apologies. Can you let me start over so that we can be friends?"

Well, he did sound sincere so what could she do. Actually, they left the library together and took a walk down the hill to the river. They strolled along the path beside the river and he bought her a glass of pink lemonade that had a little umbrella in it before they made their way back to her building. It was very hard for her to concentrate on homework after he left for home. After that day they walked together to their next class after the history class they shared. He went home every weekend. Late on Sunday afternoons Albert would come back to campus and they would walk and talk. Emma wasn't allowed to have any *gentlemen callers* in her building and there weren't a lot of things to do, still she found she was really beginning to enjoy their time together. They learned a lot about each other. She told him a little about her earlier life and how she decided to come to Glenridge. He thought she was very brave to make the trip to Michigan from Pennsylvania by herself. He talked about his dad who was a builder who built all the houses on their street. The one exception was one that wasn't finished yet. That one was being built by his brother who planned to move in with his new bride as soon as it was done.

One day Albert asked Emma if she would go to church with him and his family on Sunday morning and stay for dinner with them. He would borrow his dad's car to take her and bring her back. After having had the freedom of roaming on the big farm Emma was feeling very lonely and crowded in the small room she now shared with another person. But she told him she couldn't go with him. She had joined with a group of students who worked with children at the local orphanage on Sundays. Sometimes they played games with the children. Often they would just talk with some child and become their friend. Albert asked if he could join their group. Emma decided that maybe she wasn't ready for so much togetherness so she fibbed and told him he had to take a big, long test first. Since he worked every Saturday at his father's construction company, he decided not to join the group.

Near the end of November Albert brought her a note from his mother inviting her to come to their home for Thanksgiving dinner. It made Emma remember the big Thanksgiving dinners at the farm and she suddenly got very lonely. But she already had a commitment to serve Thanksgiving dinner to the homeless. She told Albert she would have to decline.

He was persistent. "What time will you serve," he asked.

"Well, I'm on the set-up crew so I'll work from nine till three," she told him.

"That'll work out OK. My family goes every year to help. We go earlier to get the tables out of storage and my mom starts cooking, then we go home and have our dinner."

Emma always remembered that minute while she paused to think before answering. She really wanted to go and experience some home life. Her life's goal, teaching, the two rooms and two cats in a boarding house, had remained uppermost in her mind. But would that life be enough? While Albert never rushed her about becoming someone special in his life, his intentions were very clear. If Emma said yes would she be opening a door that she could close again? Or is she making too much out of an invitation to dinner?

She told him she would accept. She seemed to realize that this first step was taking her in a direction that would change all her plans. Emma was curt and snappish when Jewel asked her what was wrong. When Emma told her she was going to meet Albert's parents Jewel jumped off her bed and gave Emma a hug.

"This is wonderful," she told Emma. "What are you going to wear?"

Emma groaned. She hadn't thought about clothes. She probably had nothing to wear that was suitable for such occasions. She made all her own clothes and had only one coat. She started to worry and thought about changing her mind.

Jewel didn't seem to notice Emma's anxiety. Jewel had other ideas.

"You should wear your navy blue skirt and striped blouse. You look great in that. We'll pull your hair up so everyone can see your neck."

See my neck? Obviously, I need educated in ways not available in books, Emma thought.

Jewel started Emma on a series of lessons about her hair. Emma thought her hair was ugly – kind of a streaky light brown. Jewel told her it made her hair look like the sun was shinning on it and was beautiful. She pinned Emma's hair this way and that and over the next few days made sure Emma knew how to do it. She insisted Emma use a bit of color on her lips and cheeks. After that Jewel and Emma became pretty good friends. Jewel was going home for Thanksgiving and hoped her parents would not make her come back to school. She did come back to finish out the term. Emma never heard from her again.

On Thanksgiving morning Emma put on her school clothes, pulled her hair back with some elastic (like she wore it on the farm) and left with her friends for the church where the Thanksgiving dinner was being held. The place was noisy as everyone kept busy. Many long tables had been set up and covered with long rolls of butcher paper. Men were putting chairs along the sides. Someone thrust some silverware in her hands and told her to set the tables. A really, really pretty young woman came up to her and asked if she was Emma.

"Yes," Emma said turning to look at her. The young woman was beautiful with long blond curls that she had loosely pulled back with a ribbon.

She thrust out her hand and said, "Hello, Emma. I'm Millie, Albert's sister-in-law. You are just as pretty as Albert said you were. I'm glad you're coming to dinner with us today."

They shook hands and Millie left to go back to finishing her assigned chore. Emma looked around the room and saw Albert. He was helping to move tables into new positions. He saw her and waved and pulled on the arm of his helper and they both made their way to her.

"Emma, this is my brother, Frank. Frank this is Emma."

"Hi, Emma," he said. "It's really nice to meet you. My wife is somewhere near here. Let me find her."

"I've already met her," She told him.

Emma's next job was to put big bowls of apples on each table. She was busy at this when a man and woman came to her saying, "Albert told us we would find you here. I'm Sydney Martin. Call me Syd," his father said. His mother added, "I'm Alberta. Call me Bertie. We're very happy you're coming to share Thanksgiving with us."

Emma tried to remember everything she had heard about meeting people and saying the right thing. She got lucky, she guessed, because someone came to get them for some so-called emergency and the meeting was brief. About 2:30 or 3 o'clock the crew that would clean up arrived. The Martin family had left a little earlier, telling Emma they would see her later. Albert stayed behind to take Emma back to her room to change and then go home with him.

"My dad and mom think you're wonderful," he told her.

"Albert," she scolded him. "Your parents don't even know me."

"They're good judges of character. Millie thinks you're beautiful."

Obviously he was lying. Emma had to admit it did give her a little boost of confidence. He went to his room on campus to give her time to change her clothes.

When Aunt Kate taught Emma to sew, she was very, very particular about fit and so Emma felt fairly comfortable when she put on her navy skirt. She liked the way it showed her ankle and just a hint of leg. Her striped blouse had a white collar and cuffs and had a short V at the neckline. She put on a gold necklace that had belonged to her mom. She started on her hair just the way Jewel had taught her. Instead of pulling it all straight back with an elastic band, she pulled it to the top of her head into a soft bun. She placed a headband (borrowed from Jewel) around the base. It was white with a blue edge and little red flowers. Then (again per directions from Jewel) she pulled little curls down around her face. She almost didn't recognize herself. When Albert came for her she knew it had been worth the effort. His eyes began to shine almost as bright as his smile. For a moment she almost forgot how good she looked and thought about how handsome he was.

Emma would never forget her first visit to the Martin home. That day she never imagined it would be her home for the rest of her life. Albert drove his dad's car across town and told her they were going to the best place in town to live. He seemed excited to show it to her. He told her about his dad and mom.

"My dad loved to build things," he told her. "When he would see a nice piece of wood he always could imagine a special use for it. He got a job helping to build houses and loved it. He and Mom got married and Frank was born the next year and I arrived a few years later. Dad worked hard, my mother managed well, and soon they had saved enough money to buy some property to build a house. My dad found a very big parcel of land about three miles outside of Glenridge. It cost much more than the money Dad had saved and seemed much too big. My Dad had a vision of a community being built there and he wanted to do it. He drew some plans showing a boulevard with trees and flowers running through the middle with big Victorian style homes on either side. He would build a garage for each house since he felt everyone would soon have a car even if they didn't have one at the time. He planned paved sidewalks along the boulevard so people could walk on them and be friendly. He went to the bank and convinced them to lend him the money to buy the property. As the homes were being built he named the street Lincoln Boulevard. Other people got interested and watched him build his first home. He had many potential buyers for the house. Instead, he kept it and moved our family into it. He built houses on either side and across the street. He was very particular about quality and if someone didn't work up to my dad's standards he was told not to come back the next day. By the time Frank was ten years old he worked along side our dad. Frank loves the construction business and couldn't wait to get out of school to work full time."

By this time Emma and Albert had arrived at the boulevard and Emma could see how special it was. Traffic moved east on one side and west on the others. Large oak and maple trees lined the center. There were gas lamp posts lining the street. Albert told her plans were already made to have them switched to electricity. The houses all looked big, beautiful, and very expensive to Emma. She began to get nervous and felt a bit uncomfortable. As Albert parked in front of the house she saw a house that seemed to be saying welcome to her.

The aroma of the turkey filled the air as Albert opened the door and called out, "We're home."

It did feel like home to Emma. The family didn't treat her like a guest; she was like one of the family.

"Come to the kitchen with Millie and me," his mother called.

"What can I do to help?" she asked.

"Taste the cranberries to see if they need more sugar," she told Emma.

It felt good to be in a kitchen again. The three women worked together and soon had the meal on the table. It was a beautiful table with lighted candles and a beautiful set of fine china that had little flowers around the edge. When Emma commented on them Bertie told her they only use them on Thanksgiving and Christmas. The dishes had come from England many years ago and been handed down through the family. Emma surely hoped she would not drop or break any. As if sensing her thoughts, Bertie told her not to worry if she breaks any, that dishes were there to be used. They talked about school, current events, feeding the homeless earlier in the day. No one questioned her about her family. They seemed to accept her as she was. After they ate, the two boys started to carry left-over food to the kitchen. Millie started to put the leftovers away. Emma was not used to seeing men in the kitchen. She learned that the two boys did dishes every night when they were younger. Emma started to help, too. Good memories of life on the farm filled her mind and she remembered how they always sang. Unknowingly, she started to hum. Before she knew what was happening they were singing the popular music. *K-K-K-Katy* and *Hail, Hail, the Gang's All Here.* Then they moved on to other songs that were patriotic: *America, I Love You* and *It's a Long, Long Way to Tipperary.* Millie had a clear, true soprano voice, Emma harmonized with alto, Albert was a baritone and Frank had a deep bass voice. They couldn't believe how good they all sounded together. Syd and Bertie called to them that they sounded good enough to be on the radio. They thought so too so they kept singing until all the dishes were done and put away.

When Albert took her home that night, he thanked her for coming to his home and gave her a hug and a kiss on her forehead. Emma was a bit disappointed that he didn't kiss her. But he had told her he wouldn't push her so she told him good-night. As she lay in bed she thought back on the day. Did she want many days like this in her future or did she still want to stick to her plan of two rooms in a boardinghouse with two cats? Somehow that idea became a little lower on her priorities.

Over the next year Emma began to spend more time with the Martins. Millie accepted her as a sister. As soon as Millie had graduated from high school she had gone to work in the office of the Martin Construction Company. She and Frank had gone to school together. They had not become a couple until one day a paperwork crisis about licenses occurred at the office and Millie was able to solve it quickly. Frank took her out to celebrate and the rest was history. Millie quit work when she and Frank got married. She still went in periodically to take care of certain projects. Syd trusted Millie completely in all serious business matters. Frank and his father could have been twins. They were both big, strong, muscular men with the bronzed look of working outdoors. Frank had started to build a house for Millie. They decided to get married before it was finished. Emma got to help Millie shop for the new curtains, rugs, and things for her house. Emma and Millie became best friends.

Emma learned that Albert, while he expected to help run the family business when he left high school, had a different dream. His mother told Emma that Albert always carried a book in his lunch pail, usually about European history, and while he ate he would read. A favorite teacher thought he should go to college and become a professor. One day he and his dad had a big talk about his future. Apparently Syd could see that Albert was not interested in construction, and told Albert that he should do whatever would make him happy. With the blessing from his father, mother, and brother, Albert enrolled at Glenridge College. He continued to work on weekends and summers with his dad and brother.

One day while Emma was visiting, Bertie took her on a tour of the house. It was a three-story Victorian house with lots of gingerbread trim. A big porch went across the entire front. The entry on the first floor led to a huge parlor on one side and a large library on the other. The library was lined with book shelves. Syd used it as a home office. There was a big dining room, a small sitting room, and a huge kitchen. Upstairs were five bedrooms and on the third floor she saw a huge attic with a ceiling high enough to walk under. In one corner there was a turret style window looking out on the street below. Emma had never seen such a grand house. Bertie informed her that someday the house would belong to Albert if he wanted it since Frank had built his own house.

At dinner one night Emma told the family about her past, her father's absence and the death of her mother. She told them about Alice and how she had started Emma on a path for an education. Bertie told her that she hoped Emma's dad would come to visit some day so she could meet him.

Emma had a good first year at Glenridge. She made friends easily and joined with a group that did volunteer work each week. She especially loved her English Literature class and found a kindred spirit in the teacher. The woman encouraged Emma to become a teacher. Albert and his family gave her a touch of home life that brought her much pleasure. Yet, she also had concerns. Albert was a very bright personable young man. His goal was to become a professor and teach European History. In the history class they shared, he had made the discussions come to life from all the reading he was constantly doing. He wanted very badly to go to Europe and travel to the places he read about. Emma worried that Albert might be a dreamer like her dad. She hadn't heard from her dad since she had come to Glenridge. *Are most men like my dad,* she wondered? *And if they are, might she be better off to continue with her first plans for her life?* Then Albert would show up with some silly trinket to make her laugh and she'd get confused all over again.

*   *   *

In 1914 a war had started in Europe. Soon the United States was sending help to the Allied forces by providing supplies and equipment.

Sometimes it seemed that the United States was gearing up to enter the war. The Army built a base outside town. Glenridge already had a small air field. The Martin Construction Company (MCC) started to get government contracts and kept very busy. There was talk about drafting all the young men into the Army. A draft was established to train men over the age of 21 for the Army. Frank was over 21 and had already registered. No one had been called up yet. There was talk of war on the news and there was a tension in the air. The allied forces in Europe were begging for help from the United States.

*   *   *

Emma had another time consuming interest. Along with other women on campus they didn't like the fact that women couldn't vote. Since the 1840's women had worked to gain this right. Along with other college students across the country they organized and started a campaign to make it happen. One day at dinner with the Martin's Emma mentioned the group. Bertie got very excited about it and told Emma she wanted to organize a group of her friends to help in the cause. Would Emma come to speak to them? Emma wasn't shy about talking among friends. Could she do it in front of a group? Emma told her she couldn't but she would send someone. Bertie wouldn't hear of it. She told Emma of course she could do it. And Emma did. Millie organized her friends and Emma spoke to them. They all worked very hard to gain the support of other women. Emma was shocked to find so many women were afraid to speak up with their opinions about the country. But she realized her mother would never have spoken up, nor would Aunt Kate. A lot of work remained to be done before women would be able to vote.

As her first school year ended, Emma realized that the year had used more than half of her savings. She needed more money to help her through her next year. She had planned to go back to the farm for the summer. The train trip would be expensive. She was not sure how she could earn any money if she lived on the farm. And she knew the farms were being sold for industrial use. One day she got a letter advising her that Aunt Kate had broken her hip and had moved to her daughter's house to recover. They thought she might never walk again. As much as she wanted to see Aunt Kate and Uncle Tom, she didn't know where she would stay. The family farm was gone. The second thing that happened was that her special teacher-friend asked her to join a small group of young women who would be presenting readings of poetry at teas and special events once or twice a week all summer. She said Emma would be a natural to give a reading and lead a discussion. She would be paid for doing it. Emma decided to stay in Glenridge. She moved into a boarding house for the summer, took care of children two days a week, did her readings, visited the Martin's, took a summer school class and attended rallies and meetings on getting the right to vote. She kept very busy. In the fall it was back to the old routine, except she had a new job. On the one day a week she didn't have classes, she got a job tutoring children who were having problems learning to read. The year seemed to fly by. Albert was asked to assist a professor who was writing a history book so his time was spent in classes, working with the professor, and helping out in the family business.

Albert and Emma continued to find time to spend together, and yes, by this time he would kiss her and she'd kiss him back. In almost every way she felt that she needed to be with him for the rest of her life. Yet every once in a while some word, phrase, song or smell would make her think about her father. She could not imagine living the life her mother had, never being settled, never having a real home. Her father was different than most men. He was a dreamer. A dreamer who put his dream first, she came to realize. Albert also had a dream: become a history professor and travel to Europe. Was such a dream compatible with having a home and a family?

*   *   *

In 1917 the United States officially declared war on the Axis powers in Europe. No troops were sent to fight at that time but the government increased the support with arms and equipment and medical help. The United States stepped up its war effort. The draft age was lowered from age 21 to age 18. This meant Albert had to register. Frank expected to be called up even though he was now a father. He and Millie had a sweet little boy with dark curly hair. They named him Harold.

*   *   *

One day Syd, Albert's father, suffered a heart attack. Bertie thought it was from all the extra work and stress. In those days, the family cared for the patient in the family home. Emma tried to help as much as she could. They were busy, difficult times for the family. Albert wanted to quit school to help care for his father and help Frank keep the family business moving. The family wouldn't hear to it. Frank got his notice to report to the Army. Because the family firm was filling Army building contracts in Michigan, and because of his father's heart attack, he was deferred at that time. Later, when Albert was called he was a senior in college and was deferred until graduation. Fortunately, by that time the war conditions had improved and Albert never had to serve. Syd did recover after many weeks.

Something else happened during that time. One day Emma was called from class and told to go back to her room immediately. She couldn't imagine why this happened so she hurried along. In the reception room, waiting for her was her father. She almost didn't know him and was sure he must not have recognized her. Emma had been a young child the last time she saw him and now she was a woman. He couldn't swing her around by her arms this time, or lift her high in the air. He was en route from one assignment to another: this time to Europe. The gravity of the war hit Emma at that moment and she felt the old love she had for him return. She had always imagined she would have many questions for him about the choices he had made. How could she ask them when she might never see him again? She was supposed to meet Albert for lunch. When she didn't show up he came to find her and insisted they join his family for dinner that night. So many years had passed without contact that her meeting with her father was bittersweet. Their lives had drifted apart over the years. Yet he seemed interested in her life and plans. He told her about living in California and for a time down in Panama where he had gotten yellow fever. She asked him if he was ready to give up the Army life now and he said he thought he was. He said he would do his duty first and go to Europe. After that he would see what he wanted to do.

"If I make it back, I'll come to see you right away," he told her.

It was not to be. Her father was killed in 1918 just before the war ended. He was buried in France.

By the time Albert and Emma were in their third year of school, they began talking about spending their lives together. There was no big proposal at the time, just discussions about when and where they would do certain things together. Near the end of that school year a tragedy occurred. Emma and her roommate were awakened by screams and smelled smoke. The building was on fire. They grabbed their robes and left the building. Flames were everywhere. The firemen and their trucks arrived. They ordered everyone away from the area. It was a devastating feeling to see the building in flames. Friends started to arrive from other buildings and call out names. Emma heard Albert calling for her. She ran into his arms and he held her tight. After what seemed like an eternity school officials came by making lists to see if everyone was accounted for and ask if they had a place to spend the rest of the night. Emma's roommate went off with her friends. Albert told them he was taking Emma to his home.

Syd and Bertie were very kind and sympathetic when they heard what had happened. Bertie put her arms around Emma and led her upstairs to an empty bedroom. Bertie gave her a nightgown and a robe. The blankets had been turned back on the bed. Emma got in and rested a little. By this time it was so close to morning that everyone was up early. As Emma had a cup of coffee, she realized that she had no clothes to wear that day.

"My clothes won't fit you," Bertie said. "You can wear a pair of Albert's pants and one of his shirts. We'll give you a belt or rope to tie around your waist and turn up the legs. See what you can find among your things and come back her to stay." She suggested they take some boxes with them. "If you don't need them I'm sure there is someone who will need them."

Albert and Emma returned to school where they learned that the fire had been started by two girls who had been smoking cigarettes early in the evening. Apparently a cigarette smoldered for a while and ignited the curtains. The girls were asleep and didn't wake up at first. They were burned very badly and stayed in the hospital for a long time. The building was about forty-five percent destroyed. Classes were cancelled. Emma was told that in another hour or so certain groups of them could go into the building to see their rooms. The fire had occurred in her end of the building. Emma expected to find a mess. And she did. Everything she owned was covered with dirty wet soot. All her clothes, as well as all her books, journals, homework – everything. She started to cry. Albert held her and told her he was sure they could restore most of it. They packed the boxes with Emma's things. Late in the afternoon they put the boxes into the car and left for home. They looked a mess. They were tired, dirty and hungry.

"We're home," Albert called out as they went in the door.

Home. What a nice word. Even though Emma had been there many, many times, that day she really felt it was home.

"Are you hungry," Bertie asked.

"Starved," Albert answered.

"I made vegetable soup today so it would be ready when you got here. It'll only take fifteen minutes to get it on the table."

"Do I have time for a bath?" Emma asked.

She took a quick bath and washed her hair. She combed it back and put a ribbon around it. She finally found a skirt and blouse that didn't smell too bad. Syd had come home early and the family was waiting for her at the kitchen table when she came downstairs.

Albert was in a very foul, sullen mood, snapping at everyone. He was disgusted that the fire had occurred. He criticized the girls who started it, the builder for not making the building safer, and the fire department for being so slow. The family knew he was hungry and probably tired since he had been up most of the previous night. He would probably not be as grouchy after eating. But Albert couldn't eat.

"Emma," he almost shouted at her. "You simply cannot go back to that building. Ever!" He got up from his chair, came to her and pulled her chair slightly away from the table and knelt down to take her hands. "You know I have loved you from the first day I saw you. I could have lost you in that fire. How would I ever live if I let something happen to you? I think we should get married right away. We can live here this summer. We'll find an apartment for our last year. I love you, Emma. Will you let me take care of you for the rest of your life?"

It took Emma only about a millisecond to make up her mind. She threw her arms around him and kissed him for an answer. Then she started to cry. The tension of the fire, the worry over where she would live, and probably the lack of sleep, all hit her. She realized how much Albert meant to her. Emma couldn't stop crying until she looked at Syd and Bertie. They had been sitting quietly through the whole proposal. Each of them had a beautiful smile on their face. At that moment Emma felt that she really had a home and a family. Syd and Bertie left their place at the table to give Emma and Albert a hug. Finally Bertie announced that she had apple pie for dessert so Albert moved his plate over beside Emma while they ate.

When they had finished eating Syd started to talk. "Emma, we're both very happy that you have chosen to spend your life with Albert. I seem to remember that when you arrived in Glenridge you had a goal in mind. Something about living in a boarding house and being a teacher. You'll soon have your degree. You can decide whether to teach or go to grad school. So you are near reaching that goal. About the boarding house . . . well, this house is as big as some boarding houses. Someday it will be Albert's and your home so you can call it a boarding house if you like. You can claim any two rooms you like for your very own." He got up from the table, walked to the doorway and reached onto the back porch. He turned back into the kitchen carrying a wicker basket. "Here's the last thing on your wish list." He set the basket on her lap. Inside were two little kittens that looked only a few weeks old. Emma started to cry again. Then she started to laugh. Then she laughed through her tears.

Albert turned to his folks and said, "I think she's happy."

It happened that an old cat had come into the warehouse of MCC. It had a litter of kittens. One of the workers had found them and told Syd, so Syd told the man to find homes for all except two of them. It turned out to be perfect timing that they were ready for a home on the very day Emma needed a home too. One was sort of orange so she named her Ginger. The other was black so she named her Pepper. They became members of the family.

When the excitement of the fire and engagement wore down, it was time to get serious about plans. They decided they needed to finish the school year. Although Syd and Bertie offered Emma a room to move into immediately, she needed to move back to the campus to finish out the school year. The school found housing near campus for the students who were burned out. Emma needed to be closer to the activities. In addition to prepping for finals, she was interviewing to student teach the next year. Albert was working for Professor Williams who kept him very busy. Emma was still giving readings of poetry at women's events and they both did some tutoring. They needed to do these things to earn money. The money from Emma's dad's college fund had been used up. She managed with her part-time jobs plus a small scholarship to stay in school. Even though Albert lived in a big, fine house, the Martins were a working family who were not wealthy.

Emma continued to work to get the right for women to vote. They held rallies. They encouraged everyone to write to the President and members of Congress. President Woodrow Wilson had said in a speech that the United States entered WWI to help bring democracy to the world. Well, what about democracy for women? Most of the western states had already given women the right to vote; the eastern states were slower to agree.

After the President's speech they had a new theme and in communities and college campuses around the country the women pursued their campaign. The mood of the country seemed to be changing and they wanted to take advantage of this momentum.

Both Emma and Albert made the Dean's List and Albert was offered a full time job as the assistant to Professor Williams, chairman of the history department. This meant that Albert needed to spend almost all of his time on campus. He needed to be living on or near the college. Frank reminded them that MCC crews would have a new small apartment complex finished in late July. He thought there was one unit that had not been leased. It seemed like the answer to a prayer for Emma and Albert. They estimated their income. If they both kept working and lived carefully they could manage the rent.

It was time to make wedding plans. They decided to be married on August 1st in the Martin family church. A reception would follow at the family home. They wouldn't issue invitations. The upcoming wedding would be announced in church. Everyone would be invited. Emma wrote to her Pennsylvania cousins to invite them to the wedding.

Emma thought about her dress. She planned to buy a nice dress that she could wear again. In late June Emma received a very big box from Aunt Kate's daughter in Pennsylvania. Emma thought it must be an early wedding present, probably one of the beautiful quilts they made. As Emma peeled back the layers of tissue paper she found a beautiful white wedding dress. It had been worn by Bertha, her father's mother, and taken care of through the years. A note was enclosed saying they weren't sure of Emma's size since they hadn't seen her for three years but they thought Emma should have it since she was the only child of Bertha's youngest son. Emma carefully lifted it out of the box and tried it on. The dress was made of soft cotton batiste. The neckline was medium high that reached to the shoulders where it dipped slightly, and short puffy sleeves were attached. The bodice was fitted to the waist which had a deep V over the tummy. A full skirt fell to the floor. Emma tried it on. It fit perfectly.

"It's absolutely perfect for an August afternoon wedding," Millie told her.

Emma couldn't understand how an open invitation to everyone could possibly work. Bertie wasn't worried. It was the way things were done in their church and community. Emma soon saw why. The neighbors on that wonderful street started working. Syd and Frank built a big arbor in the back yard. The men came to make sure the flowers were blooming and weeded. Big long tables and chairs borrowed from the church were set up on the lawn. Bessie Jensen who lived next door and her new daughter-in-law, Beverly, took over planning the menu. All the neighbors baked and cooked to plan the wedding feast. It seemed to be an accepted way of doing things.

Emma spent the night before the wedding with Millie and Frank. The next morning Millie helped her get dressed. She wore her hair up. She put a band of pink rosebuds and white baby breath around the bun. She carried a matching bouquet. Millie's dress was a soft sky blue color and she carried all pink roses. Millie and Frank were their only attendants.

The church was filled with people: mostly friends and neighbors of the family. Emma was happy to see so many of her friends from school. She really only had eyes for Albert. He looked so handsome in his suit and tie. He stood so straight and tall. He smiled at her as she started down the aisle. Suddenly it didn't matter to Emma if anyone else in the world was there. He was there. He was waiting for her. She felt like the most important person in the whole world.

They went camping in the woods for a few days after the wedding. Then it was back to the routine of getting ready for their last year of school.

Their first home was a small apartment. They had a one bedroom unit with a parlor and a small eat-in kitchen. Furniture was not a problem. The Jensens (who lived next door to Syd and Bertie) had just gotten a new kitchen table and chairs so they loaned their old ones to the young couple. Another neighbor had an extra sofa. Another had a couple of extra chairs. Albert brought his bedroom furniture and desk from home. Emma planned to use the kitchen table as a desk. Another neighbor heard about it and loaned them a desk. The unit was small with so much furniture. They didn't care. They were happy and content in that small place. Albert's folks had helped Frank get a used car when he married Millie and they did the same for Emma and Albert. Their car had a lot of miles on it. It was transportation Emma could use to get to work. They were so very happy.

Albert left early each morning for his classes. He spent the rest of the day helping Professor Williams. He was busy at first helping the new students and assisting Dr. Williams in any way he could. During that year he spent many hours researching old European papers for the book the professor was writing.

Emma began her student teaching career with a class of English Literature in the Glenridge High School. She was very nervous at first for some of the students were almost the same age as she was. She seemed to gain their respect. When they called her Mrs. Martin, she almost looked around for Bertie and realized she was also Mrs. Martin. Most of them had no interest in English Lit and she was challenged to find ways to pique an interest. She decided that instead of just reading the works either in class or at home, they could pretend they were reading it on the radio. Emma asked at the radio station for an old microphone (which didn't work) and they made a station at her desk. The students would sit in Emma's chair and *broadcast* to the class. When they got to some of the plays, she assigned each person to be a different character as they read the play. Emma got good cooperation from the students and the time passed quickly. She made many good friends with the students and the other teachers.

It seemed like Albert and Emma had very little time for each other since they both were so busy and they both had homework from the classes they were still taking. They tried to make Saturday afternoon *their* time. No studying, no work from jobs, no family time. They would go boating or hiking, or ice skating as winter came on. Their budget didn't allow for movies very often.

*   *   *

On the world scene, WWI still continued. Everyone hoped the end was near but prospects didn't look promising that it would end soon. Even though officially President Wilson had declared war on the Axis some months before, no troops had been sent to Europe. Early in the year of 1918, U.S. troops were sent to Europe. The added troop strength did make a difference. The Axis forces began to suffer many defeats. Dr. Williams depended more and more on Albert to keep him updated about the events in Europe and began to plan a trip to go there as soon as the war ended.

*   *   *

Emma stayed very busy with classes (both attending and teaching). Her poetry readings still continued. The radio station that gave her the used microphone contacted her about presenting a fifteen minute poetry reading once a week on the air on Sunday afternoon. Emma thought it was fun to prepare for and actually do. She usually started out with a humorous poem or something very seasonal. She would follow this with a poem from some well-known poet. She always tried to end with something meaningful or sentimental. An organist played background music as she read. She helped choose the music. It was so much fun for her.

They had a full, rich life even if they had little money. They were hoping to find a way to go to grad school but had to take one day at a time financially. By graduation day they decided they could at least start grad school so Emma applied for a part-time teaching position as a substitute. Her advisor said he would help her with scheduling. Albert didn't have to pay for his classes since he was working for the college.

Graduation day was a day for celebrating. At the ceremony it was announced that Glenridge College would become a University. Everyone was in a happy mood.

Two other people who lived on Lincoln Boulevard were also graduating from Glenridge so the neighbors had a big celebration for the four of them. They had ham and meatloaf and meatballs and fried chicken, potato salad, coleslaw, baked beans and rolls, cakes, pies, cookies and fresh fruit. It was a happy celebration.

*　　*　　*

In addition to the war in Europe, another cloud was hanging over the country. Some sort of influenza had hit parts of the country (and even the world they learned later). It seemed to be quite severe from the reports they heard and many people were dying. Everyone seemed to be in good health in the Lincoln Boulevard neighborhood. At least at first they did. Glenridge was not to be spared from the epidemic which swept around the world. Bessie Jensen who lived next door and Ralph Winston who lived down the street both died from the flu. Other neighbors had the flu and survived. Life and death sometimes go hand in hand. On the day Bessie died, her daughter-in-law gave birth to a baby boy they named Robert. They called him Robbie.

The first cases of the flu had been reported from an army camp first, followed by a report from a naval station and then prisons. No one was able to discover the cause. Rumors ran rampant that Germany had released a

Spanish flu germ in the United States. There didn't seem to be much truth to that since the epidemic was world-wide. That fall many cities in the United States declared that all public places must be closed. In October, 195,000 people died in one week. This included 851 people who died on a single day in New York City. The country was in a state of panic. Albert's mother, Bertie, often assisted old Doc Jameson as a midwife. When the flu hit their street she spent hours going from one home to the other assisting those who needed help. When she came home she would bathe and wash her clothes in very hot water so she would not contaminate the house.

*   *   *

Syd was not doing so well those days. His heart problems, while not critical, took a toll on him. He had less and less energy. Frank took complete control of the construction company and Millie worked almost full time in the office managing the business end. It seemed only fitting that Albert and Emma should move back to the house to help out with Syd's physical care.

There seemed to be only one thing (besides his grandson, Harold) that gave Syd any pleasure and that was Emma's two cats, Ginger and Pepper. (These were the two cats Syd gave her the night that Albert proposed to her.) She had not been allowed to take them with her back to the temporary dorm she moved into to finish out the school year. Syd said he would take care of them until she and Albert got married. This surprised the family since he had always been a dog person with little time for cats. Well, the cats thought Syd was a king and became very protective of him. Bertie just closed her eyes and pretended not to see how much time the two cats spent on his bed. If they left the bedroom for any length of time, Syd would ask where they were.

*   *   *

The summer and fall of 1918 seemed full of never-ending days. Yet it also seemed to fly by. President Wilson made a speech recognizing the contributions women were making in the war effort and announced that he would support the women's right to vote. Congress passed the bill for a constitutional amendment quickly. Ratification by the states took a bit longer. Finally Tennessee (the last holdout) ratified the bill.

Even better was in November when the armistice was signed and finally World War I was over.

The Martin house had a subdued celebration because Syd's health was failing. He spent most of his time in bed. Little Harold and the two cats continued to bring him some pleasure. He slept a lot.

Millie told Emma she and Frank wanted more children. They seemed to be unable to have them. Albert and Emma decided that they would start their family whenever Emma got pregnant. Emma had to admit she was beginning to get the urge to have a baby.

Professor Williams, his first name was Simon, began to get serious about going to Europe in the early spring of 1919. It seemed the bombing in Europe during the war had unearthed many archives buried deep in the ground. A group of scholars were planning to hold a seminar in France to examine them. The professor began to plan the trip. The university would pay for his expenses and the expenses of his assistant. Albert was worried although he wanted to go. It had been his dream to go to Europe one day. But he didn't want to leave his dad or Emma.

Just before the Christmas of 1918, Syd died with the two cats by his side. One strange thing was that when he was taking his last breath, the cats wouldn't leave the bed. After he took his last breath the cats walked out of the room and would never go back into it.

After Christmas Bertie immediately started to urge Albert to go on the trip to Europe. Albert came home from work one day with a big smile, the first they had seen for many months. It seemed that Professor Williams had a problem at home. His wife had decided *she* wanted to go with him to see Paris. He was opposed to the idea since she would be alone so much of the time. She was not one to venture out on her own. They had no children. The professor and his wife had a long talk together and decided to ask Emma to go along as a companion for her. They would pay Emma's expenses for the trip. They called it a belated wedding gift. Albert was on cloud nine and picked Emma up and swung her around when he told her. She wasn't sure she wanted to go and be a companion since she really didn't know Simon's wife. Her name was Genevieve, and when Emma had occasion to be around her, Emma found her very demanding. *Is this the way I want to see Paris*, she thought. Even on the ship going to Europe the men were planning to work so Emma would be with her every day, all day, for almost a month. That wasn't her idea of a vacation. It appeared that if Emma didn't go, Albert would lose his chance for the trip. Bertie was encouraging to Emma and ready to support her no matter what she decided. Together Bertie and Emma put together a list of all the pros and cons of going and in the end Emma said she would do it.

They didn't have much time to plan for the trip. Emma decided that if she was going as a maid she wouldn't worry about her clothes. Bertie insisted Emma was not a maid; she would be a traveling companion and needed certain things. Genevieve made many plans to shop in Paris. Emma would have loved to plan visits to museums, etc. that were starting to open again after the war. She felt very discouraged and a bit out of sorts and not very pleasant. Then one day it occurred to her there might be another reason for her foul mood. Maybe she was pregnant. If she was, could she possibly make a trip so far away? Albert had been very adamant that he would not go if Emma wasn't going. It was a dilemma for Emma. She reasoned it out. She might not be pregnant; therefore, she should not say anything yet. If she was pregnant and got sick, she would tell them she was seasick. So many times Emma wanted to share the pregnancy possibility with Albert because they both wanted a baby. But she decided to delay telling him.

Simon and Genevieve stayed in their Pullman car all the way to New York, only coming out for meals. Albert had never been to the east coast and was fascinated by the changing landscape they saw from the train windows. They talked to the people around them. They felt very important when asked their destination to be able to answer that they were on their way to Europe. The association sponsoring the trip had made arrangements for them to be taken from the train station to the docks where they boarded the Queen Ann ship to take them to France. The Williams had a suite on an upper deck and the Martins had a cabin on the middle deck. Every step they took was an adventure for Albert and Emma. The big city of New York with tall buildings – the big ship – the vastness of the ocean. It was probably obvious to anyone who saw them that they were not very sophisticated. It was wonderful to experience it all. It would take them a week or so to make the crossing. Emma wasn't sure just what was expected of her. When Gen (as she told Emma to call her since they could pass for sisters) stated she planned to stay in her cabin until noon each day, Emma felt a great freedom.

Albert would meet Simon and they would discuss and research topics they hoped to learn about at the meetings. Simon was also still working on his book and that took most of Albert's time.

Emma began a tour of the ship. She would walk all around each deck many times in the morning. She felt wonderful and decided maybe she wasn't pregnant after all. Didn't most women get morning sickness? She felt great. She got acquainted with many, many people. In the afternoon when she suggested that she and Gen walk around the deck, Gen was surprised that so many people greeted Emma. High tea was served in the afternoon which of course Gen and Emma attended. During the tea Gen announced to everyone that Emma had her own radio show and also gave readings of poetry at high teas in their home town. The social director asked Emma to do a reading. She had no books with her. She was told the ship had a large library so Emma said she would do it the next day. Gen gave everyone the impression that she had *discovered* Emma. It seemed to raise her social standing a bit on the ship. When Emma told Albert he told her Gen would be her friend for life for she was helping Gen feel important.

Albert loved the ship's library and was delighted to find a nice selection of books about other ships that had crossed the ocean. He loved to find little interesting facts that he would put into a conversation. People loved to hear him talk. When he had time he wanted to learn about the mechanics of the ship. At night when Emma and Albert cuddled in their cabin they would share their adventures of the day.

Gen became acquainted with a group of card players and spent a lot of her time that way. It was not an unpleasant trip. The time passed quickly.

When they docked in France they boarded another train to take them to Paris. *PARIS, THE CITY OF LIGHTS.* What a thrill to be in Paris. Emma couldn't wait to walk the streets. As they made their way to the hotel they could see many street vendors, outdoor cafés and artists on the sidewalks that were oblivious to the world as they went about their painting. There were museums almost everywhere. Gen saw the stores where she said she planned to spend her days.

The first evening a big open house was being held at the museum where the meetings were taking place. Spouses were invited. Emma was thrilled to walk into that magnificent building. Even Gen was impressed. Gen wasn't sure she wanted to eat any of the food since it all looked strange to her. Emma encouraged her to try some so she could tell the people in Glenridge about it. It was the right thing for Emma to say. Gen really got adventuresome for her. Once she began to open her mind to new things, she began to have fun. One day they moved around the food markets, trying this and that. They stopped and watched the artists. One afternoon an artist wanted to do a sketch of Emma but she persuaded him to do one of Gen instead. The artist saw the pretty side of Gen, not the demanding side, and the sketch was beautiful. They spent a long time choosing a frame and having it packaged to take home. Some of the old castles which had been closed during the war were re-opening and the women toured them and laughed at the life style the people must have lived. Since Gen was having a good time Emma got brave and suggested they go to the *Louvre.* Emma thought Gen might want to go shopping instead but Gen said yes, of course. It's the most important museum in Europe, she told Emma. It was so wonderful. Emma couldn't believe she was standing in front of the original painting of the Mona Lisa, the originals of Leonardo daVinci, the Venus deMilo. She almost wanted to cry she was so moved by the beauty of them. Of course, they did stop at the gift shop and buy a few prints to take home. Gen thought they would be wonderful souvenirs to give to her friends from *her trip abroad.* And they did visit the shops. Gen spent what Emma considered a small fortune on clothes. Gen listened when the saleswomen suggested certain lines to flatter Gen's body. One afternoon they went to the *Champs A L'Elysee.* They sat at a sidewalk table and had a glass of wine while taking in the local culture. Everyone seemed to move in slow motion.

Emma's favorite time of all was the early mornings and evenings. Time spent with Albert. They would walk along the Seine at sunset and watch the lights come on. No wonder Paris is called the *City of Lights.* One night they went to the top of the Eiffel Tower It was truly a magnificent scene to watch from that site as the lights came on. When the tower was built in the late 1880's it was the tallest building in the world. It was spectacular to actually be standing there atop the structure.

Equally fun was in the early morning. Emma and Albert would leave their room early, walk to the *Rue Cler* and watch the venders put their wares outside. They would stop to buy a *café au lait* and a *croissant* and sit at a table on the sidewalk having their very French breakfast. One day they took it to a park under the Eiffel Tower.

Albert's part of the trip was going well. He even was called on twice to give his opinion. Simon called him *the young man who will be well known someday.* Simon was thrilled that Gen was having such a good time. He said he hadn't seen her so enthused about anything for years.

Emma had her own reason to be happy. She knew now that she was pregnant.

On their last morning in Paris as Albert and Emma sat having breakfast she told him he was going to be a dad. At first he looked at her in disbelief. He pulled her away from the table so he could give her a big hug telling everyone within earshot that he was going to be a dad. He was thrilled. Then he started, *Are you sure?—Are you OK?* – and all the other usual things. The people smiled and gave greetings in French that Emma couldn't understand. But she thought it meant that they were wishing them well. Albert wanted Emma to go back to the room to rest. She assured him that she was fine.

While Albert and Simon were finishing up their last meeting, Emma decided to tell Gen her big news. Gen immediately said they had to go shopping for something special. She bought them a very expensive baby carriage. It was very beautiful. She had it shipped to the states. She insisted on going to the Chanel shop where she purchased some perfume, Chanel Number Five, for each of them.

Emma knew that they were leaving on the late evening train to the coast to board their ship for the crossing back home. She learned that Gen and Simon were taking the train the next morning. She tried not to question what she thought was a change of plans. She drifted off to sleep on the train. Albert woke her early and told her they would be leaving the train before it got to the coast. He seemed a bit mysterious so Emma bided her time. A car was waiting for them when they left the train. Albert told her he had arranged this side visit so Emma could visit the gravesite where her father was buried. They would have all day to spend time in the area and board the ship that evening.

Her father was buried in a cemetery of fallen Americans. The grass was neatly trimmed. She saw white crosses on the sites. It set on top of a high hill that had a distant view of the ocean in the background. Emma never forgot that day. The sky was so blue and the sun was bright. It was hard to imagine it as a killing field just a few short months earlier. There was a bench so Albert said he would give her time alone while he browsed the area. Emma told her dad about her life and the new baby. As she sat thinking she decided her dad, in his own way, did the best he could to be a good dad. Emma thought about her mother and their early life. What seemed like fun and games to a child must have been a very hard life for adults. Emma placed her hands on her belly and thought of the child she would bear. What kind of life did she want for this child? She thought about the wandering life style she had lived and compared it to the stable home life that Albert had grown up with. She made a vow to herself that day that she wanted the stability of a permanent home. *Home.* Such a beautiful word. It suddenly occurred to Emma that she had a home and she was on her way there right now. It was the first time in her life that she would be *going home.* Up until this time, when she left an area for any length of time she ended up in a new place and had to start a new life. Now she was actually going home. She would be surrounded by family. *I want you always to have a stable home – somewhere you can always come to and feel secure,* she told her baby. She did come to peace with her parents that day. Up till then she hadn't realized how much she had resented the fact that they both had left her – one through death and one through duty to his country.

By the time they arrived back in New York they felt like seasoned travelers who had seen the world. The meetings in Paris were very successful for both Albert and Simon. Simon was recognized for his contributions and Albert was recognized as an outstanding researcher. Both Simon and Alfred were excited to get back to work to finish the book. They hoped to have it done by fall. Gen was already planning an afternoon of entertaining her friends so she could show her souvenirs and tell them about the trip.

As the train approached home Emma thought about the last time she had arrived in Glenridge. A young girl, all alone and ready to start college. It had been scary that day yet it turned out so very, very wonderful. When the train pulled into the station they were surprised to see Bertie, Frank, Millie and little Harold waiting to meet them. It was a wonderful welcome. Everyone talked at once and no one heard anything. It didn't matter to Emma. *This is a family*, she thought.

Little Harold was so excited and told them he knew a secret. Emma's first thought was that she had a secret, too, which she would be sharing in a few minutes. Maybe Millie was pregnant, too. *Wouldn't that be nice so the children could grow up together?* That was not the secret. As they walked in the front door they saw that the doorway to the library had been barricaded with strips of crepe paper. Hanging in the center was a sign, cut and colored by Harold which read *Uncle Albert's Office.*

"I made the sign especially for you, Uncle Albert," little Harold excitedly told Albert as he ripped the crepe paper from the door. "Come and see your new room."

Albert just stood there not really grasping what was happening. Harold pulled him to the desk where a large envelope with his name was placed on top.

"Open it up, Uncle Albert. I'll help you open it," Harold said reaching for it. Millie pulled him back and told him to wait.

Albert carefully opened it, read it, and looked around the room, his eyes filling with tears. He looked at Emma.

"The house is ours, Emma. This is the new deed in my name. Mom, what have you done? The house should still be in your name."

"Albert, you know I can't own property in my name. The law doesn't let women own property. Your dad's will leaves the house to you and Emma.

"I don't understand any of this," he said while Harold kept asking him if it was a good surprise.

"I still don't understand," he repeated, looking around the room to see that many of his father's personal items had been replaced with his own books and knickknacks. "Somebody tell me what is going on."

Millie thoughtfully said, "Let's go to the kitchen, get a cup of coffee and talk about what has happened here. I swear you look a bit pale, Emma. We'll bring you up to date and then you both need to rest a bit. We'll have all week to catch up."

Harold pulled Albert to the kitchen telling him that he and Grandma had made cookies to welcome them home.

As they had coffee, Frank explained. "Dad's will was just what we expected. You and Emma inherited the house and Millie and I inherited the family business. We all know that it all really belongs to Mom first. For business reasons it was better to officially change ownership this way. Mom wanted to surprise you when you came back so under her direction we packed up most of Dad's things in the room and moved some of your things in. You'll have to rearrange it to suit yourself. You'll have plenty of time to go through everything. Dad was very, very proud of you. Before he died, he made me promise to see that you made this room your very own. We just gave you a head start."

Emma had never seen Albert be so humbled. He looked from his Mother to Frank to her and back to his mother. "Mom, how you can stand to see me in Dad's room, with Dad's things, sitting in Dad's chair?"

"Well, we moved Dad's books and things to the back bedroom upstairs. I'll use that as a place to go through everything. The desk is yours. You will need to buy a new chair which will fit you better. You're much taller than your father. We'll help you move more of your things in. You must make it your own office."

"Emma, what am I going to do?" he asked her.

Emma later remembered trying to get out of her chair to go to him and she remembered spilling coffee. That's all she remembered until she woke up in her own bed in a strange room. Millie and Bertie were in the room putting cold compresses on her head.

In the haze of her mind she heard Bertie say, "She's waking up now. She'll be OK. Harold, run and tell Uncle Albert that Emma is awake."

Albert came rushing into the room and put his arms around her. "You fainted. Are you OK now? Can I get you anything?"

"I don't know what happened," Emma told them as she tried to get up. "Where am I?" She thought maybe she was losing her mind.

"The family has been busy while we were gone. Mom is insisting that since the house is now legally ours we must have the big bedroom. She moved our furniture in here and moved her things into the back bedroom."

"Oh, Bertie," Emma cried. "Why did you do that? You know and we all know that this is your house forever."

"Well, good," she said with a smile. "Then maybe you both will let me stay here for a while. You need the big room. I was lonesome in the big room. I saw your father everywhere. It will be better for me to have a change of scenery. Anyway, someday you and Albert will want to start a family and the little room adjoining this one is just right for a little one."

"Tell them, Albert, tell them," Emma told him.

With a smile, Albert told his family that they would soon have a little one to use that little room.

"No wonder you fainted," Millie said. "This is way too much excitement for you on top of your big trip. Come on, Frank and Harold. Let's go home and let them settle in. We can come back tonight or tomorrow and catch up on the news."

"Wait," Emma told them. "Albert, get the big brown suitcase." She reached inside and got out a box and handed it to Harold. It was a child's set of tools, made in France. "Here, Harold, enjoy this. When you come back I have another surprise for you."

"Come back for dinner," Bertie told them. "I have a chicken casserole ready for the oven, and a salad and some rolls. I baked a chocolate cake.

We can catch up on all the news. Emma, I think you should sleep a while. We'll have many days to hear about everything."

Emma thought she was way too excited to sleep. The next thing she remembered was being wakened up for dinner. She took a quick bath and made her way to the kitchen.

Bertie came to her, put her arms around Emma and told her how happy she was about their baby news. She and Millie wouldn't let Emma help with dinner or the dishes. Harold escorted her into the parlor after dinner and brought her a dozen or so pillows (even bedroom pillows until his mother told him to stop) because his mother had told him to help Emma to be comfortable. As Emma sat there she thought about what a special family she now had. They were all nice people, doing nice things for each other.

Emma saw that it was very hard for Albert to try to move into his father's territory. "I see him everywhere," he told her. "How can I do this?"

Millie had told Emma that Frank felt the same way about now running the construction business.

"Frank said he constantly second-guesses every decision he makes because your dad is no longer here to use as a sounding board," Emma told him. It took time for the boys to move into their father's shoes. Gradually life did seem to get more normal.

Bertie and Emma fit together pretty well when it came to sharing responsibilities for running the house. The traveling Emma had done left her very, very tired and those first few weeks she slept a lot. In those days women didn't go to see the doctor until very late in the pregnancy unless there were problems. They would simply ask the doctor to stand by around a certain date. Since Emma had been under a lot of stress during the year with Syd's death, moving (twice), the trip to Europe, etc., Bertie suggested she be checked out by Doc Jameson just to be sure that all was well. He found everything fine. He suggested that she rest every day. Bertie was an experienced midwife so Emma knew she had nothing to worry about. Beverly Jensen, who lived next door, came in every day with her little one, Robbie, and Millie came often with Harold. With their help they soon had the room ready for the baby. Harold insisted that the baby had to be a boy. Albert was sure they would have a girl. A little princess. And he was right. They had a beautiful baby girl to start their family. They thought of naming her Alberta Rose for their two mothers. But Albert wanted something regal. He insisted it had to be a name worthy of a queen. He couldn't quite decide on Elizabeth or Catherine. They finally settled on Elizabeth Alberta. They would call their sweet baby, Beth.

Beth was a beautiful baby. They put her on the kitchen scales and found she weighed just a bit less than seven pounds. She had a head full of light hair and a little rosebud mouth. She was an independent baby, doing things on her schedule, not Emma's but Emma soon learned to work out compromises with her. She seemed to do everything (smiling, sitting up, teething, and walking) all well within the standards. She had a love affair with her dad and always had a big smile for him when he lifted her in his arms. Albert strutted around like he was a king.

The year was a very busy one for Emma and also for Albert. The book he and Simon had written had been sent to the publishers. After some polishing, the book was now in production. Albert was very, very pleased that in the final stages, Simon included Albert's name under his own as the author of the book. A published book means a lot in the world of academia. Albert was starting to receive requests to be a guest lecturer at other colleges. He had finished the work for his Master's degree quickly and began work on his doctorate. He was offered a full professorship at Glenridge which he accepted. But he always made time for his family.

As a new mom, most of Emma's day was spent with the baby and with all the other new moms who lived on the street. They all spent time together. The new moms were encouraged by the moms with more experience. It was wonderful to live on Lincoln Boulevard. No one ever locked their doors. Children were welcome in any home. The moms knew they would be supervised. The unwritten procedure when visiting one's neighbor was to ring the doorbell, open the door, announce your name and walk in. It worked great for them since no one had to stop doing anything to go answer the door. They learned each other's kitchens so they could get the many drinks of water or snacks for the children.

As a new year arrived they had some surprises. First, three moms on the street announced they were pregnant, including Millie. And then surprise. Emma found she was pregnant again. There would be just one year between the two children. They were all excited and looked forward to raising the children together. Millie and Frank named their baby boy, Herbert. Emma and Albert named their second beautiful little girl Catherine Rose.

Cathy was a completely different child than Beth. She had the same reddish hair as her grandmother, Rose. She was a very contented baby who hardly ever cried. Emma looked forward to all those mommy things, baby dolls, and frilly dresses just alike (with maybe one for Emma that was like theirs). Beth was moved into a big girl's room and Cathy slept in the little room off the master bedroom. Now, Albert really felt like a king with a harem. They had a lot of laughter in the home.

A very important thing happened in 1920. Finally, the year had arrived that would let women vote for the President of the United States. They took this responsibility very seriously. They held meetings trying to understand the policies of the candidates. Warren G. Harding and Calvin Coolidge made up the Republican ticket. President Woodrow Wilson supported the Democratic ticket of James Cox and Franklin D. Roosevelt. The women, women of all ages, studied the records of all the men. Some women seemed inclined to vote one way and some the other. They decided that it would make a statement if they all went together in a group to vote. They got all dressed up in their Sunday clothes, wore hats and gloves, and walked to the local elementary school where the polling booths had been set up. Some of the men tried to be funny and made a big scene trying to get out of the way of the women. They asked if the women needed help in voting. The woman took very seriously their right to vote and the right to keep that vote private. Emma felt very good that day since she had worked on the issue for almost six years. Warren Harding won that election.

As their two babies started to grow Emma and Albert saw they had very different personalities. Beth was a little more intense and wanted to do everything for herself. Cathy was laid-back and content wherever she was. Many children were in and out of the house even when they were babies. It was great having Bertie to lend a hand and give moral support to Emma when Emma was sure she was doing everything wrong. The girls thrived with all the love around them and two years later they all looked forward to their third little girl, Anne Mildred, (named for Millie). Annie had dark curly hair like her dad, and a third personality was added to their mix.

Life was good. Albert started to be recognized for his work and research; the girls were thriving. Bertie was a wonderful grandmother. Emma had time to take on some volunteer work as well as continue with her poetry readings. Life was good.

One bright sunny afternoon Bertie and Emma sat on the back porch snapping a bushel of green beans that they planned to can. Even though they didn't have a big garden just a few tomatoes, lettuce and green onions, they went to the market and bought produce to can for use during the winter. Bertie told Emma that day how surprised she had been to find Emma already knew so much about canning. As they talked, Bertie said Emma had taught her little tricks she had learned from her Aunt Kate. Emma was feeling very good as she sat and snapped the ends off the green beans. She had laid a big old blanket on the floor in the corner of the porch and Annie lay there sleeping peacefully. Beth and Robbie were in the tree house *they* built (of course with their dads' help to keep it safe). Cathy was playing with other children from the street on the tire swing. It was a very peaceful day – not too hot – and Emma just had to comment to Bertie on how content she felt.

"I'm glad." Bertie said, "I hope Syd can look down from heaven and see us today. It would make him happy to know we're OK." Bertie paused a moment. "You know, I'm feeling very strange. I have a funny feeling all over."

Emma put her pan down and walked to her. "Let's go in the house. Maybe you should lie down."

Bertie gave Emma a strange look and mumbled something to her that Emma could not understand. As Emma got to her Bertie suddenly slumped forward and fell from her chair.

"Robbie," Emma screamed. "Run and get your mother."

Emma tried to lay her flat on the floor. Beverly and Jim Jenson ran quickly from next door. Jim lifted Bertie carefully in his arms and carried her to her bed.

Beverly began to call out orders. The only telephone on the street at that time was down at the corner store. Beverly told one child to tell her mother to run to the corner store to call the doctor. Other neighbors heard the screaming and came to help. One immediately took the baby, Annie, and all the other children to her house. Another ran down the street to tell Millie, who sent that woman to the corner store to phone Albert and Frank.

When the doctor examined Bertie he told them she had suffered a massive stroke. They could pray for a miracle, he told them, which they did. Most likely she would only live a matter of hours.

Albert, Frank, Millie and Emma sat with Bertie, stroking her hand and telling her they loved her. Toward five the next morning, Bertie passed away. It was a horrible shock to them. They grieved as they laid her to rest.

Emma realized how much she depended on the older, wiser advice she sought from family members. Now she would be expected to know everything. She felt daunted and worried by such a responsibility. Emma was never sure how she managed the next few weeks. She was so thankful for the help and support she got from her neighbors. Lincoln Boulevard truly was a wonderful place to live. The street always had nice people and families living there – always ready to help each other. *No wonder I want my girls to live here forever* Emma thought.

That phrase became a joke among the children, even when they were very small. Beth said she would marry Robbie and live in his house. Cathy would marry – well, someone. It changed almost daily. She would live in the Martin house. That left Annie. Annie, who first decided she would marry her cousin, Herb, and live in the house built by her Uncle Frank. When she was told you don't marry cousins, she was quite distressed until she made up her mind that she would not stay in Glenridge; she would marry a handsome man and travel the world.

The house was very big and lonely the first few months after Bertie died.

Albert was still driving the used car his dad had bought them as a wedding present. He and Frank talked a lot about cars. One day Albert came home and said he had decided to buy a new car.

"I want to get a big car," he said. "We may have many more children and we'll need a big car."

After shopping around, he bought a Model T Fordor Sedan Touring Car. It was very expensive, $260. It was a beauty. He drove it around the block about one hundred times that first night, giving every neighbor and every child a ride in it. Emma thought it was a delightful car to drive. She had learned how to drive from her cousins when she lived on the farm.

Albert and Frank came up with a plan. The families would take a vacation together in this magnificent automobile. Albert and Frank would do the driving and sit in the front seat with Harold in the middle. Millie and Emma would hold Herb and Annie on their laps. Beth and Cathy would sit in the middle in the back seat. An attachment was available that was like a canopy which could be fastened on the side of the car. They would spread blankets on the ground and sleep under the canopy.

They gathered together the things they would need to take – camp stove, utensils, pillows and blankets, food, etc. The men kept the destination secret until Mille and Emma declared war on them. Was it to be all camping (they would take old clothes) or would there be some city visits (dress up clothes)? The men finally told the women their plans for the trip.

They would drive from Glenridge to Port Huron, Michigan, where they would take a ferry to cross the St. Lawrence River to go to Sarnia, Canada. Next they would drive to Niagara Falls. They would cross into Buffalo, New York and drive around Lake Erie and then to Detroit and home. This was so many miles to travel Millie and Emma teased them asking them if they would include the moon on the trip.

After school was out in the spring, they started their journey. They stopped at lunch time to eat the sandwiches that Millie and Emma would prepare in the morning. They stopped at many farmers' roadside markets to buy fruit. In the evening when they saw a nice level field, they would stop, pull out their camping supplies and settle in for the night. Sometimes it would be near a farm house so they would ask for permission. When they did this they often were offered a bale of hay to spread under their blankets or maybe fresh milk for the children. The Martins always offered to pay for it. No one could ever remember if anyone took the money. Sometimes the farmer's wife seemed pleased for someone to talk with. When they slept at night, Albert and Frank slept on either end with the rest of the family piled in between. It was really an adventure. They took loads of blankets to put beneath them. In the morning they had to fix breakfast and then pack everything up and stow it on top of the car and along the running boards. They talked often about how easy they had it compared to the pioneers who first traveled across the prairies and mountains to travel out west.

Niagara Falls was magnificent, something everyone should see in their lifetime. The roaring rough and tumbling water, the steep cliffs left the family stunned. They stood in awe as they first saw it. The mist from the force of the water beginning its downward slope covered them as they stood along the railing atop of the falls. It was nearly dinnertime when they first saw the falls. They were fortunate enough to arrive at the very right time of day. While they stood looking at the beauty of it all, a huge rainbow formed over the falls. They could see every color of the rainbow. It was so thick they felt like they could reach out and touch it. Millie and Emma scrambled to keep track of the children for they wanted to climb over the railing to capture the rainbow. The family stayed at a hotel that night. The next day they walked down to the base of the falls where they were given yellow rain slicker, hats and boots and taken on a ride to the base of the falls on the boat called *The Maid of the Mist*. The boat rocked in the heavy waves. Many people became afraid and were upset. Beth made her dad go with her so she could be in the most forward place, stood on the lowest rail (with Albert holding on to her), threw out her arms and shouted with glee. She loved it. The family had another adventure. They all got on a cable car that was high in the air. It crossed a gorge which is one of the few places in the world where the water changes direction. From the cable car you could see the huge whirlpool form as it spun and churned the water. The cable car looked like the basket of a hot air balloon. Instead of floating free it was secured to huge cables stretching from the cliffs on one side to the base position on the other. The cable car didn't turn around, it moved back and forth. Everyone was told to exchange seats from one side to the other when the car reached the cliffs so everyone could get a good view. Beth was thrilled. They saw many beautiful flower gardens and took many, many pictures with their brownie camera. They did one other major thing; they walked in the caves under the falls. They had to have the rain slickers for this, too, because in many, many places they were on the inside of the falls and the water splashed in around them.

All too soon it was time to move on. They crossed into New York, and a bit of Pennsylvania and all of northern Ohio as they made their way to Detroit. They camped outside of Detroit. The next morning Albert and Frank told them to put on dress-up clothes that day as they were going to a place outside of Detroit called Highland Park. They were going to see the newest automobile assembly plant built by Henry Ford. This time both Harold and Beth jumped up and down with joy. They saw structures of steel, brick and cement with many, many windows so the workers would have light. There were a few other assembly plants in the world. This one was very special. The fastest time for an old plant was 728 minutes to assemble an automobile. This plant took only 93 minutes. A car was coming off the line constantly, most of them the Model T. One out of every eight cars in the world at that time was a Model T.

Very tired, by this point, and very happy, the family headed back for Glenridge. That trip, surrounded by family, along with her first trip to Paris always was at the top of Emma's favorite traveling.

As the Martin daughters started to grow Emma and Albert could see how each one of the girls was an individual. The parents talked about how they could let each girl develop her own personality yet keep them close to each other.

Beth was the tomboy. She didn't care for dolls very much but she had a teddy bear she toted around when she was little. Beth, and even Robbie attended some tea parties for her sisters' dolls. She and Robbie Jensen, the boy next door were always together. When Robbie learned to ride a two wheel bike, so did Beth. When Beverly and Emma gave them permission to ride to the end of the block, they went around the block. When they got permission to go around the block, they went to the next block. There was always some treasure they saw just around the corner that they had to investigate. They would drag home big empty cartons which they would take to the third floor attic and make airplanes or boats of them and go on many make-believe adventures. One day Beth sneaked the world globe from her father's office and took it to the attic. She told her dad they needed it to plan their travels.

When Robbie was about eight or nine years old he decided they needed to build a go-cart. Beth took him to Uncle Frank's where they got enough wood and some left over wheels from Uncle Frank's equipment. Together, with supervision and teaching from their fathers, they put together a cart with two seats which they pushed up and down the sidewalk. This was not good enough for them. So they began to scrounge around for an engine. Off they went to see Henry Calvin who lived down the street. He was always tinkering with engines. When he saw their cart he told them he had one just the right size for their go-cart. Albert and Jim Jenson reluctantly gave permission for them to use it. They made the children promise to always stay on the sidewalk and watch out for any walkers. There was very little traffic on the boulevard during the day and one day the temptation was too much. Off they went into the street, Beth holding tight around Robbie's waist as they sped down the street. About two or three minutes later the community heard the sound of sirens in the air. Everyone ran from their homes to see what was happening. The neighbors saw Beth and Robbie getting a stern lecture from a policeman and a ticket for riding in the street. They had to go to court. The judge appeared very stern as he sentenced them to two weeks of trash pickup in the park. Jim, Beverly, Albert and Emma went to shake hands with the judge as they left. The judge told them he had never had any defendants in his court that made him smile until that day. It was the first time he ever had a case of *go-cart speeding.* He said they must be pretty smart kids to design and create a motorized go-cart.

Their next big adventure came a year or so later when Henry Calvin stopped them one day and told them about a 1922 Chevy coupe with a rumble seat that had been in an accident. The driver had been from out-of-state and said to junk it. Henry thought that maybe they could buy it for $10. The engine had some damage and the car didn't look very good. Beth and Robbie decided they would have fun working on it. Of course they were much too young to drive. They tried to convince their dads that they would learn about a car by working on it and would have plenty of time to repair it. Of course, Beverly and Emma were opposed. But Jim and Albert saw it as a fun project. Jim knew a lot about cars and said he would help the kids repair it if Albert would teach the kids to drive. They were so young they knew they had a few years to make it happen. The fathers told the kids that they had to pay for the repair parts and do the work. This was their idea of stretching out the repairs until they were of legal age to drive. As Jim taught them he made them do the work. They loved every minute of it. That car was eventually restored and both Robbie and Beth drove it for some years. They got side-tracked along the way.

One day Beth came home from a long bike ride with Robbie and announced at dinner that evening that she and Robbie were going to learn to fly an airplane. They had ridden their bikes out to the airfield and talked with the men there about taking lessons. They were only about ten and twelve at the time. They offered to wash the planes in exchange for lessons. The men good-naturedly told them they had a deal. The men never expected to see the kids again. But on Saturday Beth and Robbie showed up and they kept going back. They were shown a stack of books with charts and lessons and were told they had to learn all of it before they could learn to fly. Those men later told the families they expected the lessons to last for a couple of weeks. They planned take the kids for a ride to pay them for washing the planes. It did not work out that way. They learned to drive a car and fly a plane at the same time. Flying seemed to be a natural for both of them. They became the youngest pilots to use that field.

It was hard not to let Beth have her adventures. She was always curious about everything and studied hard to learn about things. She was a good student, helped in Sunday School each week and did her chores at home. She was learning to be a good cook at that time and often prepared dinner. She became quite an accomplished pianist.

Cathy was the cool, calm level-headed daughter. As a baby she seldom cried. When her sister Annie was born, Cathy would get her doll and do for it whatever Emma did for Annie. She loved the cats, Ginger and Pepper, and would feed and brush them each day. She became a *mother* to anyone younger than she and took care of all the kids on the street. If a child fell or skinned a knee they would run to Cathy for consolation. The older people in the neighborhood loved her because she would visit with them briefly each day to make sure they were OK. Sometimes she would carry her little doctor bag and check their hearts with her toy stethoscope. In the attic of the home she collected doll buggies and cribs and created her own hospital. She loved to go to see Doc Jameson who always gave her some *supplies* like a couple of bandages, etc. When she got her vaccination before starting school she went right home and using an ink pen *vaccinated* each of the dolls that were in the house. When Annie cried that her doll didn't need it, Cathy carefully explained why it had to be done. At school one day when a child was injured the teacher fainted at the sight of the blood. Cathy took over. She sent one child to run for help while she used her handkerchief to hold on the boy's wound. Emma remembered that all Cathy wanted for Christmas the year she was eight was a wristwatch with a second hand on it so she could check the pulses of everyone in the neighborhood. Doc Jameson had taught her how to do it. She *advised* Dr. Jameson she would someday be a doctor in his office.

This same care was applied to the critters that got injured. She brought home any injured animal or bird she saw. Albert talked with Doc about Cathy's *hospital.* Doc took time to talk to her about which animals or critters not to touch or bring home. She brought home a stray kitten once. Ginger and Pepper had ruled so long that they were very unfriendly to the intruder. She scolded them firmly and gave the kitten a home in the garage. Albert used to complain that he had no room for his car in the garage. Some of the mothers on the street would ask Cathy to come to take care of their kids so they could get a special job done.

One year for Christmas Cathy was given a book about Florence Nightingale. She decided she would become a nurse. Doc Jameson told her that was fine but why didn't she become a doctor. The next Christmas she was given a book about Elizabeth Blackwell, the first woman to be a doctor. From that point on, that became her goal in life. When she was about eleven she asked Doc Jameson if she could work for him. He gave her a job on Saturday mornings to help keep his supplies in order. She worked hard making sure that each item was in its proper place. By the time she was in her early teens she was volunteering at the hospital to play games with some of the kids who were able to do so. Just like she brought home sick or injured critters, she also brought people home. No one was ever sure how many people would be there for a meal so they cooked plenty. Like Beth (and Annie too), she had chores at home and had to keep her school work up to date. She also loved to cook and would try many new recipes.

Cathy had many boy friends when she was in high school. She became a manager for the football and basketball teams because she had *medical skills.* Once Emma overheard one parent tell another that Cathy would know what to do. Of course, the doc was always within call. Cathy looked forward to the various dances and was chairman of the Prom Committee. Shopping for her prom dress was certainly different than shopping with Beth. She had to try on every dress in blue and ended up with a full skirted style dress that flared out when she danced. There were sequins on the dress that sparkled when she moved. Her long hair was pulled away from her face and in a long page boy in the back. She looked like a princess.

Annie was their bossy child who always told her older sisters what to do. She had a knack of doing it with a beaming smile that had them doing it cheerfully. Most people knew early on that she would be a teacher like her parents. She played school constantly and made the younger children in the neighborhood be her students. It was an accepted fact that she taught every child on the street his or her ABC's, to count to 100, how to add small numbers, and how to color inside the lines. She mostly did this in the back yard in the summer. In the winter she would take everyone up to her section of the attic and hold classes. She seemed happiest when she was home entertaining her friends. Yet she kept telling every one she would not teach until she had taken a trip around the world. She spent many hours going through travel brochures and planning her trip.

In High School Annie developed a love for politics and world events. She and her dad spent a lot of time discussing what was happening in the world. She shared her dad's love of history. Annie volunteered for various local candidates for office and complained bitterly that she would not be able to be selected to be an aide to a congressman. Only boys were allowed to do that. By the time Annie was dating, Albert and Emma were so used to having any number of different boys around the house it seemed like they had sons as well as daughters.

All three girls learned to play the piano and they all could sing quite well. They would harmonize together as they did dishes each evening or when they would be cleaning the house. Their voices could be heard all over the house: soprano from one room, second soprano from another, and alto from a third room.

After Bertie had died the family was very lonely, especially on Sundays, so Emma started a new plan. Each Sunday they would invite someone home from church for dinner. Their meal was usually something that Emma could put in the oven before leaving for church. Usually the guests would be someone new to the community or someone who hadn't been in church for a while. It reminded Emma of how interesting it was in the boarding house when she was a child or the family dinners in Pennsylvania. Sometimes the girls would play the piano and sing for the guests. Very soon, neighbors heard about the *program* and began to drop by. Albert suggested that they bring their musical instruments so they could have a musicale each Sunday afternoon. Fortunately, their parlor was very large. Sometimes they had five or six guests. Often the crowd would grow to about eighteen. They were very crowded but no one seemed to notice. If you didn't play an instrument it didn't matter. You could still sing or hum along. They had some musicians who were talented. Often they were first year students. No one ever heard the mistakes. They sang and played with great enthusiasm.

One day Albert surprised Emma with a special guest who arrived late on a Sunday afternoon. When the doorbell rang one of the girls answered it and thinking it was another guest to join the music said to come in and find a chair. When Emma saw a new person come into the room, she looked – once, twice, and then again. She rushed to him as he reached out to give her a hug.

"Cousin Will!" she shouted. "How did you get here?"

Albert came over to meet him and explained. At a meeting of the professors at Glenridge, the professor who headed up the science department had brought with him a list of people invited to a seminar being held at Glenridge. Albert had spied the name of a William Wilson: Professor William Wilson from California. On a hunch he had written back to ask if he was any relation to an Emma Wilson who had lived in Pennsylvania with her aunt and uncle. Will had written back to say he was a cousin to Emma. In fact, when he planned his trip to Glenridge, he hoped he could see Emma. Albert wrote back inviting him to stay with them and decided not to tell Emma about it in case Will didn't make it.

It was such a joyful day to reunite with him and hear about the family. Will was the family member Emma rode to high school with who also wanted to go to college. The family did find a way to send him. He had become a professor of biology at a university in California, was married and had three children. He stayed with them during that visit and they visited him once in California.

Everywhere Albert traveled he would meet many interesting people whom he would invite home. He never lost his touch for learning little interesting tidbits about the places he visited. He had a list of people he corresponded with all over the United States.

One day he received a letter from a man he had met on the ship to Paris years before. This man, Alec Johnson, had been an employee of the Queen Ann. Now he was the cruise director on a new cruise ship that would be sailing from California to Hawaii. The Pink Palace, a beautiful resort hotel that was entirely pink, had been built in Honolulu. It was a big attraction to draw people from all over the world. The cruise line wanted to make the cruise very luxurious and entertaining on the trip. Alec asked Albert if he would come for a two week cruise and entertain the guests with lectures on Hawaii on the way over and back. If Albert would do it he could take his family with him to see Hawaii. He would not have to give lectures while they were in port for five days. They could sleep on the ship which would be moored at the port. During the planning Alec remembered that Emma had given a reading at High Tea. He asked if she would be able to entertain the ladies.

It didn't take too long for both of them to say yes. It was a wonderful, wonderful trip. The family never forgot seeing the beautiful palace (for it truly was a palace) nestled among the other hotels being built. The others were beautiful but not as spectacular. You could see the bright pink of the palace from miles away. There were no outside walls on the first floor. Just pillars holding up the structure. Beautiful tropic flowers filled the gardens surrounding it. Inside, everything was pink. The palace had a catamaran with a big pink sail. One day the family took a ride on it. Catamarans never make a sound and it was amazing to be sailing on the ocean. The water was so clear they could see schools of fish swimming by. It looked like you could see the bottom; of course the water was very deep. The coastline that ran in front of the hotel was very rugged. There was no sandy beach; the sand was shipped in years later to create beautiful Waikiki Beach. There was a wonderful lagoon, surrounded by more flowers where they could swim.

One night a week the hotel held a luau for the guests. The ship's crew was invited to attend. They watched the chefs roast the pig all day. That night they ate a wonderful meal which included poi which they had never eaten. They learned to eat it by dipping their fingers into the bowl and eating it from their fingers. They were given leis made from orchids to wear around their neck. They learned that orchids grow abundantly in Hawaii. Many guests were wearing traditional Hawaiian clothes; muumuus for the women and loose shirts for the men. The show was wonderful. It was traditional Hawaiian with lots of hula dancers in grass skirts, sword dancers, fire dancers and audience participation. They spent their days at the lagoon and sight-seeing. Of course, Albert was always looking for little out of the way places he could talk about in his lectures. One guest told the captain that Albert's talk had been so interesting he wanted to come back and see the things he had missed. Then it was back to the ship at night to sleep.

They made many new friends with the crew on the ship. Beth was very interested in the mechanics of the ship and made friends with the crew who let her explore it. They ate with the crew and found the crew liked to put on their own shows each night for entertainment for each other. Soon the Martin family was part of the show. The girls sang and danced and Albert, using his gift of gab, did a short talk which he made very funny and used the names of some of the crew members. Emma heard a couple of good singers among them so Albert made them come up front. They sang while Emma played piano. Two of the crew members taught them all how to dance the Charleston. This was the rage dance back home. This trip became another to add to her favorites.

The 1920's were called the Roaring Twenties and it was easy to understand why. Things seemed pretty good. A party atmosphere was in the air. Most women had to have at least one flapper dress and cloche hat. When Charles Lindbergh flew across the Atlantic for the first time, everyone realized the world was becoming smaller. Of course Beth was thrilled and hoped to be the first woman to make that flight. The League of Nations was formed which gave them all hope for peace in the world. And on the home front they enjoyed a big new innovation – talking movies. *The Jazz Singer* with Al Jolson was certainly the big hit of the century. What a treat not to have to read the dialogue as you tried to watch the screen.

All was not as good as it seemed on the world front. A young German man, Adolph Hitler, moved onto the scene. With Albert's love of European history, he wanted to learn more about the man so he read the book Hitler wrote called *Mien Kampf.* Albert expressed his concerns about the young leader. He didn't dwell on his concerns about the man at the time but he did remember it later when Hitler moved the Germany Army into many countries in Europe.

The good times of the 1920's did not last. The tragic crash of the stock market touched every citizen. With life savings gone, the dreams of families disappeared. It seemed like things got worse every day. Jobs disappeared. Businesses closed. It didn't take long before the families on Lincoln Boulevard were affected. Many children who had married and moved away came back home to live with their parents. Men would go stand on street corners hoping someone would hire them for the day. The people living on Lincoln were proud people. No one wanted anyone else to know about their troubles. Neighbors no longer ran in or out of each other's houses. They no longer saw men walking to catch the streetcar on the corner to go to work. They saw some of the neighbors taking in laundry to earn a little money. There seemed to be no hope in the country. Some of the young people tried to move to a different part of the country. The problems were everywhere. Many people sold their cars. They used the car payment and gasoline money to buy food.

The Martins were luckier than most yet not immune from the sorrow. At least Albert had a job which did not go away although he did take a cut in wages. Most women school teachers were laid off so that men could have the jobs. This worried Albert who had always supported Emma's efforts to gain equality for women. He knew of many women teachers who were the sole support of their children and aging parents. The Martins had always tried to save a little money which they planned to use for the children's education. Now that money was gone – not spent – just gone as if it never existed.

Frank and Millie were also very worried. No one who owed Frank money could pay him. He owed creditors who sold him supplies for the construction company. Frank was very worried about the men who worked for him. They had been loyal employees for many years. They had families. He and Albert spent many agonizing hours trying to find a way to help them. Finally they hit on a plan. Frank called his employees together to present it. Some people in the country still had money and were looking for a bargain. If Frank sold some of his assets – his newest equipment which made everyone's work so much easier – he could use that money to pay his staff for a while longer. They would have to go back to the old way of doing things. Frank spoke full of confidence with hope for the future. While a few younger men wanted to move on, most were relieved to still have a job. Many times both Albert and Frank would slip some money in the pockets of a man and ask him to deliver coal to heat the homes of some neighbor or family they knew who was having a struggle.

When President Franklin D. Roosevelt, Jr. was elected he encouraged people to be hopeful about the future. Emma decided something needed to be done. One day she learned that many of the children who went to school with her girls no longer brought a lunch to school. Emma knew that she had shelves of canned food in her basement. So did most of the neighbors. She called the women on Lincoln to her home to discuss the problem. Their kids were all eating well even if they didn't have any spending money for extras. Every child deserved a lunch. So they decided they would fix a lunch each day and take it to the school. Emma went to three local meat markets. She asked them to donate some kind of meat once a week. Sometimes it was beef or a few slices of ham which they would use to make soup. Sometimes it would be a small amount of lunch meat which they ground up to make a sandwich spread. Another woman went to the grocery store and asked for flour so they could make bread or buns. On occasion the grocer also donated peanut butter or cheese. At the fruit market the owner said he would donate fresh oranges or apples once a week. With the fruit and vegetables each of the women had canned they knew they could make a nourishing lunch for the children each day.

That left them with a need for milk. Emma went to the local dairy, who somewhat reluctantly agreed to bring little bottles of milk each day for a month. That month stretched into the school year. Each woman agreed to take on part of the chore of organizing to prepare the lunch. They felt good to be able to do something.

One day while out doing chores in the community Emma was sad to hear how desolate and lonely most people felt even though they had the necessities. Emma thought of another project. She heard later that President Roosevelt had thought of it first but Emma didn't know it at that time. They would get together a reading group each week. People had no money for entertainment so eagerly looked forward to the weekly get-togethers. Emma decided they should read Shakespeare's plays so that everyone could have a turn. The men and women loved reading it. They really got into their parts. They took the books home. They practiced so they could read the part with feeling.

Someone suggested that another night of the week they should all get together for a sing-along. So usually on Saturday night the group would gather in the Martin's parlor. They sang all the old songs and a few of the new. Jim Jenson said that they had to begin each session with the new song everyone was singing—*Happy Days Are Here Again.* Emma was thankful for being able to live on such a nice street; to have such wonderful neighbors. They were all there for each other. Gradually, things in the country began to improve.

Of course they had their scandals, also. At the end of their street a woman in her late thirties or early forties lived with her aged mother everyone called Grandma. The old mother never left the house. Her constant companion was a parrot that talked. He really did have a small vocabulary. The children on the street would all stop to visit her. She would let the kids feed a soda cracker to the parrot. At the other end of the street, a single man lived in the home of his sister and brother-in-law but he spent most nights in the room he had over the gas station he owned on the next street over. Well, even though the neighbors tried not to gossip they did notice that over time they began to see the single lady walking home from the gas station to Grandma's very, very early in the morning. Everyone tried to be discreet; still they began to look for her each day. Grandma lived to be one hundred years old. After she died they discovered they did not have a scandal after all. Grandma had not wanted the daughter to marry and refused to let the man come to her home. This old lady they thought was sweet and kind was really a tyrant about her daughter. The couple had married in spite of Grandma. They lived apart for many years so she could take care of her mother.

Another neighbor story concerns a young man who lived near the end of the block who fell in love at age seventeen with a young girl down the street. He would visit with her each evening until 11 o'clock when her dad made him leave. He could whistle like a bird. Each night upon leaving her home he would whistle all the way home. You could set your clocks by him. There was another character. He liked to go to the pub every Saturday night. He also liked to imbibe a little, well maybe he liked to imbibe a lot. The pub was about four blocks away. Each Saturday night about midnight he would walk home. He would sing all the way home. The neighbors all hoped the children wouldn't wake up because some of the ditties he would sing were . . . . .well, you might say they were not appropriate for children's ears. On Sunday morning he, with his family, all got in the car and went to church. It truly was a wonderful neighborhood. Emma and Albert watched their girls thrive and become good young women.

Beth and Robbie were both hooked on flying. They spent all their spare time out at the field. They did local flying. They accumulated many hours in the air. Each of them made cargo flights to Detroit and Chicago when she was sixteen and he was seventeen. Though the parents worried about them, the airport manager said they were among the best pilots he had.

In the early years, Beverly Jensen and Emma often talked about the closeness of Robbie and Beth. They were sure that they both would have many loves in their lives. They hoped that when a new love came along Beth and Robbie would be able to deal with seeing their partner with someone else. That didn't happen. The big change in their relationship came the night of Robbie's prom. Though almost two years older, he was only one school year ahead. Both of them said they were not interested in going to the prom. Beverly and Emma (as well as Cathy and Annie) insisted they had to go.

Beth tried on many dresses. She hated every one of them. They had too many flowers, or too many ruffles, or too many . . . whatevers. Suddenly she spotted a navy blue dress. Emma thought it was too sophisticated for her. Beth insisted on trying it on. It was navy blue with a very light scattering of off-white dots. The fabric was between a silk and satin. It had a slip-like top with little straps over the shoulders. It was fitted down to her knees. There was a flare at the bottom that was softly layered in the back in the same fabric that reached the floor. A touch of red was on the bottom of each layer. It fit her young body so well. She looked so beautiful Emma wanted to cry. Her Beth had grown up right before her eyes. Emma hadn't seen it until she saw her in that dress. It was expensive—$20. Beth loved that dress. Finally, Emma said OK.

Beth was wearing her hair pretty short those days. On prom day it was done in waves close to her head, the style of the day called a finger wave. Robbie brought her a corsage of red roses. When he saw her in that dress the parents could all see that he never again would think of her as his little playmate. Their relationship shifted from good friends to something more that night. They went off to the prom in the 1922 Chevy they had rebuilt. As soon as the kids left, Beverly and Jim, who had come over to see them off, hurried home. When they left, Albert went into his office and shut the door. Emma went upstairs. They knew that night that Beth was now a young woman, not a child, and Robbie was a young man.

Robbie got a scholarship to the U.S. Naval Academy. He wrote to Beth every day. She went to visit him with Beverly, Jim and Robbie's younger brother, Freddie. On the day he graduated Robbie asked Beth to marry him. He gave her the diamond ring that had been his grandmother's. Beth still had a year left of college at Glenridge. Robbie had applied for fighter training. Because of world conditions they all worried about him.

They also knew that Adolph Hitler had invaded and taken Austria then continued to take more and more of Europe. Now England was taking a beating from the nightly raids on their country. Everyone worried that United States would get into the war. Some of Robbie's graduating friends left for Canada immediately to join the RCAF so they would be able to help in the fight against Hitler. The families were all afraid that Robbie would also go enlist in the RCAF and be sent to Europe. He was selected to learn how to fly new fighter planes that were just being built. The families were on pins and needles as he completed his training. Beth did lots of griping that she was not able to enlist in the Army Air Corp. Women just didn't do those things.

In the meantime, Cathy was also growing up. She wasn't as tall as Beth. Her body was tight and firm. She was well endowed in the bust and hips with a tiny waist. She wore her reddish-brown hair in a variety of styles – pulled back into a pony tail or bun for school and hanging loose for social times. She loved to dance and attended every dance at high school or college. She spent a lot of time with a gang of both girls and guys. They were always involved in something or other. She did not give up her love of medicine. She wanted to be a doctor. By this time she had been a candy-striper at the hospital for many years. She assisted in a lot of different positions. There were a couple of boys the family thought she might get serious with but she loved everyone. She took a lot of science classes during her first years of college. She did well in all of them. She did not do as well in European history which caused her dad some concern.

Annie grew to be the tallest of the girls. She seemed to be able to eat anything and still stay slender. She kept her long, curly black hair hanging around her face most of the time. She definitely had it in her mind to be a world traveler. She and her friend, Rosemary, were cheerleaders. She was very interested in art. She had a group of her friends at the house all the time. Their home was a gathering place. Annie was the most political of the sisters and worked on several local campaigns. She was very concerned about what was happening in the world. She would sit with her dad in his office, listening to the news, and discussing world events. Albert put a big world map on the wall. They would pin little flags on it to show where the fighting was taking place.

In the United States young men between the ages of 21 to 45 were required to register for a draft into the military. By early fall of 1941, the government lowered the age for men to register for the draft to age eighteen.

The people were concerned about the war in Europe. News reports told of the bombing and loss of life. Some children were being evacuated and sent to America. The aid the United States was providing to the Allies helped but nothing seemed to be enough to end the war. Hitler was on the move in Europe and Africa. The German army went both east to Russia and west to France. In 1940 Paris fell to German rule. After a heroic battle at Dunkirk in the English Channel, the British forces had apparently stopped an invasion of England at that time.

After Robbie had completed the first part of his fighter training the family got some good news. He was being sent to Hickam Field in Hawaii to complete his training. Beverly, Jim, Albert and Emma heaved a sigh of relief. Hawaii was a long way from Europe. Emma remembered their wonderful trip there and what a good time they had. Robbie started immediately to beg his folks to come over for Christmas. He wanted them to bring Beth with them. The parents were giving it some thought.

While many families were concerned about the war, Europe seemed very far away. The country was recovering from the great depression. For the most part, life was good.

DECEMBER 7TH, 1941

Emma Martin woke up early the morning of December 7th. It was just before five o'clock and usually she didn't get up until six. *Might as well get up and get started on the day* she thought. She went downstairs, plugged in the electric percolator to start a pot of coffee and turned on the radio. The news was on so she listened briefly to reports coming from London, Africa, and all over Europe. It distressed Emma as she listened. The United States might not be in the war but it made her remember how as a young woman she had heard similar reports before the United States entered World War I. She thought about all the young men fighting over there. Well, she and Albert didn't have sons to be drafted. They had daughters.

Emma knew that Beth wanted to join the Army Air Corp but they did not accept women. Beth complained a lot about the discrimination.

Cathy had come home from school recently saying she had attended a meeting held by a woman who represented the Red Cross. The woman was trying to recruit young student nurses to join the International Red Cross when they graduated. The Red Cross supplied the Army Nurse Corp in the United States as well as nursing services all over the world. The woman was just back from Europe where she had been serving in the battlefield hospitals. She told of a desperate shortage of nurses. Cathy had met with the woman individually, still expressing her desire to become a doctor. The woman had urged Cathy to postpone her medical school plans, which would take years, and instead become a nurse. Emma could see that Cathy was seriously thinking about it. But Emma knew Cathy was serious about becoming a doctor. And that would take many years.

Annie, being more political, seemed obsessed by the war news. She and her dad, Albert, spent time every evening following the fighting taking place in Europe. Since Albert's field was history, he and Annie constantly studied current events happening in the world. They would listen to the news and look at the world map in his office.

Emma had great empathy for her friends with sons.

She stood over the coffee pot waiting for it to finish perking. She poured some into a cup. *Enough news,* she thought, *it's Sunday.* At their home Sunday meant get out of bed, start preparing Sunday dinner for any number of people, and then go to church. It was their custom to invite someone home for dinner so Emma usually fixed a dinner which she could leave in the oven to cook while they attended services. She took a nice cut of roast beef from the refrigerator and placed it in the oven to start cooking. She peeled some potatoes, carrots, and onions which she would place around the meat before they left for church. By turning the oven very low it would simmer slowly while they were at church. Yesterday Beth had made an angel food cake for dessert. This made dinner easy and quick to get on the table so that they would be ready for their Sunday Afternoon Musicale. It wasn't really a musicale; it was a lot of friends and neighbors getting together each week. Some Sundays there would be a crowd, other weeks only a few people would attend. Anyone who played any type of instrument or wanted to sing or just listen was welcome.

Emma began to hear the sounds of stirring from upstairs. Usually the girls would set the table, but since she was up early she went ahead and got the table ready for eight people. *That should do it,* she thought.

As she made her way to her bedroom to get ready for church she could hear the sounds from the bathroom.

"Annie, you're taking too long. It's my turn for the mirror," Beth complained.

"I can't hurry. My hair won't stay in place."

"It looks fine the way it is. Now move over," Beth said.

"Sorry, Beth, but it's my turn. I don't like this outfit. It makes me look fat," Cathy said as she looked in the mirror.

"You're not fat. You just have curves, Cathy," Beth told her

Hearing the girls made Emma smile. "Don't you just love hearing our girls in the morning," Emma asked Albert as she started to change clothes.

"Well, I think I'll put an end to it. I don't want to be late for church," he told her, and then called, "Girls! Get moving! Really, Emma, do you think we should consider another bathroom upstairs. It seems like we need to post a schedule around here," he told her with a smile. "But you are right. It's a pleasant sound. We are blessed with a good family, Emma. Girls," he said with a knock on the bathroom door, "five minutes and we leave."

After a search for hats, gloves, and purses they were out the door. The day was crisp and bright. After an interesting sermon and good music the family headed for home.

"Who's coming for dinner today?" Annie asked.

"We met a couple, Audrey and Ralph Curtis, who just moved to Glenridge so they'll be joining us." Emma said.

Albert added, "Clay Shipman will join us. He's back in town on business. He plays the guitar better than anyone I know. It should make for some good music this afternoon. I'm glad I held on to my guitar so he can use it."

They had a very friendly dinner. They all enjoyed the conversation with Audrey, Ralph, and Clay. By the time they were done eating and the table had been cleared, neighbors and friends began arriving for the afternoon of music. Albert got his guitar for Clay. Jim Jensen, who lived next door, brought his trumpet and a first-year clarinet student joined them as well as one violinist. It didn't matter whether you played well – all you needed was a willing heart or a joy of hearing music. It didn't matter how crowded the room was. They always had room for one more. They played, or tried to play, all types of music. Sometimes, after a song sounded especially good they would clap for themselves and want an encore. Beth, Cathy and Annie took turns playing the piano for them. Today it was Beth's turn.

The afternoon seemed especially pleasant when suddenly they were interrupted by Freddie Jensen, Robbie's younger brother, who pushed the front door open with a bang.

"Mom! Dad! Come home, come home! The Japanese have bombed Hawaii! They killed everyone," he shouted.

Jim immediately went to his son. "Stop that talk immediately. You know Robbie is there. Don't worry your mother like this. Whatever made you think of anything as stupid as this stunt?" Jim started to apologize to the others as he put his hands on Freddie's shoulders.

Freddie, almost crying, refused to be quiet and began to shout. "It is true! It is true! I heard it on the radio. They stopped my program with the news. Everyone's dead."

"Fred! Stop it!" his dad admonished him. "You probably heard an announcement for a new show. Don't you know this will worry your mother?"

Freddie's eyes were full of terror and his face was red. His body was shaking. "What will happen to Robbie?" He refused to be consoled as he thought of his older brother who was his hero.

Albert hurried to turn on the radio and the guests heard the terrible news. It was true. Freddie was right about the attack.

Beverly Jensen went to the side of her husband and son. They held on to each other for support then left for home.

Beth sat with her fingers still on the piano keys. Her face was pale. Her eyes were glazed. She sat in shock. Emma hurried to Beth's side and placed her arms around her.

The room was quiet as the rest of the guests heard the newsman reporting on the events of Pearl Harbor. Freddie Jensen had told the truth. Without any fanfare or long goodbyes, the guests all left for their homes. Perhaps they felt a need to check on their own loved ones or felt the Martin family needed privacy. Everyone seemed to be gone in a matter of minutes.

Emma tried to console Beth. "Try not to be too upset, Beth. We really don't know anything yet. This may not be happening near Hickam. Robbie might be completely away from the area on a weekend pass. It's too soon for us to know anything for sure. I'm sure we'll hear many false reports. We must wait until we get some official word."

"I know he's dead! I can feel it!" Beth shouted. "Oh, Robbie, oh Robbie," she screamed. Emma held Beth close and let her cry.

Albert could not leave the radio. Annie put the music away and folded up the extra chairs that filled the room. Cathy went to the kitchen and fixed coffee for the family. Together, the family sat, very subdued, and listened to the news.

Beth spoke quietly. "I know he's dead. I can feel it. I can feel it. Oh, Robbie, oh, Robbie." Her voice was soft, yet firm as she began to sob quietly.

Albert tried to reassure Beth and the family that the news was probably exaggerated. It probably wouldn't be as bad as it sounded. But each report seemed to be more convincing that Albert was wrong.

One hour passed, then two. There was no news from Robbie. The family sat by the radio for some time; each report seemed to be worse than the first. *This is the United States. Things like this don't happen in our country*, they thought. Beth would burst into another round of crying and the family took turns consoling her until the sobbing and shaking stopped.

Cathy and Annie quietly left the room after a time and returned with sandwiches and mugs of soup.

"I think we need a bit of nourishment," Cathy said.

"We think the Jensen's do too," Annie added. "We fixed a basket for them. Would you like to take it over, Beth, or should we do it?"

"I'll take it," Beth said. "Maybe they have some news by now. But if he should happen to call here . . . ."

"We'll come and get you," Annie told her.

After they ate Emma and Albert went next door. The scene was very somber. The Jensens had not eaten any of the food Beth had taken them.

Emma's heart ached for the agony her dear friends were going through. Emma encouraged them to eat something since she was afraid it would be a long night. They went to the kitchen where Emma made a pot of coffee. For once in her life she was speechless. She didn't try to talk much, just be with her to listen if Beverly wanted to talk. They had been next door neighbors for all of their married lives. Both women had moved into the houses where their husbands had grown up. Albert and Jim were best friends. Emma knew she could do or say nothing that would bring comfort to Beverly. Only a call from Robbie could do that.

"Would you like me to call anyone in your family?" Emma asked Beverly.

"I think it's too early to do that. Surely we will hear something soon. After all, how long can it take to get things settled and open phone lines so that the servicemen can phone home or the government can notify families."

Beth sat at the kitchen table twisting her engagement ring around on her finger as if it had magic in it that would bring Robbie home if she got it in the right place.

As soon as the women had left for the kitchen, Jim Jensen slumped forward in his seat on the sofa and put his head in his hands. "I don't know what to do," he told Albert. "What can I say to ease their pain? I already called the parents of two classmates we met at graduation. They haven't heard anything either. It must be terrible if no one has time to call their family. Robbie has been so good about staying in touch. If not with us, he would call Beth. Now, we hear nothing. Can you think of anything I can do? I can't bear to see the anguish on Beverly's face. Husbands and fathers are supposed to take care of their families. Beverly, Freddie and Robbie need me now and I don't know what to do."

Albert moved to the sofa where he put his arm around Jim's shoulders. When the women returned to the room, Jim quickly sat up straight and said, "We'll hear something very soon, I am sure."

As they sat listening to the news together, Jim did get an idea.

"I have a friend who used to be a ham radio operator. Maybe he could get through." Jim hurried to the phone to call his friend.

After a brief word of greeting, Jim got to the point.

"My son is stationed at Hickam field. We have heard nothing from anyone. Is there any chance you could get a call through so we can find out just how bad it is?"

"Sorry, Jim, I'm having no luck at all getting through to anyone. I've been trying since I heard the first news reports. Give me the unit number of your son's outfit and I'll keep trying. I'll call you immediately if I hear anything. I'm going to be sitting here all night."

The time grew late. The reality of the destruction and devastation set in. Emma and Albert stayed a while longer and then, taking Beth with them, they prepared to leave for home. The Jensen's promised to call Beth if they heard anything, regardless of the hour. Cathy and Annie rushed to Beth when they entered the house and gently led her upstairs for a warm bath and bed.

Albert and Emma continued to sit by the radio. As the reports came in they realized just how bad it was on Oahu. It would take months before they would really understand the devastation that had taken place and how futile some of the early rescue work had been. They knew that this would mean war – probably not only in the Pacific but in Europe as well. They knew this would change all their lives.

After a few hours of tossing and turning, Beth got out of bed and went to the window seat. It was still dark out, *just like it's dark in my life*, she thought. *I'll never see sunshine again.* Beth had so many memories of Robbie in the yard below her window: the tire swing where they sailed to the skies, the fort they helped to build in the big tree in the back of the yard, the various trees that became countries of the world as they had their adventures. She remembered when they were five or six years old following animal tracks in the snow. They pretended they were lion or tiger tracks. *Now he's gone. I know he's gone*, she thought.

She turned on the lamp and reached for his picture on her nightstand. She sat staring at it. She reached for the letter she had received from him on Saturday.

> *My sweet beautiful Beth,*
>
> *I miss you so much tonight. I can hardly wait till Christmas. I really hope you'll be able to come to Oahu. It's so beautiful here. It's not too hot, not too cold. It's always pleasant. And no weather to worry about when we fly. It's always good. A couple of days ago we flew over the big island of Hawaii. It's really something to see from the air. We saw beautiful waterfalls on all the islands, but they seem different on the big island. The active volcano on the island is sleeping right now.*
>
> *When it's awake the lava flows down the mountain to the ocean. It burns everything in its path. From the air it looks like a wide, black river from top to bottom. Yet, right next to it you can see beautiful green fertile land with flowers blooming. It is spectacular. I can't wait to show it to you.*
>
> *Oahu, the island we're on, is picture postcard pretty. There's a lot of ocean ships, catamarans, fishing boats, and of course, a lot of naval ships in the harbor. Most of the homes are on stilts. They are built that way to let the air circulate underneath keeping the homes warm in the winter and cool in the summer. The natives here tell a tale about the early missionaries who came from New England. They built a beautiful, sturdy church on a firm foundation. But no one came to worship. Without the breezes underneath it was too hot or too cold.*
>
> *Hawaii has so much folk lore and history. We'll have so much to do.*
>
> *Well, it's lights out time so I'll close for tonight. Don't ever forget how much I love you. You've been my other half for all of my life. I need you to make me feel like a whole person.*
>
> *Yours forever,*
> *Robbie*

Beth ran her fingers over the writing on the letter. *Is this the last letter I will ever receive from him,* she wondered? How could this be? He had always been in her life. Could she live without him? Will she have a choice? Beth knew her parents were trying to give hope to her and to Robbie's parents when they tried to convince the family that Robbie might still be alive. Beth was certain that she would feel differently if he was alive. She felt like half of her body had been torn from her. *I know. I just know I will never see him again or feel his arms around me.* She thought of the plans they had made. She would teach to provide them with an income at first. They would buy one plane at a time, buy their own airfield to have their own air cargo service and would also give flying lessons. What will she do? How can she ever live without him?

Beth heard a gentle tapping at her door.

"I brought you a cup of coffee. I thought you might be awake," her mother told her as she entered the room. "Were you able to get any sleep?"

"Not too much. I can't go to classes today."

"Of course you can't. Dad says he thinks classes will be cancelled. He and the girls are going to go to check in. I'm going downstairs now. Come down when you're ready."

Beth put on her plaid skirt, white blouse and Robbie's letter sweater. She combed her hair. She tried to arrange it to cover her cheeks which looked like they were stained with tears. She went downstairs where her mother had fixed her breakfast.

After Beth had eaten, Emma suggested that they go next door to fix breakfast for the Jensens. "I bet they didn't get much rest last night," she told her daughter.

As they made their way through the back yard they saw the light on in the Jensen's garage.

"I bet Freddie is out there," Beth said.

"Beverly told me he wants to run off to join the Army," Emma said. She pushed open the kitchen door as she called out to the Jensens. "Good morning. It's Emma and Beth."

Beth noticed that Beverly was wearing the same clothes she had on the previous day. Beverly's hair was disheveled. Beth saw her mother embrace Beverly as she said; "Sit down, Beverly. I'm going to make some fresh coffee and fix breakfast. Beth, go get Freddie. Tell him to come in to eat something." Emma began cooking.

Beth went to the garage. Freddie was sitting in the old go-cart with his hands holding tightly to the steering wheel, his head resting on his hands.

Beth tried to be calm so Freddie wouldn't worry. She pulled a small bench over to the go-cart Beth and Robbie had built when they were young children. She sat down.

"Well, seeing you on that go-cart brings back lots of memories. I cut that piece of wood right there," she said pointing to a particular board. "It was the first time I got to use the saw. This was our first car. We thought we were really hot stuff in it. After we put that old engine on, it really was great. I sat behind Robbie holding on to his waist. We flew down the street."

"Yea, but you got in trouble."

"Yea, we did," she agreed. "We were shouting with happiness one minute. The next minute we heard sirens. We knew we weren't supposed to be in the street. We had an instant when we thought we'd ditch the cart and run away. But all the neighbors came outside when they heard the police sirens so we had no place to run. Did you know we had to go to court over it? *It was really scary.* We had to pick up papers in the park every day for two weeks."

"I want to join the Army. I'm tall for my age. I know I could pass for eighteen," Freddie said very seriously.

"Well, this might not be the best time for you to leave home. Your folks really need you here. Your dad is so busy at work. Your mom really needs a man who can help her. I know Robbie always depends on you to take care of them when he's not here. Oh, I almost forgot. I came out here on a mission. My mom is in your kitchen fixing breakfast. Bacon and eggs and toast, I think. Why don't we go in?"

As they walked together to the house, Freddie told Beth, "My dad slept on the floor by the phone last night. My mom slept on the couch. They were afraid they might not hear the phone if they went upstairs."

Beth nodded. She had seen the blankets on the floor and on the sofa. She knew they stayed close to the phone. "They're very worried, Freddie. We've got to do all we can to help them."

Freddie reached over to give Beth a hug. "I'm glad you're going to be my sister."

"And I want you to be my brother."

The town of Glenridge was large enough to house a university, small air field, and Army base, yet still small enough to feel like one big family. When the horrid news of December 7th was learned, the people were in a state of shock. It seemed to really hit home that this terrible thing had happened to their country. Now they learned that their very own Robbie was in the midst of it. Everyone wanted to do something. The fruit market sent a large tray of cut-up fruit. The donut shop sent donuts and the bakery sent sweet rolls and cookies. The corner diner sent a large container of soup and the deli sent a tray of cold cuts. Neighbors quietly left casseroles on the front porch. Many people wanted to help; no one knew what to do in those early hours.

At noon, Beth and Emma returned home to find that Alfred, Cathy, and Annie had come home as the classes at the university had been cancelled. Together they sat as a family. They heard President Franklin Delano Roosevelt declare this '*to be a date in infamy*'. He went on to declare war on Japan.

After the speech, Alfred turned to his family and said, "I know these two days are days you will always remember in detail. What you were doing; who you were with. There's no question we'll be fighting a war against the Germans too. I hope our country never has another occasion to remember any other time as bad as these two days."

Beth was in and out of the Jensens during the afternoon. She had just arrived when the doorbell rang. Beth answered it. She saw three friends: Chuck Johnson who owned and managed the airfield where Beth and Robbie had learned to fly, Dave Smith, a WWI fighter pilot who taught them how to fly, and Tom Lester who knew everything there was to know about an airplane engine. Tom had insisted Beth and Robbie had to learn it all before he'd give them an OK to take out a plane.

"Hi Beth, how're you doing?" they asked as they gave her a hug and went to meet Robbie's parents. "We hope we're not intruding. We've been so worried. Robbie is like one of our own. Have you heard any news?"

"We've heard nothing. You're definitely not intruding. You helped Robbie find his passion in life – flying. Beth and flying. He told me one time he felt his life was complete because he had them both," Jim told them.

"Robbie is a natural pilot. So are you, Beth. You seem to know instinctively what to do." Chuck paused before continuing. "The first time the two of you showed up and offered to wash planes in exchange for flying lessons, I have to admit we all had a good laugh. We thought that after the first time washing the outside of the plane you'd give up. Yet you were back the next Saturday ready to start your lessons."

Tom Lester continued. "We knew you had no idea how much book learning goes into flying. You needed to know all the mechanical information before taking up a plane. You two never gave up. How old were you?"

"Robbie was almost 12. I was ten when we started washing planes. You guys always made us feel as if we were adults. We could do anything," Beth told them. "We actually got the idea when we were out riding our bikes on a Saturday afternoon. We were out by the airfield. An airplane flew very low over us. Out of the blue Robbie said, 'Let's learn to fly a plane.' We didn't have any money for lessons so we decided we had to trade something. Washing the planes was the only thing we could think to do."

Jim Jensen spoke up. "Robbie has an eager, inquisitive mind. He always has to figure out how everything works. He and Beth rebuilt the '22 Chevy. It was so beat up I thought it would keep them busy for a while before they would give up on it. They persisted. I got roped into teaching them about automobile engines. Beth's dad taught them how to drive a car at the same time you were teaching them how to fly a plane."

"Dave, you were a fighter pilot. Is it terribly hard to learn how to fight and fly at the same time? Beth asked.

"You can't learn too much about it in books. Some people have the knack for it. Some do not. Robbie had the knack. If he's ever in that situation I do believe he will know instantly what to do."

After a few more minutes, the men left.

The family went back to their vigil of waiting, waiting, and waiting. The afternoon dragged on. Each of them tried to be positive to encourage the others. As the evening shadows began to fall the family had a bleak, hollow feeling. It had now been more than twenty-four hours. They knew Robbie would have called if he could have so they wouldn't worry. Beverly got up from her chair and went to the kitchen. When Beth went to join her she saw Beverly sitting quietly at the table with her hands folded in prayer. As Beth watched, a look of peace or acceptance came over Beverly's face. Beth reached for her coat to go home for a while.

They heard the doorbell rang. Young Freddie made a mad dash to open the door. A young messenger boy from Western Union stood at the door. Freddie turned away, called for his dad, and rushed to the sofa where he buried his head in the cushions. Beth watched as the young man thrust a telegram into Jim's hands, turned and ran quickly to his bicycle. Beverly rushed to Jim's side as he tore the telegram open.

> *Mr. & Mrs. Jensen: It is my sad duty to inform you that your son, Robert William Jensen has . . . .*

With a sad cry Beverly fell to the floor in anguish. Her husband went to her side. He put his arms around her and sat beside her on the floor as he held her. They began to grieve.

Freddie left the house. He went to the garage to sit again in the old go-cart.

Beth stood; stunned for a few minutes. Then she left the house. She went to the back yard to sit in the old tire swing that hung in the big maple tree between the two houses.

They each grieved in their own way.

THE WAR YEARS

1942

Beth awakened from another restless night. It almost looked like the morning light was peeking around the sides of the window shade. The clock showed it was still early. She moved to the window to look out. She saw a heavy snow had fallen in the night. No wonder everything was so bright. Their yard looked like a sparkling fairyland – it was beautiful. A heavy wet snow lay thick on the branches. It covered everything. She saw some rabbit tracks across the yard. Beth remembered how she and Robbie liked the snow. As children they would make snowmen. As young adults, hand in hand they would walk to town. They would stop to have hot chocolate or coffee. *I need to be outside*, she thought. She dressed quickly, went downstairs to get her coat, hat, and gloves. She went outside to sit on the swing on the front porch. No snow had been shoveled: no traffic had been on the street. The scene looked like a Currier and Ives Christmas card as she looked at the big Victorian homes on both sides of the street. As Beth sat down she thought about how peaceful it was here, yet in her mind and body she felt such torment. *How could it be that Robbie has been gone almost a month? A flag draped casket. A squad from the local army base shooting their guns. The haunting sound of Taps being played by a bugler while a folded flag was presented to Beverly. Did it all really happen? How could it be that his body lies buried out in the cemetery?* Beth remembered the service.

"Morning, Beth. I brought you some hot chocolate." Beth was joined by Cathy. "Doesn't everything just look beautiful this morning?"

Beth moved over to make room for her sister. "Yea, it's really pretty. So fresh and clean."

"Are you able to sleep yet?"

"Not too much."

They sat in silence for a few minutes. Then Cathy spoke. "Our granddad was really smart wasn't he? He had a vision for Glenridge long before anyone else did. I bet when he bought all this property everyone thought he'd have a farm. Instead, he plotted out the area. He started to build these big beautiful homes. He put the boulevard in front; got the first street lights in town. He kept the yards big so kids would have places to play and parents had privacy."

"Can you imagine how Grandma felt when she moved into this big house with her two young boys? She must have felt she was moving into a mansion. Who built three story houses in those days?"

"I love this house. I hope I get to live here forever," Cathy said.

"I used to think I'd be living next door with Robbie in his family's house. You'd live here. Our kids would play together. You'd be a doctor. I'd be a professor teaching European history. I'd be teaching flying at the airfield Robbie and I would own. Now that will never happen."

"That's the way I thought it would be," Cathy said. "Most everyone on this street was born in the house they now live in. No one gets married and moves away. They get married and eventually move back here. It's what makes this such a nice place to live."

"I think Grandpa would be happy to see what good, strong houses he built. They all look so good. He really knew the construction business," Beth said.

"Yea, he did. So does Uncle Frank. He's kept the family tradition going. Do you think Grandpa was disappointed when Dad didn't go into the business?"

"I suppose he was a little. But in spite of his wishes, Grandma always said he wasn't disappointed. He wanted his sons to be happy. Uncle Fred loves the business. In a way cousins Harold and Herb are like Uncle Fred and Dad. Harold will be running the business some day and Herb will become a professor like Dad. They both love history."

"I wish we could have known Grandpa. He died so young." Cathy said.

"I'm glad we had Grandma. I bet she'd be sad if she knew about what's happening now in the world."

"Do you think things will ever be normal again?" Cathy asked.

Normal! Beth thought. *Nothing will ever be normal again.*

After breakfast Emma declared it was the day to put away all the Christmas decorations. Christmas had definitely been more subdued this season, but everyone had tried to make it as nice as possible. Cathy and Annie started to sing while they were packing away the ornaments. Before Beth realized it, she was singing along. Then she stopped suddenly as if she should not be singing. *I have just lost my lover, my intended husband. I shouldn't sing,* she thought.

Emma spoke up. "I have such nice memories of Robbie telling me how much he enjoyed hearing you three sing. He must be up in heaven smiling down right now."

"He was a happy guy," Beth said.

"Yea, he was," Annie said. "He wants you to be happy."

That night after dinner Emma made an announcement. "We have to do something to help build morale in Glenridge," Emma said. "I have an idea."

The girls began to groan and their father began to laugh. "Better get ready, girls."

"I don't have time, Mom," and "I'm very busy," and "I have tons of homework," was heard from the girls. Cathy said she might be changing majors from Pre-Med to Nursing and wouldn't have much time. Beth said she wanted to get back to help out at the air field. Emma just ignored them. "I know what we'll do. We'll put on a show out at the base."

"And just who do you expect to be in the show," Albert asked.

"Well, the three girls can sing as a trio. We'll get Rosemary, Marge, Roy and Herb to sing as a quartet."

"The boys will be leaving in a month for the Marines," Annie said.

"That means they'll be here for a month. Come quickly, girls. Let's start to practice." She moved to the piano and started to look through the music.

"What type of show do you plan?" Albert asked.

"A variety show. You can be the emcee because you have a gift of gab and can involve some of the servicemen. We'll get Miss Ethel to send some dancers. Our churches have some wonderful singers." Emma found the music she wanted and motioned for the girls to come to the piano.

"Girls, you should have expected this. You know your mother when she gets an idea," Albert interrupted.

With a moan and a groan they moved to the piano and started to sing. The girls knew their mother very well. They knew they might as well give in and do it. They knew they always had a good time when they did give in, in spite of their complaining. After about twenty minutes she said they were ready. After all, they didn't need much practice. They sang together almost every day.

"We'll open with *God Bless America* and close with *America the Beautiful.* We'll use songs with locations like *Deep in the Heart of Texas* or *Chattanooga Choo Choo* so they can sing and clap along. We use some sentimental songs like *He Wears a Pair of Silver Wings.* We'll have to learn that other new song I heard, *Remember Pearl Harbor.* It's going to be a great show."

The next day Emma drove to the base to see the commander. He was delighted and offered his support. She went to visit the churches and the local theater and soon had a plan to provide entertainment.

Beth seemed to have an improved outlook on things. The next day after classes she drove out to the airfield where she and Robbie had learned to fly.

"Beth. It's good to see you," Chuck Johnson told her. "How are you doing?"

"Oh, you know. Some days are good; some are bad. I haven't done any flying for the past two months. Any chance I could take a plane up for a short ride?"

"Sorry, Beth, there's no gasoline for pleasure flights. Why not go out and sit in any plane you want. Stop by the office before you go home."

Beth found the plane she and Robbie had used for training. It was really old, a two-seater with an open cockpit. They used a tube to talk to each other while they were flying. She sat remembering Robbie. She could see the intensity on his face when he was receiving his instructions. He wore his hair longer then. His cowlick made a pretty little curl. He liked to keep his flying helmet on to hide his hair in those days. So many little memories came back. Yet this time she could remember them and smile instead of crying. After a brief period of time she headed back to Chuck's office.

As she stepped into his office he asked, "Did you hear about Jerry and Leo? They both left to enlist in the Army. Chances are pretty good they'll be in the Army Air Corp."

"You must be lost without them. Who's taking their places?"

"Dave's been doing most of it. I was wondering if you'd have any time on weekends to make a few flights for us. Of course if you want to work full time I could use you."

"Chuck, I want to finish this last term at school and graduate. After that . . . . well, I've got a couple of ideas I'm thinking about. I'll be glad to pick up the weekend flights. Just let me know when you need me." Beth paused and then asked. "Chuck, do you have a minute more for me or are you too busy?"

"What's on your mind, Beth?"

"Did you ever hear of Jacqueline Cochran?"

"Isn't she that lady flyer who went over to England to help the women ferry planes from the factories to the air bases?"

"She's the one. Now that we're in the war, I hear she's coming back to recruit women in this country. Do you think my skills are good enough for me to apply for the program?"

"Wow, that's a big one, Beth. Your skills are great. I'm sure the training program would teach you what you need to know. To leave home to fly bombers or fighter planes . . ." He shook his head. "Do your parents know about this? Do you know what the training program would be?"

"Not yet to either of your questions. That's my next step. I didn't want to worry my folks if you thought I needed more training. I trust your opinion. I think someone's working on a training program right now. In England the women who do this type of flying are in the military. The women don't fly in combat. They fly planes or people to where they're needed. They have to learn evasion skills in case a German plane is flying over England in the same air space. Part of their training is to fly solo around the coastline of the entire country so they'll get experience with different winds, drafts, and atmosphere problems. I'm thinking more and more about applying for the program once they get it started here. I think it's what I need to do. I'd join the Army Air Corp if they'd let me. Of course that's out of the question. Women aren't supposed to fly planes or be in the Army," she said factiously.

"If it's what you want I think you should try for it. I'll help you anyway I can. If they ask for any of your records we have them here. But I wouldn't wait too long before telling your folks."

The Martin family sat down to dinner that night promptly at 5:30. Albert had asked that they eat at that time so they could have a leisurely meal together before he went to listen to Lowell Thomas on the radio to get the day's news.

"Well," he asked as they started to eat. "Why don't you start by telling us about your day, Mother?"

Emma told them about her success in getting a show organized. "And another thing," she added. "I'm going to be working with the Red Cross by being their representative out at the base three days a week. Sometimes the young men forget to write home. Their parents get worried so I'll try to act as a buffer. Some of the young men who were drafted left a wife and small children back home with no one to help them. My job will be to try to relieve their minds of as many worries as I can. What about you, Albert? How are things at the university?"

"Every day we seem to hear about more young men either getting drafted or just joining the service. Three of our young assistant professors are leaving so I have to rearrange classes and find instructors to replace them. Everyone's going to have to help. I got a call asking me to become an Air Raid Warden for our section of town."

"That sounds interesting, Dad. What will you have to do?" Annie asked.

"Help prepare the people to react in an emergency to try to keep them safe. We are not really expecting Glenridge to be hit with bombs, yet we never imagined Hawaii would be hit either. If by chance any enemy planes are headed our way, the people will have to know what to do."

"How will you do that?" Cathy asked.

"We'll have to start by making plans. We need an alert system for the people – we need a place where they could go for safety – what to do in medical emergencies – how to evacuate the city if it becomes necessary. We have many plans to make."

Annie spoke up. "Dean Whitman called me in today. He asked me to be one of the leaders of a committee to conduct a city-wide scrap drive. We need to get people to help clean up all the vacant lots, the junkyards and even their own homes to find old scrap metal. We'll get it sorted so it can be reused. Besides scrap metal, things like newspapers, glass items, and especially old tires are needed. We're going to try to make a contest out of it. We want everyone to get involved. A group of us are going to go to the schools to try to get the kids interested in buying saving stamps each week. They'll cost either 10 or 25 cents each. When they get $18.75 they'll get a U.S. War Bond that will be worth $25 in ten years. It sounds like a fun project to me."

"Cathy, didn't you have a meeting today about the new nursing program? Are you interested in it?" Albert asked.

"It was a very moving experience to hear first-hand what happened from a nurse who was at Pearl Harbor that day. She was injured and sent home for treatment. She'll be going back very soon. On December 7th, that one day alone, there were 2,300 people killed. One minute they were enjoying a beautiful Sunday morning and the next minute things were exploding around them. On that day only 78 Army Nurses were stationed at the base hospital and some of them were injured or killed. She said it was utter chaos. The hardest part was making a quick decision about who to treat first. The nurse didn't dwell on the details. She made a plea for the women to join the Army Nurse Corp, the ANC. Then Professor Starkey, the head of our nursing school, told us the program is being changed. Those women who are now in their third year will be graduating this June. These next six months will be crammed with nursing training. A few general courses will be dropped. The women joining the ANC will be sworn into the Corp the day after graduation and sent for training at an Army base for one year. After that, some will be chosen for an additional six months of specialty training."

"What did you think about it," Emma asked. "Do you think you want to change majors and become a nurse instead of a doctor?"

"Dad, I heard you say it will take at least two years or maybe more to end the war. If I go to med school it will take at least three or four years after I finish my year and a half at the university. That seems like a very long time when in a year or a year and a half I could be of help. The hospital at Hickam Field needed so much more help."

"Would most of your classes transfer to the nursing program?" her father asked.

"I've had mostly science courses. I had a talk with Dean Whitmore and he said he thought they would transfer. I have been thinking about this since I heard the woman from the Red Cross speak to us before Christmas. But I've also been thinking how I had planned to be a doctor ever since I read the book you gave me about Elizabeth Blackwell."

"Who was she?" Annie asked.

"She was the first woman doctor. She had a terrible struggle to be accepted into medical school. Only a man could become a doctor. She ended up graduating at the top of her class and still couldn't find a job."

"Well, did she ever find one?" Beth asked.

"Yes, she worked with the immigrants coming to the United States. Many of them were very ill with diseases. Women have had such a struggle to be accepted as equal to men," Cathy said.

"Your mother worked very, very hard to help get equality for women," Albert said. "I am proud of her and the role she played to get women the right to vote," he added as he reached out to take Emma's hand.

"Cathy, I can't bear the thought of having you going to a war zone. Have you made a decision?" Emma asked.

"Just talking with you all has helped me make up my mind. I will not give up my plans to become a doctor. But I will postpone it until after the war. I'll become a nurse first," Cathy said. "Do I have your blessing as I make this decision?"

"We'll always support your decisions," Albert said.

Emma wiped away a tear as she said, "We love you Cathy. In spite of my tears I am very proud of you."

The family sat silently for a few minutes as they absorbed this news.

"How was your day, Beth?" her mother asked after a minute or so.

"It was good. I drove out to the field after classes. I asked Chuck if I could take up a plane. I haven't flown for almost two months. He said there's no gasoline for leisure flights. I got to sit in a plane for a while and it felt so good. Chuck asked me to do some flying for him on weekends. I told him I would. That's OK with you, isn't it?"

"Of course," Albert said. "Everyone has to do as much as he or she can so we can get this horrid war over with quickly."

As Beth got ready for bed that night she wondered if she should have let the family be part of her planning for a major change in her life. Her parents had always approved of independence in their daughters. Still . . . . . .? Maybe she'd better wait until she got the rest of the information she had sent for.

About three days later she got the information. She took a day to study it thoroughly and then felt she was ready for the next step – talking with her parents.

"Come and sit with me, Emma. Let's listen to the news," Albert said as he rose from the table after dinner a few nights later.

"Go, Mom. We'll do the dishes," Beth told them. The girls began to sing together as they did the dishes and tidied the kitchen. Some were war songs like *There'll be Blue Birds Over the White Cliffs of Dover, I Got a Gal in Kalamazoo* and other popular songs of the day. Beth asked her sisters, "What do you think Dad and Mom would say if I told them I have changed my mind about going to grad school? Or maybe I wanted to leave home for a while?"

"Beth. What's on your mind? Sit here and tell us," Annie cried.

"Let me talk with them first. Then I'll tell you. If they say no I'll be so disappointed. Still, I'd hate to do it without their blessing. I think I'll go in now and get this over with."

"Don't worry, Beth," Cathy said. "You know Dad and Mom will always support you. Can we go in to help you?"

"I think I'd better do this on my own," Beth answered.

"Is the news over yet?" Beth asked as she walked into the library. "Are you too busy for me to talk with you?"

"We're never too busy for our girls," her mother answered and her dad said, "Come sit here beside me. You look serious. It must be something important."

Beth took a minute to collect her thoughts. "A few months ago I thought my life had been all mapped out for me. I'd marry Robbie, go to grad school, get my doctorate, and become a professor like you, Dad. And of course I'd be flying. Someday I'd move into the house next door. I'd have lots of babies. I was looking forward to happy days. Robbie's gone now. The world is changing. I just can't sit here. I can't pretend it's all the same. I feel like I have to do something. You know how much I love to fly. If I could, I'd enlist in the Army Air Corp. We know that can't happen. I read about a program being developed to let women fly. It started in England when women were recruited to do routine flying so the men would be available to fly in combat. The women fly planes from the factories to the air bases. Some of them fly a plane towing a drone so the ground forces can practice on them. The women might fly parts or people where they need to go. Jacqueline Cochran had tried to get a program like it started here a couple of years ago. Even Mrs. Roosevelt tried to help get it started. The military said no. They said that women didn't belong in planes. Jacqueline Cochran went to England. She's been helping them. Another woman, on the east coast, Nancy Harkness Love, is married to a man in the United States, who is building planes for the British. He hired his wife to recruit women to fly the planes from the factories here in the states to air bases in Canada. The RCAF flies them overseas. Now that we're in the war things have changed. Both women are trying to start programs here in the states. I have given this a lot of thought. I feel like I must join one of these groups if I qualify. When the program is set I want to join it as soon as I can. Do I shock you or disappoint you?"

"My daughters never disappoint me," Albert said in a stern voice.

Emma added, "We always want you to be in charge of your own life."

Things were quiet for a moment. Albert quietly said, "You made me very proud when you said you wanted to become a professor like me. I guess I wanted that, too. I had a flashing memory of a talk I had with my father. My dad had built up a successful construction business from nothing. Frank and I both worked side by side with him. Frank loved everything about it from the smell of the wood to the finished house. I couldn't wait to get back to the classroom. I have always loved history with a passion. The day came when we had *the talk*. I was really worried that he'd be so disappointed in me when I told him how I felt. If he was disappointed he never let it show. He encouraged me to follow that passion into academia and be the best professor and the best man I could be. He always told me how proud he was of me and how much he loved me. How could I do anything less but give my blessing to my daughter? But Beth, this is wartime."

Emma spoke. "If I hadn't changed my mind about my plans when I entered college I'd be living in two rooms in someone else's house, have two cats, and lots of books. I'd be teaching literature at the university. I thought that would be the perfect life. Then I met your father. He kissed me and my life changed forever . . . . . . .still . . . . Beth, this is wartime."

Albert asked, "Shouldn't you wait till the program is approved before making plans?"

"I want to be ready. I just know they'll have to approve it. I've got to be ready."

"Did you make a list of the pros and cons?" Albert asked.

"That's kind of hard since nothing is final yet. According to my research about what is expected, some of the cons would be that we could expect no benefits. The pay will be small. Out of it I would have to pay for my own housing, food, transportation, clothes because there will be no uniforms. If I get sick or injured, I'll have no benefits to pay the bills. The group would not be part of the military. I thought about this a lot. I think I've got enough saved. I haven't spent any of the money I've earned flying. I was saving it to buy a plane. I still have the money Grandma left me. I think I can handle it. On the plus side I'll be flying which is something I love. I'll still be young enough to go to grad school when the war is over. I wouldn't be flying in combat. I'd learn new skills." Beth paused. "Maybe I want to do this because of Robbie. He had such big hopes for how much he could help. While I can't do what he was doing, I'd still be helping fulfill his dreams. I think he'd be proud of me."

"I know he'd be proud of you," Emma said.

Albert added, "Beth, you've given us a lot to think about. Most of all, we want you to be able to do what makes you happy." He shook his head. "It's wartime. Give us tonight to look over all your material to make sure you haven't forgotten some consideration. We'll talk tomorrow."

"Thanks, Dad and Mom. I can't ask for more than that." Beth gave them her literature. She went upstairs where her sisters were waiting to hear her plans.

Cathy thought the idea was wonderful and told them she'd be joining the Army Nurse Corp in the spring. She'd be leaving right away for training.

Annie sat quietly by. "None of our lives will ever be the same," she said.

*   *   *

The next few weeks were busy ones for all three of the girls. All three had classes at the university. Cathy was technically a year behind Beth but they would graduate together in the spring.

Albert was busy with his increased responsibilities at the University as well as the civic duties he was doing. Emma stayed busy with her work at the base and also managed to put on a show at the base every two weeks. Beth was busy with school as well as making cargo flights from the airfield. Cathy was busy with classes which included hands-on experience at the local and/or base hospitals. Annie worked very hard on coordinating the scrap drive in Glenridge. Because Beth and Cathy were so busy with the extra responsibilities they no longer could help entertain at the base so Annie was joined by her two best friends, Rosemary and Marge, the two young women who had sang in a quartet with Cousin Herb and Roy. Both young men had quit college and joined the Marines.

About this time Emma got another idea. Many of the soldiers she saw at the base were very lonely. So she got busy. She talked first with the local ministers, the priest, and rabbi to find members of their congregations who could invite a serviceman to their home for Sunday dinner. Next, she talked with the Base Commander who said he would support the idea. The Base Commander may have been surprised by Emma's enthusiasm and involvement but the local clergy was not surprised. They knew about Emma and her ideas.

The early months and spring of 1942 brought a time of confusion as the country settled into a war routine. An exciting time of patriotism spread throughout the land. Times were tense. People were worried yet they remained united in an effort to do what was needed to be done. They worked to supply any needs of the servicemen to help in the fight. The United States was plunged into fighting in Europe and Africa as well as the fight against Japan. It seemed like all the news was bad. Japan was capturing many of the islands in the South Pacific. The troops sent to Africa to help the British were suffering terrible losses. Every night the newspaper had headlines about one battle or another. Albert had put a new, larger world map on the wall in his home library. He made little flags to post on the places where battles were taking place. He and Annie would pin the flags on the map each night after hearing Lowell Thomas deliver the news. There appeared to be few American flags.

Albert was optimistic. "We need time to get things together. Then we'll start winning. Don't forget, the news we get is almost always a week late here. We might already be winning." That didn't seem very possible at first thought.

The country very quickly did begin to mobilize. Young men left school and their jobs to join the Army, Navy or Marines. Industry began to retool immediately. Airplane factories began to make bombers and fighters instead of passenger planes. Ship builders began to make destroyers and battleships. The automobile plants stopped making cars. Instead they made armored tanks, jeeps, and anti-aircraft vehicles. Steel mill employees worked around the clock to produce enough steel. Textile plants and shoe factories stopped making fancy dresses and high-heeled shoes. Instead they made army uniforms and boots. Potteries stopped making fine pottery. They made porcelain parts for airplanes. Eventually even the money changed. The copper used to make pennies was needed to make ammunition. The new wartime pennies were made of steel with a zinc coating to prevent them from rusting. Now the pennies were white.

Food processing companies and farmers made supplying the military bases their first priority. Civic leaders, especially in coastal cities, met to plan ways to defend their cities should an invasion or bombing happen here in the states. With so many men gone into the service the factories had to start hiring women. This was a big shock to everyone. It was even a bigger shock when they found women could actually do the work. Everyone wanted to do something. Nothing seemed the same.

Even in one's home things had changed. People did a lot more walking and riding busses when gasoline was rationed. You only had so many stamps to buy gasoline. A little stamp on the windshield indicated how much gas you could buy. You couldn't drive more than thirty-five miles an hour. Gasoline had to be saved for the army or critical support business. Even shoes were rationed so that the leather could go to the army. Bed and bathroom linens were almost impossible to buy. And food? Well everyone was entitled to just so many ration stamps to buy things like meat, dairy products and canned goods. Sugar and coffee were very scarce. Emma always canned a lot of fresh vegetables and fruit in the summer so that helped a lot. The cities and towns had air-raid drills. While it seemed unlikely that any bombers would reach the United States, who knew what might happen. During an air-raid drill everyone had to turn off every light or cover the windows with black curtains. Albert was an air-raid warden who patrolled the streets in the dark to make sure everyone complied with the rules.

The flags in the windows at so many homes were new. They were small white silk banners hanging from a gold braid. They had a star to represent the son or husband who was in the service. A blue star meant he was in the service. A red star meant he had been wounded. A gold star meant that he had been killed. The Jensens had a flag with a gold star.

Annie, Rosemary, and Marge were recruited by their church to assist after school in a child care program for the mothers who had gone to work in factories. The USO set up a club for the servicemen to visit. The three girls went on weekends to dance or just talk with the servicemen. Just about everyone took a First Aid Course. The Red Cross was constantly conducting blood drives to collect blood to be processed to be sent to the war zones.

The three young women enlisted all their friends to write to servicemen. Usually these would be men they met at the USO club or when they were performing. They didn't forget the hometown guys, either. They wrote to men stationed all over the United States and war zones. It took from three to ten days for a letter to reach them if they were in the states.

Letters between home and the servicemen overseas usually took six weeks to reach their destination. The government came up with a new program called V-Mail; the V stood for Victory. The writer would write a one-page letter on a special form. It would be censored to make sure no one had written anything that might help the enemy. Then it was photographed onto reels of microfilm. The films would be sent by air overseas where it was reproduced to one-quarter the size of the original and delivered to the soldier. The soldiers also used V-Mail to write home. The girls bought the forms at the Post Office to write to the men. This meant the V-Mail letters could reach the person in twelve days or less instead of six weeks. The mail sent home by servicemen did not require postage. The girls spent quite a bit of money on stamps.

Every Sunday they still had company for dinner; usually a serviceman or two, and friends from church. Soon the Sunday afternoon musicales became less regular.

The spring of 1942 brought many changes to Glenridge and the rest of the country. Most families settled into a new kind of routine. The news from the battle areas continued to contain news of many injuries and death. Two servicemen who had been badly injured returned back to Glenridge to try to resume a normal life.

The city leaders met to try to find a way to honor those young men who were in the service. They decided the honor should take place in the town square so that citizens and visitors alike could see how proud Glenridge was of their young men who were serving their country.

Albert's brother, Frank, was asked to submit ideas for something that would list the names of these men. Frank worked with an architect. They tried to make it unique for Glenridge yet these tributes were appearing all over the country. The name of each man from Glenridge who was in the military service was listed on a panel protected by glass doors. They honored each young man who was killed by painting a gold star next to his name. Robbie's name had a gold star.

*   *   *

As Cathy and Beth planned to leave home, Annie wanted to be part of the war effort in the same manner. She visited the Recruiting Offices of both the Army and Navy to see which program interested her the most. She learned that if she had her degree she might qualify for Officer's Candidate School. The programs for officers interested her. She decided she would wait. If the war was still on when she graduated, she would enlist. Surely, she thought, the war will be over before then. What was that old slogan, "Join the Navy and see the World?" That's what she thought she'd do. She would join the WAVES. Her sisters might want to live on Lincoln Boulevard in Glenridge for the rest of their lives. She wanted to travel. She wanted to see the world.

*   *   *

Prior to December 7th, part of Cathy's weekly routine was to spend time with their family doctor, Old Doc Jameson. He had a son who was Young Doc. Young Doc had been drafted into the Army and was serving in a field hospital somewhere in Europe. Old Doc had always been in Cathy's life. At her dad's suggestion, Cathy talked with Doc Jameson about her decision to change her studies to nursing. Doc had thoughtfully listened to her and told her she was making a good decision. There is an urgent need for help now. She would make a wonderful doctor when and if she decided to go to Med-School. Now her schedule was so busy that she had very little time to think about any regrets she might have about becoming a nurse at this time.

When she and her class were assigned hospital duty she was surprised that she knew as much as she did. For some of her classmates it was the first time to experience working with people and even be in a hospital. Cathy was very comfortable with her new responsibilities.

She really looked forward to being home with her family for the evening meal so she could tell the family all about her new life. She even enjoyed doing the dishes. She and her sisters would sing and laugh together. The family enjoyed being together. They would take turns discussing their day. She grew up thinking all families did things this way. This was the life she wanted. She planned to continue the tradition when she eventually married and moved back to this house. On occasional days off she might have a date or go to the movies with one of her friends. But she had little personal time. She concentrated on her studies.

The next few weeks were also busy for Beth. School: flying on weekends, trying to practice for the shows at the base, most of all waiting for the mailman. Last year, she thought, I waited for the mailman to bring me letters from Robbie. Now I'm waiting for another kind of letter. She had sent for an application to fly in the program of Nancy Harkness Love. She heard back that the government had not yet officially approved such a program. Neither were applications available for the program of Jacqueline Cochran. She wrote asking how to get one anyhow. She felt certain the government would soon approve the program. She wanted to be ready. One day a letter came from Jacqueline Cochran.

It was totally unrelated to her request for an application form. Instead it was a letter informing her that her name was on a list of women fliers. If the government approved starting a program for women would she be interested in applying to join the program? If so, they needed more information about her flying record.

Beth was elated. How did they get her name? Then she remembered all the paperwork Chuck had to submit every time she made certain flights or took another test. Beth left a note for her family with the good news and headed for the airfield. It was Friday. She needed to see if she was scheduled to fly on the weekend. Besides, she wanted to share her news with Chuck. She saw Uncle Frank with a crew of his men building a new runway. Uncle Frank seemed to have crews all over town: new barracks out at the base, more housing that was needed for families of servicemen. Even some of the local businesses were expanding.

When she walked in the office she was surprised to see a classmate from her high school days working there.

"Peggy. What are you doing here?" she asked her friend.

"Sally left the office to go work in a defense plant so Dad recruited me to help run the office." Peggy was the daughter of Chuck Johnson.

"What about Norm? Who's taking care of the baby?"

"Norm was drafted before little Norm was born. He's in Mississippi now. He's getting ready to go overseas. I moved back home. I really didn't want to but I guess it was the right thing to do. Now my mom and Norm's mom help take care of the baby while I work. It's not the life I expected or wanted. What can we do? I'm glad you came by today. Dad just told me to call you to ask you to come in right away if you could."

As Peggy talked, her dad opened the door from his office. "I thought I heard you out here, Beth. Come on in. I'd like you to meet someone."

"Beth, I'd like you to meet Captain Ken Heaton. Ken, this is Beth."

Beth saw a young handsome Army officer in full uniform except for the empty left sleeve that had been carefully pinned to his side. She reached out to shake hands.

"Ken lost his arm in an air battle in Africa. He's got a new job in the Army now. It's one I thought maybe you'd be interested in so I want you to meet him."

"This is about the Civil Air Patrol the CAP. This is a group of private people who want to help protect the country. Some are sky watchers who operate mostly along the coast lines. They learn to identify and report any suspicious or unknown airplanes that fly into the area. Because of a shortage of pilots, some of the men who are too old for the army are being recruited to do some routine flying. We're trying to recruit some of the men who may not qualify for military service to join our group. Some of our members are as young as 16. The program will be run by the Army under a strict set of guidelines. I came to see Mr. Johnson, sorry, I mean Chuck, to ask if we can use his skills and his field for the actual flying. The university has offered space to train and teach all the paperwork part."

"Isn't that the same sort of program that may be offered to women?" Beth asked.

"Yes, but there is a difference. This group will only be paid for each hour in the actual air. They will only be on duty for a few hours a day. All the ground work is a strictly volunteer program. People will remain living in their own homes," Ken told her.

"Ken is looking for some good instructors. I thought of you, Beth. You have good flying skills and great people skills. You have a knack for bringing out the best in people. You would be flying. You wouldn't have to leave home."

Beth thought for a moment of how much her parents would like this program. "I'm looking into another possibility for a job." She shared her news about the letter she had just received.

Chuck said, "Beth, think on both offers. Give me the list of information you need. I'll get it ready for you if you decide to join the women's group. Talk with your folks," he suggested.

Ken added, "We'd like to get this program started right away. Do you have any other questions for me?" he asked Chuck. "If not, I wonder if I might use your phone to call for a car from the base to pick me up. They won't let me drive with one arm yet."

"If you don't mind riding in a '22 Chevy I'll drive you back to the base," Beth said.

"Does it have a rumble seat?" he asked.

"Yea, it does. Would you like to ride back there?" she asked with a smile in her voice.

When they approached the car, Ken ran his hand over the fenders. "This is a beauty. I had one just like it when I left for the Army. Did you restore it yourself?"

"Robbie and I did it together. Then we learned to fly together."

"Where's Robbie now?"

"He was killed at Pearl Harbor."

"I noticed the diamond ring on the chain around your neck. Sorry, Beth. It must have been tough for you."

"It must have been pretty tough for you to fly in combat," Beth said.

"War is a tragedy. I was shot down on my second flight. So much for seeing Africa."

"Tell me about you. Where are you from? Do you have a family?"

"Rhode Island. I have a big family of sisters and brothers."

"No wife or kids, I guess."

"No. I thought once there might be both someday . . . . ." his voice drifted off.

"Tell me about her. Does she fly?"

"She's a teacher. I took her up once. She was so scared yet I think she liked it. She needs a whole man. Not a man with only one arm."

"Did she say that to you?"

"No. But I don't want to be a burden. I just can't go back home yet. Tell me about you and Robbie. Was he a pilot?"

"Yes. I think he loved flying as much as he loved me."

"Trust me, Beth; it's a different kind of love. I understand how he felt. I wanted to fly for the rest of my life. Now there's no job for a one-armed pilot."

"Maybe so. But who could the Army get that would be any better to do the job you're doing. You know what it's all about; how important it is."

As they approached the base, Beth said, "I have an idea. Why don't you come to our house for dinner on Sunday? My mom always has a crowd at the house. It'll be noisy and fun. You don't already have plans do you?"

"I don't want to be a bother," he said as he got out of the car.

"In my family, it's kind of a more the merrier group. I have a better idea. I'll drive out to pick you up. You can go to church with us. Then we'll have dinner and I'll drive you back."

"The walls of your church would fall down if I walked in," Ken said.

"The walls of our church are very strong. They can take it. See you about 9:30 on Sunday morning." Beth waved at him and drove away.

Beth was anxious to get home to tell them about the letter she had received. She also told them about inviting Captain Heaton to dinner. When she mentioned the lost girlfriend, Annie took great offense at a girl who would drop a guy like that until her mother reminded her that maybe it was Ken who dropped the girl.

"Well, I'll have to look into it when he comes on Sunday," Annie told the family. Cathy said she was more interested in the care he got when he lost his arm.

Beth was happy to see Ken at the gate when she arrived at the base on Sunday morning. "Good, I'm glad you're here. I was running a bit late. I was worried you wouldn't wait," she told Ken as he got in the car. "My family's looking forward to meeting you. I got to warn you though, we're a nosy bunch. Annie, my youngest sister will pester you about your girlfriend. Cathy, my other sister, will pester you about the care you got when you were wounded. If they get too personal just tell them to back off. They won't be offended."

"Well, I had no intention of coming when you dropped me off on Friday. Here I am. I guess I'm surprising myself."

The family had saved seats for Beth and Ken.

"It's been a long time since I've been in church. It has felt good to sing some of the hymns I learned as a child. Going through the ritual of the service brings back many memories," Ken told Beth as the service was ending.

Beth had noticed that he seemed deep in thought.

"While I was sitting here," Ken continued, "I had a special memory of my grandmother. When anyone around her had trouble she would always tell the person, 'You may forget God; God never forgets you.' I don't think I have always been so bitter about life and the people around me. I guess I got bitter after I lost my arm. I don't know why I don't want to go home to visit my family. Down deep I know they love me. I guess I don't want them to see me without my arm. I don't want them to feel sorry for me."

"Is that a good reason to stay away from them?" Beth asked.

Ken didn't answer.

Albert claimed Ken's time as soon as they arrived home while the women put the dinner on the table. They were joined by a new couple who had just moved to Glenridge. Dinner was friendly with each person taking part in conversation. After dinner Cathy said that Ken had to come with her and they went into the library. Soon Annie chased Cathy out while she talked with Ken. Beth headed for the piano and began to take requests from the guests who were arriving for an afternoon of music. Beth noticed that Cathy came into the room followed a short time later by Annie. Ken did not immediately join them. Beth wondered if she should try to find him. As the song she was playing ended, she saw Ken come into the room with an almost peaceful look on his face. She motioned for him to come join her on the piano bench. She started on an old favorite for the next song. She noticed that Ken rested his right hand on the keys and soon began to play a descant to the music.

"Hey, you're really good on the piano," Beth told him.

"You're very kind," he told her. "I must admit, I'm starting to feel a new confidence. Maybe my life will never be the same kind of normal it was before. Maybe I can have a life with a new normal. For the first time since I was injured I'm actually enjoying myself."

As the afternoon ended and the guests were leaving Emma came to Ken, put her arms around him in a big hug. "That's from me," she said, "and now here's another from your mother. Don't forget to stay in touch with her."

"I haven't been very good about staying in touch with my family lately. I'm going to try to do better," he told her.

Albert shook his hand and told him he hoped he'd get a new arm soon. "An arm is such a small part of who you are. You are a bright young man. I think you have a bright future ahead of you."

"Did you call Sarah?" Annie asked him as she gave him a hug. She saw the smile on his face. She knew he had. "How did it go? How is she?"

"Sarah's good. I'm going to see her when I get my next leave."

When they arrived back at the base Beth got out of the car and gave him a hug.

Ken looked at her very seriously. "Thank you, Beth, for a wonderful day. I feel like I've taken the first step to getting my life back. Whatever path you take about flying I know you'll be successful."

When Beth returned home she told them about the change she saw in Ken. She thought maybe they had helped him a lot. "What did you say to him?" she asked her sisters.

Cathy began, "I told him about joining the Army Nurse Corp as soon as I graduate. I want to be the best nurse I can be. I asked what the nurses did that was good and could they have done anything better? He told me his first treatment started in a field hospital. Everyone was kind. Conditions were nearly impossible for all of them. Then he was transferred to a ship coming back to the states. One time the ship was attacked by a German submarine. He saw nurses try to hold the cots steady so the patient wouldn't get shaken so much. He said maybe the only thing bad was getting so many shots from the nurses. He said that every time he saw a nurse she had a needle in her hand."

Annie told them she started to joke with him about adding his name to the list of servicemen she wrote to each week. "Then I asked him about what sports he liked. One subject led to another. Before long he started to tell me about Sarah, the school teacher from back home. I asked him if he and Sarah were engaged. He said that he almost asked her to marry him before he left for Africa. Now he was glad he hadn't. I asked him if it was because he lost his arm. I told him that would be a silly reason when you love somebody. I told him how much we all loved Robbie. We wanted *him*. We wouldn't care if he lost an arm or leg or eye or anything. We wanted him. I told him I didn't think he was being fair to her. I told him to call her. He said he wasn't ready yet. I told him of course he was. I told him to use the phone in the hall. I took him to the phone and left him there telling him to join us as soon as he was done talking. He told me later that Sarah was apparently happy to hear from him."

"Mother, I think we have some very special daughters," Beth heard her father say.

*   *   *

The winter months passed. Spring was in the air. The family settled into a new routine. Everyone was so busy with individual concerns that time spent together became very precious. Among other things Albert was now serving on the draft board, a position he hated. Emma continued to spend two days a week volunteering at the base. Beth was flying again. Cathy was home less and less as her school load was so heavy. Annie kept busy with civic and school efforts to help fight the war on the home front.

*   *   *

The war that had begun for Americans on December 7th was not going well. Germany and Japan signed a pact to work together to defeat the Allies. Germany continued to bomb London almost every night. In addition they launched a series of bombing raids on the Cathedral Cities of England. Beautiful old buildings were demolished. Hitler's army continued their march on the eastern front toward Russia. The Germans also launched a fleet of submarines to patrol the eastern coast of the United States making travel and transporting troops and supplies to Europe very treacherous.

Japan very quickly began to capture the main islands in the Pacific area: places like the Philippines, Borneo, and the Solomon Islands. They had already bombed cities in Australia and made inroads into China.

In another sad move for our country, the United States required over 120,000 Japanese-American people to be taken to barbed-wire relocation centers to be kept under guard. Many of these people swore loyalty to our government and tried to volunteer in the Armed Forces. Some were chosen to fight the ground war in Europe.

For our government it was a time of accepting losses. They had no choice; they had not planned for a day like December 7th. But the government was quick to respond and get ready to retaliate. President Roosevelt ordered an immediate attack on the Japanese homeland. This was an impossible task since our planes could not carry enough fuel to reach Japan from any islands we still controlled. The President insisted they find a way. And they did. In April of 1942, General Jimmy Doolittle led a bombing raid on Tokyo. Japan was totally unprepared for this. The attack proved to the Japanese government that the United States had not only the ways and means to bring the war home to Japan but also had the will-power to do so. There was much cheering in the United States when the announcement was made that this had happened. But some families suffered the loss of their loved ones who died making the raid.

When the Martin family heard the news, Albert was cheerfully smug. "I told you that we would respond. I told you it would take time but we would do it. We will win this war."

*   *   *

Graduation day finally arrived. As Albert presented the diplomas to his daughters, they each gave their dad a hug. After the ceremony the family returned to Lincoln Boulevard for the annual graduation party held on their street. Two young men would be sworn into the Army the next day; the same day Cathy would be sworn into the Nurse Corp. They would immediately be leaving for camp.

On Cathy's last night home, Emma had splurged her ration stamps to buy steaks for their family and for Uncle Fred and Aunt Millie, and Cousin Harold and his wife.

"Mom, you shouldn't have done this," Cathy scolded. "Now you'll have no meat for a month."

"So," her mother said. "What better way to celebrate our daughter leaving home than a dinner like we used to have before the war started."

"Mom, are you trying to get me to change my mind?" Cathy teased.

"Is it working?" Emma teased back.

Cathy gave her mother a hug. "I don't want you to worry about me. According to the information we were given, we'll get a year of military and nursing training. Next, I'll probably have six months of specialized training. Hopefully the war will be over by that time"

"I surely hope so," Emma said. "I'm so proud of you. I know you will be the best nurse the Army ever had."

Cathy turned to her dad. As he put his arms around her he said, "I never thought I'd be sending one of my daughters off to war. I don't like this position I'm in and I don't like war. But I know I must accept it and move on. Cathy, don't ever forget about this home and how much we love you."

The following morning, Cathy boarded a train for Camp McCoy in Wisconsin. They had established a training program for army nurses at that base. She realized she had no idea what kind of military training she would have to do. She supposed she'd have to learn to march. Would she be expected to learn about guns? She had seen a gunshot wound one time in Doc Jameson's office. A hunter had been shot in the arm. It was really sad to see the damage to the skin around the wound. She knew she could not even imagine how terrible it must be to see wounds from bombs. She thought about her decision to join the nurses instead of becoming a doctor. She felt comfortable with the choice she made. Her thoughts were interrupted when a young woman sat down beside her.

"Do you mind if I sit here?" she asked Cathy. "I was sitting in the back getting more and more nervous. I have to have a change of scenery."

"Please, sit down. What's making you nervous?"

"I just enlisted in the Army Nurse Corp. I'm on my way to Camp McCoy. I have no idea what to expect. I'm starting to imagine all sorts of bad things yet I really want to do this."

"I'm in the same program. I'm Cathy Martin."

"I'm Doris Richey. Are you a nurse already?"

"I just graduated from nursing school. I was recruited through the Red Cross."

"Me, too," Doris said. "Do you believe all the promises they made us?"

"I imagine it'll probably change. I do believe they need us to learn as much as we can as quickly as we can. Is there a special branch of nursing you're trying to learn?"

"I'm thinking about surgical nursing. I suppose I'll change my mind. Are you leaving a boy friend back home?"

"No one really special. I used to think I wanted to marry Doc Jameson's son. He's an army doctor now. I wanted to be a doctor just like him. I thought we could take over Doc's practice when he retired."

"What happened? Did he find someone else?"

"Yes," said Cathy with a laugh. "He was twelve years older than me. I had to give up my dream when he fell in love with a variety of girls in high school and college."

"It must have been fun thinking about him."

"It was. He was very kind to me, never put me down or made me feel silly. He said we'd open our medical practice together. He fell in love with a home-town girl. She was so nice to me that I realized I had to give him up," Cathy said with a giggle.

"Did you really want to be a doctor?"

"Yes. I spent a lot of time with Doc. He taught me a lot. When I heard about the shortages of nurses I realized how long it would take me to become a doctor. Well, I guess I changed my mind. Here I am."

After almost two days of traveling on the train from Glenridge, Michigan to Camp McCoy in Wisconsin, the train finally got near Madison. They only had about another one hundred miles to go. They were stopped many times because troop trains got priority travel space. The women were greatly relieved when they finally arrived on base.

Cathy had only been on one Army base, the one close to her home. She thought they all must be something alike. Yet, this seemed so different. There was a sense of urgency about everything. Commands seemed to change from one day to the next. Finally, on the third day, at a meeting they learned why.

"Women of the Army Nurse Corp welcome to Camp McCoy," the commander began. He introduced various people who would be their leaders. He continued. "We know most of you were told you would receive military training for one year followed by specialized training for six months in a field you would choose. That was the plan. That plan was a luxury we can no longer afford. When Pearl Harbor was attacked we had less than eighty nurses at Pearl Harbor. We could have used 1,000 nurses. We need to get nurses to the field quickly. Our doctors and commanders in the field are begging us send them more nurses. We are in the process of developing a plan and procedure to reduce the training time. This class will be a test class to see what things we can eliminate; how we can better utilize our time. We are hoping we can complete training in six months. You are all the brightest and best as you begin this journey. You will be given the opportunity to assess your training at the end of the program and make suggestions. Are there any questions?"

"Does this mean we could be sent overseas in six months?" "Yes."

"Does this mean I get no choice in my specialty assignment?" "It could. You will be rated on many things. These ratings will be part of the final assessment."

The colonel patiently answered questions. He dismissed the group. As they walked to the barracks the gravity of how they were to serve settled on each of them. They went to bed that night not really knowing what to expect the next day.

The first few days of the program were spent on physical fitness, army protocol, self-protection, which included the use of gas masks; how to react to chemical warfare, insect control, and the critical importance of cleanliness. They began training (learning to make beds the army way) in the hospital at Camp McCoy which had 1,800 beds. The women lived in

107

barracks, shared baths. They had little time to relax. By the end of the first four weeks, they felt like they knew everything only to learn that the real teaching would begin the next week. They didn't have time to really get to know anyone very well for they learned different skills in small groups. Cathy remembered how much she loved talking with different patients in Glenridge. Here no one had time to visit. Finally, they got a break from noon on Saturday till Sunday night at 10 p.m.

Some of the women said they intended to stay in bed and sleep for 24 hours; some were already making plans to party all night long. Cathy said she wanted to take a shower that would last at least 30 minutes. Each made plans for how she would spend her time. They were a large class yet they all had a kind of togetherness, each one encouraged the other. That evening they all boarded an army bus that took them to a nearby town filled with soldiers who also had a weekend pass.

Cathy was sure she had forgotten how to dance yet when the music started and she was asked to dance she suddenly remembered every step. The group sang, danced, and partied most of the night. They returned to barracks to sleep all day Sunday. Cathy remembered how her mother started the program of inviting soldiers from the base in Glenridge to someone's home for dinner. She wondered if anyone did that at Camp McCoy. It would have been nice to be in a real home, if just for an hour or so. A place with a sofa to sit on, not an army bunk. A place to sit, to enjoy the scenery. Well, maybe she could at least do that. She asked around. She was told about a hiking trail just off base which she would be allowed to explore. None of her friends were interested so she took off alone. She climbed a big hill to a ledge she saw protruding from the top. The view was well worth the climb. She sat on the ledge and looked out over a valley. She saw a river meandering left to right. Across the river up on the hillside were buildings that looked a lot like Glenridge University. A small town was on this side of the river. She sat for a long time, thinking of home, thinking of where she might be in six months; thinking of her family. She slowly made her way back down the hill to head back to base. For a few minutes of time, she felt like she had a visit home.

The clothes for the women had become a problem. The famous white uniform, hat, stockings, and shoes always worn by nurses, was easily soiled and hard to launder. The blue cape they wore over it looked very nice but it was very hard to keep wrapped around your body, especially in the wind. The army had a solution. The women would wear blue seersucker dresses and blue suede shoes when on regular nursing duties. The dresses, being seersucker did not need to be ironed so it seemed like a good solution. But some people thought they looked unsanitary. No one was happy. They were promised they would get a dress uniform similar to the one worn by the WAC's.

They weren't too happy with their pay of $70 a month. Because they were not regular Army, they were only given a place to sleep and food to eat. Nothing else. The women had to buy their uniforms both for everyday use and dress up. They needed multiple uniforms for every day use since it took so long to wash and dry them. They were expected to have at least one clean uniform every day. The soldiers were only paid $30 a month. Still, the soldiers had everything supplied. A few of the nurses got money from home each month for extras. Most had to skimp on things. They really didn't have much time to spend money anyhow. When Emma sent Cathy two books of postage stamps, Cathy put them out for anyone to use.

The nurses had heard the story of the forty-two nurses in the Philippines who were captured by the Japanese and were now prisoners of war. The reality of war hit home as they heard it again. There would be no time to let down one's guard. Everyone was instructed to always stay alert.

The day finally arrived when the new assignments for special training was made. Cathy was almost the last to be called. She knew what some of the choices were, Anesthetists, Psychiatric, Field Hospital, Surgical, Operating Room, etc. She knew she had no choice. She was hoping for Field Hospital, Surgical or Operating Room. *Hadn't Doc Jameson prepared her for one of those,* she thought. She watched her class friends leave the office one at a time. Most seemed satisfied. By this time they all knew they had a job to do. They wanted to get started. Cathy waited and waited. Finally it was her turn.

"Miss Martin, you are being assigned to the Operating Room. Starting next Monday you will report to Major Michael Goodman. You will be trained to be in charge of the operating room, making sure each piece of equipment needed that day is sterilized and in place for the surgeon. You will be part of the medical team doing the surgery. You will count each item to make sure you have accounted for each piece of equipment before the incision is closed. You will measure how much blood is lost and how much is used to replace it. It will be your responsibility to make sure all medications are on hand ready to be administered as needed. You become an extension of the surgeon's hands. Do your job well. The surgeon and the patient depend on you."

Cathy was elated and awed at the same time. So much responsibility. Could she do it? She shook off her doubts. Confidently she shook hands with the assignment officer and said, "This was my first choice. Thank you."

There were five other nurses who were on the same assignment at this time. They met with Major Goodman. He was a tall athletic-looking young man with dark hair. Cathy noticed his hands. She always seemed to look at a guy's hands. Major Goodman's hands looked strong, yet gentle. Good hands for a surgeon, she thought. After a brief welcome he turned their training over to Mrs. Carmichael. She was a no-nonsense woman probably well over fifty years old. She looked very prim and proper in her starched white uniform. She had a curt, brisk manner.

"Your goal in this program is to insure that each patient in the operating room gets the very best care it is possible to provide. Anything less than that is not acceptable," Mrs. Carmichael said. The tone of her voice made Cathy want to say, "Yes, Maam."

Cathy had heard the same kinds of announcements in the past but Mrs. Carmichael said it with such authority that it was almost scary. To think that what you might or might not do could take a life was very heavy on the minds of the young women as they left the briefing. They hurried back to the barracks to study the books they had been given. They had to know each piece of equipment in the O.R. and what it was used for. Cathy never realized how many different types and shapes of scalpels there were. Each one was for a different use. She had to know each one. She learned what changes in temperatures could mean, signs to watch for to show the patient was in distress. The women wanted to do a good job so in their off time they practiced handing instruments back and forth; quizzing each other on procedures. They had no time for a social life. At first they just observed the surgery. Soon they were assigned small chores. Before long they became part of the team. They worked different time shifts. This was no nine-to-five type job. Some surgeries were scheduled. Many were not. The surgical team had to be ready to go all the time. Some surgeries went quickly. Some lasted many hours. They worked twenty-four hour shifts. They could go to a room for a nap if there was time in between surgeries.

*   *   *

As spring turned to summer Beth began to feel a new hope in her life. She still thought about Robbie constantly. She was also very concerned about how she would spend her future. She knew that now that she had graduated she would be embarking on a new adventure. She didn't want to think what she would do if she was not accepted into some flying program. She felt she had to be flying. *Well, maybe I should forget flying and consider going to grad school; become a professor of history.* She seemed to feel Robbie telling her to be patient a while longer. So she kept to her routine: flying for Chuck, entertaining at the base with her mom's program, volunteering at the Red Cross and helping to keep the home on some sort of schedule. With the family involved in so many things, they joked that they needed a secretary to keep them moving. Many times she was about to give up hope that she might be selected for one of the programs she was interested in joining. But she knew that Congress still had not yet given their permission for such organizations so it was with great joy she heard on the radio that the bill had finally passed Congress. Now the program could be official.

One day she finally received a letter from the group headed by Nancy Harkness Love whose program was flying planes from the factories to Canada and would now probably fly to bases in the states. With trembling hands she opened the envelope.

> *Miss Martin,*
>   *Thank you for your interest in our organization. At the present time we are enrolling only twenty-nine people in the group. Our quota was filled immediately. We will keep your application on file and notify you if there are any openings.*
>   *Nancy Harkness Love*

It wasn't the letter that Beth had hoped for. She was disappointed. She did have to admit that she knew her chances were quite small since that group had been together already – just not officially. She had already returned to Jacqueline Cochran's organization the papers they had sent her.

She thought about Cathy who had already started her training. *And here I sit on the sidelines,* she thought. But the urge to fly and the confidence of knowing she was capable to do it, kept her from feeling totally hopeless.

One evening after dinner, Beverly Jensen came from next door, looking worried. Beth called for her mom. The three women sat at the kitchen table with a cup of coffee.

"I'm very worried about Young Freddie," Beverly told them. "He's changed so much since we heard about Robbie. He's not interested in anything. He doesn't want to leave his room. We just found out that his grades are so bad he will probably have to repeat the semester. He skipped so many of his classes. His teachers certainly understand why it happened. They tried to help him. Nothing seemed to work. He was always such a good student. They have offered him the chance to go to summer school to make up the credits. Young Freddie says he won't go. We've tried all sorts of incentives. He says school doesn't matter. I guess I've been in so much grief over Robbie that I've neglected Young Freddie."

Emma spoke up. "Of course you haven't neglected the boy. He's just in his own stages of grieving. He was a good student. He will be again."

"Do you have any ideas about how we can help him? We had thought about a little trip. If he needs summer school . . . well, it doesn't seem like this is the time to take him away."

The women sat thinking of first this idea and then that. Finally, Beth said she had an idea. "I think we should stop calling him Young Freddie. Let's call him Fred." Beth paused went on. "I have another idea that might work if you and Jim think it would be OK. I think I should teach him how to drive. We'll use the old Chevy. I'll tell him I'll only do it if he gets his grades up."

"Beth, you are so busy. You don't have time to do that," Beverly said.

Emma said, "I think that's a wonderful idea. This is the summer that Robbie would probably have tried to teach him. While I know Jim could do it, it might seem like Robbie's a part of it if Beth does it."

When Beth and the Jensens told Fred that Beth would teach him to drive, at first he was very happy about the driving part but was a bit disappointed that it involved going to summer school every morning for six weeks. He said he'd give it a try. Beth insisted on seeing his homework each day before they would leave in the car. When Beth told him he was a natural for driving he was very encouraged. He would hurry home from his classes, do his homework and appear on the doorstep to see if Beth was ready to go. Very often Beth would have them stop for ice cream or a sandwich, or even coffee on a rainy day which made Fred feel very grown-up. They talked a lot about Robbie. Beth loved telling him about some of their escapades. They talked a lot about flying and about cars. Fred soon began to talk about how much he needed a car of his own. Eventually the talks included girls. One day Fred told Beth about Laurie, a girl that he just might want to ask for a date. He just happened to know that a county fair was being held not too far away and did Beth think it might be too far to go for his driving lesson. Driver's training was using up a lot of gasoline ration stamps. Beth was still young enough to get the message.

"Fred, I do believe you are right," she told him. "You do need to drive in new places. It's a great idea. Of course, I'd have to sit in the front seat with you while you drive but if you'd like to invite Laurie, she could sit in the rumble seat. Maybe we could ask Annie to go with us. We could take time to have some fun at the fair before we drive home. What do you think of that idea?"

For the first time since Robbie had been killed, Fred had a smile on his face. He looked happy. He tried to play it cool. "Well, I'll think on it," he told her. Beth knew the minute he got home that he would hurry inside to call Laurie.

When Annie came home Beth asked her if she would go on the driving lesson with her.

"Why in the world do you want to go to the fair?" Annie asked upon learning where they were going.

"Because Fred has asked Laurie Baxter to go with us. I think I'll be a third-wheel if I'm by myself."

"Is Fred really interested in girls? He's too young," Annie said.

"I seem to remember you going off with someone or other when you were his age," Beth told her.

"Well, it is rather sweet," Annie said.

The trip went very well. They all had a good time at the fair, won some silly prizes, and ate a lot of food. Coming home Beth suggested she drive home with Annie in the front seat and let Fred and Laurie sit in the rumble seat. After that trip Fred seemed to return to the once normal relationships he had before the terrible events of December 7th.

*   *   *

One day Cathy did a last inspection of the O.R. after surgery. The cleaning crew had done a great job. She checked the equipment one more time to make sure everything was exactly where it should be. Doris, her friend from the train, was on duty in the other O.R. so Cathy looked in to see if Doris was free. She was not. From the look of things the surgery had just started. Cathy headed for the lounge where she could get coffee. She had been on duty for eight hours yet she did not feel tired. She felt exhilarated. She found surgery fascinating. She sat at a table with her coffee reading yet another brochure with equipment to learn about.

"Miss Martin, you're doing a fine job in surgery." Cathy looked up to see Major Goodman standing there. "Was this position your choice or was it assigned?"

"I hoped I would get this assignment. I guess I got lucky."

He sat down at the table with her. "Did you always want to be a nurse?"

"No sir, I wanted to become a doctor. It would have taken so long and nurses were needed so I made this choice."

"You're a fine nurse. Do you still plan to go to med school?"

"I haven't decided yet. I'm going to try to be a very good nurse."

"Well, you'll have time to decide. Do you have any questions I can help with?"

"Not at this moment." Cathy was feeling a bit intimidated. She had learned that this man had a reputation for being a very tough but a very good doctor. He expected everyone to measure up to very high standards.

"I think I'll go check on our patient and take a nap," he said.

Doris came in and got her coffee. She sat down with Cathy. "Well, what's going on? A visit from Dr. G., the big man himself. I'm a little bit afraid of him. He is so precise with everything. I guess that's good. He is so business-like all the time. Did you hear the gossip about him? He never smiles or is friendly with any of the staff. He must like you if he spoke to you outside the O.R."

"Don't be silly, Doris. We only said a few words together."

"He's sort of good looking if you like a tall man with thick brown hair. I love his hair but he's a bit tall for my taste. He must be at least six feet tall."

Cathy felt really good and encouraged to receive a compliment from the doctor. The next time she stood next to him during surgery she tried very hard to do everything right.

The nurses developed a small routine. After the final inspection of the O.R. the nurses would go to the lounge to have coffee. They would compare notes, each trying to learn from each other how to be a better nurse.

"What's going on with you and *the big man?*" Doris asked her one day about a week later.

"What do you mean when you say *the big man?*" Cathy tried to appear disinterested.

"Major Goodman. It seems like I see you two having coffee in here almost every day. I even saw him smile the other day."

"Oh, Doris, stop teasing me. He may sit here but all we're talking about is surgery. Have you ever watched his hands? He does amazing things in surgery. Last week he . . . ."

"Enough about his surgical ability," Doris said. "I want to know about the personal stuff. And don't tell me you're not interested in him. I can see it on your face. What do you two talk about? Is he married? Is he stationed here all the time or will he be shipping out when we do? Tell me all the important things."

"Doris, you're naughty. He seems very nice. He is very encouraging. He has something nice to say about almost everyone. That's pretty much all we talk about."

"Don't hand me that bull," Doris said. "I saw the way he looks at you. I saw the way you look at him."

"I have no idea what you're talking about. Let's change the subject."

The next day she was not scheduled for work and decided she wanted to talk with someone in her family. She knew none of them would be home if she called so she decided to hike up the hill to the ledge where she had been before. It seemed like a little touch of Glenridge. She made her way to the top. She sat looking at the scene which reminded her of home. It was a beautiful fall day. She could see familiar trees, maples, oaks, ash, locust and others which were turning to the beautiful colors of fall: red, russet, orange and yellow. Just like the colors she saw at home on Lincoln Boulevard. Here in Wisconsin the dark green of the spruce and the evergreen trees among the colorful trees provided a striking contrast. The river was sparkling in the sunlight. She felt very peaceful. It seemed hard to imagine that a war was raging, that lives were being lost; people were receiving wounds from which they would never fully recover. She leaned back against the rocks. She closed her eyes enjoying the feel of the sunshine.

Cathy thought about her conversation with Doris from the day before. *Had she gotten into a routine without knowing it? Yes,* as she thought about it, *she and Major Goodman did seem to have coffee together quite a bit. Their talk had never turned personal. Married? Well, she didn't know. Was it important to know? She'd probably never see him again once they left Camp McCoy.* She thought about her sister, Annie. She smiled when she thought about Annie. *Annie would know Mike's whole life's history by now.* Yet Cathy did find her mind going back to the major. *I'd be willing to bet he's engaged.* She closed her eyes and allowed herself some time to think about him.

"Sorry, I thought I was the only one who knew about this place."

Cathy opened her eyes. She turned to see Major Goodman coming up behind her. "Have I discovered your secret hide-away?" she asked him.

"I think we can share it. Am I intruding?"

"Not at all," she said. "The seat is not too comfortable but the view is great."

"You're right. The air is so fresh. I like to come up here. I like to breathe it all in. When I'm in the O.R. for long hours with its own unique smell, I think about how good it smells up here. It kind of makes you forget the cares of the world. How did you find this place?" he asked as he sat down next to her.

"I asked about a hiking path one day. One of the guys at the base told me about the path. The hills and the river kind of remind me of home. I pretend it is my visit home."

"Tell me about your home."

Cathy told him briefly about her family and home town. She asked him where he was from.

"Virginia, most recently," he told her. "It's so beautiful. My dad is with the government in Washington D.C. working with a group concerned with health issues. My mother is *Miss Volunteer.* She's busy all the time."

"Where did you grow up?" she asked him.

"In a little town outside of Aspen, Colorado. It's in the Rockies. The scenery is spectacular. It was an old mining town. It stayed that way until about ten years ago. There were plans to develop the general area into a ski resort. Dad had a surgical practice. He got arthritis in his hands. He did less and less surgery. He was asked to join the Health Department in Washington, D.C. He also joined a local medical practice in D.C. as a consultant. His name is on the door. They had a place ready for me before the war started. I really love both Colorado and Virginia. They are equally beautiful. Now you tell me about Michigan."

One topic turned to another, about families, school, summer vacations, and childhood memories. Mike turned to her. "Your father must have been very proud to have three daughters; he named you all for famous queens – Queen Catherine, Queen Elizabeth and Queen Anne."

Cathy turned to him with a smile. "Now you've really made me feel good. My dad would say that all the time. Now I really feel like I've had a visit home this morning."

"Well, it's a bit past morning," he said while looking at his watch. "Since it's after three already would you like to hike back now. Maybe we could have dinner tonight. I have an old car that three of us bought to get back and forth to town. Or do you already have plans?"

"I have no plans," she told him. "That would be lovely."

He reached out his hand to help her stand. Hand in hand they walked down the hill together. His hands, the ones Cathy had admired while watching him perform surgery, felt strong and firm. They made Cathy feel safe.

Cathy was glad that none of the other nurses were around as she got ready to go out. She was feeling something special that she didn't want to share with anyone yet. She primped and fussed. She wished she had a nice dress. She knew she had to wear her uniform. She wished she had a pair of really high heels. She really didn't like the Army dress pumps. She looked at her legs. Maybe it's just as well I don't have better shoes she thought. These ugly stockings leave a lot to be desired. No silk for stockings was available anymore. The silk had to be used for parachutes. Would she ever have silk stockings again? *What's with me,* she wondered. *I've never been this nervous before.*

They went to a little Italian cafe. They shared pasta and a bottle of wine. "This is fun," she told him. "It's like a real date. Seems like years since I lived a normal life."

He smiled at her. "Well, I'm glad everything is OK. I didn't know if you had someone special in your life. I thought you might not be interested in dinner." He suddenly got serious. "Or maybe you do and he's not around now."

"No. No one special. How about you? Do you have a girl at every base or just one special one at home?" she asked him.

"No, I don't have anyone special. I guess I'm married to the Army right now. I'll be shipped out soon. I don't know if it will be to Europe or the Pacific. I guess I'll go where I'm told."

"I'll be shipping out very soon, too. Do you think we could be shipped out together?"

"I hope that can happen," he answered. "Yet, I also hope you'll be staying in the states. It's safer here."

"Can I play a special song for you and your lady?" An old Italian man with an accordion had stopped at their table. "I'll play you a happy song."

The music began. The other patrons began to clap their hands. An older man and woman got up from their table and started to dance between the tables as the music continued. Soon tables were pushed together to make room for dancing. After a few fast-paced songs with folk dancing taking place, the musician began to play *Maria Elena.*

"Let's dance," Mike said, pulling her gently to the small dance space.

Cathy felt so amazingly wonderful as he put his arm around her. He was a very smooth dancer.

The song ended much too soon. They left the restaurant. As they got to the car they stopped, embraced, and kissed.

"What a time for this to happen," he said quietly as he held her. "War is so unfair," he said as they kissed once again.

* * *

Beth still waited for the letter that would bring her hope. Cathy had been gone for some weeks now and was very enthused about her training. *If Cathy was disappointed about changing her plans to become a doctor, she hid it well*, Beth thought. *Maybe Mike has something to do with Cathy's good nature.* Beth was busy all the time yet she felt as if she were going through motions only. She wanted to get on with her life.

One afternoon as she sat on the porch, the messenger boy from Western Union arrived with a telegram for her. She hurriedly tore it open.

WILL INTERVIEW APPLICANTS WOMEN'S FLYING
PROGRAM OLYMPIC HOTEL CHICAGO ILLINOIS

FROM 10 AM TO 6 PM AUGUST 20 AUGUST 21 AUGUST 22 STOP MINIMUM HEIGHT SIXTY-TWO AND ONE HALF INCHES SUSAN MCCALLEY RECRUITING OFFICER ARMY AIR FORCE

Beth leapt from the swing. She began to dance with joy. She hurried into the house to the phone to call her dad. She left a message for her mother. She knew she couldn't reach Annie right away. She knew she would have to notify Cathy by letter. Beth ran next door to tell the Jensens and headed for the airport.

As she drove to the airport she did not let the thought that she might not be accepted enter into her mind. She was on her way. The men were very happy for her. Chuck immediately checked his schedule. He said he had a flight scheduled to Chicago on the afternoon of August 19th; would she like to have a ride? Chuck told her he had flights there about four or five days a week now so maybe he could even get her a ride home.

Beth took this as an omen that she was finally on a path to do what she was meant to do. At dinner that night Albert suggested she make reservations for a couple of nights at the hotel which she immediately did. Annie tried to be practical. She tried to discuss what clothes Beth would need. She insisted Beth must have something different than a pair of Robbie's old overalls which she liked to wear when she flew. Beth insisted she did not need a new wardrobe.

The next few days passed in slow motion as Beth waited. Finally the plane left the ground. She was on her way. She took a bus from the airport in Chicago to the downtown area and to the Olympic Hotel. By eight-thirty the next morning she made her way to the conference area where the interviews would take place. She wanted to be first in line. She was surprised to see a room full of women waiting to be interviewed. She had no idea so many women were interested in flying. In Glenridge, she was the only woman pilot.

Beth looked around the room. She saw a section with a sign indicating it was Section A – Reception. Another sign read Section B – Testing. Section C—Testing was in another location. *I guess I start at Section A,* she thought. About 9 a.m. the receptionist at Section A began handing out applications. Beth got in line. After receiving the application she was told to complete it and return it to the receptionist at Section B. It was a long application, yet pretty routine: name, address, date of birth, family, education, job experience, etc. Beth completed the form and took it to the receptionist at Section B. The young woman checked it over to make certain that all questions were answered. She then told Beth to have a seat. The next testing would begin in a few minutes. Beth chatted briefly with a young woman named Eileen Watson who was also waiting. She found Eileen had flown many different types of planes. Beth began to worry. Beth had a lot of hours in the air but they were mostly on the same type of aircraft. Soon she heard her name called. She was given the test.

"This position is part of the Civil Service program. You are required to take this test to be considered for the program," the clerk told her.

Beth walked to one of the tables and sat down. One young woman got up from the table. "I like to fly but this test is too hard for me," she told Beth as she left. Beth began to feel anxious. Beth had taken many, many tests at school. She didn't find this one too difficult. The questions were more of a general area, not specifically about flying. She completed it, checked it over, and returned it to the receptionist. She sat back down to wait for it to be checked. She was happy when her name was called. She was told to go to Section C.

The receptionist gave Beth yet another test. She was told to take her time to answer the questions carefully. This test was all about flying. From mechanical information to wind drafts; flying skill questions, flying terminology: common sense questions about emergencies. This would definitely be the make or break section, she thought. Beth tried to take her time to answer each page of questions completely before going back to review it. After more than an hour, she returned it. The receptionist suggested that Beth might want to go to the coffee shop in the hotel for lunch as it would take time to check the answers.

Beth walked down the hall into a crowded coffee shop. She could find no place to sit. She felt tired. She really needed something to eat. A hand waved to her from across the room. It was Eileen, the girl she had talked with earlier. Eileen had very dark hair worn very short. She had striking dark eyes. Grandma Bertie would have called them Spanish Dancing Eyes.

"I see you're still here," she told Beth. "How do you think you're doing so far? You must be doing OK or you wouldn't still be here. You have to leave immediately if you don't pass part of the tests. That last one was really hard I thought. Especially the mechanical part."

"I don't know about the whole test but I had a great teacher for the mechanics. He made me learn about the engines. I had to help him repair them before he would let me fly. I did notice that many of the girls are leaving. I also noticed there is still a line up at Section A. I didn't realize so many women were flying."

"I flew out of Cleveland," Eileen told her. "We had lots of women pilots. That's why it is so silly that the government won't let us fly now. If we make it into this program a lot of eyes will be on us watching to see if we're good enough."

Beth's lunch arrived and she began to eat. Eileen checked her watch and said she had to leave; that they should have her test graded by now. Eileen was getting antsy to see if she would make it to the next stage which would be interviews. "Hope to see you again. If I don't make it, good luck to you."

As Eileen left, another young woman, a striking blonde with pure blue eyes, and a voluptuous type body, came by. She asked if she could sit down. "I saw you taking the last test. I started much earlier than you. I finished much later. I'm Georgiana Berry. My friends call me JoJo. I'm from Oklahoma."

"I'm Beth Martin from Michigan. I thought the test was pretty hard. I hope I did well. Who knows? I really want to be in this program."

After some more chitchat Beth returned to the Conference Area. She met Eileen who was on her way out.

"Get ready for a long wait," Eileen told her. "They're running almost two hours behind schedule. I guess they didn't expect this turnout. I passed the test. Now I'm going for the big personal interview. Wish me luck."

Beth sat and waited more than an hour before they called her name. Finally at last she heard the call, "Beth Martin – Beth Martin." Beth made her way to the desk.

"You have passed the test," she was told. "Please exit the conference area, turn left then proceed to a door that has a sign for Air Training Management."

As Beth left the area she passed JoJo who was returning from lunch. She gave her the thumbs up sign as they passed each other. When she got to the proper area, she saw Eileen just being called into the inner offices. Beth settled in for a long wait. JoJo soon came in to join her. Eileen finally came out of the office. She sat down with Beth and JoJo.

"How was it? Was it an ordeal?" they asked her.

"Nerve-racking, I guess," she told them. "I don't know what to do next. Mrs. Grant, who interviewed me, asked me to wait out here."

Very soon Mrs. Grant emerged from her office. She came over to speak to them.

"We have had a much larger response to our requests for applicants than we expected. We're running very far behind schedule." She looked at Eileen and said, "Your next step is for a physical. It cannot be given until tomorrow." She looked at Beth. "I will interview you today but it will be the last one." Looking at JoJo she said, "I will be able to interview you in the morning at 8 a.m."

JoJo looked up and said, "I'm from Oklahoma. I'm supposed to go home tonight."

"I would suggest you change your plans. Even if I interview you next, if you pass the interview tonight you would need to be here in the morning for your physical. You can make your decision."

JoJo looked so sad.

Eileen spoke up. "I tried to get a room for tonight. I was unable to find one. I don't know what I'll do."

"I have a room with a double bed. Both of you can stay with me. We'll have a cot brought in," Beth offered. Since Mrs. Grant had motioned for her to enter the office, Beth told them, "Wait for me in the coffee shop or leave me a note at the front desk."

Beth entered the office feeling somewhat intimidated.

"Have a seat, Miss Martin. Tell me why you want to enter our program."

"I have been flying for a long time. I think I was born to fly. Now there is a need for the type of flying I'm capable of doing."

"You do have quite a resume, Miss Martin. You must have been very young when you started."

"Yes, maam. I was only ten years old. I helped to wash airplanes in exchange for lessons. The instructor made me learn all about the mechanical side. I had a lot of book lessons before he let me near the controls."

"Did you do this by yourself?"

"No, my friend Robbie was with me."

"Tell me about Robbie. Is he a flyer now? Is this why you want to fly?"

"Robbie was the boy next door. He was killed at Pearl Harbor. He had just completed training to fly fighter planes."

"So you want to do this for Robbie; to avenge his death."

"No, maam. I can't bring him back. We did hope to have our own airfield and some planes someday."

"Is that his ring you have on the chain around your neck?"

"Yes, maam." Beth suddenly didn't like the way the interview was going. She spoke up. "I made this choice because I can't join the Army or Navy Air Corp. They won't let women do that. I'm a good pilot. I don't take chances. I know a lot about planes. I'm willing to learn everything I can so I can be an even better pilot."

Mrs. Grant looked at her with some surprise. Then said. "Let me tell you about the program." She advised Beth to return for her physical the next morning. As Beth left the office, Mrs. Grant informed Beth that interviews were being conducted in New York City, Atlanta, Los Angeles, and Seattle as well as in Chicago. After all the interviews were completed the applicants would be notified. They expected the process to take about two months.

When Beth left the office after an hour and a half she found Eileen and JoJo still waiting for her in the coffee shop. That evening the women formed a friendship that lasted over many, many miles and many, many years.

The next morning the three girls returned to the testing area. Beth was informed she had passed the interview. She would now need her physical. Upon completing that test, she was ready to go home. Beth had been told that after the three days of interviews were completed the applicants would be rated. The women would be notified by telegram or letter whether or not they had been accepted.

Beth returned home to Glenridge to once more begin the waiting game. When she made up her mind that they had forgotten her, she called Eileen who had not heard anything either. She knew Eileen had so much more experience than she did. She was sure Eileen would be accepted so she didn't give up hope.

*   *   *

On the war scene the enemy still seemed to have the upper hand. In Africa, General Rommel of Germany was nearing Cairo, Egypt, and about to take the city. Hitler was moving into Russia. In the Pacific area the Americans were suffering big loses in the Philippines and the Japanese had invaded and now occupied the Aleutian Island of Attu.

*   *   *

My goodness, this is quite a storm Emma thought as she stepped off the bus and began the walk home. *It's almost as dark as midnight.* She saw that lights were on in the houses she passed. She was getting drenched from the rain even though she did have her umbrella. She remembered she had forgotten to tell Annie that there would be just the two of them for dinner. As she approached the house she was surprised to see it still dark.

"Annie, I'm home. Are you here?" she called.

"Mom, I'm here. I didn't realize it was so late. I'll get dinner started right away," Annie said as she began to turn on lights and move toward the kitchen.

Emma saw her daughter had been crying. "Whatever is wrong, Annie. Are you OK? Did we get some bad news?"

"Mom, Rich Cantrell is dead. Remember when we heard that the United States had begun bombing runs in Europe? Well, Rich was on one of those first planes. He was a gunner. The plane was hit with fire from the ground and exploded. Everyone aboard was killed."

"Annie, I'm so very sorry to hear about this. Rich was a nice young man. It hasn't quite been two years since he spent so much time at our house."

"I know, Mom. He was a really nice guy and I had lots of fun with him. After we stopped dating we still stayed good friends." Annie began to sob again.

Her mother sat and consoled her. *I do want this war to be over quickly* she thought. *How many people have to die before it ends?* Finally the crying stopped.

"Sorry about not having dinner ready. I'll get on it right away." Annie moved to the kitchen.

"Your dad has a dinner meeting at school and then a Civil Defense meeting at City Hall. Beth is on a flight and won't be home till late. Let's heat up the chicken noodle soup from last night. A bowl of hot soup will taste good on this cool, damp night."

As they began to heat the soup and set the table, Annie started to talk. "Mom, I'm so discouraged. Now two people who were close to me are dead. Cathy is already training to go to some war zone, and Beth is getting ready to leave home to fly planes. And here I sit, doing nothing. I feel like such a failure."

"War is hard on the people at home as well as in the war zones. You are doing many, many things, Annie. You have already raised over $5,000 in War Bond sales, you help at the Red Cross, and you help bring a little bit of joy and happiness to the servicemen . . . ."

Annie interrupted. "Mom, I know you're trying to be helpful but I should be doing more. My sisters always knew exactly what they wanted to do with their careers and then move back here to Lincoln Boulevard. But I don't seem to have any goals."

"Well, there's no way of knowing what lies ahead for any of us," Emma said.

"We had a letter from Cathy today. I think she's in love with her doctor friend. I hope it won't make Beth feel sad about losing Robbie when she hears about Mike."

"I think Beth will be happy for her sister," Emma answered.

"At least Cathy will know what it's like to love someone. Beth already knows. I've never had that experience and maybe I never will. I've had lots of boy friends but never one I would want to marry. Both Beth and Cathy have always known what they wanted from life and I never have. Maybe I never will," she said as the plopped herself in her chair.

"That's not so," Emma told her. "You're still exploring all possibilities. It seems to me I heard you say you wanted to become a teacher many times. You're on a path to do it. You have had excellent teaching skills since you were a very little girl. Don't you remember how often you brought younger children home to play school up in the playroom? Or the school room you had in the back yard in the summer? You taught every child on the street how to count, add numbers, their ABC's, even how to color and stay in the lines. Jane Watson, who taught first grade told me she could always tell when a child lived on Lincoln Boulevard. They were prepared when they started school. And what about the program you, Rosemary, and Marge have underway tutoring the high school students? You are doing important work, Annie."

"Rosemary and Marge only do it because they're lonely. Rosemary can't wait to get married to Roy and Marge is expecting to get a ring from Herb when he gets home on leave. I don't even have a steady boyfriend. I want to be happy like they are. Or maybe like Beth was, or Cathy is right now."

"That's because you haven't met the right man yet, or you have met him but you need time to let the love grow."

"Well, you didn't have to wait." Annie said.

"You're wrong. It took time for me to be sure your dad was the only man for me. I was frightened by the idea of caring about someone that much."

"Well, maybe it took time for you but not for Dad."

"That is true," Emma said with a smile.

*   *   *

Beth tried to stay busy and not be so anxious about being accepted into the training program.

About six weeks after the testing the telegram arrived.

> BETH MARTIN YOU HAVE BEEN ACCEPTED FIRST
> CLASS BEGINNING NOVEMBER 2ND FURTHER
> DIRECTIONS COMING.
> MARTHA GRANT RECRUITING OFFICER ARMY
> AIR CORP

At last, at last, Beth thought as she read and re-read the letter. She rushed to the phone to tell her family and went next door to tell Beverly. She went to the airfield. That evening she cautiously called Eileen since she didn't want to upset Eileen if she had not been notified. She learned Eileen had also been accepted for the first class. Eileen had already heard from JoJo who had been accepted into the second class beginning in December. Beth anxiously waited for the packet of information to arrive. She was excited about finally having the pathway opened for the journey of her life.

The family was pleased for her, yet they were anxious about her choices. They were supportive and encouraging with a somewhat heavy heart. Even though they knew she would be staying in the states, they knew she would face many challenges.

When the packet arrived, Beth found that she should report to Avenger Field in Sweetwater, Texas. She must provide her own transportation to the base. Army coveralls and flying jackets would be provided. She must provide her own clothes. Meals would only be provided when she was on duty. She read a few more pages of instruction. Beth read each one carefully until she was sure she knew them all. She was in frequent contact with Eileen. They decided to meet in Chicago to take the train together to Texas. It felt to Beth as if all the plans were now coming together.

One afternoon she spent time trying to put the things together that she would take with her. She looked about her own bedroom that had been a haven to her for so many years. She looked at the big picture of Robbie that still was on her nightstand. She held it in her hands and sat on her window seat. She remembered back to the days when she and Robbie were very young. She was glad she had so many memories of him. Almost everything in her room from pictures on her walls, to trophies they won, to mementos lining her shelves brought back some recollection of him. "Robbie, I'll never forget you and I'll always love you. I can't take all these things with me. But you will always be in my heart." She spoke the words aloud as if that would make them more official.

Emma knocked on her door to ask her if she'd like to go out for coffee. "We won't have many of these chances for a long time," she told Beth. Beth agreed to go. They talked about Robbie. Emma gently asked Beth if she was ready to let go of him yet.

"Not really, Mom, but I'm trying to be realistic. I know he's not coming back. Leaving Glenridge will be a whole new start for me. I'm not ready to start dating anyone but I don't think Robbie would want me to be alone all my life."

"Well, don't rush. You're still a young woman. Don't think about getting involved with anyone. Be open to make lots of friends without wondering where that friendship will go. You'll know when that happens."

"Mom, can I leave my room just the way it is? I know I won't be home much for a long time. You can certainly use the room if you need it. I'm just not ready to pack everything away yet."

"You don't have to touch a thing if you don't want to. We won't touch them either. If you have some things you'd like to keep private, just put them in a box. We can tape it shut. You can keep it in the closet or in the attic if you like."

"Mom, I've got one concern. It's my engagement ring. I've been wearing it on a chain around my neck. We were told not to bring anything of value with us. This ring belonged to Robbie's grandmother. I think it should go to Fred to give to the girl he marries so it can stay in his family. If I try to give it back will Beverly and Jim think I don't want it or that I'm being disrespectful to the memory of Robbie? It seems wrong to pack it away in a box. I don't know what to do."

Emma sat pondering the situation for a few minutes. "This is a situation where there is no clear cut right or wrong. Beverly and Jim love you. They wanted you to be their daughter-in-law. I don't think they would want you to give up future happiness to live your life alone. I'm sure they will understand whatever you decide to do."

Chuck had made arrangements for Beth to fly to Chicago where she would meet Eileen at the train station on October 29th. This would give them time to travel to Texas to get settled. Trains were often delayed many hours while troop or supply trains had priority on the tracks.

On the day before she was to leave her girl friends gave her a luncheon. At dinner that night Emma had a quiet family dinner. Uncle Frank, Aunt Millie, Harold, and his wife joined them. Cousin Herb was on duty in the Marines. Cathy managed to get a call through during that time so it seemed like the whole family was together. After dinner, Beth said she wanted to go next door to say goodbye to the Jensens.

The Jensens had eaten later that night. They were still at the table when Beth arrived. They were anxious to hear more details about her plans which Beth was happy to share with them. She sat with them at the table while Beverly poured them more coffee.

"Tell us about your immediate plans," Jim said.

Beth updated him about the short term plans for the next few days and what she expected over the next months.

"Robbie would be so proud of you, Beth," he told her.

"But Robbie would not want you to grieve for him forever. Don't be afraid to open your heart to someone new when a special person comes along. Robbie would want that for you," his mother told Beth.

Beth thought she would cry. This was going to be harder than she thought it would be. She reached into her pocket and pulled out a set of car keys.

"Fred, these are Robbie's keys to our car. I think he would like for you to have it now." She handed over the keys to him.

"I can't take them! I can't take them!" he began to shout.

Beth left the table, walked to him and put her arms around him. "It's the right thing to do, Fred. I'll admit Annie may ask to borrow it sometime. She doesn't need a car very often. You're a guy. A guy needs a car. Take the keys. Enjoy driving it. Of course, your dad and mom have to approve this deal and you must promise me that you'll keep your grades up."

"Mom, Dad . . . . ," he began as he looked at them. Jim gave a nod of his head.

He stood to give Beth a hug, half crying and half laughing.

Beth sat back down and sipped her coffee. Then she took a big breath. "There is something else." She reached around her neck to remove the chain with Robbie's engagement ring on it. "When Robbie gave me this ring it was the happiest day of my life. It meant we would be together forever." She paused for a moment to regain her composure. This was very hard for her. "This is a very special ring because it was given to me with so much love. I know how much his grandmother meant to Robbie. I thought I'd wear this ring forever. I'd never take it off. I'm not allowed to take anything of value with me. I'll be moving around a lot. They don't want us to wear jewelry. This ring must not be kept in a box packed away somewhere in the attic It belongs to your family so Fred can give it to the woman he marries." The tears began to flow from her eyes as she handed the ring to Beverly. Beverly refused to take the ring.

Beverly began to cry.

"That ring is your ring. Robbie gave it to you." Jim said quietly. "Robbie was so happy to give that ring to you."

"I was so happy that day. I wanted the ring I had heard about all my life. This war has changed us all. This ring must stay in your family. Robbie would have wanted that."

Beverly took the ring from Beth, held it for a minute and then handed it to Jim.

Jim sat quietly for a moment looking at the ring. With a sob in his voice he said, "This ring was worn by only two people – my mother and you, Beth; two very, very special ladies."

Beth was very happy to see Eileen waiting when she arrived at the train station in Chicago. They found departure had been delayed for an hour so they went to the coffee shop to wait. By the time the train departed and the hours it took them to get to Texas, they pretty much knew all about each other. They made their way to the hotel that would be their home for the next few days. They were surprised to find the place was filled with other women who were also part of the program. They were excited about the whole experience. Two mornings later an Army bus arrived to transport them to the base.

After all the welcomes and basic directions had been given, the officer in charge asked them, "How many of you think you know how to fly an airplane? Well, you know absolutely nothing. We will teach you what you need to know. It is extremely important that everyone does things the same way. We use one set of terms. You will learn about flying in formation. You will learn how to fly using a radio beam. You will learn how to fly in the dark. Some of you will be gone by the end of the week. Some of you may make it to the end of the second week. You have been selected as the first class because someone, somewhere in the interviewing process, thought you had the skills to become a pilot. I hope you don't let us down." With a scowl on his face and a cocky swagger to his walk, he left the area.

"Well, I guess he told us," a voice said from the back of the room. The women that day did realize they were the trail blazers for other women who wanted to fly officially with the Air Corp.

They were told that their first purchase must be a pair of beige slacks and a white shirt. It would be their *official dress uniform* at this time.

One of the first things they learned was to march in formation. They weren't sure why this was needed. No one dared to ask why. Since no one was in uniform, the group eventually became known as the *Rainbow Ladies* because they had a variety of colors in their clothing. Soon they were issued white head scarves to wrap around their hair. Someone might get hurt if long hair got caught on some part of the plane. They were issued a pair of coveralls to wear over their clothes, and they were given leather helmets and leather jackets. The outfit was called a *Zoot Suit*. For some of the shorter women the coveralls were a real problem because they were all sized for men's bodies. The women rolled them up as best they could.

The women were never told officially about another problem yet everyone seemed to know about it. Because the flying would take place with a male instructor teaching them, many of the male pilots refused to be alone with a woman in the air. Their wives would leave them, they told their superiors. Some wives banded together to protest at the base. The women in training had to learn to accept and forget the insulting remarks made about them. They were told their training was exactly the same as the male cadets in the Army Air Corp. One of the women added her own comment when she said, "They didn't have the *jealous wife* problem."

Learning to fly the Army way was different than the way Beth had learned, still she soon adapted to it. It didn't take her long to understand why everyone had to learn the same basic rules when they had to take off and land very quickly in a smooth formation.

A lot of the early training was done in AT-6's and BT-13's. They had to pass a certification test on each type of aircraft. If they failed the test they were offered a chance to take additional training on that part of the program and re-take the test. Or they could quit. No third chances would be given.

They learned to do loops, chandelles, and many evasive types of actions. Beth enjoyed this part of her training. She didn't tell anyone that Dave (the WWI fighter pilot in Glenridge who taught Beth to fly) had done stunt flying to earn extra money. One day, unknown to anyone else, he had taught Beth how to do some of the maneuvers. On the day she took her test her instructor complimented her on her skills. Beth considered this the best compliment she got during her training. Roy, the instructor had over twenty years in the Air Corp.

Learning how to trust a radio beam to guide you when all you can see is a small box that looks like a big ladybug took a lot of courage. A new language had to be learned to talk with the radio tower. Various lights on the tower meant different things which had to be learned. She had to have 30 hours of simulating altitude instrument flying. Part would be done on one type of plane and some on another plane. They had to learn cross-country flying without instruments. They always had something new to learn. About the time the women would think they had learned all there was to learn about one plane, they would find modifications had been made on the plane which meant they had to be re-certified on it.

Many days they were grounded because of the weather. On those days they studied the manuals to reinforce the things they were learning. When they began night flying, Beth was thrilled. She felt like it brought her closer to home. She remembered how her dad had taught her about the stars and constellations. She felt calm, she felt peaceful in the dark of night.

The women had a lot of physical training as well to make sure they stayed healthy. One problem that affected some of them was vertigo, a dizzy confused state of mind. Usually it would pass by quickly. One day, Kristen, one of their group confessed that she was suffering quite badly.

Three of the women had combined money and bought an old car that they used to get back and forth to town on their day off. Eileen borrowed the car. She took the girl to see a doctor in town. The others waited behind, knowing that if the vertigo continued, their friend would be out of the program by the end of the week. Finally, Eileen and Kristen returned. It seems that a bug had gotten into Kristen's ear and become infected. The doctor removed the bug, gave her a prescription. She was OK.

The harassment they suffered because they were women did not come from all the men. As the women continued to learn and be able to fly the planes, they earned new respect from everyone. Roy, the instructor, was a kind man who started to watch out for the women. He tried to help each one.

One day a notice went on the bulletin board inviting all the women for a Sunday afternoon picnic at Roy's home. It was the first time since they had been to Texas that the women had a chance for relaxation. They were told the home was on a lake so they could swim if they liked. The women eagerly looked forward to it. They hoped the dust storm that was supposedly headed their way would wait for a while. They had a wonderful picnic lunch out under the trees. Roy had a small pontoon boat on the lake and they enjoyed being on it. Roy had six children. Two sons were already in the Army Air Corp. The youngest son was just finishing high school. The three sisters were beautiful young women who sang. They brought out a guitar in the early evening. Roy built a campfire and everyone sat around it and sang along. Beth felt very nostalgic, as if she were back home for a Sunday Musicale.

It seemed like it had been so long since anyone had said anything nice to them or been so kind. The women all felt a bit misty-eyed as the evening grew to a close.

The dust storm did hit later that night. Beth had never seen anything like it. Dust everywhere. Of course they could do no flying so it was back to the books and practice marching in formation.

One day shortly after the dust storm the women were out practicing formation flying when a gusty windstorm hit the area. The planes were ordered back to base as the storm was severe. Beth was next to last in line to land.

"Do you want me to take the landing?" her instructor asked her. Beth hesitated a minute; she didn't want to wreck the plane. "I'll take it," she calmly answered him.

It was the hardest landing Beth had ever made. As they taxied to the hanger they could see the last plane coming in to land. They saw a wind gust upset and toss the last plane into a nearby hillside. The plane immediately exploded into flames. Both Beth and her instructor leapt out of their plane as soon as it stopped. They rushed to the downed plane. Beth's friend, Rose, was still on fire as they got to her. They beat out the flames with their jackets. She was still alive. Unfortunately, the instructor, who had taken over the controls, was killed. Because Rose was not military, she had to be taken to the hospital in Sweetwater where the doctors fought to keep her alive. The women knew when they entered the program that no medical help would be available to them on base. It made them angry to think that Rose had to be taken so far. Rose was in a critical condition for the next few weeks. The women pitched in a week's pay to help pay for Rose's care. Rose's husband was in the South Pacific with the Marines so the women tried to have someone visit Rose each day. Those first weeks, Rose didn't know them. Still, they talked with Rose about what they were learning. They told her they wanted her to come back. Rose was still in the hospital when Beth completed her training program a few months later.

On the lighter side, as the men got more comfortable in working with the women, things did get a little easier. The ground crews especially would play little tricks on them. Some of the younger men looked on the women as their sisters and asked for advice about the girl they left back home.

One of the girls in their group was barely tall enough to make the program. She had tried stretching herself to be qualified. She was a very intelligent, qualified pilot. The men teased her relentlessly, asking her if she brought her baby doll or teddy bear to camp with her. Soon she had acquired the name of *Teddy Bear*. While some of the women didn't think it was very nice, they could understand why. Teddy had on her zoot suit (the oversized coverall which was a size forty with the sleeves and legs pinned up) her leather jacket, leather helmet, and flying boots. She had a backpack on her back and carried a parachute in front. She was wider then she was tall. She accepted their good natured teasing. She knew she had earned their respect as a pilot.

Beth missed being home for Thanksgiving. She remembered all the big family dinners the family had each year. She and Eileen went into town. They had dinner at a restaurant. Some of the women had family members in town visiting them. Two women, who lived in the nearby area, went home for the day.

Beth seemed to feel the weight of December 7th on her shoulders as the first anniversary of that fateful day approached. She was scheduled for a late day flight on the 7th so she got up early that morning. She went to the base chapel. She had not been to church since arriving in Texas because Sunday was another scheduled work day. She found a bit of solace sitting quietly in the pew. She thought about Robbie and their dreams for the future. Then she thought about where she was now and what she was doing. She hoped her efforts were helping the country.

Beth also thought a lot about Cathy. Beth knew that within a couple of weeks Cathy's training would end and she would be shipped out. She knew Cathy was in love with Mike. Beth hoped that Mike loved Cathy. She remembered how it felt to love some one that much.

*   *   *

After Cathy's first date with Mike it was a return to training as usual for most of the nurses. But for Cathy it was a time of falling in love. After their first kiss she felt different than she had ever felt in her life. She knew her feelings were something special for this man. When she saw him as she reported for duty in the O.R. she felt a nervous chill over her body. *What if I'm just someone for a night's fun?* She had many boyfriends in the past. She knew she had never felt this way before. *I must take everything slow and careful* she thought. Yet when she saw him she wanted to feel his arms around her again. She could never forget how very special she had felt when he had come to her the next morning after they had kissed.

"I hope you're OK. Last night was really special for me. I hope I didn't scare you off and you won't want to see me again," Mike had told Cathy.

She looked up into his eyes and said, "It was special for me."

"Can I see you again? Can we have a real date?"

"I'd really like that, Mike."

The demands of training were upon them, yet they both felt a need to try to find time and a place where she and Mike could be alone. Cathy had many boyfriends in Glenridge. Mike was definitely not a boyfriend. He was so much more. They remained very professional when on duty; they were passionate when they were alone. Not too many opportunities arose when they both were off duty at the same time. Yet they made an effort to spend some time together each day. If she was on duty he would come to meet her during her break time and soon she did the same when he was on duty. On occasion they would attend the movie theatre on base or go bowling. Their growing love was apparent to all who saw them. In spite of the gentle teasing and comments, it seemed like all their friends were supporting them. After Mike took her to the Officer's Club for dinner one night she realized how serious he was when she observed how he treated her. It was the same way the married officers treated their wives.

One day when they both had a few hours off duty at the same time he asked her to climb the hill again. They dressed warmly for a light snow had fallen. The trees were bare and the scene had a completely different look. They didn't seem to notice for both were deep in thought as they knew their time together was coming to an end.

"Cathy, I can't imagine my life without you," he told her that day. "I didn't expect to find someone like you and fall in love at an Army base. I really love you, Cathy."

"I can't imagine my life without you, Mike. I love you, too. Love was not on my mind when I came here. Yet look at me now. I will always treasure the memory of each minute we've had together. Especially moments like these."

"Will you marry me, Cathy?"

"Yes, Mike," she answered quietly. "I do love you. I want to be with you for the rest of my life."

"Can we find time to go shopping for a ring?" he asked her. "I want everyone to know that you said yes and that I want us to be together forever."

"I couldn't wear it much of the time right now. I would probably have to leave it behind when I ship out. I don't need a ring to know how much you love me."

"You're probably right," he told her. "But I'll do this. I'll buy a plain gold wedding band and carry it with me till we get married. When the war is over I'll buy you the diamond ring."

They sat quietly, enjoying the moment. Then he spoke again.

"I have something to confess to you. Remember that first day I came up here and found you. It was not by accident. For some reason or other I felt very shy about approaching you to ask for a date. Even though you were very nice when we had coffee together I thought you probably already had a love somewhere else. Finally I worked up the courage to approach you but no one knew where you were when I came to your barracks. I asked everyone. Finally a young corporal who was visiting the girls said he had earlier told you about the path up here. He thought I might find you here. I knew it was now or never. When I did find you here I knew it was meant to be. Fate had brought us together. I don't ever want to be apart from you again."

In spite of their love, they both knew the time was near when they would probably be separated. How could they let each other go? To not know where he or she was or if they were safe was devastating to think about. They didn't allow themselves to imagine a life without each other. They both had a sincere desire to meet the other's parents. There seemed to be no way to make that happen. War doesn't allow for the usual routine of a courtship. They tried to be content and treasure each day, one at a time.

Finally, the fateful day arrived. They received their orders. They both would be shipping out the first part of December. They would be given a delay en route for a few days if they wanted it. Both were told to report to San Francisco in ten days. There would not be enough time to travel to Michigan to meet Cathy's family, and then go to Virginia to meet Mike's family and still get to California on time. They finally agreed they would each visit their own home and family. They would meet when they got to San Francisco. They planned to talk each day by phone.

Cathy called home to say she would be on her way. Her family was excited by the news. Her dad told her, "Cathy, we've been hoping against hope that you would get home for at least a day or two. I called Chuck at the airfield. He said Dave makes every day flights to Chicago. He can bring you to Glenridge if you can get to Chicago. He'll fly you back to Chicago for your trip to California."

Hearing Dave's voice call to her when she arrived at the airport in Chicago was second best to being home. "Dave, are you becoming a personal pilot for the Martin family?" she asked him as she gave him a hug.

"I just wish I could do it more often," he told her. "Your folks are probably already at the airfield to meet you."

When the plane taxied to the hanger, Cathy looked out. She saw her parents and Annie waiting for her with open arms.

"It's so wonderful to be home," she told them. "I think this is the most beautiful place in the world."

"Tell us about Mike," Annie pleaded.

"Annie, give her time to get settled first," her mother suggested.

"I want you to know all about him. I love him," Cathy said.

It was really fun for Cathy to tell the family about Mike and Camp McCoy, and all about Wisconsin, and her training.

"We were really surprised when we found out your training time was so short. We thought it would be a year and a half," Emma said.

"Well, so did I. I know they really need nurses badly. I'm glad I decided to go into nursing. I'd hate to think about sitting in some class when they need me. We don't know where we're going. Since we're deploying from California, I'd guess it's to the Pacific area."

"Will you and Mike be going to the same place?" her dad asked.

"All we know is that we're shipping out on the same date. We hope it's on the same ship. We hope we're going to the same place. We have no idea what will happen."

"Did you and Mike talk about when you'd get married?" Annie asked.

"We certainly did. We want to spend our life together. If we'd have had more time right now . . . ." Cathy paused. "We both want to be married with our parents with us. It's important to us to have you all be a part of a wedding. We want to get your blessing."

"Thank you, Cathy, for those nice words. We want to be at your wedding. But do remember this: you'll have our blessing wherever and whenever you get married," Emma said with tears in her eyes as she hugged her daughter.

The few days at home passed all too quickly. Cathy saw a few friends and family. She stopped in to see Old Doc Jameson. She thanked him for everything he had taught her.

"Doc, I think the most important thing you taught me was to stay in control and not panic no matter how bad things got. Some of the conditions we have heard about are very frightening. The field hospitals set up in the Philippines are out in the open with just a canopy overhead. Often times the Japanese have flown over and dropped bombs or strafed the area. It's definitely not a sterile set-up. The doctors and nurses do the best they can. One nurse had to close an incision when the doctor was hit by debris when a bomb, or maybe it was a grenade, hit the area. At least you made me practice my stitching so I'm prepared if I have to do that."

"Go with God, child," Doc told her as she left. "I'll say a prayer for your safety each day."

Cathy left home with a heavy heart. She knew she might never see her family again. She knew they were thinking it might be the last time they'd see her. They all kept smiling; still, she could see the tears in their eyes. Once on the plane to Chicago and especially on the train to San Francisco, she began to feel much better. Soon she would see Mike again.

After she checked in and got her assignment Cathy made her way to the barracks. She was thrilled when she saw Mike sitting on the steps waiting for her. *I'll always remember this moment,* she thought. *Seeing him here makes me feel very secure in his love.*

They reached for each other and embraced. They didn't care if the world was watching.

"If feels so good to be in your arms," Cathy said.

"I want you in my arms forever," Mike told her. "My parents are very anxious to meet you."

"My folks feel the same. I really wish we had time for us all to get to know each other," Cathy said as they stood locked in each other's arms.

"Knock it off, you two," one of the nurses said good-naturedly as she came out the door. "Be nice to her Doc. I don't want her crying all the way to wherever we're going."

"Yes, maam," Mike said in his most official voice.

Two nights later they were told they would be shipping out the next day. Cathy went to Mike's quarters to tell him.

"I was just coming to tell you I'm shipping out tomorrow," he told her.

"I'm shipping out tomorrow too. Do you think we're on the same ship? Do you know where we're going?"

"I bet we are on the same ship. Isn't that wonderful? At least we'll have more time together. I have no idea where we're going. I guess they'll tell us when we get there."

"Mike, we're going to have a lifetime together. I know we are."

The ship was crowded with troops going to the Pacific theatre. Cathy had never before seen so many young men in one small place. Some were cocky with bravado about how they would single-handedly win the war. Others seemed sad. Once aboard ship those men spent most of their time writing letters home. Still others were openly afraid. They sat tensely in their chairs. They wanted to talk to no one.

The medical teams on board seemed to stay together. Each day they would review and practice what they had learned. They learned the surgical people would be divided into teams of six: two surgeons, two surgical nurses, and two hospital corpsman. Whenever possible they were to stick together. No assignment of teams was made.

One day Mike told Cathy he had overheard someone say they were headed for Hawaii. Once in Hawaii they'd be separated and sent to various places.

"Mike, let's get married in Hawaii."

"Cathy, I want to marry you. But is it the right thing to do when we'll probably be separated so soon?"

"You will always be a part of my life forever whether we're married or not. I'd like it to be official."

"I'm glad you said that. I love that idea. We'll have a lot of paperwork to do. I already checked about one thing. I found out there is no waiting period in Hawaii. Once you get the license you can be married."

They looked at each other and smiled. Together hand in hand they made their way to the Commanding Officer to get the paperwork started. The CO was very understanding yet gave them a brief formal lecture suggesting they should wait. Their friends and colleagues were excited for them. They had no clothes other than their uniforms. That didn't matter. Once the ship landed in Hawaii, all they needed was a license and minister.

It seemed to Cathy and Mike that the whole ship got wedding fever. The news definitely made the long trip more pleasant. A chaplain was on board who was en route to a new assignment. They talked with him and asked him to perform the ceremony once they arrived. Their friends all wanted to come to the wedding, yet they had no idea where it would be held so no plans could be made. The other nurses on board wanted to make sure as many traditions as possible could be observed. One of Mike's friends said if Cathy would fix him up with a special nurse named Katy he would take care of getting a place to be married. As they were leaving the ship Cathy and Mike were given a nice surprise.

The CO told them they would not have to report for duty until the next day at 6 p.m. As he told them this wonderful news, he handed them an envelope with their names on it. Inside was a gift certificate. It was a certificate for one night's stay at the Pink Palace, the beautiful pink hotel in Honolulu.

"I don't understand," Mike said. "It's not open to the public. It's an R&R for the military. How did this happen?"

The commander spoke "Young man, twenty-five years ago my young son was badly injured in a skiing accident. I was told that *if* he recovered he would never walk again. A very fine surgeon worked on my son's injuries. My son made a full recovery. I will always be indebted to that man. Your father was that surgeon. What I can do for you is not even close to what your father did for me. It's just something little that I can do." He shook hands with both of them. "Enjoy the brief time you will have together."

Many nurses came to help Cathy get ready for her wedding. Katy had been introduced to the young man who was finding a chapel for them. She managed to sweet talk him into bringing a jeep to get them to the chapel. As Cathy was leaving the barracks Doris handed Cathy a small bouquet of flowers to carry. It was made of fresh gardenias and orchids and tied with a white ribbon.

"How did you get this?" Cathy was near tears.

Katy spoke up. "Fifty kisses to the guy that's driving the jeep. You might owe me something on this one. Or maybe I'll owe you. He is kind of cute."

The chapel had no sides on the building. The ocean could be seen in the distance. Young Hawaiian girls in native dress presented each of the guests a lei made of orchids as they went to their seat. Four old Hawaiian men were playing music on a ukulele, slack-key guitar, a nose flute, and a *kaekeeke*, an instrument made from a bamboo shoot, which he hit on the ground to provide rhythm.

For a few minutes the guests could forget about the war raging around them that awaited them the next day. For a few minutes they could pretend they were living in a normal world doing normal things.

Cathy and Mike repeated their vows softly and firmly to the chaplain. As they turned to greet their guests they saw a table had been placed at the back with a three tiered wedding cake and a bottle of champagne.

Cathy and Mike looked at each other. They asked, "Did you . . . . ?."

A voice spoke up and said, "The cake is with the compliments of the cook on board the ship. In his other life, he was a pastry chef."

Cathy and Mike could hardly believe this outpouring of kindness from people they hardly knew. What they thought would be two people with two witnesses and one chaplain had been turned into a real wedding. The only thing they really needed was their families. They were each able to get a call through to home to share their news. They felt the family love and support as they left the chapel.

They went to their room in the Pink Palace which had an ocean view. They didn't see the rolls of barbed wire that lined the beaches to deter an invasion. They didn't see the harbor filled with war ships and remains from the attack of December 7th. They saw a beautiful sunset. Layers of shades of pink, orange, gray and beige reflected on the water as the day ended. They were very happy. They had each other.

The next day passed quickly for them. At five o'clock they made their way to get the army shuttle which would return them to base.

The new assignments were being handed out at six p.m. The ships would be leaving the next day. No one knew where they were going. From different code letters on the orders they could tell if they would be with friends. Cathy got her orders first. After a few minutes, Mike was given his. They would not be going together. Cathy felt her heart would break. They knew when they said goodbye that neither of them would know where the other one was. The reality of the war was upon them.

They held each other close for a few minutes, neither saying much.

"Mike, you have made me so happy. I want you always to be happy. If something happens to me promise me you won't let it turn you into a bitter old man. Reach out. Take every bit of happiness you can."

"Cathy, I can't – no I won't even imagine a life without you. Don't even consider such a thing. Be very careful. Don't take chances. As soon as I can I will take care of you. I will never let you out of my sight again. I love you."

They kissed. They touched each other lips with their fingers. Each went to his/her own quarters to repack the few belongings they had with them. Mike had to report at 5 a.m. at one ship and Cathy at 6 a.m. on another. She got up very early. She tried to leave to see if she could see him one last time. She was ordered to stay in the barracks until the group left together. Sadly, she went inside to wait until it was her turn to board a ship

* * *

In Texas as Christmas approached Beth was told she would have two days off schedule. No extra time would be allowed. Beth knew she would not have time to go home, nor would most of the women. Eileen planned to visit her cousin who lived nearby. Beth knew Christmas at home would be hard on the family because both she and Cathy would be gone. Beth went shopping at the PX on base. She bought and shipped home gifts for the family. As Christmas day grew nearer, she had thoughts about trying to buy a small tree to decorate the small alcove she shared in the barracks. She also thought it might be a waste of time and money. There were rumors that some of them might be shipped out to get specialized training on the B-17 bomber. Beth hoped she would be one of the chosen for that training.

On the evening of December 21ˢᵗ Beth returned to the barracks to find two big boxes had arrived for her. She opened the first. She found a very small artificial Christmas tree along with lights and decorations for it. Inside the other box were gaily wrapped presents to put under the tree and three boxes of a slightly larger size. Beth was sure from the weight of the boxes that they contained goodies to eat. She put up her little tree. She spread the presents out beneath it. A group of them attended Christmas Eve services on the base. On Christmas morning she looked out the window at a bright warm, sunny day. This was different than Michigan Christmases where even without snow the air would be crisp and clean. She opened her gifts – a funny Santa coffee mug from Annie – clothes, stationery, and a photo album. There were pictures of her mom and dad, Annie, Uncle Frank and Aunt Millie, Harold and family, the Jensens, (Beverly, Jim and Fred) and pictures of all the crew at the airport. Beth felt like she was having a visit with the family. They were all smiling. Each one had written a note of encouragement to her. Beth looked at the picture of Fred with the Chevy. She used the phone in the communication center to call home and had a wonderful chat with her parents and Annie. She learned Cathy and Mike had gotten married in Hawaii. Now Cathy was on her way to the South Pacific. Beth remembered her last phone conversation with Cathy some weeks before. She was happy for Cathy and glad Cathy had Not waited to get married. *Sometimes waiting is not the right thing to do,* she thought as she remembered Robbie. She knew she would have taken any chance for just a little more time with him.

Around 4:30, JoJo came by to ask Beth if she wanted to go to dinner with a group of them. She did. Afterward they all went to see the movie, *Yankee Doodle Dandy* with Jimmy Cagney. It was a wonderful movie. When they got back to base Beth invited them all to her room. They ate the food in the goody boxes. Eileen came back in time to join them.

The next day it was back again to training. Beth received a notice that she was to get specialized training on the B-17 bomber. She knew it was a big heavy plane. She was anxious to get started on her training.

On New Year's Eve the women went to Sweetwater to celebrate the coming of the new year in a bistro. They laughed; they danced. It was loud and noisy. It was fun to forget the cares of the world for a little while.

The Christmas and holiday season was unlike any other the Martin family had celebrated. Mom, Dad, and Annie, Aunt Mille, Uncle Frank and Cousin Harold were all in Glenridge. Cousin Herb, Cathy and Mike were in the South Pacific. *And here I sit alone in Texas. I wish this war was over* Beth thought.

1943

On New Year's Day Beth and her group were scheduled to march in a parade early in the morning. It would be the first time they had performed the routines they had practiced so many times. The women all wore their beige slacks with white shirts. They thought they did pretty well but the drill instructor told them they needed more practice.

Beth began her new training the next day on the B-17. She loved the power, the strength of this bomber. She also had set her sights on learning to fly the C-47 lovingly called the *Gooney Bird* because of its unusual shape. She heard so many good things about it she was anxious to try it out. Three of the women began special training to fly drones for target and anti-aircraft practice. Eileen was going to be flying fighter planes. Each of the women still in the program was branching into a different field.

More than half of the women who had started training had been unable to complete the program. Those who were still in the program felt great pressure to make a good impression so the program could continue.

The group of women under the leadership of Nancy Harkness Love was called WAFS, the Women's Auxiliary Ferrying Squadron. Their function was to fly planes from the factory to bases or ports of debarkation.

Beth's group was the WFTD; the Women's Flying Training Detachment. The flying duties were more diversified.

In December of 1942, the two groups had merged. They became the WASP's. The Women's AirForce Service Pilots. There were more and more duties ready to be assigned them. Women were serving in the Army, the Navy and the Marines, mostly doing clerical work. At that time both the Army and the Navy had their own air force. With the responsibilities the women were being given, there was a need and a place for women in each group.

The top brass had already decided that even if the women of the WASP's were not part of the military they needed uniforms. The top fashion designers at Bergdorf Goodman in New York were asked to design a uniform for the WASP's. They presented two designs, one in drab olive and one in Santiago Blue. This color became known as Air Force Blue. Both styles were presented to General George C. Marshall and General Hap Arnold. They chose the blue. (They heard gossip that the drab olive uniform was modeled by an older clerk from the mail room. The Santiago Blue uniform was worn by a young, beautiful, professional model. But that was just gossip.) The dress uniform consisted of a blue skirt with a fitted jacket, white shirt and black tie. The jacket had the AAF (Army Air Force) emblem on the left sleeve. On the shoulder epaulets, the symbol of the WASP'S command was displayed. The WASP'S emblem was on one lapel. The AAF propeller emblem was on the other. The WASP'S silver wings, after they were earned, would be worn over the left pocket. The hat was a beret with a three-quarter size officer's shield pinned on front. A black leather shoulder purse completed the outfit. Nieman Marcus sent out seamstresses to measure each woman in Beth's group so that each uniform fit perfectly.

Included also was a flying uniform which consisted of an Eisenhower jacket and slacks, a blue cotton shirt with black tie and a baseball cap. Later the summer uniform was introduced which included blue and white chambray shirts with short sleeves. A beige trench coat completed the outfit. A few pieces of the uniform were provided; the WASP's were expected to pay for the rest.

When Beth listened to the news from the South Pacific she worried about Cathy as she knew the fighting was so bad there. She knew her folks must be very worried. She realized that she was getting very homesick. It had been months now since she had seen them. She would be graduating soon. She would get a two week leave before reporting to her new assignment.

Both Beth and Eileen were told they would be assigned to a post that they had chosen; Beth would fly bombers; Eileen would fly fighter planes. Based on their qualifications they could be called on for a variety of duties: flying people or cargo, and testing to re-certify experienced pilots when modifications were made to a plane. They might have to fly a drone that was being towed for target practice. They had a long list of potential responsibilities. Did they have any questions? They did not. They felt really good because they knew now for certain that they would graduate. Then Beth and Eileen were both given another offer. The second class of recruits was already underway. A new class was to start every month for at least the next six months. Would they stay to become instructors? They both thought it was an honor to be asked to teach. Since they both loved to fly, they decided to stay with their original choice.

With graduation day almost upon them Beth and Eileen started to pack up their belongings into their bags.

"It's hard to believe we've been here six months, isn't it?" Eileen asked Beth. "I got to admit I had a few times when I didn't think I'd make it to graduation."

"I don't think you ever had anything to worry about. You never had to repeat a test or seem to have any problems."

"Well, neither did you, Beth. We have really been pretty lucky. Now we're off for our first assignments. What was hardest for you?"

Beth thought a minute. "Well, maybe it was trying to forget everything I knew so I could learn the Army way to do things. I do understand why. Everyone has to do everything exactly the same way so there'll be no surprises. I didn't expect to spend so much time marching and drilling. Yet it was sort of fun when we'd chant as we marched."

"It was like being in the Army in some ways, yet we pay for our own clothes, food and housing and . . . . ."

"Well, they did give us our 'zoot suits'." Beth began to laugh. "Remember how funny we all looked trying to walk with the crotch of the coveralls being down around our knees." The girls began to laugh together.

"I wonder how long it will be before we see each other again," Beth said.

"I think we made pretty good bunkmates," Eileen said. "Do you think we made a mistake by not agreeing to stay here to train the new classes?"

"In spite of it being pretty hard, I think I'm ready to fly. We'll stay in touch. How much time will you have with your family before reporting to Florida?"

"I'm not sure. It will probably take a day and a half or more to get to Cleveland. I still have to arrange my transportation to Florida from Cleveland. Do you have your travel plans made?"

"If we can get on a flight to Chicago tomorrow I can get a flight to Glenridge from my former boss. I'm hoping to arrange a flight from

Chicago to San Francisco and to Seattle. If I have to take a train it will probably take three days, so I won't have as much time at home."

"Have you heard any more from your sister, Cathy?"

"Not since I heard she got married. We don't know where she is."

"Maybe your folks will have more news by the time you get home."

"I'm glad we have our uniforms to travel in." The new uniforms had just arrived in time for their graduation. "It should make it a bit easier to travel."

Travel from one base to another had become a problem. On many occasions they had to use public transportation to get back to base. They were given cards to claim priority for travel on planes or trains. Because the WASP'S program was not well publicized or recognized as "officially" military, some station agents refused to recognize their status. After the official and VIP travelers were boarded, the WASP'S were permitted to get on a train, plane, or bus.

That evening the remaining class members along with some of the members in the next two classes went in to Houston for a farewell dinner. It was a time to share memories of the early training; to learn how it was changing. JoJo would be graduating within the next few weeks. The three young women had become good friends. Now Eileen would be flying fighter planes from the factory to the base. Beth was scheduled to fly bombers. They knew they would have other flying assignments. Beth really didn't care too much which type of plane she flew; she just wanted to fly.

The graduation ceremony made the training now official. It felt really good to have the silver wings pinned on her jacket. Beth really missed having some of her family see it happen but travel was very difficult for civilians.

Beth was looking forward to her short trip home before starting her assignment in the Seattle, Washington, area. Early the next morning she and Eileen sat in the jump seats of an Army transport plane headed for the Chicago area. From there Eileen would head for Cleveland on a commercial flight. Beth would head for Midway Airport. She had confirmed with Chuck that Dave Smith had a flight scheduled late that afternoon. He would be flying back to Glenridge that evening.

*   *   *

Cathy found that boarding the ship in Hawaii was very different than boarding in California for the trip to Hawaii. Security was tight. Everyone moved briskly. Orders were constantly snapped at them with a reminder that obeying an order might save your life.

The nurses were given army coveralls and army boots: another change to the dress code for nurses. The nurses who were in the combat zone needed something sturdier than a blue seersucker dress to wear on duty. Often they worked in mud pits. The blue shoes were useless. Many nurses already had to climb up rope ladders on the sides of ships when escaping the enemy. Nor was it time for starched white uniforms. The women decided the coveralls were a great choice until they realized the size of the coveralls and boots. Some women stuffed sox in the toes of the boots to even keep them on. Another nurse complained that she wished she had safety pins to keep the sleeves of the coveralls turned up. Still, they all felt it was better than dresses.

Shipboard gossip said the troops aboard were headed for Guadalcanal. The troops aboard were tense and anxious.

They were taken to shore by boats between raids by the Japanese. The new nurses were frightened as they left the ship. They knew the fighting had been horrendous and the causalities were high. Wounded soldiers were everywhere. Somehow, what they learned didn't seem like nearly enough. Some of the nurses and doctors had been there since the war started. They were totally exhausted. Working under threat of constant bombing, never knowing if you might be captured, added greatly to the concern about whether or not you could save a life. Cathy made her way to the surgical tent. A nurse saw her. "Take my place," she said as she slumped to the floor from exhaustion. Cathy, at that moment, appreciated the hours spent learning to do things the army way. She could step right in. The surgeon might not even know a change had been made. No one got a day off. Usually they only had a few hours to sleep. Cathy had only a few minutes to think about Mike. She had no idea where he had been shipped. No one was able to get much sleep.

One day she received a stack of mail, her first mail since leaving Camp McCoy. She hurriedly looked through it. She saw a brief note from Mike. He wasn't allowed to say where he was. He was OK. He loved her. She read it about ten times. She turned to the welcome letters from her family and friends. My mom and dad are amazing, she thought. Even though she could tell how worried they were, they never said those words. Just upbeat letters full of love and hope.

The nurses were warned to stay very alert. The battles were fierce. Japanese soldiers seemed to be everywhere. The Americans tried as quickly as possible to evacuate the wounded to hospital ships or planes so the wounded could get to a safe place to receive care. Eventually, word came that the nurses were being transferred by ship to another post. Once again they didn't know where. They put their belongings in a pillow case and got into the back of an army truck to get to the port. Along the way they heard the scream of a plane. The truck driver yelled at them to get into the ditch on the side of the road. The Japanese plane headed straight for them. They tumbled into the ditch, one after the other, just as the plane hit the truck. It exploded. The nurses could do nothing to save the truck driver. They realized he had saved their lives. They were ordered to keep walking the ten more miles to the ship.

Cathy, once more, had no idea where she was going once aboard the ship. She hoped it might be somewhere near Mike. The ship she was on was not too large. No doctor was on board. A medical corpsman was in charge of the sick bay. A few of the so-called walking wounded had been brought on board so Cathy and the other nurses took care of them. She wrote letters to Mike and her family. She waited. When Japanese planes flew over the air space, they all had to leave the open area of the deck. One day Japanese U-boats fired torpedoes at them. They had to take evasive action. There was never a time that you forgot about the war.

One evening the ship came to a halt. After a couple of hours Cathy stood on deck in the darkness looking at the stars. She saw something moving in the water. She thought she saw a small raft type boat approaching. She ran to tell the officer on deck. He told her they were picking up the family of a man on a nearby island. This man secretly reported by radio to the Allies on the Japanese planes and boats going through the area. Because of the intense fighting on the island the man feared for the safety of his family if his mission was uncovered. His wife was nine months pregnant so he asked that she and the children be taken to safety. Cathy moved to the railing. Because the children all seemed very young, a sailor on board scampered down the rope ladder on the side of the ship. He carried each child up the ladder and handed them to other sailors on board.

"We have a real problem, Captain. The mother is in labor. She'll never be able to climb the ladder," one of the sailors reported.

"Get a stretcher," the officer commanded one man. "You stand by to assist in pulling it up," he ordered another. He looked at Cathy. "Take the kids below. Get the sick bay ready to deliver a baby."

Everyone moved. Cathy picked up the toddler. She told the children to follow her as she hurried away to find someone to help take care of them. She called to the corpsman to get the table ready to deliver a baby as she rushed by.

"I can't possibly do that, maam. I have no idea what to do."

"I'll help you. Make the place sterile."

The woman was brought in almost immediately. Cathy had never delivered a baby but she had assisted in two births. "Get the book. Read to us so we don't forget something," she told another sailor who lingered nearby.

Even in wartime, nature takes its own time in some matters. When the actual birth occurred it was fast and uneventful. Cathy soon laid a newborn baby girl in her mother's arms.

"What's your name?" the mother asked Cathy.

"Catherine. They call me Cathy."

"The baby's name will be Catherine."

The mother looked at the young corpsman that had assisted. "What's your name?"

"Robert, maam."

"The child's name will be Catherine Roberta."

Cathy and Robert reached out to hug each other.

"That was amazing," he said. "I think I want to be a doctor."

Cathy hurried to her quarters. She wanted to write to tell Mike about what had happened.

The nurses soon learned that they would leave the ship for a field hospital on one of the Solomon Islands. She suspected that Mike was somewhere close to this place. Somehow, she could just feel it.

The hospital was very close to a lot of heavy fighting. The wounded were being brought in constantly. Everyone worked long hours. They had short breaks in between. Cathy asked if anyone knew Major Mike Goodman. One doctor said he had met him at Camp McCoy. She learned Mike's unit was stationed about fifty miles away on another island. So near and yet so far, Cathy thought.

The facilities on this island were much larger than the one in Guadalcanal. The number of wounded was far greater as the battle at Guadalcanal had been winding down when they were there. In this theatre the fighting was fierce, the facilities were primitive, and they had two or three times more wounded. They never seemed to have time to clean up properly from one surgery before there was another. The army finally decided they needed to move the most severely wounded out as soon as they were stabilized. Only emergency surgery would be done. For a few days an airlift was formed to transport the wounded to Australia. Soon a hospital ship arrived in port to transport more of the wounded to Hawaii. Nurses were needed to assist on board. Cathy was assigned to be one of those nurses. She felt pretty safe because the ship had a big red cross painted on top. The *rules of war* said that no hospital ship was to be bombed. This hadn't been the case when an Australian hospital ship was bombed. Three hundred people lost their lives. The Japanese had apologized. They said it wouldn't happen again.

The ship left the port late at night. She stood on the deck, looking at the stars, thinking about Mike, thinking about home; most of all thinking about the madness of war.

One day during a break Cathy went topside. She stood near the railings, breathing in the fresh air. It was a beautiful day. The sun was bright; the waters were reasonably calm. Sometimes they could see a fleet of Japanese ships on the far horizon. Nothing had happened; the seas stayed calm. On occasion they could see a unit of planes flying overhead. They couldn't be sure if they were Japanese or American. As Cathy stood on the deck that day she began to think about being in Hawaii. Maybe she could take a walk, all by herself. Maybe she would not have to worry about hidden snipers. Or worry about an ambush every time she was in a jeep or truck. The loud clamor of the alarms interrupted her thoughts.

"Get below deck," she was told. "A Japanese plane is coming in low."

Cathy knew the drill. She hurried below. She heard the loudest noise she had ever heard in her life. She felt herself flying through the air. She heard nothing more.

Cathy started to have a beautiful dream. No, it wasn't a dream; it wasn't beautiful. Or was it? She couldn't remember. She opened her eyes. Where was she? *I'm having a dream,* she thought. She went back to sleep.

*   *   *

Beth and Eileen frowned because of the hard seats and then smiled at each other as they traveled in the Army transport plane headed for Chicago. The seats were as hard and uncomfortable as a seat could be. They tried not to notice. They felt lucky to have gotten the flight. Beth kept punching Eileen, telling her they were a few miles closer to Chicago than they were five minutes earlier.

Beth got more and more excited as she got closer to home. She told Eileen goodbye and took a cab from the Army Air Base to Midway Airport. As she made her way to the hanger area she heard a loud shout.

"Over here, Beth. Welcome home." She was so happy to see Dave waiting for her with a big hug. "You look terrific. We've all really missed you."

"Dave, you have never looked so handsome. I'm so glad to see you."

"Let's get headed for home right away. Storms are moving in."

Beth had flown this flight many times. It felt good to be a part of something from her past. As she sat in the co-pilot's seat she looked over the runway and then down on the familiar territory.

"This plane must seem pretty small to you. How many different planes do you fly now?" Dave asked.

"I guess more than twenty. It's been fun getting to try so many different planes."

"Aren't you scheduled to fly bombers?"

"Yes, part of my job will be to fly bombers from the Boeing factory to Army Air Corp bases. I'll also have to do whatever the base commander wants, I guess."

"What was the hardest thing you learned?"

"Dave, you taught me well. I always remembered what you told me when I thought something was hard. 'Don't try to learn it all at once. Break it down into sections.' It helped to make it all go a lot smoother."

"What was the most fun?"

"How quickly you can maneuver the fighter planes. Thanks to you it was fun when I could show off a bit doing chandelles and loops. You were a great teacher. I had to learn Morse code and how to use the radio. You had me prepared for that. It was fun learning to fly by radio beam. Instrument flying is really fun. Took me a few days to learn to trust the beam instead of what I could see out the window. I had to make an emergency landing once when something went wrong with the plane. I heard your cool voice walking me through procedures. Flying almost every day helped me remember what to do."

Beth looked out the window. "Hey, we're getting close to home. I don't remember this many lights."

"The Glenridge area is growing with defense plants and more people. Speaking of people, there are a lot of them who want to talk with you. How long will you be home?"

"I have to be in Seattle in ten days. If I can hitch a ride on a plane I'll have more time at home."

"Let's get Chuck to work on that." Dave taxied to the hangar area and said, "Look out the window. I see some familiar looking people."

Beth looked out to see her dad, mom, and Annie along with many people of the airport crew waiting to call out greetings of welcome.

"This is so exciting and wonderful," Beth said as she hurried out of the plane into the waiting arms of her family and friends.

It seemed like she had been gone much longer than five months in some ways. In other ways it was as if she had only been gone a day or two. It felt really good to Beth to be back in the old familiar routine: getting brought up to date on everyone's day, hearing news from the neighborhood, checking out the world news. Beth realized how much she missed them all.

"Do you feel you made the right choices, Beth?" her dad asked. "Has the training been harder than you thought it would be?"

"I thought I knew a lot more when I left home than I seemed to know after the first week of training. I felt pretty stupid for a while. We had to do things their way. Everything from marching and making beds to flying a bomber in a bad storm. I can understand why. When we fly in formation it's critical that we do. It's especially important when we are towing a drone. The ground forces use the drone to practice shooting it down so we have to do things exactly right."

"It sounds very dangerous," her mother interjected.

"It probably sounds worse than it is. Some of the girls preferred that type of flying."

"What particular plane or type of flying did you like best?" Annie asked.

"They're all so different it's hard to pick a favorite."

"How did the men react to having so many women fliers?"

153

"It was a routine job for most of them. There were some problems. Some of the wives of the trainers objected to their husbands spending so much time with women in a confined space. Some of the men fliers were upset by being certified by a woman on a change in a plane. At least two male instructors quit because of pressure from their wives, they said. We had one really nice exception, though. One of the instructors invited us all to his house for a Texas Bar-B-Q one Sunday. He and his wife were so nice. We ate by a small lake in their back yard. They had three sons and three daughters. When I asked if they sang together they said they did. So they sang for us. It made me really homesick remembering how Cathy, Annie and I always sang together. As it got dark, we built a fire on the shore of the lake. We sat around and sang."

"Speaking of sisters, have you heard from Cathy?" Beth continued. "Were you very surprised about her getting married so quickly?"

"I guess we were," Emma said. "but we want her to be happy. Here's a picture she sent home." Emma reached behind her, and handed Beth a small snapshot in a big frame. "Cathy said it was hard to find someone with a camera. They did manage to get one picture."

Beth looked quietly at the picture. Cathy and Mike both had on their dress uniforms. Cathy was carrying a small bouquet of flowers. Beth could see the love in their eyes. It made Beth think about Robbie. "I'm glad they didn't wait to get married. Who knows how long they'll have together?" she said quietly.

"They didn't have very long after the wedding," Emma said. "Cathy had written while they were on their way to Hawaii that she wanted to get married. They did manage to phone us. They got the call through right after the wedding. Then they were separated. Cathy doesn't know where Mike was sent. He'll be working in a field hospital. We don't know where she is, only that it's somewhere in the South Pacific. We won't hear from her for a month or more. Sometimes we get a packet of letters."

"Let's talk about you. Tell us about your housing," Albert said.

"It was pretty rough at first. The Army was building barracks. They weren't done when we arrived. We pretty much lived out of our suitcases the first couple of weeks. When we got settled we found each barrack was divided into ten bays. Each bay had six cots and tiny wardrobes. We had one latrine between the bays for twelve people. Inside it were two toilets, two sinks and two showers that had no doors. We all got over any modesty issues right away. We had very little room. I did put up the Christmas tree you sent me for a few days. It made the area much more pleasant. Overall, we got the same training and living conditions as the airmen on the base along with some specialized training in a few areas."

"How did you manage financially?" her dad asked.

"We get paid $250 a month. Plus we get $6 per day if we are away from the base. We didn't have much time to spend money anyhow so we did OK."

"Were there any serious accidents while you were there?"

"Just one that I'm aware of. A strong wind storm came up while we were practicing and had an instructor with us. We got a signal to land immediately. I was the second from the last. A bad updraft caught me as we were landing and we bumped and skidded. We were OK. The last plane wasn't so lucky. The wind pushed and threw them into a high embankment. The plane flipped several times and caught fire. The instructor lost his life."

"What about the pilot?"

"Rose was very badly burned and was unconscious for almost two weeks. She's still in the hospital there. We all took up a collection to help pay for her medical care."

"Are you telling me the Army doesn't even pay for that?" Albert asked.

"No, they don't. Still, we were told upfront that they wouldn't so we can't complain."

"Does the girl have money to pay for her care?" he asked.

"I don't think so. Her husband was in Borneo with the army when the war started and she heard unofficially that he was a prisoner. She has a little girl who lives with Rose's mother."

"Emma, we must get a check out immediately to help this girl," Albert told his wife.

"Dad, you're a good man. Now I do feel like I'm home. My dad is doing his usual thing taking care of everyone."

Beth slept till noon the first full day. That afternoon she headed for the airport to talk with her friends. True to his word, Dave and Chuck had arranged a flight to Chicago and then on to San Francisco. Beth made arrangements to fly from San Francisco to Seattle on an Army plane. Now she didn't have to worry about getting bumped off the train or plane by someone with higher priority. And this meant she would have an extra two days at home.

The days passed quickly. Beth and Annie managed a short shopping trip and lunch with their friends. One night the family had dinner with Uncle Frank and Aunt Millie and she learned that her cousin Herb was now serving in the South Pacific. Another night she was invited to the Jensen's for dinner.

"Beth," Jim asked her. "Do you feel you made the right career choice? Is it what you expected?"

"I guess so. I love the flying part and it is fun to be able to fly the newest planes along with some old clunkers. I love night flying. It's so beautiful to fly among the stars. It wasn't fun learning how to make beds."

"You? You had to learn how to make beds?" Fred asked.

"The Army way was a lot like Mom taught me. Although, Mom never made me be able to bounce a penny on it when I was done."

"Why? Why would you have to learn something like that?" Fred asked.

"That's another thing I learned, Fred. Don't ever ask why. Enough about me. What's new around here? How's the car working, Fred? Are you still dating Laurie?"

"Dad's been letting me use his car a lot. And my grades are better so you don't have to ask. I'm still dating Laurie."

"She's a lovely young woman," Beverly added. "Tell us about you. Have you met anyone special yet? It's time you do."

"No way," Beth said. "I'm too busy. I did make a lot of friends, both male and female. One guy and I did win free drinks when we won a polka contest one night at the club. I didn't know what to do but the guy was from a family of dancers and he had me twisting and turning. It was fun."

"How long do you think you'll be in Seattle?" Jim asked.

"I'm told I'll probably be moving around a lot. I'll probably be back in the mid-west quite often. So maybe I'll get home a little more often. The Ford plant in Detroit is pushing bombers out very fast. We'll have to keep them moving to make room for more," Beth told him.

The few days at home passed quickly. The family gathered once more for a family dinner. The doorbell rang and Albert went to answer it. When he returned to the table he was shaking and his face was ashen. He held a telegram in his hands.

"A Japanese plane flew into the ship Cathy was on. She is severely injured. She's still aboard the ship headed for Hawaii." Albert went to

Emma and took her in his arms. Beth and Annie clung together. After a few minutes Albert said, "We have to know more. Who can I call?"

"Mike's father is in Washington. Maybe he'll be able to get some news," Emma said.

Albert immediately went to the phone. The parents had already gotten acquainted on the phone at the time of the wedding. The call went through immediately. Ray Goodman, Mike's dad, answered the phone. Albert told him about the telegram. Ray advised them he had contacts in many places and would find out what he could and call them back.

Once more, the Martin family sat by the phone and waited. And waited. And waited. Beth quietly and reluctantly packed her bags to leave early the next morning. The war waited for no one. It was life as usual for the rest of the world.

Shortly after midnight Ray Goodman called with news. A rogue Japanese pilot either decided to commit suicide or had plane trouble. He flew his plane into the end of the hospital ship that Cathy was on. Cathy was gravely injured as she tried to flee the area. She was alive with severe injuries and had not yet regained consciousness. The ship had damage but was able to continue on its course to Hawaii. That was all the news available at the time. Ray was going to try to get the information to Mike. Ray promised Albert that he would keep trying to get more information and stay in touch with the Martins.

Beth went to her childhood bedroom that night. She began to cry for her sister. It also brought back the loss of Robbie. *There has to be a way to stop wars,* she thought.

The next morning she held her family close as she told them goodbye and began the next part of her new life.

*   *   *

Cathy slowly opened her eyes. The sun was shining through a window. She looked around. Where am I, she wondered? She was in a hospital bed with fresh white sheets and blankets. She saw a small vase of flowers on a table by her bed. She realized she had a tube in her arm. *I must be in a hospital. Am I on board a ship? Where am I? I've got to get up. I'll be late for work,* she thought. She couldn't move very well. Her leg seemed to be bandaged from top to bottom. There were bandages on other parts of her body. *What happened to me,* she wondered?

The door to her room opened. A nurse, dressed in a fresh white uniform entered.

"Where am I?" Cathy asked.

"Cathy, thank goodness. You're finally awake. Let me get the doctor."

"Wait. Answer me. Where am I?"

The nurse was already gone. She quickly returned with a doctor.

"Cathy, welcome back. I'm Dr. Greg Hartzell. Let me do a quick check on you. Then we'll answer all your questions."

Cathy waited while the quick examination took place, answering only routine questions. She could see her bandaged leg, no, it wasn't bandaged, but was in a cast. She could see other injuries.

"You've had quite an adventure, young lady," Greg told her. "Would you like to talk first about what you remember or would you like me to tell you what happened?"

"I don't know," Cathy answered, almost crying. "I can't remember anything right now."

"Don't let it worry you. You'll remember. You've been asleep for almost two weeks. We induced some of it to help you rest easier."

"I was on a ship. I remember that much. We were having a peaceful voyage . . . . .." Cathy paused, then slowly she began to recall about being on deck, about being ordered to go below because of the plane.

Doctor Hartzell smiled. "I'm glad you remember all that. You have apparently suffered no brain damage. You were unconscious for a long time. We've been watching you closely. What you remember is exactly what we were told happened to you. A Japanese pilot took that moment to end his life. He flew his plane into the ship. Only the front end of the ship was damaged as the plane hit. The plane fell back into the ocean."

"Did the ship sink? How did I get here? Where am I?"

"You're in Hawaii. The ship did not sink. They were able to bring the ship into port for repairs. Unfortunately you were going down the stairs in the section of the ship that got hit. The impact shoved you into heavy machinery in the area. You spent the rest of the voyage in the sick bay."

"What happened to my leg? Will I be able to walk?"

"You have a combination of broken bones and severe cuts from flying metal. You should be as good as new."

"Was I unconscious a long time?"

"You were. We were worried for a while that you might have suffered some brain damage. We see no signs of it now that you're awake. You sound very normal and rational to me. I do have a message for you though. From a Major Michael Goodman. I think you know him," he said with a smile. "Tell her I love her."

"How did you . . . . how did he know about this?"

"One of the doctors who treated you along the way had been at your wedding. He had a contact who contacted someone else. We heard from Mike as soon as you got here. We had orders that you are the daughter-in-law of a very important person in Washington. Regardless of who you are, we do try to give everyone the same kind of care, important relative or not."

"I can't believe all this," Cathy said, trying not to cry.

"You have a telegram and a letter here from your husband. Would you like to see them now?"

"Yes, yes." Now she did begin to cry.

"We'll leave you alone for a few minutes. I'll be back. Now that you're awake, we'll give you some lunch. We'll have you start your therapy very soon." The nurse and Dr. Hartzell left the room.

Cathy held the envelope, written in Mike's handwriting, in her hand. *He held this and now I'm holding it.* She placed her fingers on the side in the same way she imagined he held it. Finally she opened it.

> *My darling Cathy,*
>
> *I was frantic when I finally got word about your injuries. I hadn't heard from you for a while so didn't know you were on your way back to Hawaii. I am glad you are in a hospital where you can get proper care instead of in a field hospital. My dad got word to me that he has learned that you are expected to make a full recovery.*
>
> *He is monitoring how well you are doing. I am forcing myself to be satisfied that you will recover quickly. I will believe nothing until I can see you and hold you close to me. I love you so much. I am confident that we will have many years together.*
>
> *Mike*

Cathy read and re-read the letter. She held it close to her body. She tried to remember how it felt when Mike held her. Suddenly she felt very tired. The nurse entered the room with a cup of soup.

"Are you OK? Can I get you anything?"

"This may sound silly since I've apparently been sleeping a lot, yet I'm very tired. Would it be OK if I sleep a while?"

"You bet you can. Drink this soup and have a good rest. I'll check on you later."

Cathy awoke some six hours later, declared herself 100% well until she remembered the bandages and cast on her leg. She read the letter from Mike again, and then again. Then remembered the telegram that was on her nightstand.

The nurse entered her room. "Well, I see you're awake finally. Have a good sleep? I bet you're hungry. If you're able to sit in a wheelchair, I'll have an aid take you down to the cafeteria. I think a change of scenery would be good for you."

Cathy agreed and took her telegram with her. It was from her dad and mom.

CATHY LOVE YOU LOADS STOP KNOW YOU WILL
SOON BE WELL STOP WILL CALL YOU AS SOON
AS POSSIBLE STOP

A young volunteer wheeled Cathy to the cafeteria. Cathy asked her if there was a phone center where she could make a call.

"You have to have money to make a call," Cathy was told by the young woman. "I do have a nickel in my pocket if you can reverse the charges."

"Thank you. I'll reimburse you the nickel. I can call collect."

With the time difference she hoped the family would be home from work. She gave the operator the city and phone number. She listened while the connection was finally made. With a happy heart she heard Annie answer the phone

"I have a collect call from Hawaii from Cathy Goodman. Will you accept the call?" she heard the operator ask.

Cathy heard Annie give a scream. "Dad, Mom, come quick. It's Cathy." Annie told the operator, "Of course, we'll accept the call. Cathy, is it really you?"

Cathy spent a long time on the phone talking with each one. She learned how very worried they had been that she might not recover, or whether she might have brain damage. Whether in the field or at home, war takes its toll on everyone, she realized. With a smile, she remembered that her father would have a very big phone bill the next month. Somehow she knew he wouldn't mind it a bit.

*   *   *

Beth, who planned to sit in the jump seat behind the pilot, was invited to sit in the co-pilot's seat for the last part of her trip. She looked out the window at the Pacific Ocean as the plane left San Francisco for Seattle. One summer when she was about eight years old her parents had been offered the opportunity to take their family on a ship to Hawaii. As a child running around the deck she thought the ocean was pretty big. Seeing it from the air made her realize just how vast it really was. She thought about Cathy, somewhere on the other side of the world, thousands of miles away, still somewhere on the same ocean. She was very worried about Cathy. On the other side of the plane from time to time she saw the mountains of the west coast. They looked more rugged and higher than the mountains she was used to seeing.

"Is this your first trip to Seattle?" Leonard, the pilot asked her.

"It is. I am surprised how vast everything looks from the air."

"How long have you been flying military aircraft?"

"This will be my first official assignment."

"What will you do in Seattle?"

Leonard started to laugh when Beth answered, "Whatever they tell me to do."

"Well, you'll have plenty to do. I guess the planes are stacked up at Boeing waiting to be taken to bases on the east coast. There's always someone waiting for a plane to bring them parts or VIP's to tell them what to do next. Did you ever get a chance to fly a *Gooney Bird?* I'd sure like to fly one of those babies."

"Yes, I'm certified on them. They're great to fly."

"I guess you flew fighter planes too. I'm hoping to get transferred to a fighter unit."

"We had to get certified on many different planes."

"Look out to your right. That's Mt. Hood, Oregon. Isn't it beautiful from the air?"

"I guess we're not too far from Seattle, then. Are you based there or in San Francisco?"

"San Francisco. I make this run about twice a week."

"I hear it rains a lot in Seattle. Is that so?"

"Seattle is the only place I know that has a dry rain. I have walked around in it many times. Somehow or other I never seem to get wet. Seattle has a beautiful view of Mt. Rainier. If you get a chance, try to go see it."

The plane landed at McChord Army Air Corp base which was part of Ft. Lewis. As Beth got off the plane she was greeted by a WAC corporal who carried her gear to a waiting jeep and took her to the BOQ, the Bachelor Officers Quarters. One section of the unit had been set aside for the women of the Army. The women mostly did paperwork. She was told to report to Colonel King at 9 a.m. the next day. She was shown her room with bunks for four and given directions to the mess hall. She would be alone in the room until the next class from Sweetwater graduated. She hoped some of her friends would be transferred to McChord.

The next morning she was introduced to Colonel King, the base commander, who told her to introduce herself to the ground crew and be ready to fly. His aide, Major Wilson, would be giving her assignments. Beth stood in awe as she saw the ground crews efficiently at work; checking engines, making repairs, putting fuel in them. It looked almost like an assembly line. That afternoon, Major Wilson took her to the air field at Boeing. She looked in amazement at so many bombers lined up waiting to be taken to a base.

"You are expected to report here tomorrow morning at 0600. You will be given your destination at that time. After delivery find a way back to base. There are usually always jeeps or trucks going back and forth. Report back to me for your next assignment."

Beth was eager to begin her new job. At the appointed time she was given her first assignment. Four pilots, each flying his/her own bomber, would fly to a base in Georgia. As she taxied down the runway that first morning she felt a sense of accomplishment she had not felt before. She really had done this. *Robbie, I made it.* Into the air she flew and joined the other pilots. Together they made their way to Georgia.

Life settled into a new routine for Beth. On occasion the delivery of planes could take up to a week because she might have to find transportation back from a base on the east coast to Seattle. On a few occasions she had to fly a crippled plane back from a remote site to McChord where more extensive repairs could be made. Some days she certified pilots on changes made to an aircraft. Some assignments were more of a routine nature, like giving visiting VIP's from Washington an aerial view of the base and Boeing. It was all very impressive to see from the air.

For the first time in her life she felt as if she was living alone. She was the only one living in her section of the BOQ which meant that she had her own bathroom and sleeping quarters. She ate most of her meals in the Mess Hall. She usually sat alone. Very few women were assigned to the Army Air Corp at that time and the ones assigned to McChord lived in the other end of the building. Beth held steady and tried not to be lonely. She knew some friends from training would be joining her soon.

Beth was awakened early one morning and told to report to Major Wilson immediately.

"Miss Martin, we're cutting orders for you to fly to Phoenix ASAP. A plane that was testing a new guidance system has gone down in the desert. It appears a part has malfunctioned. We are sending with you Corporal Ed Thompson who has a new part for the plane. He has worked on this equipment since it was developed and is an expert on the part. Hopefully, we are correct in our assumptions and he can replace the part. He will be met upon landing at Briggs Air Corp Base and taken to the plane. You will have a shipment of cargo to bring back with you."

"Will I wait for Corporal Thompson?" she asked.

"No. Hopefully, he will fly back with the pilot to Seattle. Do you have any questions? If not, get ready to leave in an hour."

With a "Yes, Sir," to the Major, Beth went to her room for her gear that she kept ready to go. Most usually these trips involved an overnight stay. She never knew for sure until she got her orders. Better be ready, she thought.

Corporal Thompson was a young man almost six feet tall and thin. He looked a bit edgy as Beth introduced herself to him. "Have you flown a lot?" she asked him.

"I've never been on a plane before."

"But you're a specialist who knows how to guide the plane in the air."

"Yes, maam. But I always keep my feet on the ground."

"Well, I hope you will enjoy your first flight. Where are you from?"

"Utah, maam."

"Why don't you call me Beth? I'm not a member of the military. You don't need to call me maam."

"Yes, maam, I mean Beth."

"Do you know that we'll be flying right over Utah on our way to Phoenix? Maybe we'll fly over your hometown."

"Really, maam, I mean Beth."

"Once we get airborne we'll check it out. What's your first name?"

"Ed."

"Well, Ed, I think we can have a good flight. If you get uneasy about anything you see or hear, just tell me and I'll explain what's happening."

Beth strapped him into the co-pilots seat. As they taxied down the runway she saw his hands gripping the seat. Once in the air he started to relax and look around.

"This is fun. Isn't it beautiful up here?"

"Yes. And just think. You make it possible by keeping the planes safe and ready to fly. Tell me about your family and where you live."

As Ed talked Beth figured they could make a slight deviation in the flight plan and fly over his home area.

"I've climbed in those mountains all my life. I never thought they'd look like this," he told her. "I can't believe this trip. Do you think I'll get to fly back to Seattle?"

"I've learned not to assume anything in the service. I've always found they'll get you where they need you. Do you have a girlfriend?" she asked him.

"I sure do. Can I show you her picture?"

Beth almost felt a sob as she saw the picture. She felt as if she were looking at a picture of Robbie with her on the front sidewalk. The height difference between them was the same. Both of them had the same color of hair as she and Robbie had.

"She's beautiful," Beth told him. "What's her name?"

"Dottie. We wanted to get married when we graduated from High School. We wanted to go to college too. The Army decided for us. I got drafted right away so we decided to wait a bit before we got married."

"What's she doing now?"

"She's in college. She's going to become a teacher. Then she says she'll teach so I can go to college."

"I think that's great. What would you like to study?"

"I really couldn't decide at the time. I have sure liked working on this guidance system. Now I think I might want to study engineering."

During their conversation, Ed was constantly seeing some new wonder beneath him. "I never imagined the scenery would be so beautiful from the air."

"We're flying over Utah now. Your home area should be just ahead on your left. Maybe I can fly over that way a bit closer."

"I see the river," he said excitedly. "There's my home town. I can see the High School. I lived just to the left about five miles."

Beth made another adjustment and he began to shout. "I see our house. I see our house."

"We probably better not talk about this back at base. I'm not sure the Army would approve."

"Well, the Army might not. I certainly approve. This has been so wonderful."

Beth soon picked up the signal from Briggs field and radioed ahead asking for permission to land.

"Highest ranking officer aboard?" she was asked.

"Corporal Ed Thompson," she answered.

"Say again?" she was asked.

"Corporal Ed Thompson."

"Circle once and prepare to land."

As Beth began her descent to the ground she noticed what appeared to be a full company of emergency landing equipment moving onto the field. She was startled to see the military police in full battle gear surround the plane.

"Exit the plane with your hands up," she was told.

She looked at Ed who was white with fear. "I don't know what's happening," she told him. "We'd better do what they say."

"March this way," they were told. They were both asked to present their travel orders.

The atmosphere suddenly changed. Very sheepishly, they were told what had happened.

When the officer in the control tower was told that a corporal was the commanding officer, he thought the pilot had been kidnapped and was sending a signal for help. No one had ever called a corporal a commanding officer before. With great embarrassment they were welcomed to the base.

When Beth returned to McChord, she was told to report to Major Wilson ASAP. He smiled as she came in the office and said, "I hear you had quite an experience."

"I guess it was unusual."

"You are to be congratulated for your control of the situation. I happen to think you WASP'S fliers should be part of the military. You were the commanding officer on board. You just don't have the title to go with it. You did well. Take the rest of the day off and report back for your next assignment in the morning."

As she started to leave the office, Colonel King, Major Wilson's superior officer, came in the door. "Hello, Beth," he said as he reached out to shake her hand. "I hear you gave the Briggs base *the thrill of the day.* Job well, done. Congratulations."

"Colonel King, was there some other way I should have handled it?" she asked.

"You did fine, Beth, just fine."

Beth thought about her mother and dad that night. Now that it was over, she began to think of it as a very funny incident. She wished she could share it with Cathy. *Thank goodness Cathy is on the mend,* she thought. With the time difference between the states of Washington and Michigan it would not be a good idea to call home. I know what my mother would say, she thought. She'd tell me to write it in my journal.

The next morning she reported back to Major Wilson.

"I think you will agree that you have been kept very busy with miscellaneous flights and certification flying as well as delivering bombers. The backup of planes at Boeing continues to build. One or more of your fellow classmates will be arriving soon, probably tomorrow. We have asked for two pilots from the WASP'S. We may only get one. When she arrives we expect you to help her get oriented to the base. She will live in your quarters. I will continue to give the assignments. I would like you to introduce her to the people she needs to know and help her get settled.

"In addition, next week Brenda Marshall of the British Air Transport Auxiliary (ATA) will be arriving from London. She is your counterpart in England. She will room with you. Next week you and Brenda are scheduled to attend two days of classes at Boeing. We expect you to complete the arrangements for Miss Marshall's stay here as well as transportation to and from the classes. Ask Sgt. Joe Bosley for help. He has done this for many visitors and knows the ropes. Any questions?"

"Just one, sir. Do you know the name of the WASP'S who will be coming?"

"I have it here somewhere," he said looking through the papers. "It's JoJo something or other."

"I know her, I know her. Great." Beth left the office with a smile on her face. Later that day she was told that JoJo would be arriving that same day. She spent a few minutes making sure the room was ready for both JoJo and Brenda. She was scheduled to fly to San Francisco that evening and hoped JoJo would arrive early.

As JoJo stepped out of the transport plane that brought her to McChord, Beth was struck with how beautiful JoJo really was. She could give Betty Grable competition in the leg department. Her hair was shoulder length and a beautiful blonde shade. Her eyes were clear blue. She was perfectly proportioned with a tiny waist and a generous bust line. *JoJo*, Beth thought, *you're going to give the guys here a lot of trouble.*

JoJo rushed to greet Beth with a big smile. Beth had enough time to show her around the barracks and showed her where the mess hall was and then had to leave for her flight. "We'll get a chance to catch up later," Beth told her. "You better get ready. I bet you are already scheduled for a flight tomorrow."

During the next few days Beth completed her duties, made arrangements for Brenda's arrival and still found time to visit with JoJo. As Beth expected, JoJo was put right to work flying. Even so, it was nice to have someone to talk with who had shared at least part of her past.

The next week Brenda Marshall arrived. Beth met her as she got off the plane. She took her to the PX for a sandwich and let her settle in. Brenda had short dark hair and was about the same height as Beth. She had a bit of a weary look to her. Or, Beth thought, maybe she just looks weary because of all the stress of living in a city that gets bombed by the Germans every night. Over dinner that night in the mess hall, Brenda, JoJo, and Beth got acquainted.

Beth was issued a jeep to transport both Brenda and herself to classes at Boeing for the next two days.

As they rode along, Beth asked Brenda about the ATA. They shared information about the differences and similarities in the program between Great Britain and the United States.

"I think it's good that you are part of the official military," Beth said remembering the Phoenix fiasco. "We thought that after the first year we would officially be made part of our Air Corp. It hasn't happened yet."

Beth asked Brenda if she knew what the seminar was about.

"I'm not sure," Brenda told her, "I heard rumors about a new guidance system that's been developed. Maybe it won't be that because I heard some part of it failed a week or so ago so maybe our meeting will be about something different."

Beth remembered about Ed Thompson and the part she had carried to Arizona. "Well," she said, "I guess we'll find out soon enough. Look to your right. Those are the bombers waiting to be ferried and sent overseas."

"I can't believe how many of them are here. And they are so badly needed. What amazes me the most is that they are just setting in an open field. In London they would become target practice for the German bombers. We have to move planes away from the base in the middle of the night when we hear them coming. Now, just to see them setting in the open . . . ." Her voice drifted off.

"It must be terrible for you to live through that. Was your plane ever attacked?"

"Not yet I've had some close calls. I managed to get away with a little time to spare. We aren't trained to fight in combat. We're trained to protect the plane by moving it."

After a day of listening to lectures on guidance systems and practicing new procedures on a dummy plane, they left Seattle to return to the base. "Will you have any extra time here to look around the area?" Beth asked. "Even though I'm not an officer, I do get to go to the Officer's Club. On Saturday night they often have a show planned with entertainment. And of course there is dancing. You are entitled – no, we are entitled to have some fun after lectures all day."

"That sounds like a lot of fun. I'd like that. I fly out early Sunday morning."

The classes wrapped up just after noon on Saturday. As they were leaving the building, Brenda spotted a familiar face.

"Pieter Dekker, what are you doing in the States?" she shouted out.

"Well, hello, Brenda. I can ask you the same thing."

"I'm here learning about the new guidance systems."

"I'm here with Wing Commander Watson. He's visiting various bomber plants and meeting with the VIP's."

"I'd like you to meet my new friend, Beth Martin. Beth, this is Squadron Leader Pieter Dekker. He's a pilot (or do I need to say was a pilot) with the RAF."

As Beth and Pieter shook hands, Pieter explained that he had been on special assignment for the past few weeks. He would be returning to active flying status as soon as he returned to London.

"Are you staying at McChord?" Beth asked him. "I am trying to talk Brenda into joining us at the Officer's Club tonight. It's usually noisy and fun. If you're staying at the base, why don't you join us?"

"I am staying in the guest BOQ. I'm not much of a party animal but thank you for inviting me."

"Pieter, you know Hugh would tell you that you have to come with us. Don't make me tell Hugh that you were a party-pooper," Brenda pleaded. Turning to Beth she said, "Hugh is Pieter's best friend and the special man in my life."

"We'll see," Pieter told them.

"No, that was not an invite. It was an order. We'll expect to see you about 8 o'clock. Is that time OK, Beth?" she asked.

JoJo joined them that evening. Beth saw Pieter enter the club and look around. She stood up and called to him to join them. A crowd of people were at the table. Everyone seemed to be mingling with the other people. The dancing was already in full swing and the women rarely left the dance floor. No band was there that night, only someone playing records. When the women asked Pieter to dance, he declined saying he might dance later. As Beth finally returned to the table she thought she really should be leaving. She was scheduled to fly to Omaha the next morning and always wanted to be rested and ready. It would feel good to be flying again. She didn't like the business side of flying. The record being played was *There'll be Blue Birds Over the White Cliffs of Dover*. Pieter seemed to be lost in thought so Beth sat quietly listening to the music.. The next record was the Andrew Sisters singing the *Pennsylvania Polka*. JoJo came to the table and tried to get Pieter to dance. He had just about decided to join her when another young man came and pulled her away to dance. JoJo called to Pieter that she would be back.

"She just about had me convinced to join her," Pieter told Beth.

"Then let's not waste the music," Beth told him as she rose from her chair.

Pieter took her hand and led her to the dance floor just as the song ended. The next record was *I Don't Want to Walk Without You.* Pieter put his hand on her back and guided her around the floor as they heard the soulful sound of the trumpet of Harry James. Beth was stunned into silence. Pieter's hand on her back was firm and secure. Just like Robbie had always held her when they danced. *Well,* she thought, Pieter *probably took the same type of lessons she and Robbie had taken.* Miss Ethel, Glenridge's dance instructor, had insisted on certain postures and hand placement when she had taught them. Apparently, Pieter had the same type instructor. Still, she felt a bit unnerved as they made their way back to the table.

"I think I'd better leave all you fun people," Beth said. "I have an early flight in the morning."

"I need to leave, too," Pieter said. "Can you point me in the direction of my home for tonight? And Brenda, be sure to tell Hugh that I was a good soldier and obeyed your orders."

"See you at Livingston," Brenda told him.

Beth and Pieter walked a short way and Beth indicated she would be walking in a different direction. "It was very nice meeting you, Pieter. I hope you have many, many good flights ahead."

"It's been a real pleasure meeting you, Beth." As they shook hands, Pieter placed his left hand over their clasped hands. "I hope that someday when the war is over our paths will cross again." They each left and went their own way.

"Beth, you are being reassigned to Sweetwater," Major Wilson told her when she reported for her next assignment. "We're going to miss you. You have never complained about any assignment you have been given and have been of great help to us here."

There was a plane leaving that afternoon for Chicago, so Beth hurriedly packed her gear. JoJo was away from base so she would not have a chance to say goodbye to her. She left a note for her and left McChord.

*   *   *

Cathy looked at her body. Even after these weeks she could still see scars, bruises, and scrapes from her ordeal. She learned that flying metal had been imbedded deep into both legs which made for problems as they tried to set the broken bones in her leg. She resolved that she would try to be an even better nurse and be compassionate to the patients.

After about ten days of therapy, Cathy was advised that she was being transferred back to the states, to the Walter Reed Army Hospital in Washington, D.C. to complete her therapy. This time she traveled by plane. She wished that all the wounded could be transported by plane. It was so much easier than all the time spent on the ship. Finally, they arrived in Washington. The nurse on board put Cathy in a wheelchair to be transported from the plane to the ambulance. Cathy saw a distinguished looking man and woman waiting at the end of the ramp. They came to her with outstretched arms.

"Cathy, it's wonderful to finally meet you. I'm Joan, Mike's mom."

"I'm Ray, Mike's dad."

What started as a handshake ended up in a big hug.

"This is a wonderful surprise to be greeted this way. Mike was right when he said you were both very special."

"We know you have to go directly to the hospital now. We'll give you a few days to rest. We're hoping very soon you'll be able to get a weekend pass from the hospital. We want you to come to Virginia to see us. Mike has filled many letters full of good things about you," his mother said.

Ray added, "Mike was right when he said how beautiful you are."

"Thanks for the compliments. It's good for my morale to hear such nonsense. I'm really looking forward to knowing you both. I already knew that Mike had nice parents because he is such a good man."

Cathy was taken to the hospital. This time she was put in the therapy section. She hoped she would soon have the cast removed so she could get back on the work schedule again. She did feel like she needed a few days to rest up. The toe to hip cast on her leg seemed to weigh a ton even when she lay in bed. It was uncomfortable to sit in a wheelchair with her leg straight out. When she finally got settled into bed she thought she might sleep for a week.

One afternoon a few days later as Cathy awakened from her nap, she opened her eyes slowly then closed them again. Reality began to set it. Or did it? Could it be . . . ?

"Please tell me I'm not dreaming," she said as she saw her mother sitting in a chair by her bed.

"Cathy, dear, dear Cathy," her mother said as she quickly moved to the bed to caress Cathy. "It's me. Your dad is with me. He just stepped out to get me some coffee."

Cathy clung to her mother. She wouldn't let go until her dad came in the room. She held onto him tightly.

"I can't believe this. I'm sooooo glad to see you both."

"Not any happier than we are to see you," Albert told her. "We got the first train out of Glenridge as soon as we found out where they were bringing you. Nothing could have kept us away."

"Tell us how you really are," her mother said.

"Well, I'm considerably better than I was before you got here. How long can you stay?"

"We'll only have a couple of days. It's hard to find a place to stay with so many people trying to visit loved ones. But the nice people who live in the area have opened up their homes to help. We were able to get a place for a couple of nights. So what we don't get said today we can say tomorrow."

The hospital had put Cathy on her therapy routine right away. Somehow it seemed a lot easier when she knew her folks were waiting for her to finish her routine. She told her parents about her duties in the Pacific. She spent most of the time talking about Mike. She told them about Mike's parents meeting her at the plane when she got back.

"We have had many telephone conversations with them over the past few weeks," Albert said. "They are coming to see you later today. We're planning to have dinner together to get acquainted. They sound like very nice people."

"They have to be or Mike wouldn't be the man he is. I can't wait for you to meet him." Cathy looked wistfully at her wedding ring. "I really miss him."

"Maybe he'll be able to come home soon," her mother said.

"I hope we're not interrupting."

Cathy looked up to see the Goodman's come into the room. She watched as the four parents, who now shared so much in common, introduced themselves and got acquainted. When the four of them left for dinner, Cathy wished so much that she and Mike could have been here with her.. *I hate this war*, she thought.

True to the Goodman's word, as soon as the doctors said it was OK, a car came to take her to Virginia to spend a weekend with Mike's parents. They lived in a house on a street not too unlike her home in Glenridge except everything in this neighborhood was bigger. Every where she looked she saw reminders of Mike. Pictures of almost every stage of his life flooded the rooms: when his front teeth were missing, in his high school football uniform, to graduation from med school.

"I guess you can tell, I'm a proud, doting mother," Joan said.

"You should be. He is the most special person I ever met. I do love him. I want you and Ray both to know that. I'll always want him to have the things and do the things that will make him happy."

"Right now, the only thing that would make him happy is to be with you. We can't make that happen right now. Ray is trying his best to pull strings that would at least let him come home on leave. I know it's not fair to the others for us to do but we think he needs to be reassured that you're OK. Are you really as well as you seem? Ray has followed your medical progress. He is very worried that you might be trying to get well too soon."

"Actually, I think I'm doing very well. At least the casts are getting smaller. I don't know how long before they'll ship me back overseas."

"Surely they won't make you go back?" Joan asked.

"I have no idea. I have experience now. I'm not afraid to go back. I think this experience will help me be a more sensitive nurse."

"It was so nice to meet your family. I've talked to your mother on many occasions the last month. I know she was glad to see you."

Ray interrupted them asking if it was OK for him to come in.

"Of course," Cathy answered but instead of seeing Ray come in the door, it was Beth who rushed to her sister.

The two sisters embraced, got a bit teary. They hugged again.

"I'll leave you two alone," Joan said. "We'll have dinner at six."

"Beth, how did you know where to find me? I sent you a letter; it was sent to Seattle."

"I suspect your father-in-law had a hand in it. I have been transferred to Texas. When I got there I found I was scheduled for a flight to Washington. When I got there the CO told me a car was waiting to take me to Virginia to see my sister. The driver said he'd be back around nine to take me back to base for a flight out at midnight. Enough about me. Tell me about Mike. He's a really handsome guy. It must be so sad to not be able to see him."

The two young women had time to visit together. They shared a lovely, leisurely dinner and then Beth left. Cathy hobbled on her crutches over to Joan and Ray. She gave each of them a hug.

"Thank you, thank you. What a wonderful surprise."

"You must be very proud of Beth," Ray said.

"I'm very proud of her. Oh, I wish Mike could be here to share all this," Cathy said.

"So do I," said his mother. She was echoed by his father saying, "So do I."

When Cathy returned to Walter Reed the powers-that-be decided Cathy needed extensive therapy. The shards of metals had done far more damage than the broken bones. The days seemed long and lonesome. One day she hobbled on her crutches to the nurses' station. She asked if she could help with anything. Before long she was spending time each day working. Soon they asked her to help in the records office. It seemed like so little she was doing but at least it was something..

It took time. Eventually the casts and crutches disappeared. She still had exercises she had to do each day in the therapy section. She didn't mind. Sometimes she was able to assist someone else a little. She was very encouraging to the others. Cathy learned her way around the entire hospital. She knew the time was near when she would be discharged as a patient. She was anxious to get back to work. When she thought about it she wasn't sure where she'd go or what she'd do. She asked for an appointment at the administrator's office to check the procedures for cases like hers. Did she immediately report back to some base upon discharge from the hospital? If so what base? Would she be limited in what she could do? She had a lot of questions.

She talked with Mrs. Barber who was familiar with Cathy's record and her injuries. "You will probably not be sent back overseas."

"I need to go back," Cathy told her.

"I understand your need to try to be with your husband. After reviewing the severity of your injuries, it is better for you to be stateside for at least one year. We all hope the war will be over by then. We do need nurses here at Walter Reed. I can arrange your transfer here. We work on a rotating schedule. Are you interested?"

"Yes, I'm interested. Do you know where I'll be assigned?"

"We'll work that out. Surgical and O.R. nurses are on their feet for hours at a time. Some other assignment might be best for the next few months."

"About my housing, are there housing units here or apartments close by?" Cathy asked.

"Our units here are full. We keep a list in the office of the apartments of nurses who are transferring in and out. The apartments are on a bus line that serves the area so you won't need a car."

Cathy checked it all out. She located a unit that would be available when she needed it. It was a small one-bedroom unit with a pull-out sofa in the small living room. It was already furnished. While it wasn't exactly what Cathy liked, it would be quite adequate. Not many units were available so near the hospital. Cathy might not be at Walter Reed too long anyhow.

*   *   *

When Beth had reported for duty back at Sweetwater she had been surprised to see that Martha Grant, the woman who had interviewed Beth for the WASP'S program was now the commanding officer for the unit.

"Beth, it's good to see you again. You are gaining a reputation for being one of our stars. It will be good to have you help train our newer recruits. But we have a special assignment for you first. We need you to fly a group of congressmen back to Washington. They have been here for two days on official business," Mrs. Grant said.

The good part about the trip was the surprise visit to get to see Cathy. Apparently Cathy's father-in-law had arranged it. Beth had been worried about Cathy and though they did talk by phone it was not the same as seeing her.

But Beth had another worry. She had been very satisfied with her assignment in Seattle. The CO seemed satisfied with her work. She could not understand why she had been transferred back to Texas. She decided to find out.

"Mrs. Grant. I know I'm not supposed to ask but I've been wondering why I was transferred back here. I tried to do a good job in Seattle."

"Beth, you are becoming one of our leaders. You did a fine job in Seattle. But we need you here. We know you've been trained on the new guidance systems. Lois Miller, who was scheduled to teach our class, got very sick. We are unsure of how long she will be away. We cannot afford to waste time finding another instructor. We would like you to teach the class for the next few weeks until Lois comes back or we find another teacher. We know you adapt to change quickly and are ready and able to do this job. Can we depend on you?"

"Of course, Mrs. Grant. I do hope it's not a permanent assignment."

"This training takes priority. Can you be ready to teach by tomorrow?"

As Beth began teaching she realized that even though she had only been gone a matter of months, the training program had already been updated and revised. She took on a new respect for the leaders of the program and quickly settled into a new routine. It seemed strange to her to have a set routine for each day. She usually lived her life one day at a time, in this place or that place. Now she actually had time to sit and listen to a news broadcast.

Beth thought about how her dad was so faithful to hear the news each night. She often thought how her dad had said it would take time for the United States to get organized in its war effort, but they would do it and we would win. She had been so worried when she heard that Cathy had been injured. It was quite a relief to know she was recovering.

*   *   *

After many newscasts of death, losses, and bad news, the tide had turned. In early 1943, the United States forces had begun bombing raids in Germany at Wilhelmshaven. In February the German forces had surrendered at Stalingrad in Russia. In May the German troops surrendered in Africa. All this was just ahead of the Allied Forces landing in Sicily on a march to the German heartland. The news, although still very sad and deadly, was also improving in the Pacific. In May, the U. S. Forces had retaken Attu Island in the Aleutians. And news had just been received that we could declare that we had retaken Guadalcanal in the South Pacific. It was a horrid battle and many lives were lost. The radio newsmen in Europe reported many rumors that the Allies were preparing for some big invasion, probably in France somewhere across the coast from England. Of course no one would confirm it. On the good side, peace talks were now being held by President Franklin Roosevelt, Prime Minister Winston Churchill from England, and Joseph Stalin from Russia. In spite of the death and destruction still continuing, the coming Christmas season of 1943 held more hope than the Christmas of 1941 or 1942, especially for a victory against our enemies. The initial furor to *beat the Japs, or beat the Germans* was still there, especially as the wounded service men returned home. Hope was in the air.

*   *   *

In Glenridge, hope for a victory against the Axis forces continued. Improvement in the news coverage became more current but the country was still subdued. Annie sensed a weariness begin to set in as the country yearned for a more peaceful time. Annie worried about this. We have to keep people motivated in the cause, she thought.

She and her friends started a cookie making project. Toll House Cookies became very popular because they would pack, ship and store well. They decided that every week they would bake cookies to send to a serviceman. It was a nice idea. It was not very practical since sugar was scarce. They limited it to once a month.

They also heard about making ditty bags for the servicemen. These were small drawstring bags with personal care items inside, like toothbrush, toothpaste, nail clippers, a bar of soap etc. Annie went to see the school superintendent. She asked if the school children could be asked to bring in an item for the bags. He agreed they could ask the children. After collecting supplies they found they needed a few additional items to complete them so Annie solicited the local drug stores for donations. She went back to visit the Navy Recruiting Office to get more information about joining the Waves. She felt she needed to do more.

As the Christmas season grew nearer, Albert, Emma, and Annie hoped that Beth and Cathy might be able to come home for Christmas. But it was not to be. Beth wrote that she had exceeded her days off and would be on duty during the holidays, probably on a trip to California. Cathy, who was now working full time was scheduled to work Christmas week. Annie made an announcement at dinner that night.

"Since Cathy can't come home I think I should go to be with her during the holidays," she told the family. After a long discussion about long delays on train schedules, Annie said she would make the trip by bus; first to Detroit where she would board a bus for Washington, D.C. Cathy was thrilled and said she would meet the bus and take her home. They would get a small tree for the corner of her apartment and cook a nice Christmas dinner.

Albert and Emma finally agreed it would be nice for the sisters to be together. Annie went that day to get her bus ticket and began to pack for the trip.

"Annie, I'm over here," she heard as she got off the Greyhound bus in Washington, D.C. She rushed to her sister, hugged her and then pushed away to look at Cathy.

"You look wonderful. I can't tell at all that you were wounded."

"Well, you can tell when you look at my leg. At least I have my leg and it works well," Cathy said with a smile. "You look great, little sister."

"Stop with the *little* sister bit. I'm taller than you."

"Probably a lot smarter than me, too. We'll take a local bus to get home. I'm so glad you came. Oh, by the way, we both have to go to work tomorrow."

"What do you mean, go to work?"

"The hospital needs lots of volunteers," Cathy told her, "especially during the holidays when many of the regulars are busy at home. I signed you up to volunteer while I'm at work during the time you are here. You don't mind, do you?"

Annie reached out and gave Cathy a hug. "Now at last I can do something worthwhile instead of sitting at home," she said with a smile.

The next morning Annie and Cathy boarded the local bus to get to Walter Reed Army Hospital. Cathy had been assigned to desk duty. Cathy introduced Annie to Mrs. Brennan who gave assignments to volunteers. Annie was given a list of do's and don'ts. She was taken to the Day Room where the soldiers gathered to visit or just spend time away from their room.

"Hey Cutie," a soldier called out. "Can you move this pillow for me?" Annie saw a soldier in a wheel chair whose leg was extended out on a pillow.

"I'll be glad to do that," she told him.

"I've got an itch on my chin," said another whose arm was in a cast.

It only took Annie about three minutes to realize that they were teasing her so she started to tease them back as she performed her miracle healing powers. She went to a soldier who had just been watching.

"Any itches or aches you need help with?" she asked

"Yea," he said. "I want to talk to my girl friend."

"Can I take you to a phone so you can call her?"

"No, she's in school right now. I just miss her."

"Why not send her a letter? Let me find some paper. You can dictate a letter to me. I'll mail it for you."

"Would you really do that for me?"

"Of course," Annie said. She left to find some stationery.

Annie spent the day writing a few more letters, playing a game of gin and playing chess. She took one soldier to a big sun porch. The weather outside was very cold. The sun was shining brightly. He said he was from Florida. He told her the sun made him feel like he was home even if the air was cold outside. She helped deliver afternoon snacks to the men. The day flew by.

"See you all tomorrow," she told them as she left that night. She had a good feeling like maybe she had spent her day doing something worthwhile.

"How was your day?" Cathy asked.

"Super wonderful. I can't wait to go back tomorrow."

The girls got off the bus at an earlier stop to go to a café where Cathy liked to have dinner. They walked the rest of the way home, talking about their parents, about Beth, about Cathy's injuries, about time spent in the war zone, and of course Mike.

"I want so badly for my family to meet him," Cathy said. "I always imagined that you and Beth would be by my side when I got married. The war makes you find different ways of doing things. You learn to appreciate the little things you used to have."

"I'm so proud of you and Beth. I feel like I should be doing so much more. When I graduate I'm almost sure I'm going to enlist in the WAVES."

"Join the Navy and see the world. That sounds like you, Annie. I hope by then it is a much more peaceful world than it is now."

The next morning when Annie signed in at the volunteer office, Mrs. Brennan called to her.

"How did your first day go, Annie?" she asked

"I had a wonderful time. I told the guys I'd see them again today. I hope that was OK," Annie told her.

"Well, I know they liked you. Some of our older volunteers thought maybe the teasing might have discouraged you from coming back."

"Mrs. Brennan, I'm used to being teased. Our family puts on a variety show at an army base in our home town so the teasing is part of the territory."

Mrs. Brennan was quiet for a moment as she looked at Annie.

"I think I have a special assignment for you. Up on Ward C we have soldiers who are recuperating. They will be sent back to the war zone as soon as they leave here. They are all on the mend. They are free to move around the place as much as they like. Almost all of them have had family come to visit them here. Most get lots of mail. One young man has had no one visit him except his CO who came last week trying to find out how soon his hospital stay will end. As far as we know he has received no mail. He sits quietly in the corner in the day room just staring out the window. He is always very polite and kind, but he doesn't mix at all. He'll be discharged from the hospital in a matter of days. He has to report back to base. Would you feel like trying to break through his wall of silence? It pains me to think how lonely he must be."

"Mrs. Brennan, I'll try my very best. Are there any special things he should or should not do? Or subjects I should avoid?"

"None that I know about. I'm not expecting a miracle, just a few acts of kindness."

Annie loved a challenge. She made her way to the day room. She saw the young man sitting in a back corner looking out the big window. Annie saw a cabinet in the room with cards, games and magazines. At one table a group of men were playing poker. One man appeared to be writing letters. She saw a counter with a coffee pot. Annie walked to the cabinet. She took out a deck of cards. She took them to the back of the room to sit at a table near the table in the corner. She shuffled the cards and began to play Solitaire. After three games, she gave a very loud sigh. She got up from her chair.

"I have to get a cup of coffee. These cards are getting to me. Can I get you some coffee or a Coke?" Annie asked as she passed the table where the solitary soldier sat.

"No, no thank you," he answered.

She got her coffee and made her way back by his table. She stopped, looked at him and asked, "Did you ever have one of those days when you just can't seem to get moving? I'm supposed to be moving around here trying to be pleasant. All I feel like doing is to sit here and play cards."

He looked at her. Softly he said, "Well, you don't have to be pleasant to me. I'll stay out of your way."

"Maybe it would help *me* if I talk. Do you mind if I sit here" She quickly sat down before he could answer. "I came all the way here to visit my sister, who's a nurse. She is so busy working and . . . . ." Annie tried to think of what to say next. "Maybe I should get out of everyone's hair.

I should forget this whole thing." She placed her elbows on the table. She put her chin in her hands. She tried to appear deep in thought.

A volunteer came by to ask if they wanted anything. Annie tried to think quickly of a way to keep the conversation going.

"It's nicer here than I thought it would be. They seem to try to make it pleasant. It must be *very* boring for you."

There was a long silence. Then he quietly said, "This is the very best place to be if you have to be in a hospital."

Have you been here very long?" she asked him.

"Too long," he answered, "I'll be leaving in a few days."

"Are you going home?"

"No such luck."

"Where is home?"

"Well, it's anywhere I hang my hat."

"No wife or kids, I guess. What about your parents?"

"I only had my Mom. She died last year."

"Maybe if you took a trip back . . . . ."

"That's not in the cards for me. I'm headed back to Europe right away."

Annie felt at a loss to know what to say next. He seemed to be staring intently out the window.

"Have you been able to see any of the surrounding area while you are recovering?"

"No. I guess I wasn't interested."

Annie looked out the window. She saw the sun shining brightly on a small park that appeared to be on the hospital grounds.

"Would you feel like taking a small walk outside? I think the fresh air would do me good. I might get over this funk I'm feeling."

He hesitated just a minute. Then he said, "Yes, I'd like to be outside. I need to be outside."

Annie got worried. What if he's not allowed outside? This could be another disappointment for him. Showing great confidence on the outside, but shaking inside, she found a nurse who was delighted to see the man begin to have an interest in life. Annie collected coats, hats, and gloves. Together they made their way into the sunshine.

"I'm Annie Martin," she said extending her hand.

"I'm Tom Ross," he told her as they shook hands.

The day was cold and the air was crispy as they made their way into the little park. They saw and heard the winter birds chirping in the trees. Tom spotted a few squirrels running from branch to branch. After sitting on a bench for a while, they started to walk through the grounds until they came to a street. Annie spotted an old streetcar made into a diner featuring hamburgers across the street. She decided she was hungry.

Tom looked at her and said, "I haven't been to a hamburger shop in years."

"Let's get one with everything on it."

"Even onions," he asked with the starting of a smile.

"Especially onions," she told him.

Annie told Tom about her childhood, trying to make it funny when she told him about characters in her home town. He even smiled on occasion.

Eventually the afternoon passed. They made their way back to the hospital.

As she told him goodbye, he placed her hands in his. He asked her if she would be back the next day.

As he held her hands she suddenly felt both shivers and heat racing through her body. She had never felt this way before. She felt beautiful. She felt intelligent. She felt protected. She felt loved. He made her feel that she was the most important person in the world.

"Yes, Tom, I'll be back tomorrow."

Annie was quiet when she went to meet Cathy to go home.

"Everything OK, little sister?" Cathy asked.

"Perfect," Annie answered. "Tell me about your day."

Annie took extra time with her makeup and hair the next morning. As she and Cathy got ready to leave they heard someone knocking at the door. Annie heard Cathy scream, "Mike."

Annie stayed in the bedroom. Cathy called to her, "Annie, quit hiding. Come out to meet Mike. Mike, this is my sister, Annie."

"Thanks for coming to help take care of your sister," he told Annie as he gave her a hug.

After a few words of greeting, Annie said it was time for the bus to go to the hospital. She grabbed her coat and quickly left for the bus stop.

Annie was very torn with her emotions as she rode the bus to the hospital. She felt she should leave that day to return home so Mike and Cathy could have time alone. If she did she might never see Tom again and that was not an option for her. She had to see him again. She decided to postpone the decision until that evening.

Tom was waiting for her in the day room when she got to the hospital. His smile, the light in his eyes when he saw her made her feel so special she wanted to shout for everyone to take notice. He got her a cup of coffee. They sat together planning their day. He was free to leave the hospital and return when he chose to do so.

"Could we take another walk?" he asked her. "I brought my coat with me."

It was another cold morning as they set off walking side by side. Annie slipped on a small piece of ice. Tom reached out to take her hand. He pulled it through his arm. As they walked the streets they found a small art gallery. They found they liked the same kind of art. They had a long lunch together. He wanted to know all about Annie; about her family and her childhood. He told her about his childhood, his parents and growing up on a farm in Iowa. When Annie asked him what kind of injuries brought him to Walter Reed he answered with very short, terse words. He didn't seem to want to talk about his military life. Maybe painful memories, she thought. They went to a movie. She never could remember which one they saw. They left the theater arm in arm. They made their way back to the hospital. In the early evening dusk, he held her close. He kissed her, once, twice, and then again.

When she arrived back at the apartment, Mike and Cathy were waiting to take her out for dinner. As much as Annie hated to say the words, she felt she should offer to leave to return to Glenridge.

Cathy said to her, "Annie, did something happen at the hospital today? You seem like you're in a dream world."

"I think I should make arrangements to go home so you and Mike can have time alone. You've had so little time together."

Mike and Cathy both tried to assure Annie that she was not in their way. They invited her to join them on a trip to Virginia to see Mike's parents the next day.

"No, I can't," Annie said, almost in a hurry. "I need to go back to the hospital tomorrow. I'll fix dinner for us. Is it OK if I invite someone to join us?"

Cathy looked at her sister closely. "What's going on, Annie? Did you meet someone special?"

Annie answered. "I'd just like to make a special dinner for you and Mike."

"But . . . ." Cathy began.

"That would be very special, Annie. Thank you. Can we buy anything for you to fix before we leave for Virginia?" Mike asked with a grin to Cathy.

Cathy gave a sigh and just looked at Mike. Annie said she didn't need any help.

When Annie returned to the hospital the next morning, Mrs. Brennan stopped her.

"Annie, you've performed a miracle. We have been amazed how open and friendly Tom Ross has become. Thank you so much. I don't know how you did it."

"Mrs. Brennan, can I take him home for dinner tonight? I'll make sure he gets back at whatever time you say."

"Yes, you certainly may. Annie, but I have a word of caution for you. Tom will be leaving in a couple of days. You really don't know him very well. Be careful to whom you give your heart."

"Thanks, Mrs. Brennan. I'm OK."

Annie and Tom returned to Cathy's neighborhood. They shopped for groceries. Annie cooked them an early Christmas dinner. Cathy and Mike got to know Tom. When Mike drove Tom back to the hospital, Cathy expressed her concerns about leaving Annie alone when she and Mike left to visit his parents in Virginia for Christmas day.

"You really don't know Tom very well," Cathy said. "Don't you think you're moving a bit fast in this relationship?"

"I know I love him. I think he loves me."

"He'll be gone for a long time."

"Then I'll have to wait a long time. I know we were meant to be together. I wish Dad and Mom could meet him. I wish I had my own home here. Thanks for letting me cook dinner tonight. Now go. Have a great time with Mike's family. He'll be leaving again soon so have a good time."

The next morning after Mike and Cathy left to spend that day and next in Virginia, Annie met Tom at the bus stop on the corner. Together, arm in arm, they made their way back to the apartment. It was the first time they had complete privacy. He told her that he would like a cup of the hot coffee that she offered on that cold morning. When she brought it to him it was forgotten as they reached for each other. Tom placed his hands gently on her face. He looked into her eyes.

"You have the most beautiful eyes. I will never forget this minute. I know I shouldn't say this for it is much too soon. I love you, Annie."

"Tom, I love you, too. Why shouldn't we say it?"

"Because . . . . .because . . . . you're so young. We've known each other such a short while."

"That just means we'll have a long, long time to say the words to each other."

"Annie, I'll be gone a long time. You need to be free to have friends and lovers in your life."

"I would rather have you for a few days than anyone else for a lifetime."

Tom pulled her closer to him. He knew just how to hold her, to touch her, to awaken pleasures and desires she did not know were possible. Tom, in return was given pleasures he had always assumed were not for him. They lay in each other's arms for hours.

"Annie," Tom said quietly. "You've given me more pleasure than I thought possible. It's a pleasure I have no right to claim. I love you so much."

That evening they walked down the street to a restaurant for dinner. The night was clear and bright. They passed by a large church decorated for Christmas with red bows and green holly. After dinner, they decided to attend the Christmas Eve service at the church. It was a beautiful service for both of them as they listened to the Christmas story. They sang the familiar carols.

"Your voice is beautiful, Annie. Did you take lessons?"

"No. We always had music in our home. You are the one with the beautiful, rich voice. I know you had lessons."

"My mother was a professional singer at one time. I guess I learned from her."

"There is so much I don't know about you. How can we get it all said so quickly?"

"When I come home we'll have a lifetime together. I will come back, Annie, because now I have a real reason to come home."

"I'm sure you will, Tom. I'll be waiting for you."

The next morning, they were awakened by the ringing of the telephone. It was Emma and Albert calling to wish Annie a Merry Christmas.

"Merry Christmas, Mom. I thought I'd hear from you today."

"Did you make it to church last night?"

"Yes, Tom and I attended a late service at a church near here."

"Is Tom with you now? Could your Dad and I wish him a Merry Christmas?"

Tom picked up the phone, appearing a bit anxious about the fact that apparently Annie's parents knew about him.

"Merry Christmas, Mrs. Martin," he said in his most polite voice.

"Merry Christmas, Tom. Cathy told us we would probably find you when we called our daughter. Annie, Cathy and Mike all speak very highly of you."

"Mrs. Martin, I know you probably don't approve of my being here. I want you to know that I really love your daughter. I would not do anything to harm or shame her."

Albert got on the phone. He talked with both Annie and Tom.

Later, Annie would remember that her mother had told her that she and Albert had not been sure how to handle this *situation* when Cathy had phoned to tell them about it. They did not approve of sleeping around. Yet they sensed sincerity in Tom. Most of all they loved their daughter. Maybe they remembered how they, too, had fallen in love so quickly. Perhaps, because they remembered what a brief period of time Robbie and Beth had together, they had decided to keep their opinions to themselves. They would give Annie the support they knew she would need in the weeks ahead.

"You have very special parents, Annie. I'm glad you will be with them. If I can't be here to take care of you, I guess they are the next best."

Snow had fallen overnight. Tom and Annie decided to take another walk that morning. They saw some children testing out their Christmas sleds on a nearby hillside. Tom went to the older boys. He gave one of them a five dollar bill to borrow his sled. Together on one sled, Tom and Annie flew down the hill into a snow bank. The boys, because maybe they couldn't resist, started to throw snowballs at Annie and Tom. Of course, they had to retaliate. As they walked home they saw a big area of very smooth snow. Laughing, hand-in-hand, they ran to it to make snow angels.

That afternoon, they cooked their Christmas dinner together. They sang together; first all the Christmas music they could remember. They sang some of the popular songs.

We sound great together, don't we?" Annie asked Tom. Tom replied, "We do everything well together. I love you, Annie."

Tom built a fire in the fireplace. They made love on the big blanket that Annie pulled from the closet. Tom caressed her face, tucking strands of hair behind her ears, gazing into her eyes. As his fingers moved down her forehead he found the scar by her eyebrow.

"How did that happen?" he asked her.

"Our gang was building a human pyramid. I was the youngest and smallest so I had to get on top. It was so much fun that day." Annie smiled as she remembered. "Someone moved. We all fell. I hit the sidewalk. I ended up in the doctor's office to get stitches for the first time. They were a badge of honor for a week or so. Because I didn't cry they all thought I was so brave. It did leave a scar."

"I'll kiss it away," Tom said.

"Then I'll have to kiss your scars," she told him.

As the day went on they danced to phonograph records, shared stories of their past. They made love. They must have played *You'll Never Know* by Dick Haymes a dozen times. Knowing it would all come to an end the next day, Annie grew anxious when she thought about his leaving.

"Annie, look into my eyes. What do you see?"

"The most beautiful blue eyes in the world. They are such a vivid, true blue."

"Look again. Do you see anything else?"

Annie looked closely. "Well, the blue part has little lines."

"That's the iris," he told her. "Look again. Look at the lines this time."

"Why, I don't believe it!" Annie said excitedly. "Let me look again. Some of those little lines are making a letter *A*. I must be seeing things."

"No, Annie, you're not seeing things. Those little lines are as unique as a fingerprint. Everyone's eyes are different. My lines make a letter. Like the letter *A*. It is an A for Annie. Now you know how I knew you were the only woman I will ever love. You know you belong to me."

She kissed each of his eyes. She turned to him and said, "Tell me you love me one more time." After he said the words she placed her hands over her ears. "I'm locking the sound of your voice in my ears so I will never, ever forget your voice." They held each other close.

On the day after Christmas they each packed their bags and left the apartment. They took the local bus to the Greyhound Bus Station in

Washington, D.C. Tom would take a bus to Fort Lee, Virginia, at noon. Annie would board a bus for Glenridge at 2:30 that afternoon.

Annie thought her heart would break as she told him goodbye. She kept a smile on her lips and her eyes dry until his bus pulled away from the station. She cried as she waited for the bus that would take her home.

*   *   *

As Tom looked out the bus window he thought his heart would break. He kept smiling and waving. Annie was so beautiful standing there with her dark green coat, white hat and gloves. Her long, dark curly hair, her shining eyes were something he knew he would never forget. Why do I have to leave her, he thought; haven't I done enough already? He knew that after a time of planning and briefings he would be on a plane going back to France. It would be his fourth trip. The last time was horrid. He ended up coming home on a stretcher. Would he even be that lucky again? Before meeting Annie it didn't seem to matter if he made it home. Now things had changed.

He didn't want to make this trip. He had bad feelings about it that he had never had before. He always made a big effort not to let himself get involved with anybody or anything so that he could make this trip without any ties. That special morning in the day room had changed all that. When he saw the beautiful young woman with the long, dark hair, for the first time in his life he felt he had to know her. This from a guy who made an effort not to know anybody. He decided he needed to keep looking out the window. But he couldn't do it; he couldn't help himself. He had watched her go to the game cabinet to get a deck of cards and move his way. He was surprised when she went to an empty table near him instead of coming to his table. He knew the nurses and volunteers were trying to be kind when they tried to draw him out of his shell. He knew the other men thought it was strange that he wouldn't talk to them. He just couldn't. He was bound by his oath to keep his story to himself. He might say something he shouldn't. It was easier to shut everyone out. But that was before he saw Annie. Once she spoke to him . . . . well, he dared to take a chance that he could talk with her and still keep his secrets.

Tom was in college in Iowa when a recruiter from the FBI had come to recruit young men to join them. When they learned that Tom was fluent in French and spoke German he became the target of their recruiting.

188

Tom decided to join them when he graduated. His father died about that time. When he went home to be with his mother she encouraged him to continue on his career path. She sold the family farm, got an apartment in town so Tom wouldn't worry about her. Soon after joining the FBI, because of his language skills and his knowledge of France, he was asked to transfer to the OSS which was the secret government agency that was involved in espionage.

Of course he knew about France; his mother had been born and grew up there. He learned French along with English when he first began to talk. He learned French history along with American history.

Tom's mother, Danielle, had been a young French girl when World War I had started. One day when she was about twelve years old the Germans had invaded their village. Her dad told her to hide in the barn. He rushed to get her mother and baby brother to safety when he saw the German soldiers coming up the country lane. The young girl, Daniele, buried herself in hay as she heard the guns. She heard the screaming of her parents. When she finally came out she found her family all dead. The house had been demolished. The farm animals had been scattered to the countryside. She covered the bodies of her family with blankets. She walked away. For more than a month she walked – first one direction then another – hiding from the German soldiers. She slept under trees in the woods and in old sheds. She searched the farm fields for any leftover vegetables that might be left to rot. One day she realized she had reached Paris. It was easier to hide in the city. She saw something really strange and new to her. In spite of the war people were walking in the streets. Occasionally you would see someone singing or perhaps dancing in the street. Sometimes people threw money into cans when the singing or dancing stopped. Daniele had been told by many people that she had a very good voice so she started to sing on the streets with a can at her feet. A man and woman walking by heard her. They hired her to sing at their night club. One night a young American soldier named Joe Ross heard her. He fell in love with her voice and then with her. He was a country boy from Iowa who lived on a farm. He was teased mercilessly about his love for the *French chanteuse*. Joe pursued her. As soon as the war ended he brought her back to the farm in Iowa. Tom was born soon after. His mother never talked much about her family, only to say that she remembered gathering eggs with her mother. She never gave up singing for any one, any place, any time. She told Tom all about France, the customs, the countryside, and little bits of history. Many years later when World War II started and France fell to the Germans, Daniele began to have nightmares. Tom's father would hold Daniele close until sleep returned.

Tom knew his father adored Daniele and the little son that was born to them. Tom grew up thinking he had the perfect life.

The OSS decided Tom was a perfect candidate to go into France to get intelligence reports to help in the war. Not only did he speak French fluently he had learned a lot of German from his neighbors who had settled in Iowa years before the war.

Tom made the first two trips to France alone. He connected with the French underground movement. He got detailed information which he brought back with him. His entries and exits from the country had been uneventful. The third trip had been made with a team of four others. Tom was leading them through a field when they had been spotted by the Germans. A grenade was thrown at them landing near Tom who was in front. Tom's team fired. They killed the German patrol. Tom was badly injured. His patrol would not leave him. They got him to some underground people who treated him until he could be sent home for surgery and treatment at Walter Reed Army Hospital. The place where he met his Annie.

He was weary of the war. When the men at the hospital would sit around, they would talk about the war. They talked about their part in it. Tom couldn't talk about his work. His work was classified. It was easier to shut it all out; to talk to no one. He felt he'd never have a normal life again.

All that changed when he met Annie. He wanted to live. He wanted to have a normal life with a wife and kids. He wanted that wife to be Annie. Maybe they'd have a dog: a German shepherd or a collie, maybe.

His commanding officer had come to the hospital to see if Tom would make one more trip back. Apparently something very big was planned for the coastline of France. He and a team would parachute into France behind the lines, gather information, and be picked up by the underground members to return home. If he can get this one last trip over, he would ask, plead, and beg, not to have to do another mission.

He had to get back to have a life with Annie.

*   *   *

On the second day before Christmas when Cathy had opened her door she could not believe her eyes. It was, it truly was, Mike standing there.

They stood in the doorway embracing and holding each other close. Finally they moved inside the door. Mike kicked the door shut. Cathy suddenly remembered Annie who had seemed to disappear. "Annie, quit hiding. Come out to meet Mike. Mike, this is my sister, Annie."

"Thanks for coming to help take care of your sister," he told Annie giving her a hug before she rushed out the door.

"What a nice sister to give us time alone," Mike said as he reached again for Cathy.

"How did you get here?" Cathy asked.

"The big boss decided that the doctors should take turns on the flights that bring the wounded back to the states. So I got the assignment for the one coming to Walter Reed. We just got in around five this morning. I'll have about a week here. I do have to go back."

"This is so wonderful." Cathy said. "I had thought Christmas without you would be a nightmare. Now that you're here . . . ." She suddenly thought about Annie. Mike seemed to know what she was thinking about.

"I owe Annie a debt of gratitude for coming here to be with you. Will she be uncomfortable if I sleep with you instead of on the couch?" he asked with a smile.

"Annie will probably feel she needs to leave. I'm sure we can manage."

When Annie arrived home that night Cathy noticed Annie was almost in a dream-like state. Mike took them out for dinner. Not much was said as Cathy and Mike spent the time looking at each other. Annie seemed in a world of her own. Finally, they made their way back to the apartment.

"Cathy, I think I'd better make arrangements to go home. You and Mike need to be able to have some privacy. You'll have such a little time together."

Cathy didn't know what to say. Did she want time with Mike alone? Certainly. Even though she knew Annie understood the situation, was it fair to Annie or would she feel like a fifth wheel.

Mike spoke up. "Annie, you are very special to give up your time to come here so Cathy wouldn't be alone. Both Cathy and I have been living with many people around us ever since we met. We managed to find time alone. I want to see my folks in Virginia. I know they want us all to come down for Christmas day. Cathy has arranged time off. Their house is big. We're family now. I never had a sister before. We're going down to visit them for the day tomorrow. We'd like you to come with us."

Annie said, "Not this time. I said I'd go back to the hospital. Is it OK if I fix dinner for us when you get back? Is it OK if I invite someone else?"

"Annie, what's up? Did you meet someone yesterday? I knew something was going on." Cathy continued to be the mother-hen. "Who is he? What's his name? Where's he from? Is he married? What were his injuries?"

Mike started to smile. "Isn't she going to make a wonderful mother to our twelve kids, Annie? Of course you can invite whoever you want. Do you want us to go shopping for groceries before we head out for Virginia?"

Annie smiled. "Thank you, Mike. I'll take care of it. Don't worry about me, big sister, I'll be fine."

The next morning Annie was out of the apartment before Cathy and Mike were awake. Mike's dad had arranged for a car to be available for Mike's use. Arm in arm they walked to the car to go visit his mom and dad.

This visit Cathy was able to walk around the large yard that surrounded the house as well as tour the house. It was like a larger, grander version of her home on Lincoln Boulevard. The Goodman's had a full-time housekeeper, Rita, to run the house. Ray worked many different hours. He often had business meetings and luncheons at the house. Joan stayed busy with her volunteer work. Rita had her own little apartment in one section of the house. She was a bossy, sassy woman who obviously loved the Goodman's. Cathy was glad that Rita had accepted her when she saw how Rita doted on Mike.

"Would Rita stand on her head if you asked her," Cathy asked Mike teasingly.

"She's too old," he said making sure Rita could hear him.

"I might be too old to stand on my head but I'm not too old to wash your mouth with soap, young man. I might need to take him to the kitchen for a ten-minute time out," she told Cathy.

"Rita has always been in Mike's life," Joan told Cathy. "I had an especially hard time when he was born. I needed help. Soon after Rita came to work for us we found she was the sole support for an invalid husband. He died soon after. Rita had no where to go so we asked her to move in with us. When we moved to Washington we had this big house so we asked her to come with us. She really is one of the family. Doesn't Mike look wonderful?"

"I'm so glad to have him home."

When they arrived back at the apartment that evening, they found Annie had somehow or other managed to find dishes, pots and pans. She had a candlelight dinner ready for the four of them. They were introduced to Tom Ross. Cathy looked at Annie and Tom while they were looking at each other. How can this be? *They're in love and they just met.* A memory flooded her mind of hearing her father tell about seeing her mother for the first time on the first day of college. Albert told everyone how he had fallen in love the first time he saw Emma. This is too much responsibility for me, Cathy thought. I don't know what to do about it. Mike looked at Cathy and smiled as if he knew what she was thinking. He gave a little shake of his fist as if to say, "It's OK, Cathy. Tom's a good guy." Mike offered to drive Tom back to the hospital.

"Annie, Tom seems really nice. Do you know much about him?" Cathy asked after the men had gone.

"Only that he's leaving the day after Christmas."

"Is he going home? Is he going home to a wife?"

"No, he said he has no home any more. His dad died while he was in college. His mom died after he was in the service."

"He didn't talk a lot about what he did in the service or about his injuries. Did he talk with you about it?"

"No. All he really said was that he expects to be shipped overseas right away."

"Well, he seems very nice. Do be careful, little sis. Don't fall in love too quickly. Joan and Ray have invited you to join us for Christmas in Virginia. We'll leave tomorrow. We'll be back the day after Christmas. Their home is lovely. You will go won't you?'

Annie sat their quietly for a moment and then declined.

"Is it because of Tom?"

"Yes. I need this time to be with him."

"Oh, Annie. I think maybe Mike and I should stay home too. We can have our own little celebration here. We'll get a little tree for the corner . . ."

Annie interrupted. "NO, you will not change your plans. You must go. You must be with Mike and his family."

Cathy worried about Annie. She thought maybe things were moving too fast with Tom. She talked with Mike after he returned. He seemed calm about it all. He had made a call to a doctor friend at the hospital who didn't have much information about Tom Ross. The man told Mike he thought Tom might be doing some kind of intelligence work overseas. As Mike shared this information with Cathy he tried to reassure her.

"I never had any brothers or sisters so maybe I can't fully understand your concerns. Talk with your mother if you think it will make a difference. We can go or stay. We'll have many Christmases with my folks. I want to be with you wherever you are most comfortable."

"We'll have many Christmases to spend with Annie. Maybe I do have to let go of her. Maybe I'll call Mom just to make me feel better." She sat on the bed and made her call. The next morning before leaving she tried to give Annie some sisterly advice. Annie just smiled and told them to have a good time.

Cathy did have a good time. To be with Mike made everything good. The house was beautiful, the gifts were extravagant, the food was excellent; the love of family was abundant.

Cathy called her family to wish them a happy Christmas. She learned they had talked with Annie that morning. All was well. Cathy was advised by her mother that Annie planned to leave for home on the day after Christmas so Cathy and Mike should plan to stay in Virginia as long as they liked.

Cathy immediately called Annie who confirmed that she wanted Mike and Cathy to have private time together. Tom would be leaving by noon on the 26th. She, Annie, planned to take a bus back to Glenridge at 2:30 that same afternoon.

"Don't come all the way back here to tell me goodbye," Annie had said. "Who knows? If Tom gets an assignment near here I may be back in a month. Give Mike and his family my best wishes for a happy holiday. Thank his folks for inviting me. Thank Mike for being such a good brother-in-law. He's the best brother-in-law I've ever had."

Cathy decided she would stop worrying. Rita, who had overheard the conversation, told Cathy, "Your sister will be fine. She's strong, just like you." Cathy felt good to get such a compliment from Rita. She went over and gave Rita a hug. "Rita, I love to cook. Would you let me fix a tea tray for *us ladies of the house?*"

"No, no. You go sit down. Rest your legs. I'll fix a tea tray," Rita insisted.

"Rita, you'll be doing me a favor. I cooked all the time at home. I love to cook. With all the goodies you have around here, it will be a real pleasure to fix something for you."

Joan had come into the kitchen at that point. She gently pulled Rita toward the sitting room. "Let's go put our feet up on the furniture until our tea arrives."

Cathy could see that Rita was a bit uncomfortable. Rita was such a dear. She needed some pampering. Cathy got out the silver tea service and good china cups. She fixed some tea sandwiches. She set out some beautiful small pastries that Rita had on hand. She insisted on serving the others. Joan asked Rita to tell them about her childhood memories of Christmas. Then Joan and Cathy took turns telling Christmas stories. When Mike and his dad got back to the house they found the three women laughing and talking. Cathy insisted on doing all the clean up. When she was done, she went to Rita.

"Thank you, Rita, for letting me feel like I was back home for a little while." Cathy said.

All too soon it was time for Mike to return to the Pacific. They stayed in Virginia until the night before he was to leave. Cathy was able to observe first hand how hard it was on his parents to tell him goodbye. She and Mike made their way back to her small apartment; shared one more night together. Then he was gone. Cathy knew what war was. She knew where he was returning. She knew she might never see him again. No, she thought, I won't allow myself to think about that. I know he'll back.

*   *   *

Leaving Cathy made this departure the worst Mike had ever made. He knew he loved Cathy as much as anyone could when they separated the day after their wedding. This departure was much harder. He realized how much he needed her. More than he ever thought he would need anyone. While he was finishing med school, Mike knew he would have to spend time in the military even before the events at Pearl Harbor had occurred. The war was raging in Europe and many of his classmates were already planning, one way or another, to go to serve there. Some of his acquaintances asked him if his father would arrange for him to stay in the states.

"No one except a very few of you know who my father is. I'll go where I'm told," he told them.

Up until a few weeks ago that had been his rule. He would be a good soldier without asking for any special favors. All that changed when he learned of Cathy's injuries. He felt as if he was the only doctor in the world who could help her. He was doing that type of surgery almost every day. He knew she needed him. He knew he needed to be with her, to take care of her. They told him she was not expected to live. If she did she'd probably lose one or both legs. He would have done anything in the world to help her. Yet he could not go to her. Even if he got permission to go, she couldn't wait for him to get to her. She needed surgery immediately to save her life. Surgery couldn't wait. So he had called his dad for help. He wondered if the extra care Cathy seemed to get was because it was standard care or if it was the influence of his dad. When he had learned of her injuries he felt as if a part of him had died. He did learn he was not the only doctor in the world that cared as much as he did about the patient. He was very grateful she had such good doctors.

He knew he was treated special with this trip home to see her. Yet, he did work all of the way home. They had some critically ill patients on the plane. He got little rest. Now when they see me come back to the war maybe they'll realize the system works. Maybe some other doctor will get a chance for a break to see his family.

Thinking about families led him to think of how much he wanted to start a family with Cathy. Twelve kids should be just about right, he thought. He had seen a lot of little children roaming on the various islands. He remembered one little boy who hid in the bushes. The kid looked starved. As Mike had stepped toward him, the child fled. The next time Mike saw the same kid he went to the mess tent, fixed a sandwich, and went back to sit near the edge of the bushes. He took a small bite; he laid the sandwich down and hurried away. By the time he turned around to look the boy was gone. So was the sandwich. Mike repeated the process for the next few days. A few days later he was shipped out. He somehow couldn't get the child out of his mind. He knew there were children on every island who probably didn't get enough to eat these days.

His trip back to the South Pacific took many days on many planes. First to Los Angeles, then Hawaii, finally to some other island whose name he didn't remember. Finally, he thought, this plane is so small it must be the final leg of the trip. *I wonder what island I'm on now,* he thought.

1944

By the time the Greyhound bus arrived in Glenridge, Annie had accepted the fact that she would be separated from Tom for a while. She was excited to be home so she could tell her family and her friends about Tom. She, Rosemary, and Marge spent time together planning their future. Roy had proposed to Rosemary before he shipped out. Rosemary thought that she and Roy would probably move in with her folks on Lincoln Boulevard. Herb and Marge also were planning to live on Lincoln Boulevard, probably with his folks until he finished college. Annie would only say she would go wherever Tom wanted to go. She still had her dream to see the world but now she only wanted to do it if she could do it with Tom. The three young women started on their careers. Each of them would be doing student teaching during the spring season: Annie would teach English in High School, Rosemary planned to teach in the middle schools and Marge planned to teach kindergarten or first grade. They were all excited about their future. Even the news gave them reason to hope. When they went to the movies they saw the newsreels showing Allied victories. None of them could forget the first newsreel they had seen of Pearl Harbor. They could not believe anyone could survive such carnage. They were very encouraged to see that at last the Allies were gaining territory. Could the war possibly end in 1944?

Annie entered the classroom that first day full of confidence and a new-found energy. She made her lesson plans carefully. She tried to figure out how to make it interesting to write a sentence correctly. She asked each student to write a letter to a serviceman, a brother, cousin or friend. She worked very hard to try to make it interesting to the students and took time to help the student who just didn't like the class. Maybe it was because she was the daughter of two teachers and had learned their skills, or maybe the curriculum wasn't too difficult, but she found her days were pleasant. She still had time to be involved in community events.

She wrote to Tom every day. She wrote to him with an address of an APO number so she wasn't sure where he was. At first she knew he was at Fort Lee. When she asked him if she could come to see him he advised her he might be away from the base for a month or more at a time so it wouldn't be a good idea. He wrote to her every day. At first she received one every day; sometimes they would pile up and she would get three or four at a time. His letters were full of his love for her and his desire to leave the Army as soon as he could.

"Do you want to live in Glenridge?" he had asked her in one letter, "or do you still want to see the world?"

Annie had to think about that. He had told her how anxious he was to stop traveling around. He wanted to get settled in one place. She really did want to travel. She knew many people who got divorced when one gave up a dream for another. She didn't want that kind of marriage. Then she would remember how happy she had felt when he first took her hand or first kissed her.

"I will go anywhere or stay anywhere just to be with you," she had written back.

He had phoned her regularly the first two weeks, next once a week, then once a month. After that she had not heard his voice.

*   *   *

Beth's teaching assignment continued for the next few months. Finally Beth was glad to hear that Lois Miller had recovered and would be reporting back the next week. *I wonder where I'll go now* she thought. She hoped it would be flying and not teaching. She didn't have to wait long. Mrs. Grant told her that she was being assigned to fly to London. There would be two pilots on board. Eileen Watson would be other pilot.

Beth was elated. Just imagine. Not only was it exciting to be flying overseas, she would be partnered with the woman she met on the first day of interviews to become WASP'S. They had only flown together once before. Both were amazed at how easy they were as partners. They were to board their passengers in Washington D.C. They would stay in London until the passengers were ready to return to Washington. When Beth asked who the people were, she was told she would find out before the plane was boarded. She hurriedly packed her gear and caught a flight to Washington where she met Eileen. The two friends met, checked out their plane and filed the necessary flight plans. They learned their passengers, a Mr. Shulte and a Mr. Cleary, were two members of the State Department on some important mission to London. Fortunately, the weather was good for the long flight. They had no problems.

Beth and Eileen took advantage of the quiet flying time to catch up on where they had been during the past year. Between them they had been to almost every state.

"Did you hear that JoJo has been assigned to McChord?" Beth asked Eileen.

"I spent last weekend with her. We were both in Omaha. We spent the evening together. She was really disappointed that you were transferred just after she got there."

"Well, we got to spend a little time together. I had two days of classes with a gal from England named Brenda Marshall during that time."

"JoJo said Brenda was very nice and seemed very smart. She told me about your evening at the club and about the RAF flier who joined you. She said he was handsome and very nice."

"I guess he was handsome. He did seem nice enough. He was somewhat distracted and very quiet. At times he looked very sad. He only danced once and it was with me. He was a very good dancer. His name was Pieter."

"Did Brenda tell you about the man? She told JoJo all about him."

"JoJo didn't tell me. As a matter of fact, I left for Texas so soon after I don't believe I talked to JoJo at all."

"JoJo said he's from Austria. He was at the university in London when the Germans started to bomb London. He and his two best friends all quit school and joined the RAF. They flew on many raids together. Unfortunately, the same day Brenda met them all, they went on a mission. Hugh made it back safely. Pieter's plane was shot up and his tail gunner was blown out the back of the plane. Amazingly, Pieter managed to land the plane back at Livingston. His other friend was killed on that mission."

"No wonder he looked so sad. Can you imagine living through that?"

"Well, the story doesn't end yet. When Brenda first met Pieter, he told her that his family was back in Austria. He's not sure if they are alive or dead. He wanted to go back to check on them but the authorities won't let him."

"Oh, Eileen. How very sad for him. No wonder he looked distressed. I did hear about Hugh being his friend. Now Hugh is the man in Brenda's life. Brenda used Hugh's name to boss Pieter around."

"JoJo and Brenda think Pieter liked you a lot."

"Well, that would be hard for me to tell. We said very little to each other."

"Are you ready to let go of Robbie?"

"I think part of me will always belong to Robbie."

"Let go of him, Beth. Life goes on. Life is for the living."

"What about you, Eileen? Are you and Ronnie still together?"

Eileen started to smile as she reached around her neck and pulled a gold chain out of her shirt. On that chain was a diamond ring.

"Don't tell on me. This ring had belonged to his mother. His family sent it to me to wear until he gets home. I know we're not supposed to have jewelry. How could I leave this behind?"

"I'm so happy for you. Do you have any plans for getting married yet?"

"We want to wait until the war is over. We want to settle down in a little town away from the hustle and bustle and try farming. We've both had enough excitement for a lifetime."

"Eileen, I'm really happy for you. Where is Ronnie now?"

"Somewhere in the South Pacific. I won't hear from him for weeks and then I get a ton of mail. I sure look forward to it. I really love him, Beth."

Their radio cackled with instructions. They were directed to land at Livingston Air Field, just outside London. After landing, the passengers were met with a staff car and whisked away. Beth and Eileen were told to rest and relax for 48 hours. They should stay on stand-by for the return flight home.

They were directed to temporary quarters on base. As they made their way they heard someone call out "Beth, Beth." She turned and saw Brenda Marshall making her way to them.

"It's so good to see you. When did you get here? Why are you here?" The questions flowed as the women got reacquainted. "You showed me Seattle. I want to show you a bit of London. I don't fly tomorrow so maybe we can hit a pub tonight."

Eileen said, "That sounds like fun. Let's go, Beth. We can catch up on sleep later."

As they walked to their barracks they saw a lot of activity everywhere they looked. Planes were landing and taking off almost every minute. It was a very busy place. "Is anything special happening here today?" Eileen asked Brenda.

"It's always busy here, but it has seemed much busier the last week. If you hear three long blasts, don't get nervous. It just means that bombers or V-1 flying bombs are headed this way. If it's bombers we try to move all the planes to a safe location. If it's the V-1's we have no time for anything. We take cover. If the motor of a V-1 shuts off you can expect an explosion almost immediately."

"It must keep you on edge all the time," Beth said.

"No matter what we are doing, we try to stay alert," Brenda told her.

"Look at that landing," Beth told Eileen. They saw a plane that had been damaged yet the pilot managed to land the plane. Beth and Eileen were not used to seeing that type of activity. It was as close to the war as either of them had been. They saw the men coming off the plane looking tired, dirty, and weary. "I bet they have stories to tell their grandchildren," Beth said. "Does it take them long to recover?"

"Everyone tries. Those pilots will probably be at the pub tonight. Everyone just sort of tries to relax. We have to stay alert. Seems like the Germans have started to bomb us more often lately. Maybe they're getting worried."

"Can you ever forget about it?" Eileen asked.

"Not really," Brenda told her, "But we try really hard not to let it run our lives."

After a ride on a rickety old bus that would make a few more runs that evening, the three women arrived at the pub in the city. The place was jammed with people. It was a favorite pub for the air personnel. Brenda saw Hugh sitting at a table near the back and waved to him.

"Come this way," she told Beth and Eileen. After they arrived other airmen joined them at the table. Some would get up to dance and others would sit down. It was a very casual atmosphere.

Hugh looked up and saw Pieter enter the pub. He stood, called, and motioned for Pieter to join them at the table. Pieter looked very surprised when he saw Beth.

"Beth. I sure didn't expect to see you tonight. What are you doing here? How long will you be here?" he asked as he sat down.

"Hello, Pieter. This is my buddy, Eileen. Eileen, meet Pieter." They shook hands. "We had an assignment to bring some people to London. We're just here for a couple of days."

"Well, I hope it's a peaceful evening. I often wonder if the German pilots get as tired of their routine as we do."

The evening passed very quickly. The first couple of hours were loud and noisy. Finally the noise died down a bit; the music was a little softer and slower. Just then the alarms sounded.

"Let's go. Let's go. The bomb shelter is next door. Hurry, hurry." In an almost organized chaos the group made their way next door to the entrance of an underground tunnel. The place was quickly filling with people. Families with children were taking shelter there along with crowds from the restaurants and other pubs in the area. The air became very heavy. The shelter was very crowded.

"How long does this usually last?" Beth asked.

"Could be ten minutes or ten hours," she was told. Beth decided to try to settle in and not panic. She saw a mother with a baby and a toddler. The baby was crying and the toddler was pulling on his mother. Beth edged her way through the crowd toward them. "May I hold the baby for you?" she asked.

"Thank you," the mother said as she handed the baby to Beth and reached to pick up the toddler. "I'm trying to get home from my mother's house."

Beth rocked the baby in her arms and the child began to be calmer. A loud, loud blast suddenly occurred filling the air first with a big flash as electrical lines pulled apart. Dirt and debris surrounded them as the roof of the tunnel began to collapse. A few people began to scream. Most people just reached for their neighbor. Beth could not see the baby's mother. She hoped and prayed the mother would be OK. She couldn't see Eileen or Brenda or any of their group. They had all entered the tunnel together. She had left their side to help with the baby. Beth knew she must stay calm and try to help others.

She took off her coat, made a blanket of it for the baby and laid it under a bench which appeared to be secure. Using her hands, she began to dig away the dirt surrounding other people. She kept her eye on the baby. *No one will hurt you, little one,* she thought. As she dug she thought about the others in her group. *Were they alive or dead? What kind of bomb was it? How can people live through this and still try to have a somewhat normal life?*

Beth helped to uncover three people. One was unconscious so she laid the body out flat and returned to digging the dirt away from another. This person appeared not to be injured. Another man who was working to free himself asked for help removing a boulder from his leg. Beth crawled to help him. As Beth looked around she saw that every able body was helping someone. People began to call out names, asking if that person was safe. She could hear voices moaning and many people who were just frightened were crying. Beth realized that this shelter was a very large tunnel. She was sure that people on the outside would come quickly to help. She heard one man say that they must hurry as it looked like another section of roof was about to collapse. After what seemed like hours, it really wasn't, a hole through the debris was made from their section to another. Everyone worked together carefully to make the hole large enough to crawl through. Beth heard a cry, "My baby, my baby." Beth carefully lifted the sleeping child and passed him down the line of people who passed the baby to his mother. One by one, beginning with the injured, the people were being evacuated from the tunnel.

The unconscious woman Beth had pulled from the debris still laid on the damp floor. Beth could still feel a weak pulse.

"We have to get this person out," she shouted through the opening. "She's unconscious and needs help."

"I'm coming in," she heard a voice say. Crawling through the small opening was Pieter, pulling himself through on his belly. He called out for a stretcher to be put through the hole. Together with Beth they gently laid the woman on it and began to push it through the hole. Hands on the other side pulled it through. Pieter and Beth worked side by side to free the last of the people in their area.

"It's our turn now," Pieter finally said. "I'll be right behind you." Before they could make their way, the other section of the roof caved in surrounding them with dirt. They reached out and held on to each other as the dirt settled around them. At first they could hear no one answering in spite of their calls.

After a while they heard voices on the other side calling to them. "Is there anyone there? Can anyone hear me? Hello. Hello."

"I'm Squadron Leader Pieter Dekker, RAF," Pieter shouted out to them. "I'm with Beth Martin from the United States. We're OK, just buried in a lot of dirt."

"We've got a bloody mess, sir. The building on top of the tunnel was hit with a V-1 and collapsed. There may be another cave in. We'll work as fast as we can. Try to protect yourselves as best you can. It could take time. Should we notify anyone?"

"Squadron Leader Hugh Winchester was in here. If you can find him tell him Pieter and Beth are OK and to notify the authorities. We are both military."

"Will do, sir. I'll try to give you an update as soon as I can."

Beth sat on the earth and looked at Pieter, not able to stand because the clearance was small. Yet he had seemed ten feet tall as he took control of the situation. He looked at her and smiled.

"Did I impress you with my power to get you alone?"

Beth began to laugh in spite of the conditions.

"You'll notice that I got all cleaned up and put on my very best perfume to get ready."

They both sat on the floor in all the dust. The air was rank with odor. Beth reached up to her hair and said "I must really look a fright by now."

"You look beautiful to me," he said. "If you are trying to impress me by staying so calm, it's working."

"Are you always so funny or is it my charm that is working?" she asked.

They both began to laugh.

Pieter said, "I always like to impress pretty women. I'll bet you Hugh is trying his best to get us out of here. He never wants me to be alone with a woman, especially one as beautiful as you."

"Have you known him long?"

"Since my first day at Cotwick University. I came from Austria to attend school here. Both my dad and older brother attended Cotwick. I left home shortly before Hitler went into Austria. When that happened my dad discouraged me from coming home at first. Later he insisted that I not come home. He didn't want me forced to join the German Army. I met Hugh and Charles, another good friend, the first day. The families of both of them treated me like their son and made me part of their families."

Beth remembered what she had heard about Pieter from Eileen about his past. She wasn't sure what to say.

"You must think a lot about your family and worry about them."

"More than anyone will ever know," he told her. His voice was soft and sad. She wished she could see his face. The light making its way through the cracks in the walls was very dim around them. From time to time they thought they could hear voices. They couldn't be sure.

"Hugh knows we're here. He'll pester everyone until they get us out." After a moment or so he said, "Tell me about your childhood and your family."

"Well, that might take me two or three weeks. I guess I could start. My home is in Glenridge, Michigan. It's a town set on a hillside with a river that runs through it. My grandfather and my uncle probably built half of the town. I lived with my mom and dad and two sisters. We were always a close family doing everything together until the war started. One sister joined the Army Nurse Corp, and I joined the WASP'S. My youngest sister is still in college."

"Did your father build houses?"

"No, he was a bookworm who loved history. He chairs the history department at Glenridge University. He and my mother met the first day of college. Tell me about your family."

"I grew up in the foothills of the Alps in a small town outside of Vienna. I have . . . . .I had an older brother. He and my father were both taken to a German work camp because my father refused to fly the German flag on the top of the small department store he owned."

"Do you know what happened to them?" Beth asked. "And what about your mother?"

"I have learned recently that my father and brother were killed: my father when he refused to do any work for Hitler and my brother when he went to aid my father as he was dying."

Beth reached out in the dark and took his hand. "I'm so sorry," she said quietly.

"I heard that my mother and sister-in-law and two boys moved in together. Another baby was on the way. I heard they eventually moved to a small apartment in Vienna. I know nothing more about what happened to them." Beth could hear a sob in his voice.

As they sat there quietly in the dark, they thought they heard someone calling to them. They couldn't make out any words very clearly, but they definitely heard voices.

"We're still here. It's Beth and Pieter. We're still here." Pieter began to shout.

They got no response.

Beth was curious about Pieter's past. When he talked about his parents she felt he had more that he wanted to say but the sound of what they thought were voices had interrupted their conversation. She decided to take a chance.

"Have you and Hugh always been close friends?" she asked.

"Hugh and I will always be friends. There were three of us . . . . ." Pieter paused and then went on. "Charles was the other one in our trio. We became best friends from the first day of classes. Hugh was a local boy whose father had gone to school at Cotwick. Charles came from Birmingham. They were best friends. They were roommates with one of the largest rooms in the dorm. The school was crowded that year so their room was made into a triple. I was the third person and I really felt like a third wheel at first. But they never let me feel that way. Hugh's family was well-to-do and very social. I was invited to every social event at their home. They never made me feel like an outsider. Charles's dad owned a very large department store in Birmingham. His dad had also graduated from Cotwick. His roommate had been Hugh's dad. When my dad came from Austria to visit me, the three men had lots in common. Both families are very good to me."

"Did you become good friends right away?" Beth asked.

"Actually, we did. We were an unlikely trio. Charles was extremely handsome, so I'm told, and very, very smart. He was sophisticated in a very friendly way. I never heard him say an unkind word about anyone. He was tall with dark hair. When you first met him you might have thought he was very quiet. But he could entertain a room full of people with his wit and humor. As you know, Hugh is different, a little shorter and with blonde hair. I think he loved every girl he ever met and they loved him back. He was a stranger to no one. And there was me. At first I felt like a country bumpkin that came from another world. I wasn't as smart as Charles or had the social skills of Hugh. But somehow or other we became best friends. When the Germans began to bomb London, they enlisted in the RAF. I joined with them since I couldn't return home to Austria. We managed to stay together through training and came to Livingston together. I would give my life for Hugh as I'm sure he would for me. We didn't have the opportunity to do that for Charles." Pieter sat quietly.

After a pause Beth said, "I guess he didn't make it back to base."

"No."

"I know how it feels to lose someone," Beth said quietly.

"Did you lose someone special?" Pieter asked.

"The boy I planned to marry. He lived next door to us when we were growing up. He was a fighter pilot. He was killed at Pearl Harbor."

Pieter reached out to take her hand.

"Tell me about Charles," Beth asked.

Pieter sat quietly for a moment and softly began to talk. "It was the worse day of my life. It haunts me more than the day I heard about the death of my father and brother. Somehow I seem to remember in detail everything that happened. I keep wondering what I should have done differently to change the day. I haven't been able to talk about it."

"Maybe it would help to talk," Beth said.

Pieter paused before continuing. "Charles pulled me off my bunk and onto the floor during the night. I had not heard the alarms going off. I had been dreaming of home. In my dream I was a small boy hiking in the Austrian Alps with my mother, father, and older brother. It was a gorgeous day. In the distance I could see the snow-covered high Alps. There was no snow at our level. The grass was green all around and the sun was bright. The fields were filled with beautiful blooming edelweiss. I could see the shepherds tending the sheep. The sheep were wearing small bells so they could be located easily if they got lost. The bells sounded so pleasant and then they got very loud . . . . then louder . . . . and even louder! I woke up and realized that what I thought were bells was the alarm signal going off. Hugh was yelling at me to hurry.

'Come on, Pete, get up. We gotta move fast. Come on,' he told me.

"In a matter of seconds we were dressed and out the door rushing to our planes. Very soon German bombers would be over the base. Our goal was to fly a Liberator II bomber to a safe place until the bombing ended. The crews had the planes ready. In a matter of minutes I was in the air. It was a dark night. After I flew thru the clouds I could see a million stars. I remember wondering how it was possible that up in the sky the world was so peaceful. Below there was so much death, so much destruction. Soon I received a message to return to base.

"The three of us made our way back to the barracks. 'What's with you, man? You were really zonked out. You must have been having a dream.

Was she beautiful? Does she have a sister?' Both Hugh and Charles took turns questioning me.

'Actually, it was a nice dream. I was back home, hiking with my family,' I told them.

'Have you heard from them lately?' Charles asked me.

'Not a word. More and more I think I should head back home to find them.'

'Don't do that, old buddy,' Hugh said. 'One step into Austria and the Germans will have you captured in five minutes.'

"We decided to try to get a few hours more sleep before getting ready to make a bombing raid later in the day. At 9 a.m. we reported for a briefing and found that the target area selected that day was fogged in. The flight would have to wait until later to take off. We checked our planes, chatted with the crew and went back to the barracks to wait for the weather.

'Does it ever seem to you that we fight this war only when the weather lets us?' Hugh asked that day.

'Yea, but if we were on the ground we'd have to fight thru the fog,' Charles added. He told me I seemed very quiet that day and I told him that I thought the dream I had made me homesick. I told him how much I needed to know if my family was still alive.

"The dream I had was so real it made me homesick. I remember feeling a great heaviness inside of me.

'You should remember that your dad really wanted you to stay here instead of going home. He's a wise man. I think he must have been able to tell what was going to happen,' Hugh told me.

'Knowing that doesn't make it any easier,' I remember telling him. I lay down on my cot, pulled the blanket over my head and pretended to sleep.

"At noon we went into the mess hall for lunch. That's when I met Brenda. She and two of her team had just brought some new planes to the base. We talked about any changes that had been on the planes. Hugh was flirting with one of them and I got acquainted with Brenda. While we were talking, we heard the alarms signal for us to go to our planes.

'Fog's lifted. See you later,' we told them as we left.

"By the time I got to my plane the flight crew was beginning to board. I could hear them talking. 'Did you bring . . . . .' and 'Don't forget . . . . .'

filled the air. It seemed like most all of them carried some good luck charm that gave them some comfort to have with them.

"I checked in with each member of the crew over the intercom. I went over the checklist and waited for the signal to start my engines. This would be the sixth raid this particular crew and I had been on together. So far, everything had gone well. I moved the plane in line to wait for the take-off signal. Off we went into the early afternoon sky. I knew the targets that day were factories in France. I tried to forget that I would probably kill some innocent French workers.

"The first part of the flight was uneventful. You know the setup inside the bomber: the pilot, co-pilot, navigator, and bombardier were all located in the front cabin. Each gunner was in his own lonely place: one under the belly of the plane, one in the nose, one in the tail. There were waist gunners on each side of the plane and one on top. Since you fly bombers you probably know how lonely it was for each of them.

"Stay alert,' I told the men. I began the routine countdown. 'We're within 100 miles of target.' 'We're 50 miles from target.'

"As we got closer I heard one of the gunners call out 'We've got flack straight ahead.'

"I called out the usual alert to the men: 'Incoming flack! Man your stations. Stay alert. It's going to be bumpy.'

"The bombardier got ready to open the bomb bay doors. The plane jerked. We swerved to try to avoid the anti-aircraft fire coming from the ground. We fought to maintain control of the plane.

"After what seemed like an eternity, the bombardier announced, 'Bomb doors open! Target in sight! Alignment good! Almost there! Almost there! Bomb's away!'

"I felt the flack hit the plane. I lost control for a moment. The plane began to elevate up and down. It began to swerve to and fro. Ralph, the co-pilot and I fought hard to steady the plane. After a couple of minutes that seemed like hours, the plane rocked a little less. I knew we had been hit badly in the back of the plane. I knew we had incurred other damage. I contacted each gunner for a report.

"The nose gunner, Harold, reported he was OK but he could see a few holes in the plane. Nothing appeared to be too bad. From the belly of the plane I learned of some damage and that Roger had been hit. 'It's just my arm, I'll be OK' he told me. Richard, the waist gunner on the left side of the plane seemed to be OK. The waist gunner on the right side, Joe, advised me he had been hit. His voice sounded weak. Kevin, the gunner in the dorsal turret on top of the plane said he saw damage in the back, but he was OK. I tried three times to reach Howie, the tail gunner. Howie did not respond. I remember the silence on the plane as the men waited to hear the report from each station.

"I ordered Richard to go back to check on Howie. I will never forget his voice as he reported back to me.

'Flight Lieutenant, it's bad! Real bad! There's no tail! Almost all of the tail section is gone. Howie's gone too.'

"The training I had took control of me. I had no time to be concerned. 'Get back away from the opening. Go back to your station.' I commanded.

"I knew I had to concentrate on trying to bring the plane down safely. I wasn't sure the plane *could* land at all in its condition. If I brought it down in France or I ordered the men to parachute, *if* they made a safe landing, I knew they probably would be captured immediately. Each minute seemed an hour long. Luckily the fuel tanks had not been hit. The plane had been damaged other ways. Ralph and I used every skill we had to try to hold the plane steady. He checked off the miles one at a time. Finally at last, we saw the English Channel. If we ditched in the water we had a chance that some of the crew might survive and get picked up by the British fishermen. After a little more time had passed we saw we were approaching the home field. I radioed to base about the condition of my men and the plane. I wanted to try to land the plane but I wasn't sure I could.

"Carefully, we slowed out speed. As the plane touched the ground it bounced, skipped, slid. Finally it came to a stop. The Air Rescue Team came immediately along with fire trucks and ambulances. They all rushed to help. Some started immediately to spray the plane with fire repellant; others ran to rescue the crew. One by one we were evacuated out of the area. When I stopped to look at the back of the plane I could not believe we had flown so many miles in that condition and been able to touch down. The tail section of the plane was really gone. I stood in amazement looking at the carnage. But I felt that my heart would break. I had a picture in my mind of Howie's body floating away. I still have dreams about it. If I could have flown a little faster or slower or geed or hawed or even got to a higher elevation, could I have saved Howie? That nightmare stays with me."

211

Beth could hear the anguish in his voice. In the dim light she could tell from the slight movements that he had buried his face in his hands. She moved closer to him and put her arms around him.

"Beth, I am responsible for Howie's death. He was one of my crew. I wasn't able to save him."

"Pieter, you saved the lives of all the other men aboard the plane. It wasn't you who took his life. It was the gunners who shot from the ground," Beth told him.

"In my saner moments I know that," Pieter told Beth. "But I do keep reliving the time over and over. But my bad day wasn't over even then. After a briefing as I walked back to the barracks I learned that Charles had not made it back from the raid. No one could tell me anything at first. To feel responsible for one death was bad but to also lose one of my best friends made everything worse."

"Did you ever learn what happened to Charles?"

"Yes. His plane was hit and exploded in the air. The whole crew was lost."

Beth sat quietly with her arms around him for a time. There were no words to be said.

After a few minutes, Pieter turned to her and asked "Do you want to try to sleep?" You can lie on your coat and cover with mine," he told her.

"I don't think I'll be able to sleep. I am rather drowsy though. Maybe I'll just close my eyes for a few minutes."

"Lean on me," he said, putting his arms around her. With the time differences and their travel across the Atlantic, Beth hadn't slept for more than twenty-four hours. She seemed to go to sleep immediately.

Beth slowly opened her eyes. It took her a moment to remember where she was. The horror of the bombing flashed before her eyes. She had lived through it. She was safe. She was in a tunnel. She suddenly realized that she was lying on a cold, damp, musty floor. She was lying next to Pieter who had taken off his coat and placed it over both of them. She raised herself on one elbow and tried to look at him in the very dim light. As she watched him for a moment she remembered what she had heard about his life. What a horrid position he is in, she thought. No way for him to help his family; and his job is to drop bombs that kill both good and bad people. She was glad the United States did not have this destruction and that her family was safe. She felt great empathy for Pieter. She leaned over him and gently let her lips touch his. His arms suddenly reached out and pulled her close to him. They kissed with feeling.

Beth pulled away from him. "I'm sorry if I woke you."

"I'm not sorry."

They kissed again.

As they drew apart they could see small shafts of light entering the tunnel.

"Daylight is here. The rescue crews will be able to move faster now," Pieter told her.

"Do you have any idea of how long we've been here," she asked.

"I can't see my watch very well. I would guess at least six or seven hours. It was about 11 o'clock when the bombing started. They'll probably start drilling holes through the debris to get us out."

Almost as he said it they heard the sound of drills: one almost overhead and one coming in from the side.

"We'll have to be careful where we sit or we'll get covered with dirt from the drilling," he told Beth.

It was too noisy to talk above the drills so they sat and waited. Finally they could look up and see that the hole above them was almost clear. Voices soon called down the shaft. "Is anyone down there? Can you hear me? Hello. Hello."

Pieter called back. "We hear you. You've broken through a ceiling. I'm Squadron Leader Dekker, RAF, with American Beth Martin. We're not injured. Just tired, hungry and thirsty. What's the situation?"

"Sir, we're coming to get you through the side. Because of conditions we have to do some bracing as we go along. It'll probably be another couple of hours. Can you hear the drilling from the other side?" Pieter answered that they could hear it. "Good, that means we're in the right place. We're going to send down some water and rations. Stand away to receive them."

Pieter and Beth smiled at the word *stand*. They were lucky to be able to crawl. They crawled out of the way as the K-rations came tumbling down the hole. This was followed by a small canteen of water. Beth had never seen K-rations before. She opened the package to find two small tins – one was ground pork and the other can had some kind of processed cheese. She saw a small packet of biscuits, a fruit bar and a packet of powder to mix with water to make a flavored drink.

"Welcome to one of London's finest restaurants," Pieter joked.

"My compliments to the chef," she said as she reached for her biscuits. "I've never seen such a fine menu."

They sat and waited. The hole from above had let some light come in and the air quality began to improve.

"Tell me about the year you were sixteen," Beth asked him. They spent the morning learning about each other. She told him about her family life in Glenridge and he told her about his life in Rossbach, Austria.

"It's a small village about thirty miles from Vienna and up in the Alps. In the summer many tourists come to hike and fish. In the winter they come to ski. At one time my family home had a small barn attached so they did not have to go outside during the blizzard season. My father got rid of the barn and enlarged the big house which is made of stone. Window boxes are on all the windows and in the summer they are filled with red geraniums. My father was mayor of the village and also opened the first department store in Rossbach. It has a basement, first and second floors. My brother managed the store. Everyone in Austria is musical and loves to dance."

While Beth and Pieter talked they could hear noises coming from all directions and knew their rescuers were getting closer. Finally, they heard a call, "Stand back! We're making the final cut." The dirt fell away and they saw full daylight.

They crawled from their safe place to the opening. Their bodies were stiff as they tried to stand, and the medic insisted that they be taken to the hospital to be checked out. Beth was taken by ambulance to a hospital staffed by American doctors.

Beth heard Eileen calling to her. "Are you OK Beth? I'll see you at the hospital." The medics would not slow down for anyone. Pieter was taken back to the base hospital. They had no chance to say goodbye.

After Beth was checked out she met Eileen who had been waiting for her. A car was waiting to take them both back to Livingston Field.

"I've been so worried about you," Eileen told her.

"I'm really fine," Beth said. "And they cleared me to fly. Do you know when we're scheduled to leave?"

"Tomorrow morning as far as I know. They did tell me the time was subject to change. Seems the two men we brought over are doing something very important. One of the officers I talked with was impressed that we had flown them over."

"Do you know where Pieter is?" Beth asked Eileen.

"Brenda said he was taken to the base hospital and released for duty. She said something big must be going on because they are making more bombing raids. Brenda said that apparently she wouldn't be seeing Hugh much for the next couple of weeks because of some big mission. I guess that will include Pieter, too."

"Speaking of Pieter," Eileen went on, "did you know that he came back into the tunnel to rescue you? We had all gotten out. When we looked for you, we couldn't find you. Pieter said not to worry, he'd find you and he rushed back in. Hugh said Pieter is the most courageous man he knows."

"I want to tell him thanks and tell him goodbye. Do you think I could find him if I go look for him?"

"The base is in a lock-down status tonight. We have to stay in our quarters. I told you something big seems to be happening around here. Brenda says it's never been like this before."

Beth was subdued as she lay in bed that night. She remembered how she felt when they kissed. Now she might never see him again. *I hate war, I hate war, I hate war*, she thought as she tried to get some sleep.

As soon as the plane left London, Beth and Eileen's passengers opened their brief cases and worked for most of the flight home. The men, Mr. Shulte and Mr. Cleary, both had asked Beth about her ordeal. They looked worried and serious and wanted to get to work. Beth was quiet and Eileen didn't press her for any details.

Beth and Eileen had good weather for the flight home from London. Upon landing in Washington, Beth told Eileen goodbye and headed back to Sweetwater, Texas and reported immediately to Mrs. Grant. Mrs. Grant wanted to hear about everything that had happened, from the actual flights to Beth's experience in the tunnel, and her general overall impressions. She suggested Beth take a few days off. If she could find transportation, maybe she could go home. Beth said she'd like that.

She knew getting to Chicago was easy. There were many flights each day to the Chicago area and she felt certain she could get on one of them. She called Chuck at the Glenridge Air Field to ask if he still had flights to Chicago and he did. He arranged for Dave to meet her the next day. Next, she called home to tell them she was almost on her way.

"Beth, my darling Beth. We have been so worried about you," Emma told her daughter. "Mrs. Grant called to let us know about your ordeal in London. We were so worried. We're so glad you are safe. It'll be so wonderful to see you."

Beth threw a few things in her bag and left for the airport.

Dave greeted Beth with a hug when he saw her. He seemed almost in awe of her and her flying experience. She told him about the long flight to London.

"Did you have any interference from the German aircraft?" he asked her.

"No. We were in constant communication with the air stations and they kept us on a safe path."

"What was it like at the air field? Did you see much war activity?"

Beth knew she shouldn't talk about her activities so she answered in general terms and switched the conversation to Glenridge. Soon they touched down and Beth was greeted by her family. It felt really good to be home. She took a long bubble bath, and slept in her own bed in her own private room. It had been a long time since she had such luxuries. The next morning her mother brought her breakfast in bed and the two of them visited the rest of the day. When Annie asked her if she'd like to join Annie and her friends that evening, Beth declined..

"I'll try to see people later. I will really enjoy just having family time," Beth told her.

Beth could see that her mom and dad looked a little worried about her so she tried to reassure them that she had a very hectic schedule for the past few months and was just tired. Beth did enjoy having the old family routine back – everyone telling about their day at the dinner table, her father going in to hear the news after dinner, and doing dishes with Annie. Beth was anxious to hear about Cathy and Cathy's recovery.

The next evening Annie asked her if she had met anyone interesting. Beth smiled and said, "I think you mean have I met any interesting men. Yes, I have. I have met many. I have danced with many. I have flown in formation with many. Now, tell me little sister, how is Tom and is he still number one in your life."

"He sure is," Annie told her. "I haven't heard from him for almost a month. I'll probably get a lot of mail real soon."

"Were Mom and Dad terribly upset when they heard about my London experience?" Beth asked.

"Mom went to her room and Dad went into the library. I think they went to pray for your safety. Were you very scared?"

"It all happened very fast. We didn't have time to be scared. We just had to act. Come on, let's get the folks and I'll tell you about it."

Annie made a fresh pot of coffee and the family sat together as Beth told them about her assigned trip to London, the trip to the pub, the fun they were having, and finally, hearing the alarms and going into the tunnel. She told them about leaving her group to help the woman with the baby and how everyone worked to get people out. She told them that Pieter, one of their group had come back to get her and they were stranded for hours before being dug out.

"How did you spend your time?" Annie asked.

"We slept for part of it. I had been up for more than 24 hours and was really tired. And it was very dark in the tunnel. Dark, dirty, damp and stinky. The next morning the rescuers bored a hole through the roof and dropped us food and water and soon we were rescued."

"Tell me about Pieter." Annie asked. "Is he married? Did you both fall in love with each other while you were in the tunnel?"

"Annie, you're such a romantic. He is an Austrian who was in school in London and joined the RAF. He's flown many missions. He flew on another one just a few hours after we were released from the hospital. Dark, dreary tunnels with bombs dropping overhead is not a very romantic setting, little sister."

"Still . . . . . . well, I'll have to think on it. Do you have his address so I can write and thank him for taking care of you?"

"No, we didn't even say goodbye after it was over. He went on his flight and I went on mine."

As she prepared for bed that night she heard a knock on her door. "Hey, Beth, spring is almost upon us. If it's a nice day tomorrow I think I'll play hooky and go fishing. Want to join me?" her dad asked.

"Dad, I'd love that. Wake me up early."

Beth sat quietly as her dad drove them to the lake the next morning. At every base she had been at in the past couple of years, everything was hectic and frantic. At least she thought it was till she went to London and learned what hectic and frantic really meant.

As they drove along the river to get to the lake she marveled at the serenity of the scenery. "It's truly beautiful here, Dad. I love seeing the trees early in the season. They are a different shade of green. Look at the flowers that are already blooming. Look at the summer activity already on the river Look, there's an oriole that just flew in a tree."

"I'm glad you can still recognize nice things, Beth. Now, let's go fishing. I told Mother I'd bring home dinner. She laughed at me and said she'd be fixing chicken. Why do you think she said that?" he asked with a laugh.

They talked mainly about what was happening at the university and in the family. Finally, Albert said, "I think I'm doing all the talking. Tell me how you really are. Do you still feel you made the right choice to join the WASP's? Is flying still important to you?"

"Dad, I do think I made the right choice for me at the time. I still love to fly. But sometimes I feel something – well, I don't know what to call it. I still love to be in the clouds. You can't believe what our world looks like until you see it from the sky. Yet, sometimes I feel like flying is not enough for my life any more. I hate the thought that some of the bombers I flew were used to kill so many people. You can't believe what all the bombing in London has done to the homes and the people. Still they don't give up their hopes for a better future. Maybe always spending your time doing what *you* want to do is not the right way to live. Maybe there is something I could do to help others. I just don't know what that might be. I guess I'd better stay with what I know I can do until I make some decisions."

"War is demanding. It calls us to do many things we would rather not do. Some of the men who are fighting will never be able to live a normal life again. This war will probably be over in a year. You'll have time to decide what you want to do. Whatever you decide, I'm sure you'll do what is best for you. Your mother and I will support you all the way." They went home and had chicken for dinner. The fish all got away.

The next morning Beth got up early and went to sit on the swing on the front porch. Her mom came out and asked Beth if she would like to walk into town to the donut shop for coffee. Beth said she'd like that.

As they walked along, Emma said to Beth, "You seem very quiet this trip. I'm not surprised after all you have been through in London on top of living and fighting the war with planes and supplies all the time. Would talking about it be helpful to you?"

"I don't know," Beth answered. They continued to walk in silence. Then Beth spoke, "I guess it's me, not the war that has me confused."

"Can you talk about it? I'll just listen. Sometimes that helps." After walking in silence for a block or so, Emma asked, "Is it personal? Does it have to do with mixed feelings about Robbie and Pieter?"

Beth stopped walking and looked at her mother. "How did you know?"

"Tell me about it. Tell me about Pieter, who he really is."

"I don't know, Mom, I don't know. I've only spent time with him twice. Once in Seattle when I met him and then in London. We were introduced by Brenda who had come to Seattle from London. Pieter was in Seattle with his commander attending meetings. In Seattle he was very polite. He seemed rather quiet and sad. We shared one dance and we both went back to our barracks. He said he hoped we'd see each other again some day, and that was that. We both left Seattle the next day. When Eileen and I got to London the first person we saw was Brenda who insisted we join her that evening to go to the pub. Brenda's boyfriend is Hugh who is Pieter's best friend. Pieter joined us a little later. And you know the rest of the story."

"What makes Pieter different? I'm sure you met many men in the clubs and pubs."

"I don't know, Mom. At first I thought it was because when we danced he held me the same way Robbie did, you know, the way Miss Ethel taught us. The hand on the lady's back had to be firm. It felt so natural and good. I don't know if it was because of Pieter or because it reminded me of Robbie. Yet, when I thought about it I saw Pieter's face, not Robbie's. I didn't ever expect to see Pieter again. When he walked into the pub in London I felt very happy to see him. I wasn't sure he'd even remember me. Yet when I saw him come to help rescue me I thought he was ten feet tall. Someone who would take care of me."

Beth and her mother got their coffee and donuts and sat at the table. Beth continued talking.

"When the two of us were alone in the dark we leaned against a pile of debris. We couldn't stand up because there wasn't enough room. I fell asleep and when I woke up I could just make out the features on his face. I don't know why but I felt the need to kiss him. I just really pecked at his lips. He was awake and pulled me close and we really kissed. A real kiss. Mom, I felt something inside. Yet we were separated as soon as we were rescued. We both had early flying times. I came back to the states. I know I'll never see him again. We didn't even exchange addresses. He probably has a girl in every town. Yet if anything were to happen to him I'd really feel like I was a jinx to flyers. First Robbie and then Pieter. Worst of all is that I will probably never know what happens to him. Maybe that's OK. I don't really know him, I guess."

"What do you know about him?"

"He went to London to go to Cotwick University where his dad and brother went to school. Hitler invaded Austria and his dad wouldn't let Pieter go home because he was afraid Pieter would either be taken prisoner or forced to join the German Army. His dad and brother were taken to a work camp. Pieter told me they both were killed there."

"What about his mother?"

"She and his sister-in-law and kids moved in together and moved to Vienna. No one knows anything more."

"It must be so hard to have a worry like that hanging over your head."

"Pieter and his two best friends, Hugh and Charles, joined the RAF when London was first bombed. They all flew bombers. On one flight, Charles was shot down and killed. On the same flight Pieter's plane had the tail of his plane shot off and he lost his tail gunner. He managed to land the plane."

"Sounds like he is a good pilot and a caring man."

On their way as they walked home, Beth said, "Was it terribly wrong for me to kiss him?"

"Beth, you've heard many times about your father kissing me just after we met. And that kiss has lasted us for many years. You did nothing wrong. Kissing is good. Have you tried to locate him? It wouldn't hurt to let him know you are thinking about him. Anyone who has lost their family in this war deserves whatever happiness he or she can find. But Beth, if the kiss made you feel disloyal to Robbie, I strongly urge you to let go of those feelings. Robbie admired your strength to do whatever you wanted to do or needed to be done. He would want you to move on with your life."

The next morning Beth was awakened by her dad.

"Beth, just a bit of news for you. The Allied Forces have invaded the coast of France. This shows how determined the United States is to win this war. This will be our first step on our way to Germany."

Later that day she received a telegram from Mrs. Grant advising her to report to Andrews AFB in Washington, D.C. ASAP. Beth left Glenridge as quickly as she could and reported to Marian Turner. Mrs. Turner advised her that she needed be on standby, ready to fly any VIP anywhere they needed to be. It seemed like everything had to be done that minute. Washington, D.C. was a very busy city. The only good thing about it was that she was closer to Cathy and they could get together on occasion.

*   *   *

The new year began very slowly for Cathy in most ways. Her duties at the hospital had been geared to her strength, stamina and her therapy. She didn't have official therapy any more. At the doctor's suggestion she still worked out with the equipment once or twice a week so her leg wouldn't stiffen on her. At first, Cathy's duties had been administrative, which Cathy had not liked. She worked half days with patients and half with administrative duties. Now she was full time with the patients. She hadn't been back in surgery yet. That was scheduled now so to her it meant the doctors were sure she had made a full recovery. She still had massive scars on her legs. A good pair of silk stockings would cover that. If she could get silk stockings.

The war in Europe had taken a turn in favor of the allies after the invasion of D-Day. In the Pacific the Japanese seemed to be pulling back. It made Cathy shudder as she thought of all the civilians both in Germany and Japan who would probably lose their lives before it was over. These thoughts lay heavy on her mind as she thought about it. *I wonder if both wars will have to be completely over before Mike comes home,* she thought. She got so lonesome for him. *What would happen when he did come home? I feel pretty certain he will not want to make the military his career. Will he want to settle in Virginia? Could I be happy if I don't live in Glenridge?* They had not had a chance to talk about serious things like that. They were just so happy to be together.

One day as many nurses as could be spared were called to a meeting. A colonel from the Army Medical Corp began to speak. He told the nurses he had some good news for them.

"We are aware that you women in the Army Nurse Corp were placed in a very bad working situation as it pertains to your status. You were not civilians, nor were you Army. Yet you managed to perform heroically both on and behind the battle line. You could not officially make decisions even though you were capable of doing so and often needed to do so. We have heard that some of you suffered abuse from the Corpsmen because you were a woman. Technically, they should have reported to a senior nurse. Because of your skills and medical training you needed to make those medical decisions. The corpsmen should have been there to assist you. We are aware that while many of them did respect you and your skills, some did not because they felt that no man should take orders from a woman.

Some men said that until it was written on paper, they would not do so." The colonel raised a piece of paper in the air. "Nurses, here is that piece of paper."

A cheer went up from the group. After they quieted down, the colonel went on.

"Congress has just made the Army Nurse Corp a part of the U.S. Army. You are entitled to all the same benefits of medical treatment, education, pay ratings and commissions, etc. as any other military man. A regular Army nurse will be commissioned as a Second Lieutenant. If you serve or served as a Chief Nurse, you will be commissioned as a First Lieutenant. Nursing Directors will be commissioned as a Captain. You will receive the proper insignia to put on your uniforms so that you will be identified properly. On behalf of the President of the United States, U.S. Government and the U.S. Army I congratulate each of you on your accomplishments and your contribution to helping us win this war." He left the auditorium amidst many cheers.

Cathy was summoned shortly after to go to the Colonel's office. Mrs. Barber, now Major Barber, the director Cathy had consulted about returning to work, was in his office.

With a few short words Cathy discovered that the Colonel knew all about her nursing history as well as her injuries and recovery. He started to question her about them. Did she feel strong? Did she tire easy? And so on. Then the conversation turned to Cathy's career path. Did she plan to stay in the Army? (She had decided to wait until her husband came home. When he got home they would plan their lives together.) Did she especially want to be an Operating Room Nurse? (I will go wherever I'm needed. I'll help anywhere I can.) Major Barber sat quietly. Cathy wondered where all this was heading. *Have I slacked off somewhere? Have I caused harm to someone?*

Major Barber spoke. "We don't want to give you any assignment until you feel you have completely recovered. Do you feel you have?"

"Yes, maam, I do. I've been working some extra hours and I still feel fine. Would a new assignment mean going back to the Pacific?"

"I know you're anxious to get closer to your husband. No, the assignment would not include going back to the war zone."

"We are promoting you to become a director of the operating room and surgical nursing unit. Do you feel up to this responsibility?"

Cathy was quiet for a moment and then spoke.

"I'm very pleased to know you think I am capable of this position because I haven't been here very long. I know that I have worked hard to keep learning new things. Yes, I would be honored to accept this position. I promise you I'll do my very best."

The colonel placed the new Captain bar on her shoulder and shook her hand. "Good luck to you, Captain Goodman."

Cathy could hardly wait to write to tell Mike about her promotion. Of course, she had to call home to tell her family. And she had to call Ray and Joan Goodman.

The mail service had improved a little. She seemed to get more letters from Mike. He told her how proud he was that she was now a captain and capable of handling so many new responsibilities. She, along with everyone else, was encouraged that the allies in Europe were pushing toward Germany more each day. In Japan, the end seemed years away. *Maybe the government will send the army from Europe to help in the Pacific*, she thought.

*   *   *

The day was bright and sunny. As Annie walked home from the bus stop she saw the tulips starting to bloom in the yards. The yellow forsythia bushes were blooming and tints of pink were appearing on the blossoms of the fruit trees. *I do believe winter is over* she thought. Today was the day that she had her review about her student teaching. It had gone well. The principal of the high school had been very complimentary about her enthusiasm and teaching skills. Though nothing formal was said, she felt pretty confident that she would receive an offer to teach. *Maybe today I'll get a letter from Tom. That would make the day perfect.* It had now been weeks since she had heard from him. As she went up the steps on the porch she could see the mailbox overflowing with mail. *Yes*, yes, *yes*, she thought. *Today is the day I hear from him.* She pulled all the mail from the box, opened the door and called in, "I'm home."

She laid her books and purse on the hall table and began to look at the mail. Suddenly she saw the stamp on top of the bundle of letters – letters she had written to Tom. **M.I.A. RETURN TO SENDER.** Annie gave a loud cry and began to shout. Her parents came running.

"It can't be so. It can't be so. He can't be missing in action," she cried. "Someone knows where he is."

Albert and Emma tried to console their daughter. She wanted no part of consolation. She ran to her room and slammed the door shut. When she didn't come down for dinner Emma fixed a tray for her and left it outside her bedroom door. The next morning Emma carried the untouched tray back to the kitchen.

Emma decided to take action. She walked into the bedroom pulled up the shades and sat on the bed. Annie's head was buried in her pillows.

"Annie, you don't have enough information to assume the worst. We must try to find out something. He might have gotten separated from his outfit and they'll connect up soon."

Annie reluctantly agreed. "I know he's alive somewhere, Mom. Just like Beth knew Robbie was dead, I know Tom is alive. I'll keep writing to him."

The time was only a brief respite. About two weeks later another bundle of letters sent to him was returned with the notation – ***M.I.A. PRESUMED DEAD.***

"No, no," Annie screamed. "It can't be so. I would know if he was dead. Why are these people doing this? He's OK. I know he's coming back."

She decided to take action. She called Cathy asking her to see if Cathy's father-in-law could get information on Tom. He was only able to identify his unit as one that performed *special services*. Annie didn't know what that meant. She wrote to her senator and congressman. They sent her lists of names of K.I.A. servicemen. It shocked her to see how many men had lost their life. She could not find his name.

Annie also didn't know the names of any members of his family. There hadn't been time. She was sure he would be back. He just couldn't be dead. Part of her would die along with him if he were dead. She would know. He just couldn't be dead, she repeated to herself over and over. A small voice of reason in her head said part of her was dying already.

Annie had a moment of hope when she heard about the D-Day landing in France, maybe now she would hear from Tom. But no letters came.

Annie refused to attend her graduation ceremony or the party that was held as usual on Lincoln Boulevard. She withdrew more and more. She rarely left her room, skipping breakfast and lunch most days. She would reluctantly join the family for dinner. Then she would hurry back to her room and close the door. Emma and Albert didn't know what to do.

Their minister offered special prayers. Doc Jameson came to visit her. She refused to see anyone, even Rosemary and Marge. The days became weeks and the weeks became months.

*   *   *

In Washington, D.C. each day seemed more hectic than the day before. Beth helped out in the offices when she wasn't flying. She helped to schedule the flights as well as many administrative duties. After D-Day the whole country seemed to be reawakened to the war effort and it was like everyone could smell victory. One day when things were not quite as hectic, she decided to approach Mrs. Turner with a subject that the other WASP'S seemed to be talking about.

"Mrs. Turner, is it true that that the WASP'S program may be disbanded in the very near future?"

Mrs. Turner bowed her head slightly and in a soft voice said, "We haven't had any official word yet. It is very possible."

"What happened?" Beth asked. "I guess I haven't been listening to much news lately."

"The problem started when a bill was presented to Congress to give women full military status. This would mean insurance coverage, hospitalization, burial benefits and Veteran's status. A group, a large group, is insisting that this must not happen. They are holding protests at Congress to defeat the bill. Now they are starting to win over the press. All the Washington papers, The Post, Star, Times-Herald, Daily News and Time magazine have led the opposition to the bill. They picture the women of the WASP's as silly, pretty, participants in a frivolous program that has wasted millions of dollars. The New York Times, New York Herald, and the Boston Globe have not agreed. They have favored militarization."

"I am proud of the women who have served in this program," Mrs. Turner continued. "Yet, I do have some disappointments as well. Many of us who started this program were sure it *could* work. One concern we had was whether or not the men in the military and the government *would* let it succeed. I'm sure you faced discrimination many times. I can remember the protest rally held outside the gates at Sweetwater that was led by the wives of the pilots when we first started. They could not accept that we were trying to do a job, not look for a husband."

"For the most part, I have always been treated with respect," Beth told her. "Who is this group behind the protest?"

"They are mainly civilian pilots. For one reason or another they were not qualified to meet the very tough physical and mental qualifications to become military pilots. They were given a separate status to keep them on their job but now that women have proved they can do the job, the men are afraid they will be drafted into the Infantry. There have been protests in front of Congress. Many more are planned. Things do not look good for the future of the WASP's. We hoped that once we proved we could do the job, they would see our success. Our statistical records prove that. They should make us part of the military the way it is in England. I no longer feel confident that it will happen. At least not in my lifetime. I think about you young women who have given so much . . . ." Her voice became softer as she paused for a moment.

"I mean no disrespect, Mrs. Turner, but surely you are wrong. I've been on base. Our assignments to fly were made right down the line. I felt like one of the guys. No one doubted my abilities because I was a woman."

"But those are not the men making the decisions. We know our statistics prove we can do the job." She paused for a minute. "I hope I didn't worry you about your future with the WASP's. We believe there still is a slight chance it could continue and it could become part of the military. I have been told that no final decision has been made yet. You do not need to make any long term decisions about what you would do if it is discontinued. One thing we know. The United States is going to win the war. Always remember how much you helped."

"Thank you Mrs. Turner, I will."

Beth thought a lot about what Mrs. Turner had said about her future. She remembered a conversation back in her early days at Sweetwater when one of the women had said that she was sure the government "would kick us out as soon as they had enough men for the jobs". The rest of them saw it as a challenge to prove they could do it; therefore, there would not be a question of not succeeding. *What if Mrs. Turner is right? If I can't fly, what do I want to do? Do I want to go back to Glenridge to prepare to teach?*

Beth thought about all these things over the next few weeks as she went about her duties. She thought a lot about Pieter. One day a few weeks earlier she had taken a chance. She sent him a note addressed to Major Pieter Dekker, Livingston Field, London, England. She knew he probably wouldn't get it with such an incomplete address. She felt like she had to do something. She never heard anything back. She wondered if he even got the letter or did he get it? Maybe he decided not to answer. I'm thinking about him too much, she decided.

One day she returned from a flight to New England. She found a large envelope in her mail from her dad. Some reading material she thought. She had decided she needed a change from the base food and had stopped at a Chinese Restaurant and brought home a small container of Orange Beef and a small container of Pecan Chicken after she couldn't make up her mind which to buy. She took a quick shower, wrapped her hair in a towel, her body in a robe, made a pot of tea and sat down to enjoy her dinner and her mail.

She opened the big envelope from her dad and found two envelopes inside with a note from her dad on top.

> *Beth:*
> *Some interesting reading material. Enjoy it. Dad*

She pulled the note from the top. Suddenly she felt faint. Could it be . . . . ? The envelope on top was addressed to her father from Major Pieter Dekker. She looked at the second envelope. Beth saw only one name . . . . . . *Beth*. Beth began to laugh. She did a small dance around the room. She sat down and tore open the envelope with her name on it.

> *Dear Beth,*
> *If you are reading this it means that I have finally found you. Since I last saw you I have written and mailed you several letters in a vain attempt to find you. Up until now it was a futile effort because the mail either came back to me or I heard nothing from you. I choose to believe it's because you didn't get the letters, not because you didn't want to answer. I won't believe that until I hear it directly from you.*
> *When we were separated so quickly after our rescue from the tunnel I was sure I would see you back at the base. I was unaware that the base was in a lock-down mode. No one could give me any information about you other than you had gone back to the States. I am really sorry we didn't get a chance to say goodbye. I really wanted to know how to stay in touch with*

you. Who knows, maybe you would have let me kiss you one last time.

Anyhow, as I remembered every minute of our brief time together I recalled that you told me your father was a history professor at Glenridge University. I wasn't quite sure if you said Michigan or Minnesota. I am taking a chance. If you get this letter that means I guessed right.

I will never forget you or the time we spent together even if it was under the worst of circumstances. I admired your strength to stay calm. You saw and did what needed to be done with no thought for your own safety. I really wanted to get to know you better. Yet I do realize that you may have a really special person you care about. I don't want to complicate your life.

Still, I can't let go of you without knowing for sure. I felt something really special when we kissed — real feeling. I have convinced myself that you felt something, too. So I have to try to find you.

I know I told you a little about my family. Now that the war appears to be winding down, I know I must change the direction of my life. I need to return to Austria to try to locate my mother, sister-in law, and her three children (if the third baby survived; I heard Elsa was pregnant). I have applied for an early release from the RAF. I had applied for a release a few times before to look for my family. I was always declined, though they did give me an assignment to try to find information about them. That's when I learned my father and brother were dead. Now my request has been approved for discharge in sixty days.

When I first came to London I became good friends with Hugh and Charles. Their parents 'adopted' me as another son. They know I am trying to find you. I'll be at Livingston at the address on the envelope for a few more weeks. If you decide to write to me and it is returned to you, please send it to Hugh's family. I will enclose their address. They will forward it to me.

Right now, I'm not sure just where I will be. I will contact them.

I will not give up trying to find you until you tell me goodbye.

All my love,
Pieter

Beth's eyes filled with tears as she read his letter. *He didn't forget about me. He didn't forget about me. Yes,* she thought, *you are right, Pieter. I did feel something special when I kissed you. Is it love,* she wondered? *It could be. It could be. Maybe it's the beginning of love that needs time to grow.* She read the letter three more times before she put it down.

She turned to the letter from Pieter to her father and opened it. His name and address on the return section of the envelope was the first time she had seen his name in print. She ran her fingers over the writing. She formed a picture in her mind of him sitting at a desk writing it.

It was addressed to:

Professor Martin, History Department
Glenridge University
Glenridge, Michigan USA

Beth reached inside the envelope which her father had already opened.

Professor Martin:
I hope you can help me. My name is Pieter Dekker, Major, RAF, stationed in London. I recently met a young woman named Beth Martin.
She told me her father was a professor at Glenridge University. I am writing you, hoping you are Beth's father and that you can help me locate her. Unfortunately our flying assignments separated us before we could exchange addresses.
I tried sending a letter to Sweetwater, Texas. where I knew she was stationed. It was returned saying I did not have a complete address. I wrote to WASP'S headquarters in Washington, D.C. I had no response.
We have one mutual friend, Brenda; however, Brenda and Beth did not exchange addresses.
Beth spoke very highly of you. She told me that even in the chaos of war, she felt very secure in the love of her parents. I know that it is odd that I am writing to you, her father. My

other endeavors to reach her have failed. You are my last hope to try to find her.

I realize Beth may have a love in her life. If so, I don't want to upset or confuse her. You may use your own judgment about whether or not you should forward on to her the letter I am enclosing. If you decide it is best not to send it would you please take a moment to let me know. Please let me know that she is safe and survived our time spent in the tunnel. I will not trouble you again.

Thank you.

Pieter

Beth read the letter twice. She wished she had a way to phone him. She had an address now. Could she get through? She had no phone in her room. He's probably sleeping, she thought. But now, she did have an address.

She quickly got out her stationery. She sat down at the kitchen table to write to him. Two weeks later Beth returned home to find a letter from Pieter. Very quickly she opened the envelope to read the letter.

Dearest Beth,

What a wonderful surprise was waiting for me tonight when I got back to base. It was a letter from your father. That made it almost as good as being a letter from you. He explained he had received the letter I wrote him and had sent it on to you. He included your address in Washington. I'll owe your father a debt of gratitude for the rest of my life. I'll make it my life's goal to always know where you are.

I am hoping you were not unhappy to get my letter and that you will write to me. The mail is very slow between the countries now but I will anxiously look forward to a letter from you. I have just been summoned to see the Wing Commander. I'll close for now to get this in the mail.

I can't tell you how happy it made me to know you were OK. I will write a note to your father later, thanking him for making my dreams come true.

All my love,

Pieter

He should have my letter by now, Beth thought. She decided to write to him again.

By now, the news about the WASP's program being discontinued was being discussed by all the women with whom Beth served. JoJo was extremely upset. She said she would go lobby Congress. Eileen said she was ready to quit. Ronnie had been located in a hospital. He had been injured and returned to the States. She was anxious to go to him.

*   *   *

When Cathy got back to her apartment after work one summer night she found a telegram under her door. She had a moment of panic as she tore it open.

COMING HOME SOONEST AVAILABLE STOP WILL CALL FROM CALIFORNIA STOP LOVE YOU LOVE YOU MIKE

At first she was excited, elated, happy and walking on air. She telephoned home to tell her family. But as she prepared to call Mike's parents, she began to be concerned. Mike hadn't said in the telegram he was flying to Walter Reed with another ambulance plane. Was something wrong? Mike's mom answered the phone when she called. Joan was joyful he would be coming home but like Cathy felt some apprehension about his home coming. Joan said she would call Ray and call Cathy back. About two hours later, Ray called. He had gone to his contacts. He had no details but apparently Mike and his medical team had been under excessive stress and needed some R&R.

"Ray, you're hiding something. I can tell. Now tell me the truth. Is he wounded? What is going on?"

"Cathy, I'll be honest. It has been very, very bad for him. He has been on the front line for months now without a break. He has lost many members of his crew. He tried to keep a rotating schedule so that each one would get a small break now and then, but he took none for himself. He asked for a small break away from the battle."

Cathy shuddered as she heard the news. She knew how devoted Mike was to his crew. He had made it a point to learn about the families of each member. They had become a family. She also knew that Mike would not agree to leave the area unless he felt that he, Mike, needed to get away. She made arrangements to be off work during the time he would be home.

Joan got on the phone. "Do you want to come here to stay, Cathy? We can move a bed into the sitting room that adjoins the big sun porch. It might be pleasant for him to sit and watch the autumn flowers start to bloom. You can have complete privacy if Mike decides he doesn't want to see anyone."

"Thank you, Joan, I think that's a good idea. Ray will be able to see just how sick Mike is. He'll know if he needs help."

Ray spoke up. "Let us know when and where Mike is arriving. I'll arrange a car to bring you here."

Joan asked if Cathy wanted any of them to make any special arrangements.

"I think you've thought of everything," Cathy told her.

As the plane landed in Washington late the next night Cathy waited anxiously as she watched the passengers come down the stairs from the plane. She spotted him as he stepped out of the cabin of the plane. He looked around. He saw her just as she saw him. Cathy waved both arms in the air and hurried to the bottom of the steps. He threw his duffle bag on the ground and took her in his arms. Finally, as they pulled apart she told him about the car waiting to take them both to Virginia.

"Your folks have invited us to stay with them for a couple of weeks. I hope it's OK."

"Will you be with me?"

"Yes."

"Yes, it's OK with me."

Cathy tried to be brave as if everything was really OK. She hoped Mike couldn't see how distressed she really was. The past months must have been really, really bad, she thought. Mike must have lost thirty pounds or more. His skin color was pasty and his hands never seemed to stop shaking. He must have known she was worried because he squeezed her hands. "I'm going to be all right now," he said.

"I know you are, Mike. I know you are."

If his parents were surprised by his appearance, they never let it show.

Rita spoke up and said, "About time you came home. You're too skinny. You need some of my food to fatten you up."

Mike started to smile as he gave Rita a hug. Turning to Cathy he said, "She said the same thing to me every time I came back home from summer camp or college. Now I know I'm home."

The first week Mike spent long hours sleeping. It was not a restful sleep. It was one of jerks, spasms, calling out in his sleep. Cathy would softly rub his back or his arms until he became quiet. Rita tried to fix his favorite foods. He ate very little at first. When Cathy or his mother would ask if he wanted his dinner on the sun porch, he declined saying he wanted to eat with his family. Ray didn't allow any war talk. They talked about various relatives and neighbors.

Jake, the family's black lab, stayed by Mike's side He even slept on the floor beside Mike's bed at night. One day Cathy asked Mike to walk around the yard outside the porch.

"Doesn't this air feel good," she asked him.

"It smells a lot better than operating rooms," he told her.

A few days later they walked to a nearby park that was beautifully landscaped. It had a play area for children. A ball got away from the children and rolled into their pathway. Mike stopped and picked it up as the children came running to retrieve it. The children took time to stop to pet Jake who was always by Mike's side.

"What's his name, mister?" one asked.

"Jake."

"Can he do tricks?"

"Let's see." Mike put Jake through the usual, sit, stand, stay, shake, roll over, etc. Mike took the ball from the child. He threw it in the air. Jake caught it as it came down.

"Wow, mister, that's sure a smart dog. Do you want to sell him?"

"I don't think so," Mike told him.

Mike seemed to get a little stronger so every day they would take the same walk. Many times they saw the same children playing. One day they sat down on a bench some distance away to watch the children.

"I saw children playing on the islands," Mike said. "Rarely did you see the same kids again."

As they sat quietly Mike began to talk. "I had a very long hard trip back to the Pacific when I left you, first to Los Angeles, then Hawaii, then some larger island and finally in a two-seater plane to my post. It was close to the Marshall Islands. They are considered the outer ring of the Japanese homeland. They were fully occupied by the Japanese army. The islands were used as a supply base and port, especially for the Japanese U-Boat fleet. Our troops were planning an invasion of the islands so we would have a place to refuel our planes. Planes from there could reach the Japanese mainland and return.

"We started to set up a base hospital on the island we were on. The invasion started the next day on a nearby island. The marines invaded on two sides. The battle only lasted a couple of days but we saw so many deaths: Allied troops, civilians, and Japanese. And this was a battle for just one small island. Our crew worked around the clock. When we ran out of blood we all rolled up our sleeves to give blood. The air was so hot and muggy and the working conditions were very primitive. But no one complained. Everyone did the best they could. We set up *hot beds*. They were named that because as soon as one person rolled out another rolled in. Everyone kept thinking tomorrow it would be better and we would get a break. Our break only happened while we were on our way to another island to set up again. It seemed like Japan had taken possession of every island in the Pacific. Day after day we got no rest. We tried to get the most severely injured to hospital ships or planes but it never ended. More casualties were always coming in that needed help."

Cathy sat quietly listening to Mike. He sat deep in thought as if in a daze. He continued.

"One day when it wasn't quite as hectic, I told my second-in-command to take over. I felt such a loneliness take over my body. I went to my tent, got my picture of you and your last letters. I could see a small hill just down the beach. I decided to climb to the top and think of our time on the hill at Camp McCoy. I needed you so bad and wanted to feel close to you. But I wasn't allowed to go to the hill. It was unsecured. So I sat on the beach. For a few minutes I sat watching the waves wash ashore. I was deep in thought but I began to be aware of children's voices. Down the beach I could see a mother with three children. Two of them rushed into the water and let the waves cover their feet. One small boy couldn't run with the others. He had an extremely severe twist to his body that caused him to limp badly. I watched as he made his way to the water and heard him laugh with pleasure as the waves washed over his feet. I thought about the boy's condition. If he were in the States he could receive help. And then I thought, if I was another kind of doctor, I could help him. I had no pediatric training, we had no equipment or supplies. I couldn't help but think of how rewarding it would be to help the child. I've seen so many children who need help. Somehow I can't get them out of my mind." Mike and Cathy sat quietly for a few minutes. Mike continued talking.

"It was hard for us to get excited about the victories the Allies were gaining, both in the Pacific and in Europe when all we saw were wounded bodies and death around us. But no one gave up. Day after day, and at times all night, we worked on.

"The top brass tried to arrange a weekend or a little time off duty. But somehow or other, I stayed on duty. Not too long ago we had about an hour free and we sat around and talked about our future. I was in charge of these men and yet I never had a chance to get to know them. As I listened to them talk, especially about what they had learned and their hopes for the future I realized what a good strong team we had. Yet I realized we had become an emergency room. We patched up the wounded just enough to keep them alive and move them out to make room for more. I felt I couldn't go on anymore. I didn't know what to do about it. I went for a walk in a so-called safe area and sat on the beach again.

"They came to get me. Four little children had found some hidden grenades and thrown them. Those little arms could only throw them a short distance. They exploded. The children were severely injured. They had been brought to our base hospital because it was the only one on the island. One little boy had already died. One was covered in blood with what looked like mostly superficial wounds. A nurse took him to calm and stabilize him. The other two boys both needed emergency surgery. We divided into teams and each took a child. Two of us gave blood because our supply was gone. It was a very long night.

"When I finally lay down to rest I couldn't stop my mind from seeing their little mangled bodies. My hands were shaking. Maybe you noticed they were still shaking when I came home."

Cathy reached out to place his hands in hers. "I noticed," she said quietly.

"I realized that day I had a very efficient crew working for me. If I had seen one of them with shaking hands I would have ordered him to R&R. These doctors and nurses must have seen my condition and stepped in to help without my knowing about it. It was not fair to them. I called my commander and asked for a break. He granted it. When I told my crew I was leaving for a while I could see the glances that passed between them. They could see what I could not; I needed help. I'm sure they had times when they covered for me."

"Mike, I am so sorry I was not there to take care of you."

"But I knew you were here. And knowing that, I knew that I would be fine if I could just see you and hold you for a little while."

"I have noticed your hands are not shaking these past few days," she told him.

Mike told Cathy about the various children he had seen. "If I had been a pediatric surgeon I think I might have tried to help one other little fellow I saw," he told her. "I know you'll think this is weird but sometimes I think I would like to go back to help him and the rest of the kids."

"Would you know where to find him?" she asked.

"No. I have no idea what island he was on. They all looked the same to me after a while."

After about ten days, Mike seemed almost back to normal. He took a long nap every afternoon. Evenings were spent with the family or going out to see a movie or for dinner. He took a lot of walks, sometimes with his mom or dad; usually with Cathy. One day while they were walking, Mike told Cathy once more he thought he wanted to work with children when the war was over.

"I'd need more specialty training, I guess. I think it would be so rewarding to help a child. Would you be disappointed if I change careers?"

"Of course not, Mike. You're a great doctor already. I learned to appreciate your skills when I worked with other doctors. Not everyone has hands like these," she said taking his hands into her own

"You're such a rock to me, Cathy. How did I ever get by for so many years without you?"

"I'm here because I have such excellent taste in my choice of men," she said playfully, giving him a punch. "You can choose any career you want. I'll always be with you and support you," she told him.

All too soon Mike's leave came to an end. The family knew he had recovered from the fatigue of war. Joan had asked Ray if he could pull strings to let Mike stay stateside. Ray told her he probably could but would not unless Mike asked him to do so. They both could see that Mike was ready to go back. They knew he would not ask for favors. It was a sad parting for them, yet they had seen him go from a tired, broken down man to the strong person he was. Joan and Cathy hugged each other and cried as they told him goodbye. They knew he was doing what he thought he needed to do.

∗   ∗   ∗

Back in Glenridge Annie continued to spend most of her time in her room. She took very few meals with her family. She had no interest in helping Albert put the little flags on the world map to show the advancement of the Allies into Germany or moving closer to Japan in the Pacific. Nor was Annie interested in starting her teaching career. Emma and Albert were very worried. They were advised to give her more time to get over her grief. On occasion Emma would ask her to start dinner for them and Annie would do it but usually would not eat with them that night.

One day Emma called upstairs to tell Annie she had received a package. "I'll get it later," Annie said.

Emma carried the package to Annie. As she knocked on the door and opened it, she said, "I think you'll want this. It's from a bank in Ames, Iowa." She handed it to Annie.

Annie reluctantly took the package. "I don't think I can open it," she told her mother. "What if it's bad news about Tom? I don't know anyone in Iowa."

"Well, you won't know until you open it. Do you want me to leave?"

"No, Mom, please stay."

Carefully she cut open the tape that sealed the box. There was a letter on top. Annie slowly picked it up and began to read it aloud.

FIRST NATIONAL BANK
Ames, Iowa

Dear Miss Martin,

Tom Ross and his family were long-time clients at our bank.

We received a letter from Tom giving us your name and address prior to his last trip overseas. He asked that we forward the contents of his safety deposit box to you in the event he did not make it back from the war.

It has been brought to our attention that the government has now declared that he was killed in action.

Please accept our condolences on his death.

Yours truly,

237

Annie handed the letter to her mother. "They think he's dead."

Emma said nothing.

Annie looked inside the box. There were a few legal papers, a few photos, and a smaller box. When she opened the smaller box she found a gold locket. Inside were pictures of a woman and man. The back was engraved with the words, *I love you, J.* She held in it her hands for a few minutes staring at the picture. Finally she looked up at her mother.

"This belonged to his mother. Tom looks just like his Dad. I'm going to put it on and never take it off." She handed the locket to her mother.

Emma said nothing. She looked for a few minutes at the picture and helped Annie place the necklace around her neck. Then she put her arms around Annie and let her cry. It was the first time in months that Annie let anyone touch her.

* * *

Beth found herself in another waiting pattern: waiting to hear from Pieter, and waiting to hear if her job would be ending. The women of the WASP'S had been very pleased when General Hap Arnold, who at first had opposed the formation of the WASP'S, praised their service to the country and lobbied Congress on their behalf. But when Congress finally voted on the bill to give the WASP's full military rights, it was defeated. The lobbying from the opposition had swayed the elected officials. The official reason given was that Congress had never written a formal letter authorizing the formation of the WASP's. It had been authorized by the War Department, which under the War Department regulations, they were allowed to do. Congress wrote a new bill after that time so that an official record was on file authorizing the War Department to organize a group such as the WASP's, and to make what had happened legal. But the bill did not provide for the WASP'S to continue. It was clear that the current WASP'S organization was seeing its last days.

Morale among the women was low, yet they were determined to maintain the reputation and standards that had been set.

Beth remained stationed in Washington, DC. She spent about half of her time flying VIP's connected to the war effort around the country. The other half of her time was spent in administrative duties. Though Beth was sad about what she and the other women felt was shoddy treatment, it didn't seem to matter to Beth as much as it might have. For the first time in years she began to feel happy. She and Pieter had no plans to meet, no plans for the future. Yet, that didn't bother Beth. She knew he cared for her. It was easy for her to care for him. Everything else was just details that would take care of themselves.

One fall day she was assigned a flight to Sweetwater. She decided to see Martha Grant. It had been a while since they had talked. She was anxious to see what Mrs. Grant's plans would be when the WASP's were disbanded. Gossip said that the letters would be in the mail any day.

"Beth, I'm happy to see you. I planned to contact you this week. Tell me how you've been; what is going on in your life. You have a glow about you. Something nice must be happening."

"Well, I have no idea what I'll do when the WASP's are gone. I know I'll be OK. Remember when I was trapped in the tunnel in London. I had already met the RAF pilot when we both were in Seattle. We got reacquainted. We've stayed in touch. And . . . . . . "

Mrs. Graham interrupted. "And now you are in love. That's why you have the glow about you. I'm happy, so happy for you, Beth. I remember the first time I met you. You were still grieving over the loss of your intended husband. You were so sad. I wondered if you would stay with the WASP's. You did. You became our star pilot. Have you and your pilot talked about marriage?"

"It's too soon for that. He's from Austria. He apparently lost his family while he was with the RAF. He's trying to locate them now."

"That's very interesting, Beth, because lost families are why I was going to contact you. Sit down. Let's talk."

"There are a few international organizations trying to help family members find each other: The International Red Cross, the Mennonites, various church organizations. So many families were separated by the Nazi command. Others were separated in the bombings and ground fighting all over Europe. I have been asked to take an executive position with one of the organizations as soon as I am officially discharged from the WASP's. I will be sent to Switzerland to help coordinate information that we get from various countries and relief organizations. The task is enormous. The lists of names of missing families as well as some lists of orphaned children are long. From time to time I may need to travel to the various capitals or other cities. A refurbished C-47, a Gooney Bird, has been donated to us. Even though the war goes on we must start to help the families. We need money. I'm sure I'll spend some time in fund raising. I need an assistant.

One who can fly the plane. One who can also help in the other matters, whether it be paperwork or talking with people. I really thought about you because of your flying skills. If I remembered right, your resume included the information that you had studied languages in college. Did my memory serve me right?"

"Yes, I ended up studying German, French, and Spanish. I never used them much. I don't know how much I remember."

"I'm sure it will come back to you. At least enough to get by on. I would like to offer you the position. You will not get rich. You would earn enough to live on. It would mean moving to Switzerland. Are you at all interested in the position?"

Beth's first thoughts were of Pieter. At least they'd be a bit closer together. Maybe she could help him find his family. She thought of her own family. She had been gone from home so long that maybe she needed to go home. Maybe she could help her sister Annie who was grieving over the death of Tom. Beth knew about that type of grieving.

"I'm really, really interested. I have no idea what I'll do when I leave the WASP's. This sounds like a fantastic opportunity for me." Beth became more subdued. "I remember telling my dad not very long ago that I thought it was time I would do something to help someone else."

"Take a few days to think about it. Call your folks. I'll call you the first of next week."

Beth thought of little else the next few days. As she expected, her folks told her they'd support her decision. Her mother sounded wistful about Beth leaving the country for even a little while. Beth knew Emma would never tell her not to go.

Shortly after, *the letter* came. It was dated 1 October 1944, and was signed by H.H. Arnold, General, U. S. Army, and Commanding General Army Air Force. It was addressed To Each Member of the WASP's. It sounded sincere. It was complimentary about the WASP's. It was the death knell of the program. It didn't matter if the women were angry or if they were sad. The program was over.

Along with her fellow WASP's, Beth grieved over the end of the program, even though she was luckier than most. She had another job to go to. Many, perhaps most, had to start all over again. She was proud of her service in the WASP's. Of nearly 2000 women who were accepted into the program, over one thousand earned their wings, flying over sixty million miles on every type of aircraft. Thirty-eight WASP members lost their lives in flying accidents. They had a proud record to leave behind.

Beth decided to call her parents. She told them she had decided to accept the job offer in Switzerland.

"Beth," her mother said, "you grew up in a house and a neighborhood where people take care of each other. You also suffered the loss of a loved one. Maybe you can combine these two experiences. You can be of real help to the people. I can't imagine living through something as horrid as losing your home and being separated from the family you love. I can remember how I felt when I didn't know where my father was. I was lucky. I had family around me. I can't even imagine how it would be to not know where any of your family is or even if they're still alive."

"Beth, are you doing this to be closer to Pieter?" her father asked.

"Dad, he's becoming special to me. We've had no chance to get to know each other except through letters. If I'm in Europe, I may have a better chance of finding out."

"I'm glad to hear you are thinking this through," he told her. "If you decide you two have nothing in common, will you still be satisfied to stay there? You must think about the responsibilities of the job you are taking."

"I will think about that, Dad. Thanks."

Her dad continued, "Did I tell you that Pieter has written to me twice? Both times he wrote to thank me for sending him your address. He is concerned about many things: the people and his town which is shattered. The people are turning to him for help and leadership in the same way they turned to his father. He's very concerned about locating his brother's children. I'm sure he told you that he has heard his mother and sister-in-law were killed by the German police. He's concerned over how he will earn his living. He is carrying a very heavy load right now."

"Yes, dad, I do know."

"I will say this much for him. In spite of his troubles he didn't complain about them. He is trying to make plans to handle each one. He seems very sincere in how he feels about you. I'm glad you're taking time to see where it will lead with him. You both are two nice people. I would hate to see either one of you get hurt any more than you have already been hurt in the past."

Beth thought a lot about her conversation with her dad and mom. They really are here to help me, she thought. She and Pieter were writing to each other every day now. She knew they were growing closer through those letters. She had written Pieter telling him of the job offer. Because the mail moved so slowly, she had not yet heard back from him.

Mrs. Grant asked Beth to visit a relocation center in Washington D.C. to get ideas on how the office was set up and find resources for supplies. She hoped to take the C-47 full of supplies when she went to Switzerland. She would be in charge officially in one month. Even though they would be working in an established office, Mrs. Grant had decided while on a short visit in Switzerland that there were many opportunities to make it more efficient. Beth visited many office supply places. She was very encouraged with the offers of supplies that were donated. One firm gave her reams of paper; Konica offered a mimeograph machine to make copies of important papers. Another firm donated boxes and boxes of index cards so they could set up a filing system similar to that used in libraries. Instead of writing the names of the families in books, the cards would have names of people. One company offered to supply four desks and desk chairs if she could find some way to get them to Switzerland. Beth stayed busy from sun-up to sun-down and filled many notebooks with entries.

Beth had spent the month of November preparing for her move to Switzerland. Now it was time to make the move. Although she got a letter from Pieter almost every day, he had not mentioned anything about her move to Europe. She didn't know if it was because of slow mail or if he was having second thoughts about having her in his life. She saw another letter from him when she returned home after attending a class all day about how to raise money for charitable causes. She didn't like the idea of asking anyone for money and she didn't like the instructor. Beth was not in a very good mood as she sat down to read the letter.

> *Dearest Beth,*
>
> *I am floating on one of those beautiful clouds you and I have flown through. What a wonderful surprise to know you are moving to Switzerland. It makes me so happy to know you will be even a bit closer. Of course, I wish you were moving to Austria. I'll look on this as step one.*
>
> *I have had really serious thoughts about leaving Austria. I wondered if I should try to move to your country. It's really so important to me to see you again. I know I want you in my life. When you really get to know me, and the baggage I must*

carry for a while, I don't know if you could ever be happy here. Austria is very different than America. And I do want you to have a life of happiness.

I came back to Austria because I needed to know if my mother and Elsa, my sister-in-law, and the children were still alive. If they were dead, as I heard they might be, I would then be free to go wherever I wanted to go. Something happened. The people in Rossbach welcomed me home with open arms, telling me they now know their town will recover. They told me I was like my dad who tried to take care of everyone. After being completely over-whelmed by their love, I began to feel a responsibility to them. How could I tell them I was only here long enough to find my relatives? How could I leave Austria when it is possible my mother might still be alive?

Even more important, how could I live without you in my life if there is a chance we could spend our life together? Could I leave Austria and go to America? I decided I need to talk with you. First and most important is to know how you feel about me, not just for a night of passion, but for a lifetime.

My town, to me, is just as beautiful as it was while I was growing up. Yes, it's true, the town is shabby. Many buildings were destroyed. The people are just barely staying alive. Yet there is a spirit of hope among the people that it can be restored to its full beauty. The snow-covered Alps that surround us, the green fields of edelweiss, the tall trees and the sparkling lakes are part of my heritage.

Somehow, I have the feeling that I could restore this community. These are people who were a part of my childhood. As for my search for my family, I got a new lead today that may help me locate Elsa's mother. That will be step one.

You may remember hearing about my friendship with Hugh and Charles Merriman. After Charles was killed, his parents continued to stay in touch. I just heard from his dad who is going to be in Switzerland in December and wants me to meet with him. Now that I know you are coming to Switzerland, I will make sure to be there too. When I let you know how much I love you in person I want you to know what a confused schlep I am.

I love you, Beth.
Pieter

Beth sat their quietly reading and re-reading this passionate letter. *Am I really in love with him? Could I spend my life with him in a strange country with people who are strangers to me? Could I make him happy enough to forget Austria if I said I wanted to live in America? Would it have been better to hear these things in person instead of a letter? No*, she thought, *I know if he put his arms around me and told me of his love, I'd just melt. He probably would leave if I told him I wanted him to live in the United States. Could he ever be happy in my country?* Beth knew she must be sure of what she'd be doing – giving up her family and her town to make a new life somewhere else. *If I don't make the right decision both of us will be unhappy for the rest of our lives.* She could read from his letter that his heart is in Austria. She spent a restless night tossing and turning. She was leaving the next day to fly to Switzerland.

Mrs. Grant had flown the Gooney Bird with the supplies earlier and was already in Switzerland. She had arranged a hotel room for a week for Beth. Beth was able to hitch a ride on a plane full of relief supplies. Beth thought a lot about Pieter and about her family. She had told them about Pieter's letter and his plans for the future. As usual her parents were careful about what they said. As the plane landed, she gathered her gear, stepped on the tarmac and looked around. She could see the Swiss Alps in the distance. The scenery was really beautiful. Switzerland had remained neutral in the war so she saw no remains of the bombings Beth had seen in London. She made her way through customs and out of the hangar area.

"Beth! Beth!" She looked up at the call of her name and there was Pieter rushing toward her. She ran to him. "How did you know when I was coming? How did you get here?"

"I called Mrs. Grant when I got here. Did you get my letter telling you I might be here?"

"Yes, but I didn't expect to see you at the airport."

"I couldn't wait to see you." They kissed passionately.

"I love you, Beth."

"I love you, Pieter."

Finally, they pulled apart and made their way from the airfield. "I'll take you to your hotel to get settled. I have a meeting scheduled with Mr. Merriman in one of the banking buildings in an hour. I have no idea what it is about. He made it sound very important and almost insisted I be there. When I heard you were coming the same day I headed for the airport in Rossbach and in exchange for giving flying lessons for the next year, they let me use a plane to fly here."

"I'm just glad to see you. I'm very happy to see you."

"I wish I didn't have to go to the bank. The Merriman's have been so kind to me over the years. Charles was a very, very good friend. He was like my brother. His parents often introduced me as their *adopted* son. Maybe this meeting won't take long. If you need to go to the office, leave a note at the desk for me, or I'll leave a message for you if it gets late."

Beth got settled in her room and then called Mrs. Grant.

"Did you connect with Pieter?" Martha Grant asked her when Beth called.

"Yes. Thank you so much for telling him when I'd be here."

"Take tomorrow off. Plan a full day when you come in the next day. We've got a lot of work to do."

Beth's room was tiny yet spotless. The bed was made up in pure white sheets and blankets. She took her white towels and went down the hall to take a bath. Before she saw Pieter she had planned to take a nap. Now she spent the time trying to arrange and rearrange her hair, putting on one outfit and then another. She wanted to be perfect when she saw him again. He had never seen her out of uniform. She thought about all her confusion about her relationship with him. When she saw him, when she felt his arms around her, she knew her love was real and the other things would just have to be taken one at a time.

After a long three or so hours Beth was informed that a Mr. Dekker was waiting for her in the lobby. She hurried down the three flights of stairs. Pieter was waiting for her.

"Somehow or other, I never thought a day like today would ever happen in my life," he told her as they made their way to the lobby to sit in a quiet corner. "Having you here beside me is more than I hoped for. Beth, something big, very big, has happened. Doug Merriman has arranged a loan, a big loan for me at the Swiss bank. It's enough for me to restore and refurbish the department store my father owned and also rebuild our family home. I couldn't believe what he was saying." Pieter sat there shaking his head.

"Start at the beginning," Beth told him.

"Well, we met in a small room at the bank and after a waiter brought in coffee, Doug started to talk about the time he met my father. Doug had a small department store outside Birmingham, England, so they had retailing in common. His store was not damaged in the war. He explained that he no longer is interested in it. Since Charles died, he and Margaret have put their life on hold. He told me how much he wanted Charles to take over the business. He told me he and my dad had laughed about both men having sons who didn't seem that interested in sales." Pieter paused. "It was almost like having a visit with my own dad for a little bit. Anyway, Doug asked me about the store in Rossbach and my plans for it. I told him how confused I had been about staying in Austria. He asked me if my confusion was complicated by my feelings for you. I told him I love you and you love me. I told him we haven't talked about our future. He talked for a while about Charles and how much he missed him. He said he and Margaret felt they had to do something that they are sure Charles would want them to do. He had taken it on himself to talk with the bankers in Switzerland and would guarantee a big loan for me so I can bring back the family business. Payments on the loan are deferred for three years. Doug had already talked with the bank and based upon his knowledge of retailing and the banker's knowledge of financing, the business end can be settled as soon as the papers are signed. He has offered his expertise and support to make it happen. He said he is doing it in memory of Charles. I'm still stunned as I sit here. It's more money than I could have imagined. He already has most of the papers prepared for me to sign. Beth, I'm still in a state of shock."

"It sounds to me like he loves you a lot. If you decide to accept it I think it will make him feel like he's sharing a bit of Charles with you. Think how many jobs you would be bringing to Rossbach. Think how it would encourage the people when they see the town come back even better than it was before. Pieter, how can you say no to him?"

"Beth, I don't want to live the rest of my life without you. If I do this I'm making a commitment to stay in Austria. Do you think you could ever be happy living away from the United States? Do you think you could be happy there?"

"Pieter, right now I feel like I could be happy wherever you are. I want you to be happy. Living with you in Austria now will be different than it was before the war. The countries used to be so far apart. Air travel is going to bring us all closer together. I'm sure we can work together to make it happen."

"Doug and Margaret have asked us to join them for dinner tonight. Are you too tired from the trip? I'm sure they'll understand."

"Pieter, this will be our first time together as a couple. Yes, I'll gladly go with you. We have many things to talk about but we'll have a lifetime to do it. I'll go up and get my coat."

Mr. and Mrs. Merriman were very kind and gracious to Beth. It was obvious that they adored Pieter and really wanted to help him in the same way they had expected to help their own son. They weren't pushy about the relationship between Pieter and Beth.

Pieter took Beth back to the hotel. "Some night, very soon I hope, I'm going to ask you if I can stay the night. I know you've had a long trip and a very long day. So I'll leave you till tomorrow morning. Sleep well, beautiful Beth."

The next morning Pieter arrived early for breakfast and then he and Beth went to the bank to meet again with the Merriman's to sign the loan papers. The amount of the line of credit established would let Pieter restore and stock the store in the way Pieter's father would have done it. Without the loan it would have had to be done one part at a time. Pieter talked about how many jobs it would bring to the people and how encouraged they would be.

"Pieter, if the war had not happened, what were your dreams for your life?" Margaret asked him

"Probably to live in a little cabin high in the Alps, fish and hike all summer and ski all winter. Oops, I probably shouldn't say that to someone who has just endowed me with enough money to restore a town."

They all laughed as Margaret said, "Well, you'll just have to work smarter so you'll have time to do that too."

They told the Merriman's goodbye and Pieter had to leave for home. They both knew they had commitments ahead: Beth to help to find missing family members and Pieter to help to rebuild a town. They also knew that they loved each other and together they would find a way to build a life together.

Beth felt at home almost immediately when she reported to the office. She was warmly welcomed and got right to work. She saw many, many volunteers who came in to pour over lists of names of missing family members. Some orphanages and churches had sent out lists of names of people they had taken in during the war. When a name was located, the family would be notified of a possible match. If the agency could help in arranging a reunion, they tried to do so. A good day for the workers was when they got even one match. Using the cards Beth had brought made them a bit more efficient because cards could be added or deleted easily. The writing on some of the lists was hard to decipher – sometimes they would complete two cards, each with a slightly different spelling. Beth sent out letters to the mayors of many towns and cities, and church leaders, asking them for information on anyone they had taken in. Beth remembered something from her flying lessons. When a problem is too big, break it down into little pieces.

She was surprised how quickly she made friends with the people. Volunteers from all over the world were helping. The main part of the work force was the Swiss citizens, all eager to help. They invited Beth into their home and their family life. She found a small, extremely small, apartment: two rooms with a shared bath. She was happy. And the high point of each day was when she came home and opened her mail. Her family and friends in Glenridge kept the letters flowing. Best of all were the letters from Pieter.

He was really a hero in his home town as he went about his new projects. He told Beth the people were so enthusiastic that they often worked overtime without pay. Pieter set up a series of goals and as each one was met, they would stop and have a half-day festival. This meant the families joined the workers. They brought with them food of many kinds. Though none of them had a lot, they shared what they had. They brought their music with them and danced into the night. A letter told Beth about how encouraged he was about the progress the town was making. Even though the war continued in the Pacific, Europe was beginning to rebuild.

* * *

Cathy went back to her duties after Mike left. She thought constantly about Mike and his desire to work with children. She thought of those wonderful hands of his. She knew he would be a kind, gentle doctor. Maybe before very long, they'll have children of their own. She laughed when she remembered Mike telling Joan that he and Cathy would have twelve kids. I don't think so, dear Mike, she thought. Maybe three or four would be nice.

One day the administrator brought to her attention that she still had about ten days of leave time accumulated. Cathy thought about her family in Glenridge. She was really worried about Annie. Dear, sweet Annie who had fallen in love with Tom while she was with Cathy and Mike. Annie still refused to believe Tom had died since they didn't find his body. Cathy understood why bodies were not always recovered. She had seen war. Annie had not. Cathy knew that Annie's depression was a form of illness but she didn't know how to help her.

I think I'll go home to Glenridge for Christmas if I can, she thought. She did her Christmas shopping, first for Mike and Beth and shipped them off. She got gifts for Ray, Joan and Rita which she took to them, and gifts which she would take with her to Glenridge. It seemed like a long train ride. Finally the train pulled into the station. Cathy was so happy to see her mom and dad waiting to greet her. For the first time in her life she thought they looked older. She could see the worry lines on their faces. Though outwardly they were exuberant about her homecoming (and she knew how happy they were to see her) Cathy realized that the worry over Annie, over Beth's safety, and her own ordeal had taken a toll on them both. Still, with much joy they made their way home.

Annie came out of her room long enough to greet Cathy, then said she was tired and went back to her room and closed the door. Cathy could see why the family was concerned.

Cathy decided to try to make this as nice a Christmas as possible. Last year, Emma and Albert had to celebrate alone. Beth was gone, and Annie and Cathy were together. Well, sort of together. *This year we'll have to celebrate,* she thought.

The next day Cathy went to the attic and brought down the boxes of ornaments. Cathy and her dad went shopping for a tree. Albert put the lights on and said he was done. So Cathy and her mom trimmed the tree, sharing happy memories as they hung each ball. They had many ornaments that were handmade when the children were small.

"Maybe I should start sorting these ornaments so you and Beth can put them on your own tree next year," Emma said. "Hopefully, this is our last war time Christmas."

"Funny you mention that," Cathy said. "Just the other day I was thinking that Mike and I haven't really talked about what we'll do after the war. I know that he will want to get out of the military. He mentioned that he may want to work with kids. I just don't know what we'll do or where we'll go."

"You'll have time to think about that. Do you realize that 1941 was the last Christmas we had as a family? I think the world will be changed forever. We must remember we are a family even when we're in different states or countries."

Emma planned a big Christmas dinner. Uncle Frank, Aunt Mille, Cousin Harold and his wife and kids, and the Jensens from next door were there. Cousin Herb was still somewhere in the Pacific and Beth was in Switzerland. Still it almost seemed like old times. Annie did come to the table just long enough to eat and returned to her room. After dinner, the family went into the parlor and sang all the Christmas carols. For just a little while it seemed like the days of her childhood.

"I wish Mike could be here and see how Christmas is supposed to be celebrated," Cathy said rather wistfully.

"You'll build your own traditions with your own children," Emma said.

*   *   *

In Europe, the American and British forces were inching their way closer to Germany from the west and the Russian troops were getting closer from the east. One by one the various countries were being liberated. In the Pacific a terrible battle and loss of life was occurring as the fight for Iwo Jima went on.

Another year of the war came to an end.

1945

The year of 1945 started with people having more optimism than the previous three years. Everyone hoped that the war might finally be coming to an end. In February President Roosevelt, Prime Minister Churchill and Premier Stalin met in Yalta to develop the terms necessary for Germany to surrender. In the Pacific that month, Manila in the Philippines was retaken and General MacArthur returned to the island. In March, Iwo Jima was retaken after weeks of heavy casualties. But the war did continue and lives were still being lost each day. April 12th was a very, very sad day. The world was informed of the sudden death of the President of the United States, Franklin Delano Roosevelt. Harry S. Truman became the new president.

*   *   *

In Switzerland Beth settled into a new routine with enthusiasm. Any day the relocation group was able to connect a family became a special day. Mail came regularly from home. But most important in her life was her growing love for Pieter. She looked forward to his letters telling her about Rossbach. *Could it be my home someday,* she wondered.

One day she received a very sad letter from Pieter.

> *Dearest Beth,*
>
> *It is with a heavy heart I write you. Because I felt torn about spending time at the worksite in town, the need to find my family, and mostly my desire to be with you, I turned to the good people here and asked them to ask their relatives in the surrounding areas if they knew of any family named Dekker or Ulrich.*

That was Elsa's, my sister-in-law's, maiden name. The plan worked.

One old lady remembered that she knew a woman who was named Hulda Ulrich.

Her daughter had married a man with the name of Dekker. This woman didn't know where the Ulrich daughter was but she did know where the mother was. I found it was a small town on the outskirts of Vienna. The old woman was living in a home for old people and was unaware of her surroundings. The people there gave me the name and address of the woman's oldest daughter, Marta. I knew Marta was Elsa's sister.

Marta recognized me immediately. Her first words were to ask if I knew what happened to the children. I said I didn't. I asked if she knew what happened to Elsa and my mother. Marta told me she did. They both were killed by German fire. They are both buried in a local cemetery. She told me that after my dad and brother were taken to a work camp, Elsa and the children moved in with my mother. Our house was taken over by the German army and the family had to leave.

They made their way to Vienna and moved in with Marta. Soon that house was taken, too. They found a two-bedroom apartment in Vienna and moved in. It was crowded with three adults and six children. They spent most of their days in one of the parks along the Danube River. They spread a blanket on the grass and let the kids play. Many people did this and the parks were always crowded. One day they were at the park just in front of the Fetter Building which housed the Gestapo, the German police. It was a very hot, sweltering day. The windows in the building were opened. The Gestapo housed prisoners on the fifth floor in a section that faced the river. A prisoner, an Austrian, who was being questioned, decided to kill himself by jumping out the window. The body fell right where my family had spread the blanket. As he fell to his death, machine guns were fired from the guards on the ground and the guards in the windows. Many women and children on the ground were killed. Marta and her three children were gathering stones along the river They were spared. My mother and Elsa had thrown themselves on top of the children. The women were killed instantly. The police made everyone go home and wouldn't let anyone near the scene. Marta left her children with neighbors and returned where she saw the bodies of Elsa and my mother. She could not find the children. She saw some children's bodies, but they weren't Kurt, Georg, or Maria, my little niece who was born after I left Austria. She tried to find the children but had no success. She claimed the bodies of Elsa and my mother. They are buried in the Heinz cemetery. She took me there. While at Marta's she went to her desk. She removed a small bundle tied in a handkerchief. Inside I found the wedding rings of my mother and Elsa. At least now I know for sure about my mother and Elsa. My search for the children must go on. I love you, Beth,

    Pieter

Beth felt like her heart was breaking when she read the letter. She wanted to be there for him, to comfort him, to put her arms around him. *What am I doing in Switzerland when I should be in Austria with him?* How could she get to him? How could she let him know that she would stay by his side? He had to visit Switzerland once a month to meet with the bankers. She knew he'd be here in two weeks. She'd tell him then. No, she thought, I'll write him right now.

    My darling Pieter,

      My heart aches for the loss you must be feeling right now.

      I wish I could be with you. I wish I could hold you in my arms. I want to be with you forever, to share your sorrows as well as the good things in your life. I want to be with you for the rest of my life. I think it is time that I come to Austria to be with you.

      We must talk about this when you come here in two weeks.

    Beth

Beth wondered about her job? She knew the work must go on. They must work harder than ever. They must work to find the three Dekker children. Surely, someone, somewhere had crossed paths with them. She had to find them. She had already pasted the names of Kurt, Georg, and Maria on each desk. She had to find them; she just had to find them.

In Switzerland, Beth talked with Mrs. Grant and told her of her love and concern for Pieter as well as her concern to fulfill her obligations to her job. Mrs. Grant listened quietly. She asked Beth if she had told her parents of her decision. Beth confirmed that she had not done so. Mrs. Grant asked Beth if she could meet with Pieter when he arrived that weekend. Of course Beth said yes. She was puzzled about why Mrs. Grant wanted a meeting. Beth was very surprised when Mrs. Grant opened the meeting with a question for Pieter.

"Can I hire you to fly a plane to Washington, D.C.?"

"I don't understand," Pieter said. Beth added, "I don't understand either."

"I was just notified that a large shipment of supplies for the relocation centers in Europe is setting in storage ready to be shipped. We have a critical need for the supplies here. I will be assigning Beth to make the trip. We like two pilots on board for a trip this far. I would like to hire you to make this trip with her. But perhaps your schedule is too busy."

"Mrs. Grant, I can't believe this," Beth said. "Oh, Pieter, could you get away?"

"Mrs. Grant, I can't believe this either," Pieter replied. "Of course I'll get away. I love Beth and . . ." he paused just a moment. "Could we stay long enough for me to go meet Beth's parents; even for just a day or two? I have something important to ask her father."

Mrs. Grant smiled. "The plane must be back in time to be serviced for a flight on April 26th. If you can fit that in your schedule, well, the plane is prepped and ready. Have a good time."

"Mrs. Grant, you are a grand lady," Pieter said as he reached to give her a hug.

Beth was almost at a loss for words. She kept saying, "Oh, Mrs. Grant. Oh, I can't believe this." She turned to Pieter who took her in his arms.

That same afternoon they left Switzerland in the old donated Gooney Bird for Washington, D.C. They felt very lucky, the weather was good. While the skies were not entirely safe from German fire, there had been no war activity in the area of their flight plan. Beth got lucky too. When she called her parents the call went right through. Often the calls were delayed for hours.

This was the first time Beth and Pieter flew together. Beth looked at Pieter. "I'm so happy to be making this flight with you. I always feel good when I'm flying and to have you by my side makes the day perfect."

"Are you upset with me?" he asked her.

"Why would I be upset?"

"Because I said I want to talk with your father. You do know I want to ask him for permission to ask you to marry me."

"Hmmm," Beth said. "What if he says no or what if I say no."

"I'll have to kidnap you. I'll take you away without permission," he teased back. "Seriously, Beth, I know we love each other. I come with so much baggage. Are you ready to leave your home, your country and your way of life to be with me?"

"Yes, Pieter, I am. I love you."

"Do you think we could get married while we're in Glenridge? You will say yes when I officially ask you, won't you?"

"I'll think about it," she teased. "I've decided already. I'll say yes. I'm not sure if we can get married that quickly. Let's try."

"Will your folks be surprised?"

"I doubt it. My folks are very resilient to change."

Somehow this trip didn't seem nearly as long as the other trips. When they landed at a small field outside Washington, D.C. they heard shouts of "Beth – Pieter! Over here." They looked around. They saw Cathy waving her arms in big circles. Standing next to her . . . . could it really be . . . . . . ? It was. It was Dave. Beth ran to them both while Pieter talked with the ground crew. He took care of the shutdown procedures. Pieter quickly made his way to them.

Cathy reached out to give him a hug. "I'm Cathy, Beth's sister."

"I'm Dave, private pilot for the Martin family," Dave said with a smile on his face and an outstretched hand.

"Dave was my first instructor," Beth told Pieter. "How did you know? Did Dad call you?"

"Yes. We have been making routine flights here for the last year. He said you were limited for time on this trip so I figured I needed company on the flight. It's a much smaller plane than that one, though."

"It'll be perfect."

The flight to Glenridge passed very quickly. Cathy and Annie sat in the two pull-down seats. Pieter sat in the co-pilot position. Albert and

Emma, and many of the airport personnel, were waiting for them when the plane landed.

As Emma and Albert greeted Pieter, Pieter turned to Albert.

"How can I ever thank you enough for sending my letter on to Beth? I had about given up hope I'd ever find her again."

"Just always be good to her," Albert told him.

"Do I have your permission to ask your daughter to marry me?"

"I want Beth to be happy. You don't need my permission."

"Hey, Beth," he shouted across the crowd to her. "You dad said it's OK for me to ask the question. Will you marry me?"

"Yes, Pieter, yes," she shouted. She ran to him.

The happy crowd made their way home. The talk soon turned to a wedding. Could it possibly be arranged? Pieter was so used to traveling between countries that he carried his citizenship papers with him.

The citizens of Lincoln Boulevard responded, as usual, planning a wedding reception for the back yard unless it rained that day.

On a bright afternoon, on April 22, 1945, Pieter and Beth were married in the church she had attended all her life. Emma brought out her wedding dress, the one nearly one hundred years old that both Emma and her grandmother had worn. Beth tried it on. It fit her perfectly. Annie was still grieving for Tom but did agree to stand with Cathy as Pieter and Beth spoke their vows. The day stayed beautiful. They had enough food for an army to feed the crowd who stopped by to offer congratulations.

All too soon they were taken back to the Glenridge air field where Dave was waiting to take them back to Washington, D.C. and a return to Switzerland.

Spring had arrived in Switzerland. The fields were becoming green, the sun was shining brightly; spring flowers filled the meadows. Shepherds began to take their flocks of sheep up into the Alps for the summer. Beth marveled at the beauty of the world as they landed.

Mrs. Grant was very understanding about Beth leaving the program. She asked her to stay on until May 5th when her replacement would arrive. Beth was pleased to know the person would be JoJo. She knew JoJo would follow the procedures already in place. They were beginning to show some results.

*   *   *

On April 30th, the world was advised that Adolph Hitler had committed suicide. The end of the war in Europe grew nearer. On May 2nd, the final German forces in Italy surrendered to the Allies.

*   *   *

Pieter had returned to Switzerland the sixth of May so he and Beth could travel back to Austria together. He took care of his banking business that day while she completed duties at the office. A party had been planned for the next day to say goodbye to Beth. It was a celebration none of them would ever forget for on May 7th, 1945, the German forces surrendered to the Allies. The war in Europe had come to an end.

Now, of course, the biggest party of all was to celebrate the end of the war in Europe.

Pieter and Beth celebrated. As they said their goodbyes and were walking out the door a voice from one of the workers cried out, "I FOUND THEM! I FOUND THEM! Beth, Pieter, WAIT!"

They returned to the desk of the worker who handed them a new list which had just come in from Northern Italy. Included on that list were three Dekker children: Kurt, Georg, and Maria.

Along with December 7th, Beth knew this was a day she would never forget – this time a day which she could share with the man she loved.

*   *   *

On May 7th, Emma knocked on Annie's door calling out to her, "Annie, the Germans have surrendered. The war in Europe is over. Come down and hear the news with us."

They sat in front of the radio, elated that one battlefront was now peaceful, but mindful of the battles still going on in the Pacific. A subdued celebration was held in the land.

"Dad, I think it's time we take down at least some of the flags on the map," Annie said.

"You are so right. Let's do it right now," Albert told his daughter.

"I'm going to fix us a special desert to celebrate," Emma said as she hurried to the kitchen.

The next morning Albert knocked on Annie's door. "The sun is shining and I feel like celebrating. I'm going fishing. Want to come with me?" Albert asked.

"Yes, Dad, I do. I'll get dressed and be right down."

As Annie and her dad sat in the small row boat on the quiet lake surrounded by the tall spruce trees that reflected into the still waters, Annie spoke to her dad.

"There are still good things left in the world, aren't there Dad?"

"Absolutely," Albert told his daughter.

"I've been pretty hard on all of you, haven't I?"

"Nothing we can't take. We've been worried but we've always loved and respected you."

"I really loved him, Dad, even if we didn't have much time together. Is that hard for you to understand?"

"Not at all, daughter. I knew from the minute I saw your mother that I would love her forever. I've never changed my mind."

"I think I could accept Tom's death if I had seen his body or even talked to someone who was with him. Maybe that's why people have funerals. So you have a chance to accept what has happened; a chance to say goodbye."

"Maybe so, Annie, maybe so."

Each day Annie began to live her life again. She still had times of wanting to be alone. She spent more time with the family each day.

One day a letter came from the school board asking her if she planned to return to classes that fall. Annie talked to her dad and mother.

"I think Tom would want me to move on with my life," she told them. "I'm going to try to get a new start. I need to go to work. I don't think I'm interested in teaching English Composition. Dad, how can I find a new field? I do want to teach."

"I agree, Annie. I think Tom would want that for you. He would be proud of you. I know I am. About the job . . . well, there are tests you can take. I suggest you go talk to Roger. He's principal of the high school. He might have suggestions."

"Mom, will you go with me so I don't lose my nerve?"

"Of course I will. Let's go first thing in the morning if Roger can see you. Let's have lunch at the tea room. We need a girl's day out."

Roger Winters was very happy to see Annie. He was anxious to get the staff set for the fall term. When Annie told him she wasn't interested in teaching English he began to smile.

"Actually that's very good news. The teacher we brought in to replace you loves her job. She's very good at it. We do have a real need for someone to teach the new curriculum with the Civics/Government program. It's a new program with all new books and methods. A six week course is about to begin to explain and teach the program. I think you might be just the right person to try to stimulate our young people to become interested in how our government works. Would you be willing to give it a try?"

Annie knew it was the place for her. She started her classes immediately. She eagerly looked forward to the upcoming term.

*   *   *

The patients, doctors and nurses at Walter Reed celebrated with the rest of the country when the war in Europe was finally over. But along with the celebration it was also a time to remember the many, many thousands of lives that had been lost.

Surely, Japan will realize that now we'll have twice as many forces, and they will surrender, Cathy thought. But the war in the Pacific went on.

Cathy decided that even if the war was to last another year or two, she would allow herself to think for a little while about her future with Mike. She thought about his letters and the changes in his career he was considering. Did it really matter to her? They need doctors everywhere. Is it important to her to go back to Glenridge? What if Mike wants to return to school to specialize in another branch of medicine? I'll go wherever Mike wants, she thought.

*   *   *

Beth's first view of the small town in Austria where she would make her home was from the air. It looked so beautiful. The Alps in the distance were snow covered but it was early May. Spring was waking up. In the distance she could see the shepherds taking their flocks of sheep to the higher elevations. Flowers were beginning to bloom; the trees had the fresh green leaves of early spring. As the plane taxied to the hanger they saw a crowd of people from the town of Rossbach holding up signs written in

English that said *Welcome Beth.* Pieter stepped from the plane. He waved to his friends. Beth remembered enough German to acknowledge their greetings. Much to her surprise, Pieter made a public announcement and introduced her as his wife, the woman he loved. He shared with them the news that the children had been located. Since they all had been trying to help him in his search, they all began to clap and cheer. Beth phoned Mrs. Grant who had offered to locate the orphanage. They left almost immediately by train for northern Italy where they hoped to find the children.

Beth worried about how the children would react to Pieter; and especially how they would react to her. Only Kurt was old enough to possibly remember who Pieter was. When Beth was working she had witnessed one reunion that was bittersweet. Good because the children would now have a home, yet sad because the children were almost like robots as they met their family. Beth had no idea what to expect.

They met with the Mother Superior who was in charge of the orphanage. She had talked to Kurt to try to solicit memories of his family so she could try to make certain who Pieter was. Fortunately, Kurt remembered the names of his grandparents and a few events. She then asked Pieter the same questions. When she was satisfied she took them to a room to wait. The door opened. There stood three children; a boy about nine or ten years old with the sad eyes of an old man, a boy about six or seven, and a little girl.

Mother Superior started to introduce them to the children. "Children, this is your Uncle . . . . ."

"Uncle Pieter," Kurt cried. He rushed to the arms of his uncle. As Beth looked at him she saw what appeared to be a look of relief or a look of astonishment. She thought about how long it had been since this child had seen a familiar face. Yet he recognized some family trait in Pieter. He began to cry uncontrollably. Pieter held and comforted the boy.

Beth looked at the other children who were waiting at the door. They looked puzzled. They were very worried when they saw their big brother crying. Beth reached out her arms to embrace them.

"It's OK," she said in her broken German. "Pieter is your uncle. He will take care of you."

The children began to cry. The Mother Superior quietly left the room.

Kurt finally composed himself and resumed the rule of caretaker of the younger children.

"Georg, Maria. Come to say hello to your Uncle."

Beth would never forget the picture of Pieter sitting with the boys beside him on a sofa with Maria at his feet as they tried to get acquainted. Over time Pieter and Beth learned how Kurt took care of his younger siblings. Many people had offered to take baby, Maria. But Kurt would not let the family be separated. When he learned that he, Kurt, was to be taken to work in the fields, he took the children and left the group in the night. He insisted they had to stay together. The younger children obeyed Kurt as if he was their father. They learned the children spoke mainly German. They had picked up some Italian along the way as they made their journey. Sometimes a family would take them for a while, or they would be with another group of orphans. Having the toddler sister who had to be carried made for many problems.

They completed the necessary paperwork at the orphanage and left by train for Austria the next day. The children had never been on a train. Georg and Maria were very anxious. They wouldn't do anything unless Kurt told them it was OK.

"I'm glad we didn't tell the people at home when we would be returning. I do believe a large welcome would overwhelm them." Beth told Pieter.

Pieter's family home had been occupied by the Germans as an office building during part of the war. Pieter had already had all the old traces of their occupation removed. The rooms had all been repainted but there was still much work to be done. Pieter had only a bed and a few pieces of furniture. He ate very few meals at the house.

When Beth, Pieter and the children arrived at their home they found a nice surprise. Additional beds had been set up; three single beds in three separate rooms. The beds looked fresh and clean. They saw a kitchen table and six chairs, dishes and cookware and a stove and even food in the cupboards. Pieter's neighbors had been busy. The children were tired so after eating they showed each child his or her own room. Pieter and Beth would share the big bed in the biggest bedroom. Before going to bed late that first night they looked in on the children. Three beds were empty. On the floor in the third bedroom they found Kurt, Georg, and Maria asleep on the floor. Beth took a couple of blankets off the beds. She covered the children as they lay quietly sleeping. As Beth covered them that night she prayed that God would help her be a good parent to them. When a neighbor gave Maria a doll and little cradle they put it in her room. After that she stayed in her room to take care of her baby. Pieter asked the boys if they would like to share a room. They liked that idea and began to sleep in their beds.

Beth remembered those first few weeks as being tense. They were almost scary. Beth went into a new home in a new country with a new family. Communication was hard as Beth struggled to remember her German. Pieter was the brick that held them all together.

*   *   *

The world's attention had turned to the war in the Pacific. Most people were betting the Allied Forces would be planning an invasion of the Japanese mainland very soon. Concerned people who had followed the D-Day landing in Europe knew of the heavy, heavy causalities that had occurred. No one wanted any more lives to be lost.

Unknown to most people, the United States had developed a secret bomb, an atomic bomb. A decision was made that this bomb would be dropped on a Japanese city. Hiroshima was chosen. On August 6, 1945, the first atomic bomb was dropped on that city. The world was shocked at the destruction and devastation that occurred. The Japanese army fought on. On August 9, 1945. a second bomb was dropped on Nagasaki, Japan. On August 14th the Japanese officially agreed to an unconditional surrender. The formal surrender papers were signed on September 2, 1945. The war that had started for the Americans on December 7, 1941, had finally come to an end.

*   *   *

The day the Japanese agreed to the unconditional surrender there was dancing in the streets all over the world. People got out of their cars in the middle of the street to sing and dance. Church bells rang in every American city. In small towns the sound of fire sirens filled the air.

Cathy was at work when the announcement about the war's end was made that August evening. The joy of hearing the news spread quickly. Windows were opened so the patients could hear the celebration. Those patients who were able to walk went outside. Anyone able to sit up for a while in a wheelchair was taken outside. It was a joyous night in the land. Cathy stayed all night at the hospital. As she left the hospital the next morning she stopped in the chapel to say a prayer of thanks that the war was over. And she prayed that God would keep Mike and everyone else in the war zone safe. She knew the news of the surrender would take time to reach the many Japanese guerilla troops hiding in the hills.

Cathy decided she would remain at Walter Reed until Mike came home. She wasn't sure when he would be discharged from the army. She thought a lot about their future. *Would Mike want to go back to school to specialize in Pediatrics? He was so touched by the many children he saw. Or will he want to join his father's practice in Washington, D.C. Did she want to go to med-school now to fulfill her dream of becoming a doctor.* They had been married nearly three years but had actually spent only about a month together. *Would they want to start a family?* Cathy had many questions about her future. *I guess I'll just take one day at a time,* she thought.

It was almost two months later before Mike was transferred to Chicago to be mustered out of the army. This would be a new start for Cathy and Mike. One that they would be living as civilians. He had been very tired the last time she had seen him when he had been home on R&R for a couple of weeks. He was very worn out at that time. Cathy wondered what awaited her.

Cathy knew that Mike put her first in his life. She wasn't surprised when he asked her to meet him in Chicago when he was discharged so that they could get a car to drive to Michigan because he wanted to meet her parents. After a visit in Glenridge they would drive to Virginia where he would decide what he would do in the future. It sounded very wonderful to Cathy so she arranged for her discharge from the Army Nurse Corp in time to meet him.

They had a joyful reunion in Chicago. They went shopping for civilian clothes for Mike. Cathy had already shopped for her civilian wardrobe. Neither of them had ever seen the other in any civilian clothes other than around the house when he was on leave. He got a new suit which they tailored for him that afternoon; slacks, shirts, sweaters and a jacket. He looked so handsome in his civilian clothes.

They went shopping for a used car. There had been no cars built for civilian use during the war. They went to about five car lots without finding a car he liked. Finally he found *the* car; a 1941 Chevy deluxe. It looked so huge. The running boards were concealed; the headlamps were blended into the fenders. It had beautiful white wall tires. It was a dark maroon color. It really looked like new. They were told it had *only been driven by a little old lady on Sunday afternoon when it didn't rain.* As a brand new model the purchase price was almost $1,000. Since this had a *few* miles on it and Mike was a returning soldier, the salesman offered to let them have it for only $750. Prices had gone up because there were so few cars available to buy. Mike asked to take it to a Chevy dealer for inspection. The salesman wasn't happy but he didn't want to lose a sale so he said OK. It passed inspection with flying colors. The dealer suggested Mike offer $500 which Mike did. They finally settled for $600. They left for Glenridge feeling on top of the world.

Emma, Albert and Annie were very happy to see them and made them feel so welcome. They stayed up most of the night talking. The next day Cathy introduced Mike to Uncle Fred and Aunt Millie, cousins Harold and Herb, who had just been discharged from the Marines and to all the neighbors and especially Doc Jameson. Young Doc had returned from Europe some months earlier. He was taking over more and more of the practice. Young Doc and Mike had many things in common to talk about as Young Doc had been a field doctor in Europe with the Army. Old Doc asked Cathy if she'd like to assist him with a couple of his patients who had come in for a routine visit. These were people Cathy had visited when she was a child. It was a fun time for her. Young Doc invited them to his house for dinner.

"Do you think I'll be able to convince Mike to come to Glenridge to practice," Young Doc asked in a playful manner when he was sure Mike was listening.

"He's a wonderful doctor," Cathy said. She turned to Young Doc. "I thought you were saving that place for me."

"You know you can't trust Young Doc to keep his word," his wife said. "Didn't he tell you he was going to wait for you to grow up so he could marry you?"

They all were laughing and having a good time when the phone rang. "It's your dad. It's urgent," his wife said handing Young Doc the phone. They sat quietly hearing Young Doc ask one or two word questions. Then he hung up.

"There's been a huge gas explosion over in Milltown. They're going to bring the more seriously injured over here because we have better facilities at the hospital. Sorry, I have to leave."

"Can Cathy and I be of help? We're both used to dealing with emergencies," Mike asked.

"We sure could use you both. Our staff is small."

The ambulances had already started to arrive just before they arrived. A nurse gave them hospital gowns to put on over their clothes. The men immediately went to assess the situation. Cathy worked at the entrance with the regular nurse to triage the patients, trying to get the more seriously injured in for care more quickly. More than thirty people were admitted that night. Some injuries did not appear too severe; a few were quite bad. Two of the regular surgeons from the hospital had gone to the site of the accident in Milltown. They were assisting on the scene. About four o'clock in the morning Cathy was driven home by one of the hospital staff who lived near their area. Mike stayed on at the hospital until almost noon the next day. He had helped perform surgery on a young man. Mike didn't want to leave him until his vital signs improved.

"What a difference to do surgery in a clean sterile room," he told her when he arrived home. His eyes were shining. He really did not appear tired. For a while he looked like the old Mike Cathy had fallen in love with at Camp McCoy. The look he had on his face was a common one among surgeons. A look that said I've done my best. I think the patient will be OK.

When Mike got up later that afternoon he insisted on going back to the hospital to check on *his* patient. As usual, Emma and Albert had gone over to Milltown to help some of the residents who no longer had a home. Cathy went to the kitchen to prepare dinner. It seemed like old times for Cathy, only better because now Mike was here. The family had dinner together, sitting around the table talking about the events of the day.

The night before they left Glenridge they called Mike's folks who were awaiting their homecoming. Mike told his dad about their new car. He gave him their license number and told them they planned to head down through Ohio to Pittsburgh to get on the Pennsylvania Turnpike to travel to Virginia. They were going to make it a leisurely trip, stopping often when they wanted. It was a late fall that year. Although the air was a bit crisp, the fall colors were beautiful. Cathy felt so happy, so content. As Mike and Cathy talked with his parents they heard Rita call to his mom to ask what special thing they wanted to eat.

They said goodbye to Cathy's folks early the next morning and began their trip. They didn't make it too far. When they stopped for lunch they ended up taking it to a small town park on a lake. They sat on a bench planning their future.

"I am really surprised that I enjoyed working at the hospital the other night. A month ago I would have told you I never wanted to see another OR in my life. I got such satisfaction of repairing that young man," Mike told Cathy.

"You saved his life, Mike."

"Someone else would have stepped in."

"Who, Mike? Only Young Doc was there to do it all. He had other surgery. Don't be modest about your skills. Be practical."

Mike sat quietly, deep in thought. "Maybe it's the small town atmosphere I liked. I think I could be happy being a doctor living in a small town."

They sat for a long time that afternoon in the park before leaving town. There were no big motels in those days. Mostly they found small cabins along the roadside. That night as they sat in their room Mike brought up the subject again.

"I grew up in a small town not too far from Aspen, Colorado. Do you think you could be happy living in such a small community?"

"Anywhere you are is where I want to be."

The next night they stopped in another small town and got a room in a small hotel.

"Are you here for the festival?" the owner asked.

"What festival?"

"The Homecoming Festival. It's a street fair with vendors, a big Ferris wheel and other rides. And of course, the homecoming football game at the high school.

They went to the high school football game. Then they went to the fair. They had such a good time. The people were so friendly. Mike wanted to look around the little town the next morning. They saw a charming little house with a "For Sale" sign in the front yard. The house had a white picket fence around it. Shutters of light blue were on the white house. Colorful chrysanthemums were planted along the walk leading to the front door.

"Could you be happy in a house like that?" Mike asked.

She was so happy to see him enthused about anything. She told him she could be happy living anywhere he was. Small town, big city . . . well, if Mike was there that was where she wanted to be. They visited the street fair again that day before leaving to travel a few more hours before stopping for the night. The next morning they crossed the state line into Pennsylvania where they got on the turnpike. They would have no more little towns to visit until they left the turnpike half way across the state.

"There's been a State Police car following us for a bit. Oh, boy, he's just put his lights on. I wonder if I've been driving over the speed limit," Mike said as he pulled the car off the side onto the berm.

"Are you Doctor Michael Goodman?" the officer asked.

"Yes, sir. Is something wrong?"

"We had an alert come over the radio advising us you would be traveling this way. We have been requested to have you call your home as soon as possible."

"Do you know what's wrong?"

"Sorry, I don't. There is a rest station about fifteen miles ahead with a phone. If you'd like to follow me, I'll escort you a little faster."

Mike thanked him and they headed for the rest stop. They could not imagine what had happened. They were glad they had given the families the make of the car and the license number before they left Glenridge.

When they arrived at the rest stop Mike parked the car. He headed for the phone booth and Cathy headed for the coffee counter. She saw Mike's face go white, his head drop. She waited patiently for him to finish talking. They made their way to a quiet table in the corner. With tear-laden eyes he told her that his mother and Rita had been out shopping for groceries. On their way home they had been broad-sided by a drunk driver. Rita had been killed instantly; his mother was not expected to live. They sat quietly, finishing the coffee. Together they made their way to the car for a drive straight through to Virginia.

They went right to the hospital where his dad was waiting. They sat with his mother for almost twenty-four hours before she died. They took the bodies of both Joan, his mother, and Rita back to Colorado for burial.

*   *   *

The summer the war ended was an awaking time for Annie. She never really accepted Tom's death, but she did move on with her life. The course she took to teach the new Civics class had renewed her passion for teaching. She was excited about the new lesson plans she was creating.

Annie looked at her clothes one day before school started and decided she needed at least one new skirt and blouse to wear to class. While she was in the dressing room she overheard two women talking about her.

"Did you hear? Annie Martin got the new job all the teachers wanted."

"Well, you know why. Her dad and mother probably arranged it for her. She's not qualified at all."

"I thought maybe it was because she was young. She's enthusiastic and the kids could relate to her."

"No, I'm sure someone did some favors. The job should have gone to old Mr. Peters. He knows everything about teaching. He's been at it for forty years."

Annie was hurt and angry when she heard the words they spoke. The special course she had to take was very intense and difficult. She hurriedly dressed and ran out of the store. She went to the largest department store in town and asked for the personal shopper to help her. She spent a lot of money that day but it was worth it. The shopper helped her get the proper fit and enough pieces of a wardrobe to put together many different looks. It was wonderful for her morale. Finally, feeling much better, she stopped to buy some lipstick at the drug store. She took time to get a cherry coke. While at the counter drinking it, two young girls came in. They sat down next to her. They had an interesting conversation.

"Did you hear Miss Martin is coming back to teach?"

"Oh, that poor thing. Isn't it just too, too sad about her boyfriend. I hope she finds time to tell us all about it. I want to hear every little detail. I bet we'll spend hours hearing about it."

"I don't think I could bear it. I'd probably cry buckets of tears."

Annie was shocked. Had she become a topic of conversation in town? Did people pity her? She felt ashamed and embarrassed. What could she do to change things?

Well, she did something. She went to the most expensive hair salon in town. They cut her long dark curly hair into a short bob. One of the girls who worked there asked her about her make-up as they were starting to carry a new line. Annie let them teach her how to apply the different items. She went home with a new persona but much poorer.

Annie went to teach her new class full of confidence. She informed them she was to be called Miss Annie instead of Miss Martin. She was afraid *Miss Martin* might have a reputation to live down. She told them their first assignment was to write by hand the Preamble to the Constitution. After that they would study it. She was happy when the class responded. She told them she would give them extra credit if they worked on some political campaign. Most addressed envelopes for men who were running for the school board. The class attended a meeting of the school board and the city council. They attended a court proceeding one day. In class they held lots of debates. Most debates lasted at least two days. If a student was for a cause one day, the next day that student had to present a case against the cause. Annie wanted them to learn to see that each cause has two sides and most usually there are both bad and good issues in each side. The students all responded very well.

Annie's teaching became her life. Her friends were constantly trying to fix her up with dates, but Annie always declined. Cousin Herb and Marge had gotten married and moved in with Uncle Fred to help take care of Aunt Millie who was ill. Their house was just down the street from the Martin house. And across the street Rosemary and Roy had moved in with Rosemary's parents.

*   *   *

As the Christmas season of 1945 neared, there was an air of joy in the air that the war was finally over.

Beth, Pieter and the three children celebrated their first Christmas together in Austria, making new traditions to be followed in the future.

Cathy and Mike had moved in with Mike's father in Virginia. They blended the traditions of each of them into a new way to celebrate the holidays.

Emma, Albert, and Annie, along with relatives and good neighbors on Lincoln Boulevard once again celebrated the old familiar traditions they knew and loved.

FIFTY YEARS LATER

Beth sat on the lawn swing in the back yard of her home in Rossbach admiring all the flowers in her yard. The red geraniums were still blooming in all the window boxes on the house, and chrysanthemums were beginning to bloom in the gardens. *This is not much different than the back yard in Glenridge,* she thought. Though she appeared deep in thought, her mind was flitting from one nice thing to another.

"Am I interrupting some deep concentration? Or would you like some coffee?"

Beth smiled and took the cup. She moved over on the swing so Pieter could sit with her.

"I'm just enjoying this beautiful day. And you know, I have just decided the world is pretty small after all. Living here in Rossbach isn't all that different than Glenridge."

"You're a remarkable woman, Beth. Not every woman would leave her family, her home, her country for a whole new way of life in a new country with a ready-made family."

"It's not all that different. Air travel, computers, and cell phones have changed things. Glenridge doesn't seem that far away."

"Yes, but you gave up your dream of living next door to your family home, living next door to your sister . . . . ."

"But I got a new dream and a wonderful family. I wouldn't trade my life for anyone."

Pieter started to smile. "Remember our first days with Kurt, Georg, and Maria? I think we both wondered what we had gotten ourselves into. I bet you had many thoughts of leaving then."

"Now you know I never had those thoughts but I do remember how incompetent I felt. Do you remember how hard it was for Kurt to give up the responsibility for Georg and Maria? He had been their sole support and only family for so long it was hard for him to let it go. He didn't trust anyone," Beth said. "And he was only ten years old. I was trying to learn to speak the language and be a mother and a wife. When their Aunt Marta offered to move temporarily to Rossbach to help us it was wonderful. Marta was full of encouragement. I remember one day when Kurt told the kids they didn't have to listen to me. I sent him to his room. 'I'm a failure as a mother,' I cried. But Marta just laughed and laughed.

'Why are you laughing?' I asked her.

'You have just become a mother. Kurt was testing you. He went to his room. He didn't run away which he might have done before.' Marta was very good to us."

"Most of my acquaintances were surprised at how quickly Kurt adapted to both of us. Remember right after we brought them home and the town threw a wedding celebration for us. Maria and George fit right in with the crowd and started to make friends. Kurt stood back and would not even eat the food or talk to anyone. I had more than one person tell me it could take years for him to adjust to a home life."

"I do remember that celebration," Beth said. "It was wonderful. I remember thinking that everyone in Austria must be musical because so many people came carrying an instrument. I had never seen an alphorn before. It was longer than I was tall. I remember that Georg even danced with me."

"Yes, and I danced with Maria, but Kurt sat on the sidelines like a tired, sullen old man. I worried that he might never get over his experiences and be able to live a normal life. But over time he changed. Now he's a clone of your father."

"They did form an instant bond when Dad and Mom were here. He took Dad fishing and from that moment on he was by Dad's side constantly. I was never told what Dad said to him but Kurt got interested in history, like Dad, and now he's made a career of it," Beth said.

"Your dad never treated him like a child. Actually, Kurt didn't have much time to be a child. But do you remember the day the adoption was final?"

"I sure do. The first time we talked with them about adoption was one of your finer moments."

"Really?" Pieter said with just a hint of modesty in his voice.

"Yes, indeed," Beth said. "Remember how we were advised not to push adoption until the time was right and we would know when that was? Well, I hadn't believed it up until then. But when we told them I was pregnant I will never forget the sad look on their faces. Maria asked us where they would be sent when we had our *real* children. I told them they were our real children. You quickly spoke up and asked them if they would let us adopt them so that legally we would all be one family. You gave them the choice."

"I do remember," Pieter said. "They were full of disbelief at first but were more concerned about what they would call us, Mom and Dad or *Vater* and *Mutter.*"

"It worked out well that they call us Mom and Dad. That let us use *vater* and *mutter* when we talked about their birth parents," Beth said. "I was always glad that Marta felt comfortable telling them about their real parents."

Pieter and Beth sat quietly remembering old times.

"I remember another special day in Kurt's life," Pieter said.

"Which day is that?"

"When you were trying to teach him at home his school lessons and the other two kids were in school. Remember, you were trying to help him catch up for all the years of school he had missed? And he got mouthy with you and didn't want to study?"

"I do remember," Beth said. "He didn't want to go to school and have to sit in the same room with the younger children. He had no opportunity to go to school during the war years. The school here had worked out a program for him to study at home for a time. He wasn't very interested. I was out of ideas to motivate him. So that day I told him he had to go on errands with me and he mouthed off again saying he wasn't going to any stupid store. I told him we weren't going to the store, we were going to the airfield. I was teaching flying there at the time to pay back some of the teaching time you had run up when you flew to Switzerland to see me. Anyhow, Kurt mouthed off again saying he hated the air field. I told him this time he was going to get his first flying lesson. He was stunned into silence. He never complained about school after that. I do believe that was the day when he finally accepted me into his life. And he even learned to love me. I think I always loved him."

"Well, he not only learned to fly a plane and love it the way we love to fly, but he has ended up as a professor of history at the university."

Pieter and Beth sat quietly remembering the past.

"What day are Hugh and Brenda coming? Is it Thursday or Friday?"

"It's Friday. Brenda said she can't wait to get to the lodge and relax."

"Do you think we should backpack up or take the car?"

"Brenda's had some ailments so I think we'd better drive up there."

The friendship between the four of them had continued for more than fifty years. They visited back and forth. Their favorite place to visit was the lodge in the Alp's.

Many years earlier when the Merriman's had loaned Pieter money to restore the family store and home, Margaret had asked Pieter what he'd really like to do with his life. He told her about a place high in the Alps where his family used to visit on overnight hiking trips. There was a lake there that was as clear as glass. It was a wonderful place to fish. And there were many, many hiking and skiing trails. It was a very special place to Pieter because of all the family memories.

About five years after Pieter and Beth were married the Merriman's came to visit them. Doug was interested in seeing the restoration that was taking place in Rossbach. Doug and Pieter hiked up to the special place that Pieter loved.

Doug also fell in love with the location and thought Pieter should build a lodge there; one that would be special enough to attract the high end spender. He said that since Pieter had repaid most of the loan Doug had advanced to him, he was willing to invest to build the lodge if Pieter was interested.

Of course Pieter was interested. It quickly became his dream. But there was a major problem. The town records had been destroyed during the war. No one knew who owned the property. Pieter searched but could find no records. He paid for a professional search to be made. There were no records. Pieter, Beth and the children liked to backpack and spend time there but it seemed the dream to own the land could not be fulfilled.

Pieter and Beth's family had increased with the birth of three more children, Frederick Albert, named for the baby's grandfathers, Greta, and Charles, named for Pieter's friend, the Merriman's son, who died during the war.

One day Kurt had come to his parents with a proposition.

"When Grandpa Martin was here he told me that the attic of our home could be made into more bedrooms. I think I should have a room up there. That would free up a room down here for the other kids. I could have more privacy, too. These kids don't give me any time alone."

"The ceiling isn't high enough up there to do that," Pieter had told him.

"Grandpa knows all about construction so I asked him in a letter. He says that's not a problem. When we get a new roof we'll just have the ceiling raised. Didn't you say we needed a new roof?"

Pieter answered, "Well, I guess I did say that. And we could use the room." He thought for a few minutes and then said, "Come on, Kurt. Let's go talk to an expert."

Arrangements were made for work to begin quickly.

Pieter and Beth decided to check out the space before the builders arrived. They had not been up there except for a quick look around years before. It appeared to be empty. There were a few small windows under the eaves to let in light. They went to look out the windows and came across a few boxes. Beth opened a couple and saw they appeared to be filled with old clothes.

"We must send these to Marta for the folk dancing troop. Or maybe the local theater group would like them. This is a treasure," Beth said.

Pieter called for the boys to help him carry the boxes downstairs. Beth began to go through them. Buried deep in one box, below all the clothes, were several large envelopes with a note on top. Beth called to Pieter to come to the room while she read the note which had been hand-written.

> *It is our hope we will all survive the war. This year, 1939, has brought us all many challenges. We don't know what lies ahead for any of us.*
>
> *It is our hope that these papers will remain hidden until one or both of our sons find them. Know that we love you both very much. We have always been so proud of each of you.*
>
> *May God always bestow his greatest blessings on you.*
>
> *Greta Dekker*   *Frederick Dekkar*
> *September 1939*

Inside one envelope were special family pictures: Greta and Frederick's wedding picture, baby pictures of the boys, the wedding picture of Karl and Elsa along with the baby picture of Kurt. There were many other pictures taken around Rossbach showing how the town had grown.

Inside another envelope were special papers, wedding and baptism certificates, land titles to property, and a copy of their will. They wanted an agreement worked out between the boys. They knew Karl loved the store so maybe Karl could have the store and Pieter could have the property. They didn't care. They just hoped it could be worked out peacefully and that each son would have a happy long life.

Pieter took the papers to his study to read them.

"Beth, come quickly," he called a few minutes later.

Together they read that his father had purchased some special property high in the Alps that was a special place for the family. He hoped that his sons would find an oasis there when the cares of the day grew heavy. This was the land Pieter loved so much.

Pieter began to weep as he held the letter in his hand. All through the war and the years after it, Pieter had to remain strong to take care of the family and the responsibilities left behind. He cried for the loss of his father and mother, brother and sister-in-law, for his friend, Charles, for Howie the gunner he had lost when the tail was blown off their plane, and other friends he had lost. He cried for the horrid destruction that had nearly destroyed his homeland.

Beth held him in her arms.

When Doug Anderson learned that Pieter owned the property he suggested making the lodge quite a bit larger than they had first thought about. He offered to put up any needed funds, saying he was sure that the lodge could be rented out year round. It could be a source of income for Pieter and Beth. Pieter loved the purity of the land and wasn't too happy about developing it at first. But when he learned he could control the use of the land (no ski-lifts or motor boats allowed) he began to warm to the idea. His goal was to do what his father wanted: keep the land as pristine as possible. Pieter wanted to provide a haven to go fishing or hiking in the summer; hiking or cross country skiing in the winter. Cross country skiing in the Alps includes a lot of hills He wanted to create a place to enjoy the environment.

Construction began almost immediately and the finished lodge was beyond their expectations. Beth's cousin, Harold, who had taken over the construction company in Glenridge, sent them lots of information about the latest technology developed during the war. The conveniences were modern and up to date yet the lodge itself maintained an old world charm. The main building held three suites and ten single rooms. A big dining room, a reception room, a large indoor swimming pool and a spa were on the main floor. A two story smaller building next door had a small gift shop, hair salon, and coffee shop on the first level. Over the shop were ten small apartments where the employees could live. The lodge became a small, but high class resort. Not really snobby high class, just special enough to attract the affluent customer. They hired a couple to manage it for them. Doug and Margaret Anderson brought some close friends to spend a week there when it opened. Word soon got out about it. Many people came from all over Europe and the United States. The lodge became booked up all year round. Some people liked to come in the summer to fish; others enjoyed the quiet ski trails in the area. The family always set aside some time each year to gather the whole family together. Over the years the family had become quite a tribe with six children, their spouses and their children.

Hugh, Pieter's best friend from college and the RAF, and Brenda, Beth's friend from London, got married about the same time that Pieter and Beth did. Soon after the lodge opened, they came to Austria to visit and had fallen in love with it. Now they were coming back for another visit.

On Friday when Hugh and Brenda arrived, Pieter drove them up to the lodge. The two couples were in a two-bedroom suite. That night they sat in the living room with a fire in the fireplace. They could see an early snow falling outside of the big windows. They began to relax and get caught up on family news. They began to remember their days during the war, especially the time they were caught in the tunnel.

As they reminisced Hugh asked Pieter about the time that Pieter had been transferred for special duty in London. This had happened right after Charles was killed and Pieter had lost one of his crew. Pieter had been transferred to London for a special assignment.

"When you got back to Livingston some weeks later you never mentioned about what you did in London. All I ever knew was that you somehow ended up on a trip to the states and you met Beth. Was your assignment horribly boring? Did you miss flying?"

Pieter sat very still for a couple of minutes. Then he quietly said, "I guess I can talk about it now. I made a trip undercover to Austria. I had tried to leave the RAF to go check on my family. Of course my request was declined. But the commander knew how very concerned I was about my family. The British Intelligence and American OSS needed someone to obtain written information and pictures that had been secretly passed through relatives from Poland to an Austrian citizen. It was Frederick Dieter who lived in Rossbach. I volunteered to make the trip. I was flown to Italy where underground workers arranged transportation to Austria. I was on my own. A lot of my travel was on farm carts. I did a lot of walking. I was disguised as a very old man. I had a wig with long white hair and an old, very long overcoat. I wore the worst shoes anyone has ever seen. German patrols were everywhere. I kept muttering to myself. I spit on the ground a lot and apparently did it well enough to get through the patrols. I knew Frederick Dieter. I knew where he lived out in the country. I finally made it to his home. He saw me coming and came outside the small shack where he lived.

'Go away,' he shouted, 'I have no food.'

"I walked fairly close to him. I quietly identified myself with a password and told him who I was. From the look in his eyes I know he was shocked to see me. He never let it show in any other way.

'We're being watched every minute,' he said. 'They suspect me of transferring information. We will not go inside,' he told me very quietly.

"I pretended to beg for food, offering my hat to him. He threw it on the ground. With many gestures he indicated he wanted my coat. I shook my head to indicate I would not trade my coat. He went inside, came out and handed me a large, hard roll. I stood and broke off small pieces of the roll. I quietly asked about my family. He told me he had definite word that my father, who had always been outspoken about his dislike for Adolph Hitler, had continued to do so very openly. The Germans used my dad as an example of what would happen if you didn't obey the rules. They arrested him. My brother fought to get him released. They both ended up being taken to a work camp for resisting arrest. My dad remained stubborn. They beat him every day. One day he couldn't get up and my brother ran to him. The guards opened fire. They both were killed. As Frederick told me these things he would wander the area, kicking up the dirt and appearing agitated. I asked him about my mother, Elsa and the children. He said the last he heard was that they were in Vienna. He very quietly told me to trade coats with him. He suggested I leave right away. He told me to be very careful. He reached over and took the hard roll from me and with gestures indicated I could have it back if I would trade my coat for it. He passed the roll under my nose as if to tempt me. I used every curse word I could think of. Finally, reluctantly I traded coats. He ordered me off his property. I'm sure I heard a lot of snickering from the woods nearby. I began my walk back to Italy. Occasionally I'd get a ride a short distance. After a couple of days I met more underground operators who eventually got me back to London. I guarded that coat with my life."

"Wow! You're quite a hero," Hugh said. "You never told a soul about it."

"What happened to Frederick?" Beth asked Pieter. "I don't remember meeting him."

"When I came home I learned the Germans had killed him. Someday I hope the story of how brave he was will come out. Even though it's been fifty years I think it's still too soon. His relatives are in the area. The hate that went on among neighbors at that time still lingers in some places. I don't want to say anything that could bring harm to anyone."

"Did you ever hear about what was in the coat?" Brenda asked.

"They were pictures of the death camps and also locations where the death furnaces were being built to kill the Jewish people. They were sewed in the lining of the coat. Since I had put my life at risk, they let me view some of them. I was sworn to secrecy. This is the first time I have ever told anyone. The CO for my assignment arranged for me to travel to the states on a visit to Seattle before I reported back to Livingston. When I was in the States, I met my Beth," he said reaching out to take her hand.

As Beth listened she thought, *now I know why Pieter had such a melancholy look when I met him in the states.* There is never a good side of war.

During the visit Brenda and Beth talked about their flying days during the war. Brenda had been officially military and had some benefits.

"Were you sad when your days in the WASP'S ended?" Brenda asked her

"My pain was eased by the knowledge that I would be coming to Switzerland and I would be closer to Pieter. But yes, I often think back to my days in the WASP's. I learned so much about the world during my time with the group. Where else would I ever have had the opportunity to learn to fly so many different kinds of planes? I do believe that we women were treated unfairly. When the WASP's were dissolved, the government ordered that all of the records be sealed. It made us feel like the group never existed or helped in the war effort. It was very hurtful. The men in Congress refused to recognize us. Those records were not unsealed until many years later when President Jimmy Carter and Senator Barry

Goldwater insisted on their release. Still, it was all done so quietly that no recognition was given to anyone. But my life has been good."

"How and where are the kids now?" Brenda asked.

"All six of our children are happy well-adjusted individuals. Kurt is a quiet thoughtful man who lives in Vienna with his wife, Alina, and two daughters whom he adores. He teaches at the university and lectures on Ancient History around the world. If he has nightmares about the events of his childhood, he hides them well. Yet his interest, his support goes to those people who live in war-torn areas. Oh, yes, like Pieter and I, Kurt did learn to fly a plane. In fact, all the kids learned to fly.

"Georg, like his birth father, was a retailer at heart. By the time he was twenty-two he had finished college. He took over more and more responsibility for the Dekkar Department Store in Rossbach. He married a beautiful young woman, Beate, who was a model. She brought with her a love and knowledge of fashion and how to dress. Soon the fashion end of the store began to blossom. Georg was approached about opening another store in Vienna, which he did. He spends his time between the two stores, but Rossbach is always home. They have a son and daughter. Their home is just a few miles from our home so we get to see them often.

"Maria surprised us all when she said she wanted to be a scientist. We had no scientists in our family. She studied very hard. She joined the United Nations in Switzerland working in their medical labs. She married Mark, an American fellow scientist. They are quiet people, happy with their work and with each other.

"Fred (our first natural-born child) is an independent spirit. He got interested in politics while in secondary school. He studied political science. He served as Mayor of Rossbach for one term. After that he went to work for the national government. He lives in Vienna with his wife, Ingrid, and son and daughter.

"Greta (our second natural child) had a bit of her mother in her I'm afraid. She couldn't wait to learn to fly. She was most happy tinkering around engines. She worked for various airlines. She had a zillion boy friends until she settled down with Alec, her husband, and family of five children. She still teaches flying. She reminds me so much of my mother. She is such an independent spirit.

"Charles, (our youngest) is so like Pieter. He is a very caring man, always watching out for others. On any given weekend you find him hiking in the Alps. He took over the management of the lodge. He has made it a great success. He has been asked to open other lodges like it. He loves nature. He's concerned about world pollution. He and his wife, Elise, have just one child, a son who looks just like Pieter."

"Have you missed living in the United States?" Brenda asked her.

"As I get older I think a lot about my days of growing up. I had wonderful parents who accepted me as I was. They didn't try to make me into someone else. How many parents would let their ten year old wash airplanes to pay for flying lessons? Or be so patient when they got in trouble with the law for speeding down the street on a go-cart. I still remember the wind blowing my hair. I thought I was going more than one hundred miles an hour. I remember how Lester at the airfield kept making me hand him tools so I would learn how to repair a plane before I could fly one. I remember the way I felt when I soloed for the first time. My mom and dad were on the ground (grinding their teeth I'm sure) but all cheers for me when I landed.

"I can remember singing with my sisters. Our love of music is something both Pieter and I brought to our home. We've always had a lot of music. I have especially enjoyed the special time I spend each year with my sisters. Sometimes we meet at one or another's home; sometimes our husbands come along. We have met in places all over the world. One of my favorite places was when we met in Switzerland. I got to take them on the cogwheel train up the side of the Alps. There are so many curves that at times if you are sitting in the middle of the train, you can see both the front and back of it. It is so steep you constantly feel you will fall off. When my sisters found out we would come off the mountain by a cable car they began to be frightened. We laughed so hard that day as we shoved them in the car. The picture we had taken remains in a frame on my desk."

"I do often wonder if I had not been in the WASP's how I could ever have met Pieter. I refuse to believe that we were not meant to be together. When a young woman from a little town in Michigan meets a man from Austria and they fall in love in a tunnel in London . . . . .well, that's hard to believe. But that's what happened."

"Do you ever get lonely for your home and family?" Hugh asked.

Beth reached over and took Pieter's hand. "Often in the mornings we will take a cup of coffee to the swing in the back yard. We take walks through our community, stopping to chat with the neighbors, checking on those who are unable to get out. It's a routine we both enjoy. It's a routine I would probably keep if I lived back in Michigan. Austria is my home now. Pieter and the children are my family. My life is good."

*   *   *

"Hey, Cathy," Mike called. "Let's take a walk over to the park. It's such a beautiful day."

Cathy grabbed her jacket and hurried to join him. Romeo, their dog, came with the leash in his mouth to join them. He always responded to the word *walk*.

"Do you remember the first time we walked to this park?" Mike asked Beth.

"How could I forget? It was when you came home on R&R from the Pacific. I remember how we had Jake with us and the kids came to play with him. Is it possible it's been fifty years since we did that? Where have the years gone?"

"Do you feel old now?" he asked her.

"I really don't. I can remember my mother telling me about a friend of hers. A woman who just a bit older than Mom had to move to the County Old Age Home. She was just over fifty years old. Of course she had no family to help look after her, but can you image anyone just over fifty today being considered that old?"

"Well, you'll never be old to me. I don't think you have had enough time to think about getting old. Your energy is amazing. But of course that's why I wanted to marry you," he told her with a smile.

He continued, "Have you ever wondered what would have happened if we had gone back to Glenridge to live in your family home the way you planned all your young life?"

"I do think about Glenridge. Of course Annie lives there so I can go back whenever I want. When the war started in 1941 it changed the lives of so many people. I don't want war, but do you think we would have met had we both not been sent to Camp McCoy?"

"I think we would have met anyway. I really can't imagine spending my life with anyone but you. One thing happens and then another and before you know it everything has changed. Like your dream to become a doctor. Sometimes I do wish you had not given up that dream. You would have made a wonderful doctor," Mike said.

281

"I gave up that dream because I thought it was the right thing to do. But I also think about how you considered going into pediatrics. Do you ever wish you had made that choice?"

"Not really. I try to remember that when I do surgery on a young father or mother that it's just as important for a child to have a parent. But I remember you telling me how you and Beth planned to live next door to each other, surrounded by friends. You must miss it sometimes."

"In a way, we have the same type of neighborhood here. The families have been in the same homes. They look out for each other. And of course, both you and Pieter have been great about getting the families together."

They sat quietly for a few minutes. Mike said, "I see a smile on your face and I bet I can tell you what you're thinking about."

"I bet you can't."

"You were thinking about our Jeff and the time Beth, Pieter and all the kids came to join our family on a trip to Glenridge. We sure had a house full of people."

"Well, you are right. I did just think of that trip. It was wonderful the way the kids all got along so well."

"That visit was more important to me than I ever told you," Mike said.

"Oh. Well, tell me now."

"That visit taught me a lot about families. I was an only child. I didn't even have any cousins close to me in age or location. I had been a bit apprehensive about the trip for I envisioned a lot of people in a house with everyone wanting to do their own thing. Instead, one person would suggest something and everyone looked forward to doing it for the most part. And yet no one got offended when someone needed private time. The kids all acted as if they knew the cousins so well. When Pieter and I took the kids to the cabin on an overnight trip to fish it was as if they had been best friends all their life," Mike told her.

"I remember that trip. Beth, Annie and I acted like teen-age girls. We giggled and laughed. We must have sung our way through all the music in the house. We had a great time just visiting and sharing memories."

"You were blessed with a good family," Mike said.

"I was impressed with how all the kids took turns cooking and doing dishes. But I guess I should not have been surprised. It's the way Beth and I were brought up," Cathy told him. "It seems to me I even remember you working in the kitchen."

"Well, you know I do cook a great breakfast. It was fun having someone other than you or our family giving me compliments." Mike smiled as he remembered.

"I remember that. I also remember that it was on that visit that Jeff decided he had to learn to fly a plane because his cousins had learned how. I had a vision of my mom and dad getting the same news from Beth and Robbie."

"Your dad told me one time that he saw and heard a passion in Beth and Robbie's voices when they announced they would learn to fly. I do believe I saw that same passion in Jeff. I was always glad he had to learn the mechanical side of flying before they let him in the air. Jeff always had a special glow about him when he'd return from lessons," Mike continued.

"Jeff was happiest when he was flying, I do believe," Cathy said.

"I'm sure he would have changed in time but it was amusing how flying came before girls or parties or . . . ."

Cathy interrupted. "He was quite charming with the ladies as well as the girls. I think they all loved him. In spite of his social skills in many ways he was a bit of a loner when it came to his personal life. I always imagined him as a dad with a big family of kids."

"He had a lot of respect for his cousins, especially the three older ones and what they had endured as young children. He was a caring young man. But I think that on the visit we all had together Jeff felt so important at first because he had been to Glenridge many times and loved showing off a bit." He paused and went on. "We did have a crowd. There were fourteen of us to sleep and use two bathrooms. How did we survive?" he asked with a smile.

"I still miss Jeff every day, even after all these years," Cathy said.

Mike reached over to take Cathy's hand. "I miss him, too. But I don't think there was anything we could have done that would have changed his mind about quitting college to fly helicopters in Vietnam."

"I know," Cathy said quietly. "When you and I were on our way to the Pacific in 1942 I remember how so many of the young men couldn't wait to get to the battlefield. Jeff had that same bravado. When I think back about being notified of his death, well, it's hard to remember that he was a young man, not a child, and entitled to make his own decisions."

Cathy sat quietly remembering that fateful day. Instead of a telegram like the Jensen's had received when Robbie was killed at Pearl Harbor, she received a visit from an officer and an Air Force chaplain. But the service remained the same: the flag draped casket, the folding and presentation of the flag, the same fly-over of the planes, the gun salute and the haunting sound of the bugler playing *Taps*.

They sat for a few minutes remembering.

Cathy spoke softly, "I got pregnant so soon after the war ended. Your Dad needed us here. Sometimes the plans we make when we are young are not the best for us when we grow older," Cathy told him.

"You are so right," Mike said. "I didn't think my dad might ever get over the death of my mom. You were so very good to him. I guess life is what happens when you're making other plans," he said.

Cathy sat remembering how Ray had gone into a state of depression when they returned to Washington after their trip to Colorado to bury Joan and Rita. Ray and Joan had planned to return to make their home in Colorado when he retired at the end of the year. Ray had already said he was tired of big city life and yearned to go back to the mountains. He blamed himself for not agreeing to leave Washington as soon as the war was over. He was full of self blame. If they had left Washington in September, Joan and Rita would not have been on a street in Virginia in October. Mike and Cathy had tried to comfort him as best they could. His friends were wonderful to him, ignoring his self-imposed isolation. They continued to come to see him. Sometimes, they would just sit with him, saying nothing.

Cathy was happy when Ray slowly returned to a normal life when he found out Cathy was pregnant. He was very protective of her and encouraging to Mike as he debated his future.

The medical firm Ray had joined in Washington was eager for Mike to join them. Mike agreed to do so. He really seemed to settle into the job nicely. He liked the people and as he said, every place needs some good surgeons. It was just assumed that they would stay on in his father's house. Ray slowly resumed his old friendships and returned to his volunteer work.

Cathy had a pregnancy of a lot of morning sickness but all those memories disappeared quickly when Jeffrey Michael was born. He looked just like Mike in his baby pictures and he had the same beautifully shaped hands: the hands of a surgeon. He brought great joy not only to Cathy and Mike but to his grandfather. Ray doted on the boy. Their second child, Beth Ann was born two years later.

Cathy's life was very busy with a husband who was a doctor, two babies, and a father-in-law who had a lot of company in the house. Cathy had been called on to continue the charity work Joan had been involved with. Before their deaths, Rita had been there to help Joan keep things moving. Cathy only had Louise who came in to clean house once a week. Occasionally she would baby-sit for Cathy. Mike and Cathy decided to ask Louise to move into the house. Rita's apartment unit in the house had been empty.

Louise had two grown children who had left the area. She was happy to have a new home and family to care for. The children loved her. On most occasions she ate with the family. Ray went back to entertaining his friends at lunch time.

Following the tradition established by Emma, Cathy and Mike always invited someone home for Sunday dinner. It became a time of interesting conversation for them all.

One Sunday their guest was a missionary back from Africa. Over dinner she talked about her work, especially with the children. Mike asked a few pointed questions about the medical conditions in Africa. He found there were few or often no doctors within an area of many miles. Mike told the woman about the children he had seen on the various islands in the Pacific. Cathy could see the wheels turning in Mike's head. When he came home a few days later he informed Cathy he had invited three doctors he worked with at the hospital and three of his Army friends to come to dinner the next week, she was not surprised.

"Have you also invited our missionary friend or is she out of town?" she asked Mike.

He started to grin. "How did you know?"

This was the first of many visits the group made to go to Africa to work with the children. Cathy and other doctor's wives collected supplies and equipment for them to take with them. Soon the doctors recruited their friends who had a variety of specialties. Their original plan called for each doctor to give a month each year to go there. They hoped to send two or four doctors at a time. It took almost a year to plan and get all the legalities out of the way.

Cathy could see that Mike was very excited as he left for Africa. He had often dreamed of the children on the islands who had stolen his heart.

"Maybe I can't go back to those islands and help them but I can help others," he told Cathy.

He came back from his first trip tired but elated. "Children with physical handicaps are shunned and accused of being possessed in some of the countries. We can help give them a chance to live a normal life."

The second trip he made he asked Cathy to go with him to assist in surgery. With Ray and Louise both at the house, Cathy said she would go.

But Mike had a surprise for Cathy. He had invited Beth and Annie to come to South Africa to join them at the end of Mike's term. One of Cathy's favorite pictures was one taken by Mike as Cathy and her sisters tried to bargain with a street vendor over the price of a wood carving Annie wanted to buy. They had no experience in the art of bargaining. But it was a fun time for all of them.

After that first trip, Cathy often accompanied Mike on his trips. Eventually the doctors involved joined with the group from France, Doctors' Without Borders.

"Enough memories," Mike said. "Why don't we walk to the café for lunch?"

"Sounds like a good plan to me," she answered.

"Have you talked with Beth Ann?" he asked.

"She and Joe and the kids will be here Sunday for dinner. I can't wait to see the kids. Young Joe reminds me so much of Jeff, always wanting to know how everything works."

"Well, Beth Ann and Joe are good about letting the kids find their own interests. I guess we did that too. Did you ever think Beth Ann would become a surgeon like me?"

"Of course, I did. Didn't she become your shadow as soon as she could walk?"

Mike gave Cathy a bright beautiful smile. "She did do that, didn't she?"

"Are you fishing for compliments?" Cathy asked him.

"I hope we were good parents," he told her.

"I'm glad times changed enough so that Beth Ann could become a doctor. Times were starting to change for women when I thought about it, but I know it would have been a struggle for me. Unfortunately, it took a terrible war for the work of women to be recognized."

They were both quiet as they continued their walk to the café. They often had these quiet spells after they had talked about Jeff. Jeff had been the idol of his parents and especially his grandfather's eyes. What Jeff wanted, Jeff got. And Jeff loved his grandfather. He might get angry with Cathy or Mike when reprimanded about missing a curfew or driving too fast. He never raised his voice to his grandfather. He loved and respected him. It was a mutual admiration society. When Jeff died, Ray lost his will to live. He died less than six months later. They took his body back to be buried next to Joan in his beloved Colorado.

Mike and Cathy had gone through the motions of living after Jeff's death. Mike put all his energy into his work. He worked many long hours. Cathy didn't want to leave the house. As the weeks went on, Mike realized that he and Cathy had just been going through the motions of living. One day Mike came home and said Cathy was going on a trip. He and Pieter had talked. They felt she needed to be with her sisters. Annie flew to Virginia. Together Annie and Cathy flew to Austria to visit Beth. They went up to the family lodge in the Alps. On one hand it had the solitude and quietness Cathy craved. On the other hand her sisters made her laugh. Pieter drove up to take them home. That was what Cathy thought. Instead of taking them home he took them to a plane headed for India. Pieter had some business meetings there for a week so insisted they join him. When the sisters had a chance to ride an elephant they all bought saris just alike. They climbed up into the basket. Pieter took pictures of them. Cathy came home from that trip still sad about the loss of her son. But now she accepted his passing and tried to move on with her life.

"Did you remember that we are hosting our dinner group next week?" Cathy asked Mike.

"That'll be fun. What kind of food will we have?"

"I'll have to decide tonight; maybe Cajun with a couple of different fish. We've done a lot of the European countries lately so I'd like to try something different. It's been fun to try so many different foods."

"I agree," Mike said. "Some of the food we've tried has been really good but some has been pretty weird."

As they entered the café they heard calls of their names. They saw another couple who lived on their street having lunch.

"Come join us," they were invited. They sat with John and Terri who lived on their street.

"John has had a terrific idea and we want you to join us. We are going to form a dance club. We'd like to have eight couples. The dance studio over on Elm Street will rent out the room and provide all kinds of music two nights a month. If we want to learn new dances they will provide a teacher. It should be a lot of fun. Will you be able to join the group?"

Mike spoke. "Cathy and I went to an Italian bistro on our first date. We danced to *Maria Elena*. How about it, Cathy?"

"I think it sounds great. Do you think they'll teach us line dancing or maybe hip-hop?" Cathy asked.

"Hip-hop?" John asked. "I'm hoping we can learn square dancing."

"Forget square dancing. I want to learn the Latin dances," Terri said.

As Cathy and Mike walked back home after lunch, they reflected on how busy and yet satisfying their life had become. They both volunteered at an inner-city health clinic one Saturday morning a month and Cathy worked with young unwed mothers. But they still had time to pursue their individual interests and find new ones to share.

Sometimes Mike and Cathy play the *what if* game. *What if* Cathy had become a doctor? Or *what if* Mike had gone into pediatrics? Or *what if* they had moved to a small town. Or *what if* they had moved to Glenridge or Colorado. They have no regrets about the choices they made. They live their life one day at a time. Somehow things work out. Of course they would like to have Jeff back. What parents ever get over the loss of a child? They try to take comfort in knowing they got to have him for twenty years. Now they have happy memories of him.

Cathy loves to share the happy memories of her childhood living in Glenridge with her daughter and grandchildren. She loves to take her family back to visit with the friends and relatives on the street.

Each spring when she sees the old fashioned petunias break through the ground, the ones she transplanted from Glenridge, she thinks of her Grandma Bertie and how much she loved the petunias. She remembers what good caring parents she had. She thinks of her mom and dad. They set a very high standard to live by. It was their teaching, love and support that made her the person she is, the woman Mike chose to marry. It is with his love and support that she continues to have a good life.

Now Cathy and Mike are in their seventies. They still walk hand in hand to the little park they visited all those years ago when he was home on R&R. They still find pleasure in the little things in life.

*   *   *

Annie came out on the porch and sat on the swing. She had a cup of her favorite coffee with her. It was a beautiful day. The sun was bright on the trees that lined the boulevard in front of her house. The leaves, with their mixed colors against the blue sky made the area look like a picture puzzle. As Annie sat she thought about how much she loved this house. Could she ever seriously consider selling it?

She had just gotten back from visiting with her friend, Esther, at the new Retirement Village which had been built just outside of town. Esther had been one of the first to move into an apartment and was urging Annie to sell and move there too. Esther's apartment had one bedroom and a tiny kitchen. She said her furniture had been oversized for the unit so she purchased new to fit the space. She ate most of her meals in the dining room in the main unit. She loved the companionship of the people around her. Two other friends, Doug and Janet, had moved their old furniture into their own small condo on the campus. Doug's big chair seemed a bit large for the room but it helped him feel very much at home. They did all their own cooking. Everything at the Village was up-to-date and very convenient. Medical service was on call which made Janet feel very comfortable since Doug had some medical problems.

Annie loved being in her own big family home. Cousin Herb lived just down the street with his son and daughter-in-law, John and Christine. Rosemary lived just across the street. But what if she were to get sick? She didn't want to be a burden. And if she waited until she got sick she might not be able to make the move.

Annie lingered on the swing for a while. Her thoughts were interrupted by the ringing of the phone. She went inside to answer.

"Hello, Annie." It was Herb. "I'm in the mood for some good fish. Do you want to ride over to the fish market for dinner?"

They usually had dinner together a couple of nights a week. When Marge, one of Annie's best friends, had married Herb they had moved into the house where Herb had been born. After his parents died he and Margie remained in the family home. When Margie became ill some years later, his son and wife, John and Christine, had moved in with them. Now Margie was gone but John and his family stayed on. Herb said he liked to go out to eat a couple of nights a week to give the family some privacy.

Annie said she would go. "But, Herb," she scolded, "You will change from your white tennis shoes and those horrid striped slacks, won't you?"

"Annie, Annie. I look so handsome in this outfit. Why do you want me to change?"

"Sometimes you dress like a clown and you know it. Christine tries so hard to keep you looking neat and up-to-date and you give her such a hard time. You simply must make more of an effort to look neat."

"Annie, were you always so bossy or did you just get this way when you got so old?"

"Well, I'm younger than you so watch what you're saying. I'll be ready in fifteen minutes."

While they were driving to the restaurant Annie wondered if she should tell Herb about her visit to the Retirement Village. She decided to wait until she made up her mind for sure, because he was sure to raise a fuss. He detested any kind of change.

They saw a lot of friends as they made their way to the table. They had a glass of wine as they waited for their food to arrive.

"You'll never guess what Danny's into now," Herb said. Danny was Herb's teenage grandson.

"What is it this week?"

"Surfing the net. He's finding all kinds of weird websites. He found one that's apparently used to locate missing people. There was a posting looking for a woman named Martin who was working at Walter Reed Army Hospital in 1943. Wasn't Cathy there about that time?"

Annie got a pained look on her face. "Yes, but her name wasn't Martin then. She was already married to Mike. She was there from late summer of 1943 till the end of the war. I remember it very well. I went to spend Christmas with her. It was the year I met Tom."

"Tom Ross," Herb said shaking his head. "I know that remembering that period of time can be painful for you. Let's change the subject."

"Not painful Herb, just poignant. It was sad that it ended the way it did but I wouldn't change a minute of it. It was the most wonderful time of my life."

Herb looked at his cousin who was like a sister to him. "You know something, Annie? You're quite a gal."

$$* \quad * \quad *$$

When Herb arrived home that night he was greeted by his son, John, and John's son, Danny.

"Did you ask her, did you find out the year, Grandpa" Danny asked.

"Ask what?" John said. "Is something going on I should know about?"

"Yes, Danny, I asked her. Annie was visiting Cathy for Christmas of 1943.

"Great news, Grandpa."

"What's going on?" John asked again.

Danny looked a bit sheepish.

"You'd better tell your Dad," Herb told Danny.

"I was surfing the net and found a site looking for people. I've been to this site a lot. There has always been a listing for someone named Annie Martin who worked at Walter Reed Army Hospital in 1943. This last time instead of saying she *worked* it said *volunteered*. Do you think someone could be looking for our Annie? Do you think it could be Tom? I think I'll go answer the letter and ask why they want to know."

"Danny, I do not approve of your answering inquiries on the web. You never know who you are dealing with. You may respond this time but if you get any more queries, I must see them. Understood?"

"Yes, Dad. I understand."

Herb spoke up. "Danny, Annie went through a lot at that time. Don't say or do anything that might bring danger to her or might cause her pain."

Danny went to his computer.

$$* \quad * \quad *$$

From: <dmartin@hotshot.net>
To: <bwebster@earth.net>
Sent: Wednesday, October 10th 10:00 PM
Subject: Annie Martin

I have a cousin named Annie Martin. She visited Walter Reed in December of 1943. Why do you ask?

Danny

*   *   *

As Annie brushed her teeth to prepare for bed that night, she thought about Tom. She hadn't thought about him for a while. *He's probably gone by now. Maybe he's been gone for more than fifty years. Gone but not forgotten. Never.*

In spite of her grief, she had lived a good life. She had met Paul, who was a fellow teacher. Paul was a kind, gentle man. Annie was teaching her Civics classes at the High School and Paul transferred there. He appeared to be a lonely, but caring man. He would stay late at work or even come in on Saturdays to help his students. Annie had learned that his wife and two small children had been killed in a violent auto crash. He escaped with only minor injuries and could not reconcile himself to the fact that he'd lost his family while he lived. He sold the family home and moved from the area. He bought a small house on a lake just outside of Glenridge and began teaching in the High School. Paul was always friendly and took his turn with after-school activities, but he would never attend any of the social functions among the teachers.

One day a terrible snow and ice storm hit the area during school hours. Classes were dismissed early. All the cars in the teacher's parking lot were snowed in. Many of the cars wouldn't start. Paul had a Jeep that he had parked close to the exit of the lot. He took as many people as he could to their homes and came back for the others. Annie was the last to be taken home.

She asked him in to warm up before he continued his journey home. They turned on the radio while they had coffee and learned that all the roads surrounding the town were impassable. Annie invited him to spend the night in the guest room. When she got up the next morning Paul was already out shoveling her driveway and sidewalk.

That was the start of a beautiful friendship. They would spend time at her house which was closer to the school or at his place by the lake. One of their favorite times was sitting on his front porch watching the sun set on the lake.

But most of their time was spent talking about their past. He told her about his loving wife and his beautiful children who had been killed by a drunk driver. He told her how he wanted to die also; that he didn't feel he could go on with his life. Annie understood his feelings. She told him about Tom and her refusal to accept his death. Many times the tears would flow from both their eyes as they remembered certain things. But soon they began to remember the good times instead of the loss each had suffered.

He remembered the joy of seeing his children learn each new thing: walking, talking, throwing a ball with his son or having a tea party with his daughter and her dolls. He remembered his wife and how beautiful she looked on their wedding day. At first he remembered these things with tears in his eyes, but as the story would be told over and over again, he began to remember more and more good things. Eventually he was even able to smile or laugh as he told a story.

Annie, too, began to smile more and even laugh as she remembered some special moment with Tom.

After about three years of companionship, one day Paul said, "Annie, you are my best friend. You know me better than anyone. You brought joy to me when I thought my life was over. I know you have feelings for Tom that you'll never forget, just as I can't forget about Isabel and the kids. But life is for the living. I know I couldn't go on if anything happened to you. I want you by my side forever – when I go to bed at night and get up in the morning. I really treasure each moment we spend together. We are not yet forty years old. We still have a lifetime ahead of us. I want to spend that time with you."

"Paul, I know that Isabel will always be a part of your memories, just as Tom will be in mine. But I agree. It is time for us to let go of what's already gone and look ahead. I realized the other day that you are an important part of my life. I don't think I could go on without you. I think we both have pretty big hearts. We have room for each other along with our memories."

Paul took her in his arms and kissed her tenderly. Soon after that with Herb and Marge by their side, Paul and Annie were married.

They had twenty-five years together, to share the problems of the world, to share vacations, holidays, and to share the joy of being alive and having someone with whom they could spend their life.

When Paul suffered a heart attack and died suddenly, Annie buried him next to his beloved Isabel and the two children. She planned to be buried next to her parents in the family lot.

When Annie went to bed that night she had a very restless sleep. Her dreams moved from Tom to Paul to apartments to some memory of her childhood in her home.

When she finally awoke the next morning she realized she had slept about an hour later than usual. After dressing she went downstairs, put two Danish pastries in a bag and went over to Rosemary's.

"Hello, it's Annie," she called out as she opened the door. "Where are you?"

"I'm in the basement. Come on down," Rosemary said.

"What are you doing down here so early?" Annie asked.

"Just looking at the junk. Did you ever see so much? Look at that old gas stove in the corner. Mom used to come down here to do her canning. Look at all the Mason jars on the shelf. Whatever am I going to do with all this stuff? It overwhelms me to think about it."

"I brought some rolls. Let's have coffee. We both have lots to talk about," Annie told her. They made their way to the kitchen.

"Bob Brewster was here yesterday," Rosemary began. "He is eager for me to get the house ready to sell. Apparently Clair called him and told him she is anxious for me to make the move to be near her in Chicago. She put a deposit on a unit in a retirement community near her. I know she loves me and is trying to take care of me because she's my daughter. Even though I know it might be best for me, I can't reconcile myself to giving up this house. It's where I was born; it's where my children were born. It was home for Roy and me from the day we were married. I still see Roy everywhere even though he's been gone for years." Rosemary sat quietly with her chin in her hands.

"Well, I know you've already given this a lot of thought. And I do know how much Clair loves you. She's worried about you being here with no family. But I also understand how you feel about the house. I feel the same way about my house. I did go visit Esther and Doug and Janet." Annie told Rosemary about her visit the previous day.

"How serious are you, Annie? Could you really do it – could you sell the house?"

"I'm still thinking. But, like you this morning looking at all your things, I have no idea what I'd do with everything in the house. I haven't been up in the attic for years. It probably still looks the same. Whatever will I do with everything? I do think it is time now for me start getting rid of things."

"Do you remember how much time we spent in that attic? We had so many good times." Rosemary paused and then continued.

"Bob suggested that I do a checklist of small things to be done to update this house to help it sell more quickly; like the leaky faucet in the bathroom and the tile that needs replaced. I guess I'll have to look for someone to do those small jobs."

Annie spoke up. "Just ask Herb to do them. Remember he is the son and grandson of carpenters. He's pretty handy with small things."

"Annie, I couldn't ask him. He's so busy with his volunteer and his community work. He would never let me pay him for doing it. I'm afraid if I ask him about someone I can hire to do it he'll think I don't trust him to do it right. I'll have to think on it."

"Well," Annie said. "I think I'd better go home and start on the attic today."

"I'll go with you," Rosemary said.

Together they made their way to the place where they had spent so much of their childhood. They looked at the little round table with two chairs where two dolls still sat waiting for the tea party to start.

"Tea, Rosemary?" Annie said as she picked up the doll size cup and saucer. Rosemary picked up the doll with a china head and soft body.

"There's Cathy's hospital over there. Whoever thought she'd stay with medicine all her life?" Rosemary asked as she saw doll cribs, buggies, and cradles all lined up. In another corner were the remains of old cardboard boxes that Beth and Robbie had used to build airplanes and boats to see the world.

"School time," Annie said as she stood among the makeshift schoolroom she had created.

"Oh, Annie, whatever are you going to do with all this? Children today play with modern electronic things."

"Maybe I'll call the Children's Theater. They might be able to use some of these things in their plays. It's time they go."

That night Christine called Annie inviting her for spaghetti that evening.

"Annie, you seem rather quiet tonight. Are you feeling OK?" Christine asked her.

Annie told them about being in the attic that day. "I guess I'm deep in memories today," Annie said. "But it's time I think about getting rid of things."

"Why do you want to get rid of everything?" Herb asked. "You're supposed to leave it for someone else to get rid of when you die. Christine is right. You do seem to be rather quiet these days. Annie, do you have a medical problem you don't want to talk about?"

"Herb, I'm fine. But if you must know, I am thinking seriously about selling the house and moving to the Retirement Village."

"That's the most stupid thing I've ever heard you say." Herb was almost shouting. "You don't know anything about that place. It's terrible."

"Actually, Herb, it's very pleasant. I was out earlier in the week. And I didn't tell you because I knew you'd have a hissy fit just like you're doing right now. I'm not going to talk about it any more tonight," Annie said.

"Can I have some help clearing the table?" Christine tactfully asked. She was used to the bantering between the two cousins. It didn't worry her. She knew this was their way of competing to see who would have the last word.

"I'll help," said Annie. As they finished clearing the table, Annie told Christine that she did have a little problem she needed help with. She told Christine about Rosemary needing help but reluctant to ask Herb to help her.

"Dad would probably get a lot of pleasure of doing it for her," Christine said.

"Rosemary would never agree to let me ask him for her," Annie said.

"No problem," Christine said. "I'll just talk with Dad about Rosemary trying to get the house in good shape and suggest he ask her if he can help."

"Christine, you are so smart," Annie said as she gave her a hug.

*   *   *

Later that evening, Danny brought his father an E-mail letter that he had just received.

From:	<bwebster@earth.net>
To:	<dmartin@hotshot.net>
Sent:	October 11th 10:00 PM
Subject:	Annie Martin

You asked *why Annie Martin?* A very good honest man met someone named Annie Martin in 1943. He always wondered what happened to her. He was a patient at Walter

Reed; she was a volunteer. He does not know I am looking for her. He has a birthday coming up and I would like to surprise him with cards from old friends. Can you tell me if your Annie ever volunteered at Walter Reed?

Bill

* * *

Annie decided it was time to start down-sizing her possessions. Annie had already donated most of her father's papers to the university and her mother's papers and journals had been given to the local library. Beth and Cathy had been through most of their things and taken those things they wanted to keep. She found the old trunk full of dress-up clothes the girls had played with and put them with the dolls and furniture to be given to the theater. She felt a small pang when she added her first blackboard and *teaching* desk to the lot. But it was time to let go of those things. Danny had come over and carried some boxes of papers to the library.

She was lost in time when she heard the doorbell, followed by a friendly, "It's me."

"Come on in, Herb," she called. "I'm in the library."

"Did you want me to pick up sandwiches or should we stop somewhere," he asked.

"Oh, my. I didn't realize it was this late. We'd better stop on the way," Annie said.

One afternoon a week Annie and Herb volunteered at the local hospital. Herb usually would take people in wheelchairs for X-rays or tests to and from their rooms. Annie worked in the Children's Ward. Often she would visit or play games with them. Danny made sure she knew how to play the latest electronic games. Sometimes she would tell them or read them stories. But Annie had a special knack for talking with the parents, trying to reassure them that their child was getting good care.

As they drove along, Herb asked Annie, "Are you serious about selling the house?"

"Not quite yet. I'm still thinking about it."

"Well, it's making me think seriously about what I should do. I never expected to end up living with John and Christine. When Margie was sick for so long and they moved in, I don't think even they thought it would be forever. But after Margie died and they stayed on, one year became two and . . . . ."

"I know, Herb. Sometimes things just happen. But I know for sure that they are very, very happy with the living arrangements. Christine has told me so, many, many times. She has made it her home."

"Yes, I think she has. That's why she and John should always live there. It's me who should find another place. Maybe I should check out the Retirement Village." He was quiet for a few minutes. "There is really just one thing that's keeping me from looking into it. I really don't want to live alone."

"And I don't really think I could live with anyone. I've been alone since Paul died. I like my independence."

"Well, you're my cousin and best friend. But you're much to bossy to live in the same house as me," Herb said with a smirk in his voice.

"And you're too old and grouchy to live in a house with me."

As Annie lay in bed that night she thought about the conversation she and Herb had about the Retirement Village. *I guess it's part of growing older and having a time when we need to make changes in our lives. I never thought about the fact that Herb might be lonely. He needs a woman in his life. Esther would love to be married. So would Ruth. Or what about Jenny? She is a sweet woman.* And then Annie had a brilliant thought: *Rosemary. Rosemary doesn't want to leave Glenridge but her daughter doesn't want her to be alone. Rosemary and Herb along with their spouses, who had died, were best friends for all their life. Why doesn't she, Annie, get Herb and Rosemary together. How would she do it? She'd figure out something.*

Annie, with a smile on her face, settled in for a good night's sleep

*   *   *

Danny made a copy of the E-mail response he got back from bwebster. He wasn't sure what reaction he would get from his dad when he showed it to him. He knew his dad wanted him to forget the whole thing. But Danny loved Annie. He had heard about the love story between a man named Tom and Annie that had ended badly. Maybe this would be something nice for Annie. He knew he might get in trouble if he answered it since he only had permission to respond to the first E-mail. It was decision time. He took the letter into the living room where the family was watching TV.

"I got a letter back from bwebster," he told his family as he gave his dad the letter.

"What letter? What's going on?" Christine asked.

John told Christine about the first letter and then read her the letter Danny had given him.

"Let me have some time to think on this, Danny. I'll respond if we think it best."

John, Christine, and Herb discussed the letter.

Herb finally spoke. "We're assuming this could have something to do with Tom. It may not. Maybe we need more information. It could be something that would give Annie a lot of pleasure. But let's not mention it to Annie until we know for sure what it's all about."

"I'll write an acknowledgement back but give him the opportunity to shut the door on this correspondence," John said.

From	<jmartin@anchor.net>
To:	<bwebster@earth.net>
Sent:	October 13th 9:30 PM
Subject:	Annie Martin

Hello, bwebster! I am John Martin, father of Danny, who has communicated with you regarding Annie Martin. I would prefer that if we continue to be in touch, you communicate with me instead of my young son. My cousin, Annie, was a volunteer for a brief time at Walter Reed in the time period you named.

As much as I would like to help you to help your friend, I am having very mixed feelings about doing so. My cousin met a young soldier and fell in love. He didn't make it home from the war. Annie suffered a serious deep depression for more than a year and even after recovering, never forgot him. I am not comfortable talking with her about that period of time. I hope you will understand my concerns. Best wishes to you in your search.

John

*   *   *

Annie continued to go through boxes of papers from the attic. One day she came upon the box containing her letters to and from Tom. She decided to read them one last time and then she would burn them in the fireplace. They were extremely personal to her and she hated the thought of someone else reading them. She held them in her hands for a few minutes. *Sometimes it seems I can feel you close to me* she thought. *I don't think I'm ready to let go of these letters today. Maybe tomorrow.* She closed that box and reached for another.

This box was very special. It held the very personal items of her dad and mom. She pulled out the picture frame holding the picture of Emma and Albert on their wedding day. Her dad always kept it on his desk. There were various special pictures of the family vacations. Annie sat in solitude and thought about her parents. They had always been so encouraging to their children. They took joy in watching the girls grow. If the girls ever disappointed them they hid it well. Annie remembered how excited they had been to go to Austria to see Beth shortly after the war. They had a wonderful visit. Emma got sick shortly after they returned. They learned that cancer had invaded her body. Even though medical care had improved over the years, pancreatic cancer was still a mystery. Emma had died after a few short months. Albert was never able to recover from her death. He resigned his position at the University and lost all interest in everything. He joined Emma in death before the year was over. Annie looked at the pictures and mementos in the box. *This box will stay with me forever,* she thought.

The next box held papers from her teaching days. She took time to read a few. It was very enjoyable to re-read some of the papers she had saved. One of her students had become mayor of Glenridge. One had become a congressman. He had been a fun-loving rascal of a student. She set his papers aside. *I think I'll send these papers to him.* She found a very well-written paper from a young girl who had gone on to become the president of a small university out west. Annie was interrupted when Rosemary and Herb came in the house.

"I've been making some small repairs at Rosemary's and now I'm going to take the both of you out for pizza. Get your jacket," Herb told Annie.

"I'll meet you," she told him. "I need to drop off some things at the Goodwill Center."

Annie smiled as they left without her. *Maybe my plan to get them together is working.*

* * *

From: <bwebster@earth.net>
To: <jmartin@anchor.net>
Sent: October 17
Subject: Annie Martin

John,

Thank you for your e-mail. I know my prior e-mail was a bit vague.

You deserve to know the truth. The veteran I wrote about is Joe Ross, my step-father. He fell in love with someone named Annie Martin in December of 1943 as he was about to leave the Walter Reed Army Hospital to return to duty in Europe. He was seriously wounded there, both physically and mentally. He suffered from amnesia. He had no idea of his name or where he was from. This continued for almost two years before he recovered. He was identified as Joseph T. Ross after he remembered he had worked for the FBI. As he was recovering he kept saying the name, Annie. My mother was his nurse. She made it her goal to locate Annie. It was some time before he remembered Annie's last name. After a long and detailed search for Annie proved fruitless, he and my mother were married. My birth father had died on December 7th. As my mother lay dying years later, she made me promise to keep looking for Annie. A few weeks ago, a friend mentioned about volunteering at a hospital. Joe said Annie had been a volunteer.

This was the first time he had remembered this information so I changed my on-line search to include about being a volunteer.

As much as I would like to know if your cousin is the Annie we've been looking for, I have no desire to upset her life. Joe still talks about Annie. I feel an obligation to Joe (and my mother) and perhaps even to Annie to at least make an effort to locate her. Please give this matter some thought.

Bill

*   *   *

Annie had just poured a cup of coffee when she heard the doorbell followed by "It's me." Rosemary came to the kitchen. "I'm so upset this morning. Bob Brewster called again last night trying to push me into listing the house with him right away. And you better know this: Herb is a mess worrying about you moving."

"Forget Bob Brewster. He's just looking for a fat commission. Our houses sell very fast in this neighborhood. But what's this about Herb?"

"He thinks Retirement Villages are places where you go to sleep in your wheelchair all day. He says you don't understand what you're doing."

"He is so wrong. It's lovely out there. Some of the units have a view of the woods that you can see into, and some have a view of the lake. They're beautiful. Maybe I should take him out to see them. He might rest easier. I think we should go this morning."

"Well, if you do go, come back for lunch at my house. I couldn't sleep last night so I got up and made an apple pie. I'll fix some soup to go with it."

Annie called Herb. He finally agreed to go look at the campus. He was pleasantly surprised. He managed to criticize some things, but that was his way of admitting he could have been wrong. Annie decided she would want a two bedroom unit and took some measurements.

"I see a big round couch here with a colorful throw rug," Annie told him.

"Is it wired for the internet?" he asked her.

They returned to Rosemary's for a delicious lunch. As they finished eating, Rosemary told Herb to go into Roy's library, sit in the big chair and watch TV.

Herb had a fit. "I can't sit in Roy's chair," he said.

"Herb, it's just a chair. Go, sit. I'll make us a cup of tea."

As he made his way to the library he very loudly compared this old stately home to the new modern condo at the village.

"You don't see crown molding like this at that place. Look at these nice big rooms. Look at the stained glass windows. Look at the beautiful hardwood floors. Look at the high ceilings. Look at these beautiful old rugs. They don't belong in a condo."

Annie and Rosemary just smiled as they listened to his tirade.

Rosemary took him his tea. When she came back she was crying. Annie was furious.

"What did Herb say to you? Did he offend you? I'll straighten this out." She started from the kitchen.

"No, no, no," Rosemary cried. "It's not that. He's sitting in front of the TV sound asleep. He's so peaceful. It just reminded me of how Roy did that. I'll never be able to have memories like this if I move to Chicago."

Annie decided to be brave. "Rosemary, I think you and Herb should get married. He's a lonely man who constantly thinks he's in the way at his own home. You want to stay here but your daughter doesn't want you to be alone. I think it's a perfect solution to both problems."

"Me! Marry Herb? What a crazy idea." The tears were gone. Rosemary was very indignant. "Well, I never."

"Well, you've known each other forever. Both Roy and Margie would smile from heaven if they saw you together."

Their voices must have gotten louder because Herb came back to the kitchen

"Are you two fighting?" he asked.

"Certainly not. Why would you say such a thing," Annie asked him.

"Well, I thought I heard loud voices."

"I need to go home," she told him. "You left your hat at my house. Come and get it right now or I'll throw it out."

As they walked to her house she decided it was time for step two. "Rosemary is very lonely. She doesn't want to move to Chicago."

"I know that. I think it's terrible that her daughter is making her move."

"Her daughter loves her. She doesn't want her mom to be alone. She has no family here to help look after her."

"We've always looked after her."

"Yes, Herb but it's not the same as family." Annie swallowed hard and decided to go ahead. "I think you and Rosemary should get married. You can move into her house. You worry about John and Christine having little privacy. This would give them privacy. You'd have company all the time. You really need to think about it."

"You just think you can boss everyone don't you? I never heard such foolishness. What about you? Living alone in some stupid modern condo without any family around. Who do you plan to marry?"

"Herb, I was blessed twice in my life to have the love of two good men. One that was the love I will never, ever forget. The other was a good man who didn't try to make me forget the first. I will never marry again."

Herb left the house in a snit. Annie didn't worry. She knew her cousin well enough to know she gave him something to think about.

Somehow, Annie could not get Tom Ross from her mind. She went back to the box where she had placed the letters he had written her along with the letters she had written him that had been returned. She sat in her room until dark that night, reliving every minute she spent with Tom. *I don't want to think he is dead. That leaves one alternative. He didn't want to come back to me. Somehow I just can't believe that. He really loved me. He must be dead. Will the heaviness I feel in my heart when I think of him ever go away?*

On the bright side, her little matchmaking was working well. When Annie *didn't feel well* and couldn't go to an Alumni dinner with Herb, he asked Rosemary to go. For a couple of weeks it seemed they became a threesome. Then Rosemary's daughter visited. She saw what was happening; how the two of them were becoming a couple. She cancelled her plans to move her mother to Chicago.

*   *   *

John gave a lot of thought of how to respond to the latest E-mail from Bill Webster. He talked with Herb.

"Do you think he could be a scam artist who thinks Annie may have a lot of money? Or maybe some step-son with an infirmed old man on his hands that he wants to unload?" John asked his dad.

"Could be," Herb said. "Or he could actually be for real. Maybe Tom *was* badly injured and lost his memory and that's why Annie didn't hear from him."

"Do we take a chance, Dad, or just ignore all this?"

"Can you look him up on the Internet?"

"Let's do that now."

A search of the internet for Bill Webster revealed that he was the head of the Oceanic Institute in Portland, Oregon. His father was John T. Ross who headed Ross Investigations, a firm that specialized in corporate espionage. Mr. Ross had retired.

"I guess I'll respond carefully," John said.

> From: <jmartin@anchor.com>
> To: <bwebster@earth.net>
> Sent: October 18th
> Subject: Annie Martin

> Bill:
>
> I admit I was surprised by your last e-mail. The man my cousin fell in love with was named Tom Ross. Do you know if the "T" in his name is for Thomas? Annie went to visit her sister for Christmas in 1943. Her sister, Cathy Martin Goodman, was a nurse at Walter Reed and encouraged Annie to spend some time trying to cheer up the troops. According to the family's memory, Tom was somewhat of a loner. Annie became his friend and soon fell in love with him. They only had a short time together. Right after Christmas Tom left for a new assignment and Annie returned home. They corresponded over the next few months. One day all the letters were returned with a stamp indicating he was missing in action. A little while later more letters were returned with the stamp indicating he had been declared dead. She never heard from him again. She tried every way possible to get information, (even enlisted the help of her Senator). For almost a year the family thought she would never get over the loss of Tom. She became very ill during that time but finally did recover. She could not accept that Tom was gone from her life. Many years later she met and married a good man and they had twenty-five years together before he died.
>
> I'm confused about what to do. It could be devastating to them both if they were to get their hopes up about meeting each other and then find these are two entirely

different people. I share your concern about what to do. Let's think on this.

John

Almost immediately John received an E-mail.

From: \<bwebster@earth.com>
To: jmartin@anchor.com
Sent: October 18th 9:00 PM
Subject: Annie Martin

Joe's middle name is Thomas. He was named Joseph Thomas Ross, Junior. His parents called him Tom. Do you know if your Tom came from Iowa?

Bill

When John read the E-mail, he turned to Herb. "Do you know where Tom is from?" he asked.

"I think it was Iowa. I know he went to school there," Herb told him.

John went back to the computer.

From: \<jmartin@anchor.com>
To: \<bwebster@earth.net>
Sent: October 18th 8:00 PM
Subject: Annie Martin

Bill:

My dad thinks it was Iowa. He knows Tom went to school in Iowa.

My dad and Annie grew up together. They are each other's best friend.

Dad is urging us to try to figure out how we can solve this mystery.

Like he said, they both are getting older. If the Tom and Annie we know are the people we suspect they might be, should they have the right to make a decision about whether or not they want to risk a disappointment about meeting? I have to admit it is beginning to sound like Joe and Tom could be the same person. Let me tell you about Annie. She grew up in a happy home with her mom, dad, and sisters Beth and Cathy. She met and fell in love with Tom while she was visiting with Cathy. Annie is currently going through old letters, etc. which is taking her on a trip down memory lane. She's talking about her time together with Tom.

She remembered that Tom's father apparently died before he went into the service and his mother died just after he joined the FBI.

He said he had no other relatives. If you can use any of this information in your talks with Joe, please feel free to do so. Do you think it's time for us to talk with them about it or consider some form of contact between them?

John

Christine knocked on the door of John's study. "I brought you both some coffee," she told John and Herb. "I think it's time you tell me what's going on. You two have been spending a lot of time on the computer lately and seem very secretive. Danny thinks he knows what's going on. Well, I don't know and I'd like to know. Does it have to do with those E-mails?"

"You are so right, Christine," Herb said. "Better tell her the whole story, John."

Christine was near tears when she read the E-mails that had been sent between John and Bill Webster.

"Do you think it could be Tom? Oh, wouldn't that be wonderful for Annie. But what if it's not Tom? It would kill her to get her hopes up and then find out he's not Tom. What are you going to do?"

John checked his E-mail one more time. "Looks like maybe we might not have to decide." He shared the latest letter he had just received.

From: <bwebster@earth.net>
To: <jmartin@anchor.com>

Sent: October 19th 9:00 PM
Subject: Annie Martin

Annie's information about the death of 'Tom's' parents agrees with the information that Joe gave us. I am having many concerns about going forward with a reconciliation. I'll be in touch when I reach a decision.

Bill

"I guess we sit and wait now," Herb said.

*   *   *

Annie seemed to be consumed with thoughts of Tom. She had gone thru spells like this before. *I know I will get over it. Yet, the thoughts pressure me day and night. I wish I had been able to find some family member I could have talked with. I really tried but I had no luck finding anyone. I pray that I will be relieved of the burden that I feel from time to time. I can't allow myself to slip into the darkness that I was in all those years ago. I must try to move on with my life.*

She reached for a stack of magazines on her night stand. One was a travel magazine with an article written by a person just back from Oahu – a person who had lost a loved one on December 7, 1941. She read it twice. *Could it be an answer for her?*

The article told of a tradition that had been started at Pearl Harbor after the floating memorial was built over the USS Arizona that lies on the bottom of the harbor. Guests riding on tour boats drop leis of flowers on the water and let them drift as a memorial to their loved ones. Annie had always felt that if she could have attended a funeral for Tom that it would have been a way to say goodbye to him and make it easier to accept his death. That didn't happen. It made it easier when she said goodbye to her mother and father. It made it easier when she said goodbye to Paul when he was taken so suddenly. A service for Tom when she learned of his death would not have been very meaningful since she was the only person in Glenridge who knew him. But the anguish of not saying goodbye had stayed with her all these years.

As she lay in bed that night she tossed and turned for a bit and then the answer came to her. She would go to Hawaii. She would hold her own memorial service for Tom by dropping a lei in the water. *I know that Tom didn't die on December 7th, or even in Hawaii. But he was a victim of the war that started that day. I will do it in memory of Tom, the man I truly loved. The man I can never forget.* She fell into a peaceful sleep.

The next morning she called her travel agent who had helped her plan her trips all over the world; the trips with Paul and also with her sisters. She asked to be booked into the Pink Palace, the Royal Hawaiian Hotel. She would go at the end of the week.

Christine called and invited Annie for dinner that night. Annie said she would go.

I will tell them of my plan to make the trip, she decided, *but I will keep my plan for the memorial to myself. That will be my last private time with Tom. Then I will come home and make a deposit on the condo at the Retirement Village. I will sell this house.* She felt at peace with her decision.

"I have some news for you," Annie told the family as they had dessert that night. "I'm taking a trip to Hawaii. I'm leaving this weekend."

"You can't do that. You can't make that trip alone," Herb told her. "Or is Rosemary going with you?"

"No, Herb, I'm going alone. I am not too old to make a trip alone. You might be but I'm not."

Christine spoke up. "Annie, I think that's wonderful. But John and I are also going to Hawaii. We're celebrating our anniversary a month early. Would you mind if we travel with you? I promise you we'll give you all the private time you want."

"Well, I guess I don't mind. You do know I can make this trip alone don't you?"

"Of course," Christine said, ignoring the glare from John and the coughing spasm from Herb. "But it will be company for me on the way over. You know how John likes to sleep on the plane."

John got up from the table saying he had to make a phone call.

"Annie, are you in your second childhood? First you decided to sell the house and move, and now you're making a big trip alone. What are you thinking of?" Herb asked.

"That I don't want to become an old grouch like you. Now let's get busy and do the dishes."

*   *   *

John had received a phone call from Bill Webster at the end of last week. Bill had apologized for not answering John's last E-Mail promptly. He admitted that he needed time to absorb the fact that Annie seemed to be the person for whom he'd been looking. He admitted he had been reluctant to accept that fact. Tom had been a very good father to him and he didn't want to see his dad get hurt, nor did he want to lose him. But how could they make it work? Should he and his wife come with Tom to Glenridge? Or should Annie, John and Christine come to Portland? Should they find some neutral place? Should they tell Tom and Annie before the meeting? They had many questions about how to make it happen.

John made the phone call to Bill. "It seems my dear cousin, Annie, may have solved our problems. She has decided to take a trip to Hawaii. She got her tickets for this weekend. My wife informed Annie that we also had a trip planned there. Do you think you and your wife and Tom could meet us? I'll try to work out the details. Maybe if we all get together and they get to talking they will be able to make the final decision about who they are."

That seemed like a good plan to Bill. 'For better or worse we are committed now," he said.

*   *   *

Annie was a little worried as she packed her bags. She had made trips with John and Christine in the past. Yet, everything seemed a little different this time. She really had a feeling that they had not planned to make this trip. To her eyes, John had looked very surprised when Christine had announced they were going to Hawaii. Things seemed so tense between them. Maybe John has some medical problem he's worried about. He's always been strong and dependable yet he walks around with a worried look on his face. Maybe the trip will do him good, she thought. *But they better give me my alone time. I must have time to say goodbye to Tom.*

The trip to Hawaii was uneventful except for the fact that John walked all the way. He didn't walk on water, but he did pace the aisles every time the *fasten your seatbelt* sign went off.

"Christine," Annie asked. "What's wrong with John? Did you make him come on this trip because you didn't want me to go alone?"

310

"I would never do that. He's just got a lot on his mind. I think this trip will do him good."

As they neared Honolulu Annie looked out the window. She could see the Royal Hawaiian Hotel, the Pink Palace, nestled among the other hotels along the waterfront. She remembered the first time she had seen it from the ship when her parents took the family there. She remembered seeing it from the air when Paul and she had joined with Beth, Pieter, Cathy and Mike for a week. It had really changed over the years. Now there was a big white sandy beach. Sun umbrellas dotted the shoreline. Sailboats and catamarans were sailing on the clear water. It was so beautiful. They had taken a late flight out of Chicago so the sun was rising as they reached the hotel. Annie told them she would see them for dinner that evening. She went to her room and unpacked her things and then put on her swimsuit and cover-up. She headed out to sit on the beach. The beach boys set an umbrella over her head and towels in the chaise to sit on. The sun was warm. It felt good on her weary old bones. She watched the families walking by with the children trying to catch the waves. She saw young lovers walking hand in hand. She drifted off for a long afternoon nap. As she walked back through the lanai she could see the tables ready for the evening dining. She freshened up and joined John and Christine for dinner. She wasn't sure whether or not she wanted to tell them about her plans for the next day. She had one thought that it might be nice to have them with her. On the other hand, she wanted some alone time to say her goodbye. As they separated to go to their rooms, she told them she had plans for the next day.

"Try to join us for breakfast around 9:30." John requested.

"No, I think you and Christine need to have a whole day to yourself. I'll be up and out early."

John took both of her hands in his. "Annie, do me this one favor. Please meet us for breakfast. We have friends joining us from Portland, Oregon. I want you to meet them. It's really, really important to me. Please do this for me."

Of course, she had to say yes. She was a bit disappointed. She putzed around the next morning waiting till the appointed time. She put on a pair of slacks and a knit top. Then she decided that maybe she should be dressed a little better. The Royal Hawaiian is a pretty fancy place. Maybe these friends they're meeting are business associates. She changed her clothes. She put on a white cotton top and a long white skirt with touches of blue in it. She didn't like the way the neckline looked so she reached for her jewelry case to look for a necklace. She found the locket that had belonged to Tom's mother, the one she had worn for years like a wedding ring. The locket hit her neck in just the right place she thought. She had gotten a little sun the day before. *Instead of my usual pasty skin, I think I have a bit of a glow.* She felt pretty good as she made her way to the dining room.

John and Christine were waiting for her. The maitre'd escorted her to the table. The restaurant in the lanai extends openly to the sandy beach. The sun was shining brightly and the ocean was sparking in the sunlight. The maitre'd seated her with her back to the ocean view but what could she say?

She saw a couple enter from the lobby, a couple about the same age as John and Christine. They were escorted to their table. She was introduced to Bill and Dorothy Webster.

"My step-father made this trip with us. We expected him to be with us now. Apparently he took a walk on the beach. I'm sure he'll be here soon," Bill said.

To Annie the conversation seemed a bit strained and not quite natural. John and Christine were usually very out-going on occasions like this. Even the Webster's seemed tense.

They began to chat. Bill suddenly looked toward the water and said, "Here comes my dad now."

"Sorry, I'm late, everybody. The day is so beautiful and the sun felt so good . . . ."

Annie heard a voice behind her. She suddenly felt as though she might faint. She tried to turn and rise from her chair. She was shaking so hard she thought she might fall. She felt a chill run up and down her spine yet she felt that all her blood had rushed to her head. Her heart began to throb.

"That voice . . . that voice," she cried loudly as she turned around.

"Annie. Oh, Annie. Is it really you?"

It was Tom; her Tom, Tom Ross. They reached for each other. They held each other close, then backed away to look at each other.

He didn't see the gray hair or lines on her face or slightly stooped shoulders. She didn't see the bald spot or weathered skin or slight paunch of his belly. To Annie, Tom looked exactly like the young soldier she had told goodbye more than fifty years earlier. To Tom, Annie was still the

312

young girl with the dark curly hair in a green coat waving to him. They had no need for words. Being in each other's arms was enough.

"The scar over your eye; it's still there," he said touching it gently with his finger.

She looked into his eyes. "I still see the A in your eye. Oh, Tom, is it really you?"

They stood holding each other for a few minutes. The entire restaurant had gotten very quiet. Annie felt as if the world was standing still. She looked over at John and Christine. She looked at Bill and Dorothy. All four of them were sitting at the table with tears streaming from their eyes. Actually, there wasn't a dry eye in the entire restaurant as the other patrons realized the reunion they were watching.

Tom and Annie looked at the family and then each other. "Oh, Annie," he said. "Today is a set-up. I couldn't figure out why they were so insistent I come with them on this trip."

Annie wanted, almost needed, to sit down, but she didn't want to leave his arms.

Bill spoke. "The maitre'd has a small private room next door. Let's move to the room so we can talk."

Clinging to each other, they made their way out of the dining room. It was a small room with two couches and four chairs. A tray was placed on a table with a big urn of coffee, a basket of sweet rolls, and a plate of fresh fruit. "We can have this room for as long as we like," Bill told them.

Tom and Annie sat next to each other. He pulled her close to him.

"I don't understand yet just what is happening, but I thank you from the bottom of my heart for making this day the best day of my life," Tom said.

"Tom, I thought you were dead," she said finally reaching a state of accepting that he really was her Tom.

"I know you did. Everyone did. I guess I was close to death. When I finally woke up, I knew I had to find you." He paused. "It's a long story. But how did today happen?" he asked Bill.

"Dad, you know I promised Mom that I'd never give up trying to find Annie for you." Bill then looked at Annie. "Annie, my dad looked for you for fifty years. He never forgot you. For a long time he could not remember your last name. When he did remember we started a search. Do you have any idea how many Annie Martins live in the United States? We had your name posted in newspapers all over the country, especially in Washington,

D.C. Then computers became popular. I put the same posting on the Internet that we had used before to try to find you: *I'm trying to locate Annie Martin who worked at Walter Reed Army Hospital in December 1943.* One night a few weeks ago when we had company one woman mentioned that she was going to volunteer at the hospital. You, Dad, said that Annie was a volunteer at Walter Reed. That was the first time we had heard that so I changed the posting from *worked* to *volunteered* there."

"I do remember that night," Tom said. "I tried for many years to forget about you, Annie. I never could. I hoped you had met someone who would be good to you. I hoped that you had a good life. The Lord moves in mysterious ways on his own schedule. I'm not sure if Betsy first told me about God or if I remembered about Him through my stupor of amnesia. First, I remember praying that God would help me learn who I was. I did find out. After I remembered who Annie was, I prayed that I would be able to find you. Just a few weeks ago I remember sitting on my porch, looking at the mountains. I prayed that somehow God would let me remember just one more thing, some little thing that might lead me to you. I thought it would be in the form of a city or location. I remember the night Bill, Dorothy and I were visiting with Ruth Nelson. I remember her talking about volunteering at the hospital. I do not remember saying anything about Annie being a volunteer. Did I really say it or did you, Bill, make the connection in your mind that this was new information to help in the search? It doesn't matter at all. God got the message and it was just what I asked for. I am a happy man." He shook his head in amazement. "Tell us what happened next."

"I got back an e-mail the next day from a Danny Martin who said his cousin had been there at that time and why did I want to know."

John spoke up. "Danny is our youngest son. He's a computer geek. I wasn't sure he should answer Bill's posting. I was angry at first for I didn't want him communicating with people we didn't know. Bill responded back with a rather lame reason for the posting. I wrote back a terse note saying he should not communicate with my son. I took over the communication. I'll confess I didn't know what to think. I wouldn't do anything in the world to hurt you Annie. I didn't know whether to let you decide what to do or protect you."

Bill went on. "I guess I felt the same way. I have been helping Dad look for you for so long, that I thought it was another wild goose chase or maybe some phony who likes to play games. The more we communicated the more I had to realize that maybe we had found you."

"Annie, you really stunned us when you said you were coming to Hawaii," Christine said. "John and Bill had finally decided that it would be up to the two of you to decide if you wanted to take a chance to see if you really were the same two people who were in love all those years ago. They weren't sure how to make it happen. None of us wanted to put either of you in a situation that would be uncomfortable for you. We really couldn't be sure that you would know each other after all these years."

Annie got off the couch to give John and Christine a hug. "Now I know why you were so antsy lately. Thank you, thank you, thank you." She turned to Bill and Dorothy. "Thank you so much for not giving up."

Dorothy said, "We were worried that you might have moved on with your life. Joe, or Tom as you call him, was sure you were married since you thought he had died. Yet he wanted to be sure that you were OK. We did not want to put either you or Dad in a position that might shock and later disappoint you. We really couldn't be one hundred percent sure if you were Dad's Annie. Even if you were, we couldn't be sure if you wanted him in your life after all these years."

"And the E-mails had the name of Joe, not Tom," John added.

"My name is Joseph Thomas Ross. My dad's name was Joe so the family called me Tom."

"By the way Annie, you owe me ten bucks. I paid the maitre'd to seat you so you would be able to see Tom come in the door," John said with a smile.

"Instead I took a walk and came in the other way," Tom said. "I'll always be by her side from now on," he told them.

Dorothy spoke up, "Dad, I almost had a heart attack when I found the note you shoved under the door this morning about taking an early walk. I know sometimes you walk for an hour or more."

"Sorry about that Dorothy. I never imagined a surprise like this. I don't understand yet how all this communication went on so quickly."

"E-mails, Dad," Bill said. "I brought the whole set with me. You can read them later."

"In our effort to protect you both, we played cat and mouse for a while, you know, asking questions. We then tried to confirm answers," John said.

Annie thought of Herb and some questioning of her that had occurred. "Does your dad know about this? Was he in on this?"

"Of course. While you were playing cupid trying to fix Dad up with Rosemary, he was encouraging Bill and me to arrange a meeting between the two of you."

Bill spoke up. "I apologize to both of you for I held up this meeting for almost three weeks. Dad, do you remember when I was a child and had nightmares? You would come in and comfort me. You stayed with me till I went back to sleep."

"I remember," Tom told him.

"I always told you I couldn't remember the dream. I lied to you. Those dreams were always about you finding Annie and leaving me so you could be with her."

"Bill, I am so sorry. I didn't know what it was doing to you," Tom said.

"After you married my mom, the dreams went away. I always kept looking for Annie. I really never expected to find her after all these years. When I realized that maybe we had found her, I guess the little boy in me came back. I had nightmares again. I tried to convince myself that Annie would want nothing to do with you and you would be hurt all over again. I had to have time to process all this."

Bill continued. "I think I knew from day one that we had found you, Annie. But I do know now I'll never lose him."

Tom got up. He went to his son and put his arms around him. Dorothy came over to sit by Annie. They probably had gone through a box of tissues by this time.

"What happened to you, Tom?" John asked.

"Most of what I will tell you is what I was told by others. Technically, I was not in the army. I worked for the government in the OSS (which became the CIA). After leaving Annie I was sent for paratrooper training. I was to be dropped behind German lines in France to gather information in preparation for the D-Day landing. I had made this trip three times before. My mother was a French war bride who came to the states after WWI. French was a second language in our home. I also spoke German. I'm told that five of us made this drop behind the lines that day. A German patrol saw us and opened fire. My chute landed in a tree. They saw me and shot an extra round at me." Tom paused, looked around. With a look of surprise he said, "Now I remember it. I remember looking down.

I remember seeing my crew lying on the ground. I remember hearing a German call out, 'There's one in the trees.'" Tom paused, deep in thought for a moment and then continued. "I heard the guns. I remembered nothing else for almost two years. After the Germans left, the French underground worker who was our contact person climbed the tree and cut me free. He took me to some secret place where they tried to doctor me. They did enough to keep me alive. I was in a coma. None of us on that mission wore dog tags so no one knew who we were. It wasn't very long before the Allied troops landed on D-Day. I was turned over to the Americans. The Army treated me in England for a while. I was sent back to the east coast. I still remained in a coma. Finally, they sent me to a Veteran's hospital in Portland, Oregon. Through all this time no one knew who I was. They called me Joe with a number. That's how all my records were filed."

Bill then took up the story. "My mother was a new nurse when she married my father who was a sailor. They had met in a club just a couple of weeks earlier. My grandparents wanted nothing to do with my mother. They never felt my mother was good enough for their son. Within a month my father was shipped to Pearl Harbor, leaving behind a pregnant wife. He was killed on December 7th. My mother went through my birth with just friends to help her. She went back to work at the hospital. Joe was one of her patients. My mom took great interest in her new patient. One day she heard him mumbling something. It was the name, *Annie*. It was the first time anyone had heard him try to speak. She assumed Annie was his wife. She tried to get a conversation going. He kept mumbling, "Annie." Then a miracle happened. Joe (or Tom) opened his eyes. He didn't know who he was or where he was. He remembered nothing. The doctors said he had amnesia. They held no real hope he would ever remember his past but were encouraged that he had remembered the name Annie. It could be a clue that in the future he might remember some things. They told him that he might eventually recall part of his memories, but they encouraged him to make a new life."

"Betsy was a wonderful nurse," Tom said. "We started to talk every day: the weather, mostly or just anything in general. Betsy started to question me about Annie, who she was, etc. I couldn't remember a thing. I would get very frustrated. It was so scary to not know who you are. I had also forgotten how to do most things we take for granted. While the wounds I had were healed, I had no physical therapy all this time. I had to learn everything again: how to walk, how to feed myself, all the other things of everyday life. I got very discouraged. I wanted to die. I felt that everyone expected me to do everything. I was not able. One day, Betsy came back to the hospital on her day off and brought Bill with her. He was around five or six at the time. He brought me a picture he had colored. I still have it. He was a kind, gentle child who touched my heart. He demanded nothing of me. He accepted me as I was. I looked forward to his visits. I remember one day a therapist was in the room. I was very frustrated and angry when Betsy and Bill came in. Bill came to me, laid his little hand on my face and said, 'I'll help you." And he did. Sometimes he would bring a toy truck or other toy with him. I remember us throwing a soft ball from the bed to a chair."

"I remember playing cars with you on the floor," Bill said. "For the first time in my life, I had someone other than my mother who seemed to care about me."

"What neither of us realized at the time was that Betsy was sitting and listening. She was making notes from my conversation with Bill. She gave them to the doctor who was treating me for the amnesia. One of the main goals was trying to find out who I was. One day I remembered that I had worked for the FBI. I had been fingerprinted when I joined them so they were able to confirm who I was: Joseph T. Ross, of Iowa, hired by the FBI. I was put on loan to the OSS. Now I had an identity. They were able to track the mission I was on. Unfortunately, I had nothing personal in my records other than where I had lived, gone to school and the names of my mother and father, now deceased. I was constantly advised to make a new life."

"My mother wasn't satisfied with that," Bill said. "She had heard him say *Annie*. Annie must be important to him so we must find her."

"Betsy was relentless about it, almost to the point of annoying me," Tom said. "She was very good to me. She took me from the hospital for a day at the beach with Bill, and next for a holiday, then for a weekend. She had a tiny three bedroom house not far from the hospital. Finally after another year or so I was released. Betsy took me home with her. I loved it because of Bill. He was always a joy in my life. One day while Betsy was pestering me I remembered that Annie was a wonderful woman I had fallen in love with. I could see her dark curly hair, her beauty. Betsy went through every phase of my life. Eventually I did remember where we had met. Soon after that I remembered your last name. Betsy acted like she found gold. She contacted Walter Reed. She found there had been three nurses named Annie Martin working during the time I was a patient. Over the next six or seven months we tracked them down with the help of a detective. One had been on leave during that December; one was an older woman who now lived in Alaska. The other lived in Florida. I made a trip to Florida. She was not my Annie. I decided I needed to try to create a new life so I asked Betsy to marry me. She was a bit reluctant at first; her heart really belonged to Bill's birth dad. We understood each other. Finally she agreed. We were married soon after. There was only one snag, her ex-in-laws. They felt she was very disrespectful to get married again. They begged her not to let me adopt Bill. We compromised. I would adopt him. He had been my son from the first day I met him. As a compromise we decided he would keep his birth father's last name. It didn't matter to me. I knew he was my real son."

"He's a real dad to me," Bill added. "He's the one who came to me in the middle of the night, who rode in the ambulance with me when I broke a leg playing football, who helped me find a second passion in my life – studying the oceans. My first passion is Dorothy and the kids."

Annie sat there hearing her Tom tell of his anguishing times. She remembered how she had felt when she couldn't accept the news of his death. He had been alive all that time. If she had just known he was alive how different their lives would have been. They reached for each other again.

Bill spoke. "When my mother died she made me promise that I would never give up the quest to find Annie. The internet has now made that happen."

Tom suddenly looked at Annie closely. "Is that . . . is it possible that the locket you have on belonged to my mother?"

"Yes, Tom, it did." She told him about receiving the letter and the locket from the bank.

"We've both been through a lot," he said quietly.

One of the hotel employees came knocking at the door to ask if they wanted lunch brought in. They decided to go out to celebrate together.

Over lunch they asked about Annie's past. She told them about trying to locate some record of Tom and her physical breakdown. She told them about marrying Paul, who grieved over the death of his first wife, just as Betsy had grieved for her first husband. She told them about teaching school.

The next two days were perfect in every way. Tom and Annie did everything together. The sat or walked on the beach, took catamaran rides. The went on a sundown dinner cruise. They talked a lot about the years they were apart. They also talked about their future. They decided to get married before leaving Hawaii. There is no waiting period in Hawaii so it could happen immediately.

Annie, Dorothy, and Christine went shopping for a special dress. At one of the stores she was asked why she didn't choose a traditional Hawaiian bridal dress called a *holoku*. She wasn't sure what that was but decided to look at it. After looking at many she chose a version suitable for a woman of her age and size. It was made of cotton in a princess style with a high neck and long sleeves. The fit was on the loose side. The original *holoku* looked something like a nightgown. They were originally designed for the queens whose average height was five feet and weight was around 300 pounds. A young woman wearing one usually has a train on it. The *mature* bride omits the train or has only a short one. Annie said she guessed she was a bit on the mature side (she's only in early 70's) so she had no train. She wore a lei of pink orchids around her neck. Tom wore a traditional white Hawaiian aloha shirt with tan slacks and a green maile leaf lei. They were married on the beach at sunset.

John and Bill took lots of pictures. Thanks to computers they were able to send them immediately to Tom's grandchildren back in Oregon. They also sent them to Annie's family in Austria and Virginia. Of course one went to Herb and Rosemary.

Bill and Dorothy and John and Christine all left for home after the wedding. Annie and Tom stayed on for another week then flew to Portland where they were warmly welcomed. All Tom's friends and family had known about the *search for Annie.*

Annie was so excited when she met Tom's grandchildren. They were so open and friendly to her. She was so pleased, no, thrilled and touched, when they asked her if it was OK for them to call her Grandma. Tom had a condo in Portland which had a big porch on it where they sat and saw a beautiful view of snow covered Mt. Hood.

After a few days there so Tom could pick up some clothes, they headed for Glenridge. What a welcome they had. The neighbors all knew about Tom. As usual when anything happened on Lincoln Boulevard it was an excuse to have a party. The party they had was wonderful. Tom got to meet everyone, even Herb, who kept smiling like a snooty cat. Annie said it was because he had kept a secret from her.

As Tom and Annie sat on the swing on the front porch. she remembered how many times members of her family sat there and talked about their future plans. Most specifically about Beth's and Cathy's plans to live on this street forever and Annie's plans to have a life traveling to see the world. World War II changed those plans. They moved away and she remained here. She remembered what loving parents they had. They made the girls believe they could do anything. They helped their daughters to become strong, independent women. It didn't matter where they lived. Annie wished her parents had lived long enough to see that the way of life and the standards they set for their children are still in place; in Austria, in Virginia and yes, even in Glenridge. Annie hoped that they now know that she and Tom have found a life together after all the years of being apart. Albert and Emma Martin were two very special people.

Every time Annie looks at Tom she still sees the tall handsome young soldier with the dark hair and sparkling eyes and a quirky tilt to his cap that she met all those years ago. He stills see the young girl with the long dark curly hair that stole his heart and gave him hope for the future.

The had a brief conversation about where they'll live. It doesn't really matter. They decided to keep both his condo in Oregon and her house in Glenridge for a while so they can keep in touch with all their families. They are already planning a trip fairly quickly to get together with her sisters and their husbands.

Maybe, Annie thought, *it is because I expected to spend my life alone, that it makes every day now so special. The years that we missed being together are not important anymore. It is important that we are together today. Having Tom by my side has made my life very meaningful. It has made me very happy.*